THE
LITTLE COFFEE SHOP
OF
TERRORS

HAZEL GRAVES

avon.

Published by AVON
A division of HarperCollins*Publishers* Ltd
1 London Bridge Street
London SE1 9GF

www.harpercollins.co.uk

HarperCollins*Publishers*
Macken House,
39/40 Mayor Street Upper,
Dublin 1
D01 C9W8
Ireland

A Paperback Original 2024
2
Copyright © Stephanie Campisi 2024

Stephanie Campisi asserts the moral right to
be identified as the author of this work.

A catalogue record for this book is available from the British Library.

ISBN: 978-0-00871892-3

Set in Birka by HarperCollins*Publishers* India

Printed and bound in the UK using 100% Renewable
Electricity at CPI Group (UK) Ltd

MIX
Paper | Supporting
responsible forestry
FSC™ C007454

This book contains FSC™ certified paper and other controlled
sources to ensure responsible forest management.

For more information visit: www.harpercollins.co.uk/green

Hazel Graves is an Australian author based in sunny Southern California. The author of more than a dozen titles for young readers, Hazel has at long last embraced her natural inclination for swearing and double espressos in *The Little Coffee Shop of Terrors*, her first published book for adults. When not writing, Hazel spends time roasting coffee with her husband (but not in a murderous way) or browsing vintage markets for oddities that just might find their way into a book.

*To Wes, for the laughs, the love, the excellent coffee,
and for supporting me in this silly career.*

Contents

A Bitter Taste

Adele's chest heaved. Her ears rang with the light-headedness of holding that high C; her throat demanded lozenges for the same reason. She'd given the audition her all, spurred as much by the white-hot fear of not being able to make rent as by her passion for musical theatre.

But this was Broadway. (Well, Off-Broadway. Off-Off-Broadway, if she was going to be technical about it.) Everyone was faking it. Even the ones who'd made it.

Holding her position, Adele unleashed a brilliant grin courtesy of a ten-day regimen of teeth-tingling whitening strips. She twirled lightly in the canary-yellow dress she'd convinced herself wasn't too on the nose for the audition. Out in the empty theatre, Ekaterina and Alejandro, who'd sung and danced with her all the way from Nashville to New York like her own personal Rockettes, were up on their jazz-shod tiptoes, mouths open in pride.

There was no doubt about it. She was the next Belle.

It was finally happening. After years of singing her heart out fuelled only by ramen and the insatiable desire to make it in the

City, the stars were aligning. This was Adele's Manhattanhenge. The part was hers.

But then: disaster.

Adele's phone rang, its shrill vocals blasting from the pockets of the jeans she wore beneath her audition dress.

Oh shit! Not now, Mom!

She slapped at her pocket, trying to end the call.

Richard Cuttle II, the theatre's perennially unimpressed casting director, pulled out the red pen everyone secretly called the Guillotine.

Her head was about to roll, and all because Boomers refused to text.

You see, when it came to musical theatre, Richard had many rules, including no plastic protectors on sheet music (the glare!); a costly fine for approaching the audition table (the audacity!); and a blanket ban on faux-British accents ('Save it for the West End, darlings.'). But the most important one, the one he adhered to like a particularly zealous barnacle, was *no phones*.

'All my years of expertise. Experience. *Passion*. And you do this.' He gestured like Don Corleone, if Don Corleone were dressed in a hot-pink suit and a beret. 'I could be in my cute little Cottage Food Law–approved kitchen baking up a storm.'

Adele's dreams of playing Belle had slipped away on the banana peel of an unintended etiquette breach.

Maybe she could rescue this situation enough to play Mrs Potts. That would be fine. Not ideal, but fine.

Chip? She could take Chip.

Just then, the theatre doors swung open, spotlighting two statuesque brunette clones. They stalked down the aisle like

2

shimmering Akhal-Teke horses, hair extensions swinging and highlighter powder glistening.

Adele's smile faltered.

'*Bozhe moi*,' mouthed Ekaterina.

'*Dios mio*,' mouthed Alejandro.

'Well, fuck,' mouthed Adele.

'Pardon?' Richard cupped a hand around his ear.

Wincing, Adele turned off her microphone and stepped down. Her soul was crumpling like the wrapper of the Shake Shack burger she'd seen Richard – who was extremely vocal about his veganism – sneak into the trash can before her audition.

She'd come up against the Nivola sisters before. Everyone had. Theoretically there were only the two of them, but given how omnipresent they were, Adele suspected there were at least eight. Their names graced every playbill, every tabloid gossip page, every donated wing in a twenty-mile radius.

Honour and Gracie Nivola rode upon the coat-tails of their parents with the intensity of a chariot rider avenging a loved one's death. And what impressively tailored coat-tails they were: a celebrity Narchitect mother (the force behind the anti-homeless infrastructure that broke skateboarders' arms and spiked pigeons) and an ageing oil magnate father, who had not cast a reflection since the earliest days of his career.

It wasn't that the Nivola twins weren't *good*. They were devastatingly beautiful. They sang like Dolly. They moved like Jagger. And with their promises of support from the bank of Mom and Dad, they swept the floors with their competition like a possessed Swiffer. Who'd turn down a supremely talented cast member who'd also pay the wardrobe bill and arrange for your musical to have its own limited-edition branded prosecco?

As Honour Nivola took to the stage, Richard clapped his hands, then clasped them as though he were crushing a butterfly inside them.

'I think we've found our Belle!'

Not a butterfly. Just Adele's dreams.

I Need to Venti

Standing at her favourite sink in the plushly carpeted art deco bathroom of the Sun Theatre, Adele splashed her face with water, then dabbed herself dry with the toilet paper she'd stolen from one of the booths. Hugging the roll, she slumped down on one of the creaky leather couches in the powder room area.

Now she knew how Nessarose in *Wicked* felt. This was where tenacity and hard work got you: squished by a house.

At least in Adele's case it was a metaphorical house. Although, having grown up in Tennessee, being squished by an actual house was a very real fear every time the tornado sirens went off.

Having appeared with the silent black-clad grace of a stagehand, Ekaterina waved a flask beneath Adele's nose. 'You look like a girl in need of some emotional-support vodka.'

Adele flinched: the vodka was more rousing than bath salts.

'I think you accidentally bought floor cleaner.'

'Keeps the insides fresh.' Flicking her pink hair, Ekaterina looped her arm through Adele's, playing the cheerful friend, which was usually Adele's job.

Adele wiped her nose with a strip of toilet paper. 'What if I'm just not meant to do this?'

'Of course you are,' said Alejandro, touching up their hair by the mirror. Alejandro's magnificent coif required constant retouching. 'What else are you going to do with your life?'

Adele couldn't decide whether that was a motivational statement or a demotivational one.

'How about we people-watch at the park?' suggested Ekaterina. 'It's wet, so there'll be dogs in raincoats. Your favourite.'

Adele *did* love dogs in raincoats. But not right now. She needed a cry, just not the happy type that dachshunds in frog hats and Pomeranians in plastic jackets inspired. An ugly cry, with clumped eyelashes and a mouth twisted in rictus. An ending-of-*La-La-Land* type of crying.

'I'll catch up with y'all later. I need a few.'

'Be good to yourself.' Ekaterina's purple lips came in for a quick kiss on the cheek. 'Remember: cheap wine is as effective as the expensive stuff.'

'Wiser words have never been spoken,' added Alejandro.

The duo flounced out.

Ugh. Adele's phone was at it again. She let it ring out: she wasn't in the mood to tell Mom about her latest failure. Her parents were always so supportive, and Adele was . . . well, *not quite meeting expectations*, as her ninth grade report card had said. (That had been the year she'd discovered musical theatre.)

After unwrapping the commiseration cake pop Richard had given her, she shoved it in her mouth. The confection was drier than Adele's pipeline of work.

She sighed.

She'd spent her entire twenties and these first few years

of her thirties chasing the dream of . . . all right, not exactly *stardom*, but something in its orbit. Something that meant intrigued nods at dinner parties and perhaps some free stuff from up-and-coming brands, and ideally a nightly standing ovation from an adoring crowd. But every time those ambitions had started to coalesce into a playbill with her name on it, they were whisked away by the cackling witch of nepotism. Why couldn't *she* have a fairy godmother with a Rolodex? And not the neighbour back home who'd decided she was fit for the part simply because her name was Angel. Well, Angel-Rae. Which was even worse.

Spitting the rest of her inedible cake pop onto the frilled lapels of her yellow audition dress, Adele stripped off and stuffed the dress into the tampon bin.

She'd lost auditions before. Plenty of them. But this one smarted. Mostly because it ran right up against the cut-off she'd given herself for making it in the city, and which she'd already extended a few years after realising it wasn't going to happen before her thirtieth-birthday deadline.

And, if she was honest with herself, because *she* wanted to whiz along the bookshelves in the Beast's library set piece, dammit!

But life wasn't a fairy tale. It wasn't even a musical. You might have your 'I want' song, but that's usually where things ended. It had for Adele, anyway. She was Moana on her island, passionately wanting more. Eliza Doolittle rhapsodising about all things *loverly*. Dorothy dreaming of a place beyond the rainbow. An overqualified temp worker wondering why it had been so long since the staffing agency had placed her at a job.

Adele squared her shoulders as she stared out at the evening cityscape through the thickly gilded theatre doors. *You wanted this, Adele. You'll get there. And if you give up now, you'll never know what might have been.*

Out of the frying pan, into the deluge.

While Adele had been inside the theatre watching her career plummet between her unpedigreed fingers, the moody summer skies had been having a good old blub on her behalf. Ordinarily, Adele was fine with weather-related melodrama. And melodrama generally, honestly. But she wasn't even wearing sensible shoes.

The billboards of Broadway were stippled in the pouring rain. Headlights and horns formed a storm of their own as they stop-started through puddles. Drenching torrents spilled off umbrellas and newspapers, gurgling towards the gutters and whisking away garbage from overfilled trash cans. Adele pulled a cardigan from her handbag and hoisted it over her head, going full Hunchback of Notre Dame as she sheltered beneath a canopy here, some scaffolding there.

Was there a belltower she could hide away in while she licked the wounds of her ego? Ideally somewhere closer than St Patrick's.

Positioned beneath the generous overhang of an awning, a robed busker whacked away at a hammer dulcimer. His tip bucket was as dejected as Adele's spirits. Someone had stashed half a bagel in there, and not even one with lox. As she tiptoed past, his gaze followed her. *Are you not entertained?* his eyes shouted gladiatorially.

Adele scrabbled about in her handbag for some change, tearing a nail as she fought a war against lip glosses and the ring of keys she'd been gradually adding to since she'd moved out of home. That was the rule of keys: never remove, only add. The same as teenage Adele's rules for applying makeup.

Distracted by a jostling group of students somehow impervious to the rain, she threw a crumpled note down into the busker's basket. Shit. A twenty.

Never remove, only add, she thought sadly, as the busker prestidigitated it into his pocket without missing a beat. She caught a flash of a wad of cash – he had more notes than Bette Midler's 'Rose's Turn'. Who'd have thought busker life was so lucrative? Maybe she could join in, add some vocals . . .

No, Adele. Don't let musical theatre pull you back in. Remember Jersey Boys. *When you get home you'll call the temp agency and beg to stuff envelopes. Maybe you can get a gig running Excel mail merges.*

Oof. A stranger's elbow took a solid shot at her shoulder, sending her spinning like Gene Kelly around a lamppost.

'That's what I keep telling the *client*,' boasted a tall, glasses-wearing guy dressed in an impeccably starched suit and carrying what looked like a Very Important Briefcase. He flagged down a cab in that magical way that only native New Yorkers can, hurling himself into the back seat as he yabbered confidently about RSFs and capital improvements.

Maybe he'd let her ride with him to the subway. She waved hopefully.

No luck.

The cab whizzed off into the evening, hurling a curtain of oil-rainbowed water over Adele. As its moisturising properties crawled down her scalp and up the hems of her jeans, she felt as small as she'd ever felt in her life. Which, at five foot one, was saying something.

For years, she'd held on like a stubborn guest star in a

daytime TV show. She'd endured basement apartments and $25 sandwiches and Hades-hot apartment thermostats and the flasher on the Q line. And here she was. Unemployable. Unhireable. Unremarkable. The city had beaten her. It was over.

'You win,' she muttered, stepping aside to avoid a woman pushing a double stroller comparable in cost to Adele's first car. And second car. As she did, her heel caught in a grate. Down she went, flopping like Sondheim's *Merrily We Roll Along*.

The only saving grace of the moment was that everyone around her was too busy racing to make their rent money to bother filming her humiliation for TikTok. Instead, they split around her like a chorus line, shoes tramping and phones glowing.

Her phone was buzzing again.

Not now, Mom!

That was it. This not-so-prodigal child was booking the first flight home.

Well, the cheapest first flight home. Ideally with alcohol.

Where Have You Bean All My Life?

After three subway delays and a detour around two rat gangs fighting in the street, Adele slumped on the futon in her apartment. Well, not *her* apartment, precisely. For the past six months she'd been subletting the kitchen portion of a studio apartment from Lane, a thundercloud of a girl who was a whiz when it came to sound effects and musical theatre soundboards. Bad attitude aside, she could make anything play like a Dolby.

Fortunately for Adele (if unfortunately for musical theatre) Lane was rarely around. By day – and often by evening – she was a paralegal at a law firm in Midtown, one of those ones with five names, each increasingly silly, etched into its marble façade above a sculpture of the scales of justice. This meant that not only was Adele able to claim the oven as a shoe rack and the fridge as a closet, but that she could also raid Lane's designer wardrobe whenever she needed to. Which was often.

'I promise I'll pay you back for the Belle dress,' whispered Adele, peeking through the tropical fish shower curtain that separated her kitchen abode from the part of the apartment a human was actually meant to live in.

Good, she was alone. Which meant she could embrace her inner gremlin without fear of being judged. Not that Lane did much judging – she was always too tired. The only thing she had time for was following up about Adele's portion of the rent.

Which was due next week.

And Adele had given the busker her last remaining twenty, which meant that she was down to a few crumpled ones, some ornamental buttons, and the laminated ten-dollar bill she carried as a memento of her very first paid theatre gig.

Adele rolled over on her futon, trying to put a positive spin on this whole situation. She was famously talented at finding the silver lining in the category-four hurricane, but today the sunshine wasn't coming.

'All right,' she told herself. 'So you're jobless and living in a kitchen apartment that is a *far* cry from the Brooklyn brownstone dream that the aspirational television of your childhood promised you. But you have your health, and your friends, and your extremely cheap wine.'

She took a swig from the bottle, grimacing. On a day like today, even her Anything But Chardonnay rule went out the window.

Adele's phone was ringing again.

At least her phone company hadn't cut her off yet, which was generous given that she couldn't remember the last time she'd paid the bill. Probably around the last time she'd been paid, which was for a surrealistic ad campaign Ekaterina had dragged her to, all the way out in Trenton. She still wasn't sure what it had been advertising. But the French would love it.

She answered.

'Sorry, Mom. It's been a shit day. I just . . .' She sighed. 'Do you mind if I come home?'

'Come home?' said a sharp New Yorker voice that had none of Mom's Tennessee twang. 'What nonsense is this?'

Adele sat up like she'd been chastised by one of the Catholic nuns at her secondary school. To this day she felt uncomfortable wearing nail polish – apparently a sign she intended to make herself beautiful for the devil. Obviously the devil loved a good mani-pedi.

'Who is this?' Adele wiped at the wine she'd just spilled all over herself.

'This is Celia Fjutcha.'

Adele giggled. 'And this is Seymour Butts.'

'So *not* Adele Forrest, grand-niece of Doralee Forrest?'

Oh. Perhaps this wasn't a prank call. 'Well, I am the first bit. I'm not sure about the second bit. Who's Doralee?'

'Your great-aunt. Absolute icon of the borough. Died a while back.'

'I'm sorry to hear that,' said Adele, who was, even if the name Doralee didn't ring a single bell.

'Yeah, well. I'm sorry for your loss, but not so sorry for your gain.'

'My . . . gain?' Wasn't that a brand of laundry detergent?

'She left you some stuff. Look, come down to my office in the morning. We'll go over the paperwork.' There was a crackle as Celia covered the receiver to yell something about planets being in retrograde. Momentarily, she came back on the line.

'Sorry, doing some consulting for my sister there. Anyway. All I'm saying is today's your lucky day. Depending on how you define lucky. And day. Tomorrow: 8 a.m. sharp.' Celia rattled off an address in Flatbush. 'Don't stand me up, kid. I'm a busy woman.'

Adele stared down at her phone. Could Celia be for real? Or

was this some sort of elaborate identity-theft scam like the one that Uncle Timbo had fallen for, and which had cost him his retirement, his dignity and his best-functioning kidney?

No, she couldn't think like that. Imagine if Charlie Bucket had turned down his Golden Ticket! He'd still be sharing a bed with his entire extended family. And Gene Wilder would never have been immortalised in the Condescending Wonka meme.

The tiny kitchen window's Venetian blind made a sound like an indignant slinky as Adele yanked its strings. Squinting through the blind's wonky slats, she pretended she was gazing out at the glorious Manhattan skyline instead of the graffitied wall of the adjacent building. Maybe, somewhere amidst the light pollution, there was a shooting star up there making dreams come true.

And she owed it to herself to chase after it.

Better Latte than Never

Adele awoke to a slamming hallway door and a crust of drool running from lip to chin in a perfect facsimile of the Roosevelt Island Tramway route. The sun hammered on the window between the impotent blades of the Venetian blind, spangling the dust in the air. It was a wonder that an apartment this small could even collect dust. Where did it go? Did it pay rent?

Hang on. What time was it?

Unless she'd hallucinated that call during her chardonnay haze – which was possible given the questionable quality of the plonk – she had somewhere to be.

She checked her age-weathered phone: half past seven. Not an egregious time to get out of bed, but definitely not enough time to race into Brooklyn before eight. But she'd do her best.

Sneaking into Lane's part of the apartment, she took a cursory shower that hit the important bits, then threw on an outfit of paperbag trousers and a striped shirt (Lane's), which she tied off with a thrifted Ferragamo belt (her own!) to reduce the inevitable pirate comparisons. In mere minutes she was clattering down the urine-ripe stairs – a better bet than the

15

elevator, which took so long it was definitely visiting other dimensions between stops.

Did she have time for a coffee? Definitely not, but also . . . did she have time for a coffee?

Half an hour later, holding a double-sleeved takeout cup whose contents were still tongue-scaldingly hot, Adele stood outside an odd red-brick townhouse. A dual sign jammed into a daisy planter out the front advertised legal services (*Celia Fjutcha – ground floor*) and psychic services (*Willa Fjutcha – first floor*). So that explained the debate about planets in retrograde.

The very definition of higgledy-piggledy, the building wore a skirt of metal shutters between its steps. Every few minutes, hot air blasted up around the skirt, which a series of rivets held down like Marilyn Monroe had her iconic white dress. Of course: a subway vent.

Could this possibly be legit? Was she about to be murdered? This definitely seemed like an excellent place for murdering. She caught the eye of a passing bicycle courier in case someone needed to verify that she'd been here.

'What?' he snapped.

She held up her hands in apology.

Somewhere in the humid depths of the neighbourhood a church bonged the half hour. Fashionably late, but not flagrantly late. She'd explain that she was a creative. That usually bought you an extra few minutes.

Steeling herself, Adele took a deep breath infused with the aroma of cooking fish, rotting bananas and burning rubber. When it came to stenches, the city never disappointed.

In she went.

Inside, the building was a Rubik's cube of carpet and sun-faded wood panelling. You could see the bits where nervous hands had traced, leaving sweaty prints in the polish, like the heel prints Adele's Pops would impart on her parents' coffee table when he visited. Everything smelt like old ladies: rose-shaped soaps and potpourri and hand lotion. There was definitely a smiling crocheted toilet paper doll lurking in the bathroom.

An old guy in a newsboy cap emerged from a twist in the corridor, intently tracing the lines on his palm. Seeing Adele, he thrust his hand at her as though seeking a high five. A Southerner at heart, she tentatively went to oblige. She couldn't abide someone else feeling rejected. During college she'd ended up going out with a wrong number purely because she hadn't wanted the guy to feel bad. She'd spent a whole year being called Terri and pretending she liked baseball.

'What does this look like to you? Do I seem like a bad guy? Like I got skeletons in the closet?' The faux high-fiver said it with such force that his dentures lost their grip on his gums. He sucked them back into place just in time, then traced the lifeline on his palm.

'I . . . don't work here,' Adele stammered.

'You pay all that money, you expect some good news, is all I'm saying. Got a Band-Aid? Maybe I can cover this thing up.'

Adele dug about in her giant handbag. She grimaced as she found yesterday's torn nail, but then came up with a bandage. 'It's Paw Patrol. I hope that's okay.'

Peeling the Band-Aid, High-Fiver slapped the smiling faces of Rubble and Chase over his lifeline. 'Should keep me out of the hospital. Anyway, if you're heading up there, good luck.'

'Oh, I'm not here for a reading. I'm here for the lawyer.'

High-Fiver guffawed. 'Where do you think I came from?'

Well. Adele was sure she'd have a good comeback for that later. But for now, onwards.

Celia's door was bright orange, except around the edges where the paint had long chipped off, showing ribbons of white undercoat and dark wood. It looked like a reincarnated Cadbury Creme Egg.

'Open!' came the shout, before Adele even had a chance to knock.

Celia's office was decorated in Sixties style, with tapering wood and thick chrome everywhere. Adele suspected that it had remained this way since the actual Sixties, and that Celia – who sat deep in a vinyl executive chair with a ferret in her lap – had simply aged in place as the world had changed around her. The ceiling had dropped several inches with decades of accumulated cigarette smoke layers, which Celia was presently adding to in defiance of every anti-smoking law in the state.

Adele held her breath, the way her family always did when they drove past a cemetery and were trying not to inhale the resident ghosts. At least ghosts weren't cancerous.

Waving Adele in, Celia doused her two in-progress cigarettes in a cup of purplish tea. Clamping one hand down on the ferret, she grabbed for Adele's with the other, shaking it up and down like the shark in *Jaws*.

Adele wrested it back, relieved that she wouldn't have to learn to write with her left hand. 'Sorry I'm late.'

'Eh. I said eight so you'd arrive for nine.' Celia stroked her ferret. The creature's murderous eyes regarded Adele as it clutched a pet potato. 'I know how you musical theatre types are. You save all your timing for the stage.'

'Yeah, well. My musical theatre career is in the rear window.

'I'm done.' Adele plunked herself upon a burnt-orange armchair, which creaked alarmingly. Mid-century furniture wasn't designed for plunking.

'Famous last words.' Celia reached for a pile of papers as spotty and dog-eared as a family of Jack Russell terriers. 'Anyway, we're here because you're Doralee's heir.'

Adele gawped. 'Heir? Of like . . . an estate?'

Was Adele about to become a Disney Princess, Anne Hathaway style?

Perhaps Celia, for all her chain-smoking and ferret-toting, was a real-life fairy godmother. Finally, a pumpkin carriage instead of a decorative gourd painted like a Thanksgiving turkey.

Grimacing, Celia grabbed a pair of purple glasses and jammed them on her nose. 'Estate is a strong word. But you do get a coffee shop. I see you're a fan.'

Adele glanced down at her coffee cup, the contents of which were still too hot to drink. She'd grabbed it from Jittery Joe's, which served the cheapest drip coffee within walking distance to her apartment. With a tip it was still five bucks. Add a pastry and that was her food budget for the week. Addiction was a rough thing: sometimes she resorted to eating Folgers out of the tub.

'A coffee shop,' Adele muttered, bewildered. She loved the idea in theory: what girl hadn't dreamed of pottering around a quaint shop that sold coffee, books and plants in equal measure? Perhaps even vintage records. And handmade pottery from local crafters . . .

The lyrics to 'Somewhere That's Green' started bubbling up within her.

No, no singing in a lawyer's office. Lawyers and singing

didn't go together. Except in *The Producers*. And she didn't have the range for that.

'There's an apartment as well. But you're in charge of clearing out Doralee's *many* personal effects. Hoarder tendencies.'

Blinking as this all sank in, Adele gave a delirious titter. Could it be? A roommate-free, *rent-free* existence in the greatest, most expensive city in the world?

Free from the existential weight that had floated up off her shoulders to join the layers on the ceiling, Adele probably stood at a towering five foot two, maybe even five foot three. This must be what it felt to be a trust fund kid.

Nepotism! What a wonderful thing!

'Keys.' Celia shoved a profuse keychain bristling with New York totems across the desk. 'Don't ask me what's what.'

Adele toyed with the array of keyrings: a rose, a Statue of Liberty, a stovetop espresso maker, a tiny guitar. Behind every one of them was a story that belonged to this Doralee she knew nothing about. There was a whole life represented in this keychain, and now suddenly it was Adele's.

'Why me?' she murmured, twirling a blown-glass ornament between thumb and forefinger.

'You're her closest living relative.'

'Geographically? Or genetically?' As far as she knew, she'd never even met Doralee. Her mom had joked about a wild aunt living in the City, but Adele had always taken it as a vague cautionary tale and nothing more.

'*Creatively*,' said Celia, with an expression that said *you silly goose*. 'You know that Doralee got her start just like you did?'

No wonder the poor woman had died. It must have been from stress. Or malnutrition.

'She had Broadway in her sights as well. Never made it,

although if you ask me, she damn well should have. She had a voice that gave you goosebumps. And the woman could *dance*. But she dated the wrong guy – a star who ran her reputation into the ground at the same time he was busy running around behind her back. One day she shot him.'

'Wait, *what*?' Adele let go of the keychain, worried it might somehow channel her great-aunt's propensity for violence over to her.

'With a peashooter. A prop, back before all this safety stuff we've got today. Not on purpose, probably, but how are you gonna argue otherwise when you've been jilted? Got him right in the eye with a dried garbanzo. He never looked straight after that. And she never auditioned again.'

Adele boggled. Aunt Doralee had been a real character.

'After all that scheiße, she opened the shop. This was way back. Seventies or so. Anyway, she built quite the community. The darling of the counterculture, some called her. Gave Iris Apfel the inspiration for those enormous glasses.' Celia leafed through a stack of documents, licking a gnarled finger to separate the pages. 'Doralee wanted her estate to go to someone with similar dreams. I went through your family tree. You were the only other one who made it to the City from . . . where was it?'

'Sweetwater, Tennessee.'

Celia shrugged. 'Is that where Dolly's from? Eh. Don't care. So, there are some stipulations. One. You must keep the shop operational for a year. Two. You must be the *active* manager, which means being on site and doing whatever it is coffee shop managers do. Three. Ben stays.'

With each point, Celia's fingers curled like the proverbial monkey's paw.

'Questions?'

Adele had *so* many questions. More than in *36 Questions: the Podcast Musical*. But what was that thing about gift horses and mouths? Not that she wanted to look Celia in the mouth with that pack-a-day habit.

'That all sounds . . . fine,' she said, as evenly as she could.

Celia plucked a knife-like fountain pen from her blazer pocket, uncapping it with a wrench of her teeth. 'Sign in about twenty places, and we're off to the races. Well, I am. Got a bet on a filly called Mustang Sally. You can do whatever you want with the rest of your day.' She scrawled something on the back of a CVS receipt. 'There's the address. And here's my sister's card. My clients get twenty per cent off, and vice versa. Bargain.'

Stashing the receipt and the glittery card in her handbag, Adele riffled through the papers, scribbling her name over and over in thick green ink. It wasn't the same as providing an autograph, but it was close.

A solo apartment, a business, and coffee . . .

These were a few of her favourite things . . .

No, Adele. No singing.

Celia hefted the ferret onto the padded shoulder of her blouse. 'It's been grand. You aced this audition, kid. Any problems, you know who to call. My sister.'

And like that, with some familial preferential treatment, Adele's fortunes changed.

Outside, it started pouring again, but this time she was singing in the goddamn rain.

Only in New York.

Into the Grind

Here she was. On the threshold of her new life. Well, the flower-patterned welcome mat of her new life.

With its sunflower planters and hand-painted signage and bold diagonal perch on a street corner covered in murals, Riffraff Coffee Co seemed like the perfect architectural incarnation of Great-Aunt Doralee. Well, according to what Adele knew about Doralee, which had been filtered through Celia, a vague memory of a family photo album, and the first page of Google.

Doralee had apparently been many things. A consummate flower child and socialite, she'd been the kind of woman who lived to be, well, *that kind of woman*. Who loved, lived and ate indiscriminately. Who had a mind, and who spoke it: well, and often. Who inspired all sorts of caustic gossip from envious suburbanites. Who didn't want to be buried, but rather eaten by cats. (It had reportedly been a strange funeral. Lots of sneezing.)

And the kind of woman who bestowed coffee shops and apartments upon down-on-their-luck relatives. Which Adele had absolutely no complaints about.

Adele took a fortifying breath. Immediate regrets. Trash day was still on the horizon, and the stench of the piled-up garbage bags was so strong it had practically solidified in the air. Was that a rat eating a pizza near that weird-looking exhaust pipe poking up from the basement?

'Pizza rats are my four-leaf clovers,' said an impressively sun-weathered woman who'd emerged from the coffee shop with a cart bursting with plants and flowers – and wearing a crocheted dress to match. Silvery hair swinging, she shoved the cart into the back of a tiny three-wheeled van, which teetered alarmingly. 'How can you not love this city?'

She waved demonstratively as she pulled out, leaving Adele laughing in agreement.

The city was the spiritual opposite of her tiny hometown in eastern Tennessee, where the skyline consisted of Walmarts and Dollar Generals, and where the opportunities were equally stunted. And where driving a tiny three-wheeled van full of plants might get you shot.

Hmm, what was that?

Adele squinted as the stifling mid-morning sun glinted off a pattern of glass bricks set into the sidewalk lining the scrabbly red brick of the coffee shop. If you peered down, you could see the shadow of machinery and storage boxes. A basement level. Now there was an opportunity for expansion. You could capture the goth market.

'You going in? Princess needs her puppuccino.'

Adele stepped back, realising she was blocking the pathway. A French bulldog in a wagon smiled up at her, its smooshed face a topography of wrinkles.

'She gets mad if she doesn't get her fix,' said Princess's owner, a guy in a short-sleeved puffer vest and an armful of rubber charity bangles. With a practised hand, he tossed a knotted bag of dog poop in one of the pungent trash cans that lurked around the back corner of the shop. 'And it's late. She's usually two in by nine, and it's quarter after.'

Was a quarter past nine late in the coffee world? It seemed that way. But let's face it: there were morning people, and then there were musical theatre people.

In a manoeuvre honed by experience, Princess's owner shoved open the door with his hip and rattled the pram inside. He held the door for a second, waiting for Adele to take it.

Come on in: the coffee's fine, read the hand-painted sign.

All right.

In she went. Enter stage left.

A string of bells jingled merrily as the front door sagged closed behind her. The street *parfum* of sun-warmed pickles and sweaty cheese gave way to the warmth of freshly ground beans and buttery cronuts.

And it looked as delightful as it smelt. Hardwood floors polished by decades of caffeinated feet sloped at odd angles beneath a hodgepodge of seating upon which the butts of various regulars were happily planted. Two students, broccoli haircuts melding into one single *broccolo*, browsed the board game collection stacked on an old writing desk in a corner nook. A woman with a baby snoozing in a carrier napped herself in a love seat in a recessed area bursting with potted succulents. Vibrant prints and photographs smothered almost every inch of the patched and crumbling walls – ooh, she loved that one of the aurora borealis! – and a pothos vine twined across the cracked stained-glass windows like a flower crown on the head of a festivalgoer. All around came the happy murmurs and chitchat of people sipping their drinks or nibbling pastries.

Taking it all in, Adele broke into an enormous grin.

Yes, the place had its quirks – like that cooing pigeon walking along the fireplace mantel and the ominous sign on the light switch saying: *do not use – risk of death*. But it was hers. She'd bring the same confident energy to it she brought to every one of her disastrous relationships: *I can fix him.*

Speaking of men.

An affable barista in a *very* well-fitting Henley shirt worked his magic behind the counter, banging out coffee grinds into a knock box and hissing foam into cappuccinos. With that swoopy dark hair and green eyes, he was probably rolling in tips. And phone numbers.

Which the gaggle of Lululemon-clad women crowding the counter were sidling his way as he blended together their bespoke, sugary concoctions. It was a high-stakes gig: when it came to frappés, soccer moms had expectations as high as their scrunchied ponytails.

As Adele waited to get the hot barista's attention to explain the whole Surprise New Boss situation, something fuzzy brushed against her leg. She jumped. Had Pizza Rat snuck in with her?

A cat.

Mrow. The cat's eyes were yellow moons in his black face. His chest was a white bib, and his tail was a dark puffball with a frizzled end. Adele wondered what had happened there. Had he used it to stir a too-hot latte?

Of course. This must be Ben! Doralee's third stipulation finally made sense.

She knelt to give the cat's fuzzy head a scratch. 'You're a well-dressed little guy, Benny Boy. You don't usually see tuxedos out of Fred Astaire movies and funerals.'

A woman in rhinestone-studded glasses and a Stevie Nicks shawl squinted over her crossword. 'That's Ember, love. Ben's behind the counter.'

Adele straightened, blushing furiously. 'I guess it's an easy mistake to make.'

She wouldn't mind seeing *him* in a tux. Or even just the bow tie part.

The woman cackled as though she'd read Adele's mind. With her floaty tie-dyed dress and veritable chain mail of silver jewellery, she definitely looked like she had clairvoyant capabilities.

'I'd rub either of their bellies,' the woman confided.

'*Reba*,' admonished an old guy with the remnants of his hair scraped up into a ponytail. He sat a few tables over with his Birkenstocked feet propped up on a chair, reading an age-rippled paperback with its cover missing. Adele wondered why they weren't sitting together. They looked made for each other. She bet they could spend all night listening to Phish while gorging on Ben & Jerry's.

Catching Adele's thoughts, Reba scoffed. 'It'll never happen. Too much water under that Brooklyn bridge. Anyway, I like your energy. You strutted in here like you own the place.'

Adele fiddled with her watch, which she'd picked up from a street vendor in exchange for a few of her ornamental buttons. (She really was serious about this new punctuality schtick.) 'I, um, actually do.'

Reba's blue-rimmed eyes widened behind her witchy glasses. She leapt to her feet in a waterfall of colour and tassels. 'Well, perm my hair and call me Jerry Garcia. You're Doralee's grand-niece! The failed Broadway star – but aren't we all! You'll do fine here, so long as you don't try to change anything. *Anything*.'

Oh good, thought Adele, squinting at a spot of sun streaming in through a hole in the ceiling.

'Have you met Ben yet? No? Ben! Get your tuchus over here!' shouted Reba, voice scratchy as a nailfile. 'Bring cookies. They're on the house.'

Smiling broadly, Ben handed the soccer moms a teetering stack of iced coffees that probably totalled the combined heights of their overscheduled, out-of-sight kids. Then, with a pointed look at Reba, locked the cookie display case.

Reba shrugged. 'Worth a try. Here! Come here!'

Throwing a cleaning rag over his shoulder – oh, to be that cleaning rag – Ben picked his way over to them, effortlessly bussing tables along the way.

Leaving his stack of crockery on a nearby table, he leaned in with a grin and propped his elbows on Reba's table.

'Stuck on a clue, Reebs?'

He had a soft Australian accent that did strange things to Adele's knees. She rarely thought about her knees, but they were failing her right now. She braced against a chair, feigning nonchalance.

'Stuck on *you*.' Reba giggled, twirling a clicky pen stamped with the words *Dyer on the Mountain*. Reba's business, Adele guessed.

Birkenstocks harrumphed.

Ben turned his sparkling green eyes on Adele. It suddenly felt so hot in here that she worried the sprinklers might go off. Were there sprinklers? Was anything in this place up to code?

'Hey, stranger. I'm Ben.'

'So I hear.' Adele furtively fanned herself. 'I thought you were the cat.'

28

'I've heard worse. If you need help remembering what's what, I'm the barista, roaster, schmearer of bagels, mopper of floors, and all-round good bloke.'

'Don't forget live-in caretaker,' added Reba, pointing to the ceiling.

'Love my work so much I sleep here,' said Ben – *possibly* sardonically, although who could tell with Aussies – clocking Adele's extremely interested upward gaze. 'Meanwhile, Ember . . . does that.'

Ember was licking his unmentionables.

'I don't do any of that,' said Adele.

'Good to know,' said Ben. 'Nice pirate outfit,' he added.

Adele put her hands on her hips. Would a pirate wear a belt like this? Really?

It was probably time to build her own wardrobe of basics instead of always borrowing from Lane's. Especially given the whole moving to Brooklyn situation.

'So . . . I'm Doralee's great-niece. Or something.' Adele wasn't sure how to bring up the whole inheritance thing. It sounded so . . . *hoity-toity*. Before all this, she assumed she'd inherit nothing more than genetic predisposition towards a horrifying illness. Or maybe one of Meemaw's swan lamps. The pink one with the scotch-taped crack down the side.

'Adele Forrest,' she added.

'Adele Forrest,' Ben repeated, pronouncing her given name the Aussie way: uh-Del. She could get used to that. He regarded her, making her wish she'd done more with her hair than pull it into a messy bun. 'Doralee mentioned you. I can see the resemblance.'

'Really?'

'Maybe in fifty years. Well, welcome to Riffraff. Looks like you're an early bird, so we'll get along like a house on fire.' A pause while he topped up Reba's coffee. 'I'm taking the piss.'

'He means teasing,' translated Reba, happily gulping her coffee. 'How about some Baileys with that, love?'

'It's nine, Reebs. And our liquor licence has lapsed.'

'It's after 5 p.m. somewhere, Benny boy. And you think *I'm* going to rat you out? Ooh!' Reba's mug jittered as the floor rumbled beneath them. Unless that was Adele's knees again? She looked askance at Ben, whose cheerful expression had turned dark. He folded his arms, revealing a rainbow of tattoos that started at his wrists and presumably kept going . . . *Focus, Adele*.

'Most excitement I've had in a while,' said Reba. 'Gave me a thrill.'

'*Reba!*' groused Birkenstocks.

Reba winked at Adele.

'That'll be the roaster. Nightmare bloody thing.' Ben seemed suddenly distracted, as though he'd remembered something important he had to do. Maybe his phone was buzzing with missed calls from the soccer moms.

'What kind of . . . capacity does it do?' Adele knew nothing about coffee roasting, but she wanted to steer the conversation back to its pleasant beginnings. And to learn more about Doralee and her relationship to Ben.

The door tinkled. A younger guy in a flawlessly tailored outfit and glossy shoes had strutted in, briefcase swinging like he was spoiling for a fight on the floor of the Stock Exchange. Seeing no one behind the counter, he aggressively slapped the service bell. Adele cringed – the guy from the cab that had drenched her the other night!

'There in a tick,' called Ben. He turned back to Adele,

who was hiding behind a coaster. 'I've done up to about . . . a hundred and twenty kilos? Whatever that is in American. Where's Ember? He's not downstairs, is he?'

He sounded worried.

'I can go check.' Especially if it meant getting out of the sightline of Splashy Stockbroker.

'No.' Ben clamped a hand on her shoulder. His eyes stormed. 'New owner or not, the basement's out of bounds. It stays locked at all times.'

He gestured at the basement door, which bristled with a penitentiary-chic row of locks. The only possible entry was via cat flap, which apparently Ember made good use of.

Adele faltered. What was with the mood shift? Was he on drugs? Or was he extremely vigilant about OSHA policies?

She wished Doralee had explained *why* it was so important that Ben be here. Perhaps stability was a vital part of his post-prison rehabilitation. Maybe he was Doralee's secret love child. Or perhaps his ridiculous good looks were all that stood between Riffraff and bankruptcy. It was probably that one.

Well, Adele never had been one to shy away from a challenge, especially one that came with free room and board and a nearby subway stop. If she could audition with 'Bring Him Home' from *Les Mis* while delirious on cough syrup, she could handle Ben.

Do You Want Room with That?

'So you're, like, moving out.' Lane was not impressed, but also, not *not* impressed. Upward mobility was the whole goal of the City. Regarding Adele's duffel bag, she bit savagely on a carrot, leaving black lipstick marks on its orange hide. 'Does this mean I get the oven back?'

'And the fridge, if you want it. You can put your sound stuff in there.'

All right, so maybe it was a touch pre-emptive to tell Lane the news about her new place, which she hadn't actually seen yet. But hoarder hovel or not, there was no way Doralee's apartment could be bad enough that Adele would prefer being squished into a kitchen over a rent-free spot of her own three blocks from her new business. She hoped.

'And you're going to pay out the year, right.'

Lane said this so matter-of-factly that Adele almost agreed. But then she remembered that she was dealing with a paralegal. 'Am I even on the lease?'

'Well, no, but like, as a courtesy.'

'Then, no. Sorry. Although maybe I could . . . No, sorry.' Adele's southern upbringing made saying *no* so difficult.

Lane finished her carrot, green crown and all. Adele was both horrified and fascinated. She'd seen Lane eat apple cores and kiwi skin before, but this was a new one.

'Worth a try. I *can't* move back in with my dad. Living above a funeral home stops being cool when you're sixteen.'

'If anyone can make it cool, you can,' said Adele, encouragingly. For better or worse she'd skipped the teenage emo phase in favour of the weird theatre kid phase. Although she had watched a lot of *Six Feet Under* with Meemaw.

Lane picked up her phone, fingers flying as she started a group text for a new roommate. 'It's been, like, grand.'

Closer to thirty grand, actually.

But better, cheaper days were ahead!

With anyone else, Adele would've attempted a hug. But hugging Lane was like a PDA with a saguaro. Prickly. And probably illegal in Arizona.

It was with a spring in her step that Adele hurried down to her subway stop – a spring that lessened slightly as she grappled with the overstuffed duffel bag, but a spring nonetheless. She hadn't felt this light on her feet since she'd helped Ekaterina dial in the umbrella stage flight scene in *Mary Poppins* (she'd played the under-understudy). She even considered jumping the turnstile on the way out, but a conductor gave her a warning look: *I know you musical theatre types.*

Clattering up the grimy stairs, she emerged from the dank chrysalis of the subway into her new neighbourhood – and immediately began humming 'A Whole New World', because how could you not? If she squinted, she could see Riffraff at the bottom of the hill! Her commuting days were as over as skinny jeans.

All around, massive oaks knotted their leafy fingers over the streets, distracting from the fact that their roots were erupting from the sidewalk like wooden volcanoes. Cars snuggled up against each other in a demonstration of seriously impressive parallel parking. A soiled mattress leaned against a nearby lamppost, surrounded by an almost intentional circle of milk cartons. A passing babushka scowled at her as though Adele had single-handedly caused the Soviet Union to fall, then spat a mouthful of sunflower husks her way, like a wizened AK-47.

Adele waved – it never hurt to be on good terms with your neighbours – then checked her phone. According to Google Maps, she was here. But where exactly was Doralee's apartment?

A furious ginger tomcat sauntered out from between two wrought-iron double gates, its tail wafting in the mid-morning sun. *The Jellicle Ball is this way, baby.*

Well, obviously it didn't say that, and definitely not in Andrew Lloyd Webber's voice. But Adele followed the cat, as any good human would do. Cats always knew where they were going. Or at least they confidently pretended to, like that one guy in a group who was always like, 'It's right up here. A little farther . . .' when in search of a new bar.

Adele pushed open the gates, gasping as they revealed a charming European-style courtyard filled with colourful café furniture and hefty planters bursting with hydrangeas and ferns and Talavera pottery chickens. Framed by gently glowing fairy lights, four brightly painted doors overlooked the courtyard, each with its apartment number outlined in ornate script. One of the doors was yellow with purple flowers painted all over it.

Aha. Adele knew that pattern. She spun through the keys on Doralee's chain until she found the key that perfectly matched the door. It looked like it had never been used.

Adele put the key in the lock, twisting the doorknob as she did. Hang on. It was already . . .

As the door swung open, Adele clapped her hands over her mouth so that she wouldn't scream. Her duffel bag huffed with ennui as it fell to the ground.

The apartment resembled the fallout from the 1968 sanitation strike condensed into 800 square feet. Celia's description of it as a hoarder house had been a euphemism that would echo through the ages, like the high notes in *Phantom* or the scathing critical response to the stage adaptation of *King Kong*.

But beneath the bursting tote bags and the half-painted canvases and the teetering photo albums were what a model's casting agent might call *good bones*. Elaborate cornices and ceiling roses. The gloss of oak floors. The mint green and blush pink of Fifties decor.

She could do this.

'Want some help?' A stunning older woman with a profuse head of silver curls and mud-stained floral overalls appeared in the doorway. 'This is *not* a solo job.'

'Oh hey!' said Adele. 'You're the plant lady with the three-wheeled van.'

'And fellow Pizza Rat fan.' Her smile was so high-wattage it could power an IMAX. 'Kyra, with a Y. My parents were Lynyrd Skynyrd fans, bless them.'

Adele shook Kyra's free hand – the one not holding a watering can. 'I'm Adele, with the standard vowels. My parents are Adele fans, but I predate her celebrity by a few decades. I'm Doralee's grand-niece.'

'I was wondering when you'd show up.' Kyra regarded Adele with kohl-lined eyes, nodding slowly. 'You'll do. You'll do. You've got that same Doralee spark. Heart of gold, loyalty of a terrier, spirit of an adventurer. Hoo! The parties she'd hold in this courtyard! Rumour has it that we're on every watchlist known to the Home Office. And INTERPOL. And the karaoke police.'

'And Marie Kondo, by the looks of it.' Adele reached a toe into the apartment, nudging an overflowing box of doilies with a clear and obvious escape plan. Where was she going to put all of this stuff? Maybe she could cart it down to the giant trash cans behind the coffee shop.

'Everything brought Doralee joy,' said Kyra. 'You see the problem. You know what? Give me one sec.'

Setting down her watering can on one of the tile-topped courtyard tables, Kyra disappeared behind the blue door opposite Aunt Doralee's. Adele ran a hand gently over the pom poms of the hydrangeas and allium growing explosively in their pots – they reminded her of Mom's garden back home. She was opening and shutting the mouth of a snapdragon to the rhythm of 'Summer Nights' when Kyra returned with a pan of brownies, two pairs of gardening gloves and a roll of trash bags.

'These are beautiful,' said Adele, releasing her hostage snapdragon.

Kyra paused to deadhead a drooping purple flower. 'Never met a plant I couldn't nurse back to life, hardiness zones be damned. I worked at Prospect Park for years. Although the highlight of my career was consulting on the Bryant Park bathroom flowers.'

Adele grinned, pulling on the pair of sunflower-patterned gloves Kyra had passed her. 'Peeing in that bathroom was the highlight of my career.'

'The showbiz life, huh?' Kyra waggled her gardening-gloved hands like a chorus girl.

'I couldn't take the glitz and glamour anymore.'

'Ah. Meanwhile, I can't take the boredom of retired life. I have my plants in Riffraff, a bunch of boutiques. Got my greenhouse gig up at the cemetery. I even do ghost tours up there when the moon's full. By the way, if you want to make a call, that cemetery's the place to be. These apartments are like a tin-foil hat – they keep the signal right out. The electrical here's been wonky since the electromagnetic storm of '94, but who's complaining. Be thankful for the peace. Such that it is,' she said, as an ambulance siren split the air.

Adele chuckled, shuffling sideways into the apartment, which was still and quiet, probably because it was pinned by the weight of hundreds of decorative boxes and photo albums. She bit her lip: the apartment was so laden with Doralee's presence that she could almost see her great-aunt curled up in the striped armchair in the corner, beading one of the bracelets that hung from the metal tree stand on the side table.

The apartment was full of memories and personality. A sunflower-gloved hand on a dusty hatbox, Adele hesitated. It wouldn't be right to toss it all. Doralee's legacy obviously mattered to her, or she wouldn't have gone to the effort of arranging such a complicated will. Adele owed it to her great-aunt to sort through everything and find a home for it. Maybe a museum would take the photo albums. And a yard sale might work for some of the knickknacks.

'Quite the place, ain't it?' Kyra's cheerful voice broke into her thoughts. 'Let me tell you: if you're walking in Doralee's footsteps, you're going to be kept on your toes. The coffee shop is an icon, but I hear it's got its own challenges.'

'You mean Ben?'

Kyra gave Adele a quizzical look. 'Do I sense some tension?'

Adele cleared her throat. 'No tension. I think.'

'I see.' Kyra waggled the baking sheet in front of Adele, unleashing a heady combination of chocolate, butter, and the fragrance of the skunks who'd hide out beneath Adele's porch back home. So cute. So pungent.

'So potent.' Adele boggled as she took a bite. In a few minutes she'd be able to see through space and time.

Waggling her eyebrows, Kyra daintily popped a brownie square in her mouth. 'Right? Well, let's get to work before you're asleep on your feet.'

Behind them, the wrought-iron gates squeaked, and the courtyard filled with tipsy chatter and the rustle of takeout boxes.

'*Ky-ra!*' came a sing-song voice. 'Who wants *phở*? We've got about a million rice paper rolls here for you, too. Some start-up placed an order and didn't pick it up.'

Someone had set up a speaker: the whiny electronic strains of 'Mr Roboto' started pouring into the courtyard. Adele straightened in delight. She adored a good concept album: it was the musical theatre gateway drug.

'I'm here with the young Doralee,' called Kyra, eyes sparkling as she watched Adele fighting the urge to pirouette. 'We're tidying.'

'Food is *fu-el*!' called the courtyard voice. Leaning back through the door, Adele could see it belonged to a grey-haired guy with a diligent side part and a passion for ear piercings. He seemed to have a chess piece speared through his left earlobe. Huh. She hadn't known a rook could move in that direction.

'I hope you don't mind if I sing.' Adele had definite plans to belt out the 'Mr Roboto' bridge at the top of her lungs.

'We judge the quality of a party by the quantity of its noise complaints,' said the guy. 'Bring that chest voice, honey.'

Caution! Contents Hot

The bells adorning Riffraff's door jingled as Adele sauntered through at the heinously early time of 8 a.m., excited to put in a proper, honest day's work in a place where she wouldn't be critiqued and found wanting by the Richards of the world. There'd be no auditioning. No dance routines to memorise. No pancake makeup. Best of all, she might even get paid!

The very idea made her want to break into song. But that would be counterproductive. And her voice was raw from last night's garden party, which had carried on long into the star-misted night.

Inside, the coffee shop was sultry with the humidity of hot drinks and the hotter barista. Not to mention the buttery aroma of freshly warmed croissants and the tiny doughnuts that a machine behind the counter was busy frying. The pops of green from the pothos-smothered stained glass and the succulent table displays added to the jungle-like feel.

Reba and her longing would-be beau had staked out what seemed to be their usual spots, and a few other customers sat carefully positioned with a table or two between them, like a human-populated game of Tic-tac-toe. A pale Slenderman of a kid sipped at a carton of coconut milk as he roughed out an architectural drawing of a bridge to go with the popsicle-stick model beside him. Meanwhile, behind a fortification of empty coffee cups, a group of teachers graded a monstrous stack of essays with the trepidatious despair of the last few survivors in a zombie movie.

Sitting on top of what Adele assumed was a broken record player – jazz crooned tinnily from a cheap CD player next to it – Ember presided over the shop as he daintily licked a paw. A paw that had probably just come from a litter box. Adele tried not to think about the logistics of that. Or what the Health Department might think about the logistics of that.

'Good morning!' she proclaimed, warranting a glare from the teachers. Adele grabbed a stack of mini doughnuts from the jar on the counter and popped them on a tray. She bussed them over, bashing her shins on a lurking steamer trunk on the way.

'Here. Y'all deserve this,' she said, blinking back tears of pain.

'There aren't enough doughnuts in the world,' whispered one of the teachers.

'I know,' said Adele, apologetically. 'I was a student once.'

Ben raised his eyebrows as she hoisted herself upon a cracked bar stool positioned around the counter. 'Wow, here at eight. Right on time to miss the morning rush. And I'm docking those doughnuts from your pay.'

Adele glanced up from the bruised shin she was inspecting. 'I thought eight was a decent—'

'Not in coffee. Five is a sleep-in.'

'*Five?*' The very concept was more painful than the shin-gouging she'd endured. The only time Adele had been up that early was to secure Taylor Swift tickets. 'Are you in bed by dusk?'

'The hermit life suits me. Plus my commute's short.' He pointed upstairs. 'That's off limits as well.'

'Can't have your boss in your bedroom.'

Adele was mortified even as she said it. The intrusive thoughts were strong today. It'd been *days* since she'd unleashed her emotions on stage, and apparently they were coming out in her attempts at small talk instead.

Fortunately Ben was too busy to notice her melting into a puddle of embarrassment. He was trying to interpret the order of a customer jabbing wildly at the menu while arguing about his divorce proceedings on speakerphone.

'Almond milk, and no, she's *not* getting the Paris pied-à-terre. I'll burn it down before that happens. And the airline miles are mine. *She* ran up that credit card debt, Louis. Tell her she can take the lovebirds. Resentment birds. A lid? And a double sleeve. I hate the feeling of hot coffee in my hand. No, not you, Louis.'

Adele helpfully rearranged the napkins while Ben poured the guy something frothy with a squirt of cream on the top. Hopefully not cyanide, although from the way the guy was talking about child support, he probably deserved it.

Meting out exact change – and no tip – the divorcé reached over the counter for an extra sachet of sugar, then stomped off on his way.

'What a wanker.' Ben shook his head as the guy strode out the door, yabbering about who deserved the Williams-Sonoma ice-cream scoop. 'Can't get off your phone, mate?'

Adele pushed an origami napkin swan Ben's way. 'So, where do we start?'

In the thick of it, it turned out, because a group of construction workers vibrant in high-vis vets had sauntered in. Adele was no fortune teller – although she did have the business card of one in her wallet – but she predicted the shop was about to run out of pastries.

Setting out a series of to-go cups in anticipation of the workers' order, Ben prodded an elbow at the huge dual brewer. With its chrome styling and red central switch, it reminded Adele of HAL 9000. Oh God. Was he suggesting that they wipe out all of humankind?

'Reckon you can put on a couple of fresh pots? One normal, one decaf.'

'Sure thing. Give me a second . . .'

Adele pulled out her phone, browsing YouTube for a tutorial. Ben swiped it from her, pointing to the hand-painted *No Wi-Fi* signs sitting next to the succulent planters on each table. *Look up from your phone! Talk to a stranger!* they griped.

'This is an analogue environment. Even the cash register is offline. You're gonna love that when it's time to do the books at the end of the month.'

'Wait, the books?' Adele hoped he meant curling up with an Agatha Christie novel.

Ben tapped a drawer marked *Out of Sight, Out of Mind.* 'It's your place. I just work here. And live here. And regret my life decisions here.'

Adele grimaced. Her dream of pottering around a quaint coffee shop was turning out to be way more administrative than she'd imagined. Would she also have to do taxes?

'So. Espresso drinks?' Ben propped an elbow atop the hulking espresso machine, which was the most intimidating thing Adele had ever seen. All that hissing and humming:

43

it was like if the Tin Man were possessed by a winged monkey.

Adele beamed. He was offering to make her a coffee! Now there was a job perk. 'Sure! Cream, three sugars, a pump of caramel.'

Ben gave her the same look of chagrin the teachers had. 'That's . . . sacrilege. Also, caramel has three syllables. Bloody yanks. So, that's a *no* on working the espresso machine, yeah?'

He cocked his head as though giving her a chance to revise her answer.

Adele squinted at the gleaming Italian machine. If she could handle the ballroom choreography for *West Side Story*, she could figure out an espresso maker. After all, generations of aspiring (and failed) Broadway performers had managed it. All you had to do was put the cup on the tray, waggle the silvery spoon thing into that black circular bit, press some buttons, and make some banging noises. Or something like that.

Ben steered her away from the machine before she managed to break something. 'How do you feel about washing dishes?'

Adele pouted at the prospect of lipstick-stained mugs and caked-on pains au chocolat. 'Anything else?'

'Bussing tables? Cupping? Ordering beans? Replenishing Kyra's succulents?'

These were getting more and more esoteric. Although maybe that was because Adele was listening more to his accent than what Ben was actually saying.

'Do you have even a skerrick of knowledge of coffee?'

'A . . . skerrick?' Was this a metric system thing?

'It means a bit,' called Reba, standing up in a profusion of tie-dye, like a hippie peacock.

44

'Ta, Reba,' called Ben.

Adele winced. She was making a hash of this whole business-owner thing. And in front of this . . . no, not hot barista. *Employee*. She had to look at him through impartial eyes. Ones that wouldn't get her sued for creating a hostile work environment.

'I'm more of a people person,' she explained, with a wave to the customers dotted about the place. 'Maybe I can focus on the clientele. And cleaning this place up. You should see the magic I worked on Doralee's apartment.' A few square feet of it, anyway.

'You're living in Doralee's flat?' Ben's tone was measured, but she could see he was processing this.

'As of last night. Kyra and I . . .'

'No wonder you were in late. You were up all night talking about plants.'

Yes, talking about them. That was it.

Ben leaned over the counter, giving Adele an exquisite glimpse down his shirt. Wow, he really hadn't held back when it came to this whole tattoo business. Or the gym.

Eyes up here, Adele!

'You know, Kyra gave Doralee that pothos. Audrey III,' said Ben, pointing. 'That thing's about thirty years old. Just keeps growing, too. Another few years and it'll have taken over the whole borough.'

Wrenching her gaze away from Ben, Adele turned to marvel at the trailing plant that climbed so languidly across the stained-glass windows, its leafy tendrils curling towards the sun. Imagine having a friendship – not to mention a plant – that endured for decades. It said something about Doralee, and about Kyra. She reminded herself to text Ekaterina and

45

Alejandro later. She'd been so busy with this coffee shop stuff that she hadn't even updated them about what was going on. They probably thought she was angrily tormenting an opera house wearing a half-mask. Or that she'd fled back to Tennessee. Whichever was worse.

Speaking of Tennessee, she'd also completely blanked on calling her parents. Although that was mostly because the reception in Doralee's apartment boasted fewer bars than the main street of Adele's hometown (a dry county), and when she'd plugged in the toucan-shaped landline she'd found amongst the stacks of decorative boxes, she'd shorted out the whole block of apartments. Twice.

Ben drummed his hands against the counter. 'Righto. If you're gonna be my boss, you're learning how to make a decent cuppa. C'mon.'

He lifted the half-door that separated the work area from the rest of the shop, inviting her through. His fingertips brushed the small of her back as he guided her over to the machine. Adele flinched: she felt as though she'd been set alight.

Ben glanced down at his hand, blinking. 'Are those rubber-soled shoes?'

Adele lifted her foot in a delicate passé. 'I can tell you that they're lovingly fashioned from the cheapest material available to humankind.'

Ben shoved aside a stack of saucers. 'Well, you'll get some static, but rubber's non-slip at least. But toes are a no-go.'

'You're not a feet guy?' Adele asked innocently.

Ben blushed, fumbling the saucers. 'It's a work safety thing. Close-toed shoes in case you drop something.'

'I'll wear socks and sandals tomorrow,' promised Adele. Oh, but he was fun to tease! 'Now let's do shots.'

Ben sighed. '*Pour* shots. This is our La Marzocco, also known as the workhorse.'

Adele gave it a pat. 'The machine that keeps this place running, huh?'

Ben cleared his throat. Had his gaze shot down to the mysteriously off-limits basement? 'More or less. But for now, you're going to sit at the kiddie table.'

He steered Adele over to a smaller version of the espresso machine covered in stickers. A piece of tape marked *training* sat crookedly across its front.

'You can mess around to your heart's content back here.' He handed Adele the big silver spoon thingy, which was surprisingly heavy.

'That's your portafilter. It's what the espresso machine pushes hot water through to make the extraction that will become your espresso shot.'

Adele nodded as though this made sense. She was more of a doer than a listener, at least according to the guy at Home Depot when she'd tried to return some wall hooks with a giant chunk of drywall attached. It would all come together after a few tries. She hoped.

'This is your grinder.' Ben tapped a squat black demon of a device with a red light peeping out from under a metal mouth, then pointed to a fancier brass one next to the La Marzocco. 'And that. Hold your portafilter under it—'

Adele shrieked as coffee spewed out of the machine and into the portafilter. And also all over her bare toes. Ben silently pointed at a broom in the corner as he went on with his lecture.

'—then tamp it with this little bloke here.' He showed Adele a springy wooden device used to flatten the ground coffee into a dry puck. It reminded her of the ink stamp she'd used at her first job.

'Once the grinds are level, lock her into the group head like so.' Ben's hands guided Adele's as she locked the portafilter in place. They fit over hers seamlessly, like tattooed matryoshka. 'Pull the shot . . .'

Closing her eyes, Adele pressed the button he'd indicated. The machine hummed, and twin streams of molten coffee filled the tiny espresso cup Ben had placed there. She squealed excitedly at the result. She felt like Jack Skellington stumbling into Christmas Town!

'Pretty decent shot there, kid. So that's the espresso, which forms the basis of all the coffee drinks worth drinking.' Ben propped a forearm on the kiddie-table surface top, feigning a thoughtful expression. 'So there is where it gets contentious. The long black – the Aussie way – versus the Americano. I'll reckon you can guess which one's the right way to do it.'

Adele pretended to think long and hard. 'I'm going to go with not the American way.'

'Fast learner.' Ben shot her that disarming grin. 'Our way preserves the crema. The American way—'

'Shoots it to smithereens?'

'You're not far off.'

'*Down Under loves its crema; in the States we love our creamer . . .*' sang Adele, sotto voce.

'What was that?' Ben raised an eyebrow.

'A mnemonic,' said Adele. 'I can remember anything so long as I have a ditty. I sang the entire Periodic Table of the Elements for a talent show once.'

'Did you win?'

Adele laughed. 'I did not.'

Biting back a smile, Ben showed her how to pour both an Americano and a long black, in case a peevish Karen or a homesick Aussie tourist came in. After a few disasters – an off-centred tamping incident and a shot that missed the cup entirely – Adele managed a pour that looked like something you could actually serve without drawing the ire of an undercover coffee cop. Or the interest of the *Kitchen Nightmares* film crew.

'Hey, look at that!' She jumped up and down, clapping.

Ben seemed pleased. 'Why don't you take that out to Reba and see what she thinks of it.'

Adele did. She would've added a pastry, but the construction workers had made short work of their remaining stock. She carried the cup over to Reba, who was working methodically through her crossword.

'Dad to Glengarry, Glen and Ross,' Reba mused, spinning her pen.

'Mamet,' called Ben, not missing a beat.

Hmm, so he might not be a musical theatre type, but maybe he was a *regular* theatre type. It was the lesser of the two mediums, but still a socially acceptable choice.

'Of course!' Reba scratched the answer into the page. Her tie-dyed blouse floofed dramatically as she moved, like a rainbow emergency parachute.

'I could've told you that,' muttered Reba's would-be beau as he slurped on his iced coffee. Adele felt bad for him. Did he sit there all day hoping Reba would talk to him?

'As if, Frank.' Reba signalled for him to shut up. 'Do you like the theatre, love?'

'So long as it's musical. Although those days are behind me. This is me now.' Adele gestured around the shop.

Reba downed her coffee like a kraken might an unsuspecting sailor. 'Scarred, are we?'

'Opportunity heals all wounds.' Adele cleared away Reba's extra dishes. How many cups of coffee had she ordered today? Should she intervene on behalf of Reba's doctor? Was there a defibrillator behind the counter?

'Look at Little Miss Sunshine here. Good for you. Oh look, it's Ember! Here, puss puss puss. Here, sweetie. Don't talk to that old windbag. Talk to me!' Reba pulled out a can of tuna from her tie-dyed robes and cracked it open. Ember, who was twining around the bare, skinny legs of Frank, glanced up, tempted. Brined fish reek wafted through the air with the lingering intent of an elevator fart.

The floor rumbled, and Adele grabbed at a nearby chair. Was that an earthquake? Was New York City even on a fault line?

She wasn't sure what to do. She waved at Ben, trying to get his attention. But he was disappearing down in the basement. They must be running low on beans.

'I'll take that. Why don't you taste that coffee and give me your thoughts?' Adele grabbed the stinky can from Reba and coaxed Ember outside. This took some doing, as cats are their own bosses, even when there's a pungent meal of tuna on offer. Finally, the well-dressed tuxedo kitty trotted out the door and out to the street, crackly tail waving as he polished off the tuna.

Adele watched him eat, enjoying the warmth of the sun on her arms and the ceaseless passage of the neighbourhood passers-by. There was always something going on: an enormous truck doing a fifty-point turn to get around a tight corner; a hungry crowd gathering in wait for the tamale lady; a guy going for a jog in a three-piece suit; someone on a unicycle carrying a bunch of helium balloons; the goat yoga instructor next door chasing a wayward billy goat down the street. And the pigeons and rats. Always the pigeons and rats.

'I hope you're not leaving that cat out here,' snarked a fixie-wheeling hipster in a topknot. His guyliner flashed as he narrowed his eyes. 'They kill native birds, you know.'

Oh yes, the native birds of the concrete jungle, Adele wanted to say, but obviously didn't. Confrontation was so . . . confrontationy.

Instead, she broke into a cheerful rendition of 'Feed the Birds' as she watched Ember eat. Singing usually cracked through the defences of whoever was being a jerk to her. She'd learned that during elementary school, when a tall, thin-lipped boy called James had decided he had it out for her. He'd ended up being her understudy in the school play, and they'd bonded over Back Street Boys lyrics.

Smoke belched from the coffee shop's basement, drawing the attention of Ember's golden eyes. And the hipster's.

The song hadn't worked its way into his heart – the guy apparently wasn't a Julie Andrews fan – but the air pollution had.

'You need a better afterburner on that roaster.' The hipster gave his handbrake an indignant squeeze. 'Climate change is coming for all of us. I pan-roast at home in my apartment, and there's never smoke like that. Here, smell my shirt.' The hipster stretched his Hawaiian shirt, which had a patterned ascot shoved into its neckline, in her direction.

Adele took a step back, affronted by both the challenge and the violently bright fashion choice. 'I am . . . okay, actually.'

The coffee shop door swung, and Ben raced out. His sleeves

51

were shoved up his arms, revealing a swirl of tattoos that looked like they'd taken inspiration from the Italian Renaissance, together with lines and lines of text. Finally, a proper look at what his shirt cuffs had been hinting at all this time. Although she'd need to get up close to properly read the script . . .

Ahem. Adele.

'There you are! And Ember too. I thought— Is this guy bothering you?' Ben's green eyes were an unearthly shade in the strong sun.

The very hot sun. Adele was suddenly rather warm: was it heatstroke?

'Adele?'

'Oh! Um, not at all,' she replied finally, in a voice that meant, *yes, please for the love of Barbra, save me*. With an undertone of: *please carry me upstairs and have your way with me*. No, no, retract that. Could you retract subtext?

'He's telling me about how he roasts coffee,' she went on, flustered. 'Y'all would probably get along.'

'You're the roaster?' Topknot had suddenly changed his tune. He patted around at his (tight, burgundy) trousers. 'We should swap cards. I love to nerd out on coffee.'

Ember wound himself around Topknot's legs, meowing plaintively. Ben frowned, like he was making a decision about something. To be fair, Adele did the same thing when a guy offered to exchange numbers with her. Although as a dude, Ben's decisions were probably less fear-driven. It wasn't like he had to gauge split-second what decision was least likely to end up with him dead. The calculus of being a woman was as tough as actual calculus.

'I usually roast in the evenings, but I reckon I can fire her up now. We've got a bespoke machine, an import. She's pretty

52

special: you haven't seen anything like her before. And definitely won't again. What do you reckon? Wanna take a look?'

Topknot's eyes lit up. 'Lead the way! We can talk ventilation.'

'Sure, mate.' Ben gave Ember's head a scratch. 'Adele, mind the shop? It's quiet right now – just Reba and Frank having one of their usual lovers' tiffs. But make sure no one comes down to the basement. Opening the door can stuff up the roast.'

Adele puffed up like a delighted Violet Beauregarde as she followed them back inside. No more kiddie-table espresso machine for her!

A Tall Order

The cheerful warmth of Riffraff hugged Adele as she took her place behind the counter. She smiled: she was coming to love every quirk of the shop and its steady stream of offbeat visitors. Things had settled down now that the office workers and students had clocked on for the day, so she availed herself of Meemaw's advice: *time to lean, time to clean*.

Popping a Mamas & the Papas album on the sad player, she filled a milk pitcher with water and gave the pothos a drink, rubbing its glossy leaves. It was such a healthy-looking plant, especially for its age. Kyra really knew what she was doing. Adele would have to send some of her special plant food mixture back home to Mom. The dogwood natives would love it.

Frank was playing Connect Four by himself, looking longingly at Reba as he placed every tile. Harrumphing, Reba scooped up her crocheted handbag and shuffled off to the bathroom.

Walking by with her cleaning rag, Adele grabbed a red tile and popped it down a chute.

'Your turn,' she said, polishing a table while Frank

considered where to place his yellow token. 'So, how do you know Reba?'

'We're married,' said Frank, with incredible matter-of-factness. His tile rattled into the rack.

Adele dropped her rag in Reba's coffee. 'You're what?'

Frank raised his left hand. A huge skull-topped band adorned his ring finger. 'About thirty years now. We met here, as a matter of fact. Doralee always said this was a place for bringing people together. Which is why the two of us keep coming back here, I suppose. Even after everything.'

Before Adele could ask what he meant by *after everything*, the bell at the front door jingled. A posse of teenaged girls sloped in, dressed in oversized clothing and oversized attitude. Adele grinned. She loved girls at this age: they were all preparing to take on the world. She saw her own big dreams in them. Oh, to be sixteen and to know fully in your heart of hearts that the world was going to give you everything you deserved.

Still, if they brought it up, she'd assiduously steer them away from a career in the theatre.

'Hi y'all! Is there anything I can get for you?' She inwardly begged the universe that they'd only ask for espressos and bottled water, and not whatever concoction was currently going viral on TikTok. 'The cookies are incredible.'

'We know,' said a girl, wearing an oversized Nirvana shirt that incongruously featured a picture of Hanson. Her braces flashed as she spoke. 'Ben lets us help out here sometimes. I stamped those sleeves.'

She pointed to the Riffraff-branded sleeves stacked up by the counter.

'And Rivka painted that wall,' she added, gesturing at a

bright yellow alcove lettered in a bulging Seventies script with the words *Coffee: because sleep is for the weak*.

'Thanks, Trix,' whispered a girl in head-to-toe purple, staring ardently at the hardwood floor. (It *was* a memorable floor.) 'Frank helped. He does all the signs around here. Even the menu board.'

Adele hadn't paid much attention to the menu board, but she did have a chuckle at the name of the day's roast: *Hannibal Delectable*.

Frank's Connect Four board rattled as he pulled out the bottom tile holder. 'I'm a man of many talents.'

Adele could see that. 'Nice work.'

Trix shrugged indifferently. 'It's kind of zen. And Ben's pretty famous around here, so it's cool to work under him.'

Adele raised an eyebrow. She hadn't realised Ben's barista skills were so lauded.

'Is Ember around?' asked the third girl shyly. She wore a headband with cat ears on it, and carried a cat backpack. Even her earrings were cats with springy tails. She had more commitment to her bit than Lorelei Gilmore. *Chaya*, read her cat-shaped nametag.

'Ember!' Adele looked around for the shop's resident terror, but he must have followed Ben and Topknot down to the basement. 'He's usually wherever the sunshine is, but right now he's helping out with a roast.'

The lights flickered as she said it. She hoped the building had enough juice to power the roaster *and* the espresso machine. Maybe there was a reason Ben roasted at night.

'Right. Speaking of, can I get some beans? It's my dad's birthday.' Trix grabbed a bag from the shop's rattan merchandise shelf, giving it a squeeze. 'Is that the roast date?'

That was a Ben question, not an Adele question. But he was busy downstairs with Topknot. And he'd been as serious as the throat-slitting scene in *Sweeney Todd* when he'd said, *we're not to be disturbed*. Coffee roasting must be an involved process. Adele was imagining something like baking a soufflé, where opening the oven door could result in the whole thing collapsing. Or maybe the part in brain surgery where you pulled out a clot.

'Let me get you some super fresh stuff. Just to be sure.' Grabbing a scoop, Adele filled a fresh bag with beans. She sealed the bag with the laminator machine sitting on top of the bar fridge – laminators and label makers were the two machines she knew how to work – then stuck a vinyl Riffraff sticker from a nearby bowl on its front. Almost done. All it needed was a curly bow . . . There.

'Wow, you ornamented it.' Trix held it up to the light, inspecting Adele's handiwork. 'That's so cool. Are you a scrapbooker? I know that stuff's huge with your generation.'

Ouch. An insult of Shakespearean proportions.

'She's an actress,' called Reba, easing herself back into her seat. 'Musical theatre.'

'Like, on Broadway?' marvelled Chaya, her cat-ear headband bobbing in excitement. 'We perform, too. At school mostly, but we're starting to do community stuff. We're working on *Tender Morsels*. Trix wrote it.'

Trix blushed. 'It's an early work.'

Do something else! Adele wanted to say. *Anything* else! Spare y'allselves!

Instead, she cheerfully blurted, 'Well, let me know when opening night is, and I'll definitely come see it.'

The girls exchanged excited looks. Adele fizzed inwardly: she knew how validating it felt to have a fellow creative interested in your work. Never mind that she wasn't a *real* Broadway actress.

'Now, what are y'all drinking?'

She regretted it as soon as she said it, because the girls blurted out a full algebra equation of milks and sugars and syrup pumps. Was it legal to give kids that much sugar? What exactly were sago pearls? She hadn't been this discombobulated since trying to go off-book for 'I Am the Very Model of a Modern Major-General'.

'One second.' Adele pulled out the coffee-stained cheat sheet Ben had directed her to after he'd busted her trying to google the instructions for the brewer. She ran a finger over it, trying to find anything that resembled what the girls had ordered. It was like trying to decode the Rosetta Stone.

'Here, let me. Coming through, toots. And you, love.' There was a rainbow of tie-dye as Reba squeezed past the girls and ducked back behind the counter. Helping herself to an oatmeal cookie, she said, 'Now, what were you girls after?'

The teenagers repeated their untranslatable orders. Reba nodded sagely, then directed Adele to fetch cups and mugs while she pulled out the milk frother.

'I used to help Doralee out, back in the day,' explained Reba, as they mixed and stirred and rattled around vintage-looking drink shakers. Adele was impressed: Reba still had it. She could give a chorus line a run for their money.

'Plus I spent years selling grilled cheese sandwiches to absolutely shitfaced hippies on Shakedown Street. You learn to reach across the aisle. Catch!' Reba tossed a cocktail shaker at Rivka, who caught it with a shy giggle. Reba spun a tall glass along the counter. 'Now, pull that lid off and pour that in here.'

Rivka carefully poured the contents of the shaker into her cup. Her hennaed hands shook, but she finally set down the emptied shaker with pride, wiping her palms on her purple jumpsuit.

Reba considered. 'Now, we don't have sago pearls, but we *do* have chocolate chips. Will those do?'

The girls conferred, then nodded their consensus.

Adele grinned as she sprinkled chocolate chips into each drink. When she was done, Reba produced four long sundae spoons, handing them to the girls one by one.

'I can't believe you knew all the recipes for those drinks!' said Adele, watching the girls slouch off to the big communal table to sip at each other's drinks and scribble in each other's school planners.

Reba knotted her silvery hair into a bun, through which she stabbed a bombilla straw. 'Oh, I have no idea once you get past the basics. But it's hard to go wrong with chocolate and condensed milk.' She handed Adele a spoon of her own. 'Now let's clean this delicious mess up.'

You Mocha Me Crazy

Adele was scraping her spoon around the bottom of the can of condensed milk when the shop door jingled. It was Stockbroker Guy. Again. He strode in with the stiff-backed, hyper-alert confidence of someone riding an invisible Segway, setting down an elegant leather briefcase on the counter with the care and precision of a concert pianist about to break into the *Rach III*.

'Espresso. Neat,' he said, tapping away on his phone.

Adele was too intimidated to ask, but weren't all espressos neat? Maybe the terminology referred to a new trend she was way behind on. Like when she'd thought that Pacojets were rocket jets. (Alas, this was not the case.) But she wasn't going to risk looking foolish in front of the guy who had seen her go ass over tap shoe along Broadway. She made a note to ask Ben later. Or to look it up at the first place that had phone signal on the way home.

'Coming up,' she said, around a mouthful of solidified sugar-milk. There was a reason her mom hadn't allowed condensed milk in the house.

Hiding beneath a curtain of grown-out bangs, she tamped the shot and prepped the La Marzocco.

'*Weigh it out and tamp it down and muscle it on and push on through*,' she sang under her breath. '*Do the thing the customers demand that you do . . .*'

The machine hummed happily as it pressed hot water through the grounds in the portafilter. Look at that! The crema was magnificent. Ben would be proud.

'Here you go.' She slid the cup along the counter, then took the hefty black Amex the guy handed her. It was as sharp and thick as a sushi knife.

'I'll need a receipt,' said Stockbroker Guy, still typing. 'You're new here? I haven't seen you before.'

'Actually, you have,' admitted Adele as she scribbled *four dollars* on a carbon pad that had last been used for Doralee's grocery list – apparently her great-aunt had been addicted to hummus. 'Yesterday. And the other night on Broadway. During the rain. You were getting into a cab. I . . . was getting splashed.'

Stockbroker Guy's glasses gleamed as he leaned across the counter to get a better look at her. Up close, he smelt of high-end cologne and leather car seats, and there was a certain polish to him, like he'd been buffed with the chamois of intergenerational wealth. With his slicked-back hair and tailored suit, he was the opposite of Ben, but he *was* kind of cute. Maybe it was the confidence. Or the twenty-dollar bill he'd popped in the tip jar.

'No. I'd remember.' He flashed a grin so white it was almost translucent. 'I'm excellent with faces.'

Well, at least Adele hadn't made a bad impression. In fact, she hadn't made any impression at all.

Looking for something to do to hide her discomfort, Adele rinsed the portafilter. Something about this exceedingly well-put-together guy made her shy. Did that mean she was interested in him? Or did it mean that she should stay away?

Based on her past experiences, it was both.

'Donny,' he said, holding out a hand. A watch that cost more than Adele's in-state undergraduate degree in Theatre Studies flashed on his wrist. The watch probably opened more doors than her degree, too, she thought sadly.

No, enough of that. She was living the dream. She had her own coffee shop! Her own, only slightly rat-infested apartment!

Her own hot barista, she thought idly, wondering what was taking Ben and Topknot Guy so long. How long did it take to roast a batch of coffee, anyway? She didn't know much about it, but she assumed that it was similar to making popcorn. You put it on the stove, let it go for a few minutes, then took it off the heat before the pops turned into a nuclear explosion.

Donny tucked the receipt into his fancy briefcase, then carefully wiped at an invisible spot on its supple brown hide. 'Vachetta leather. Can't be near water. So you're . . . the shop assistant?'

Adele flushed. 'The owner, actually. It's a new development.'

'Look at you! Your LinkedIn inbox must be overflowing.'

'Mm,' agreed Adele. She felt as lost as the time she'd learned the wrong choreography to *Footloose* and had twirled off stage right.

'Maybe dancing *should* be banned around you,' her high school theatre teacher had snapped.

Donny chugged his espresso, then turned the cup upside down on its saucer. 'Well, I bet you have some ideas to make this place shine. I mean . . . look at it. It's got a long way to go. I'm guessing your P&L is heavy on the L. And selling it's going to be near impossible. Decent footfall, but you've got the cemetery at the top of the hill, and the wonky zoning in this area. Not to mention all the ways that this place skirts code. What're you paying? Is it triple net?'

This was like one of those anxiety dreams where Adele found herself in school trying to fill out an exam using a piece of damp spaghetti. At least in those dreams she could awkwardly swim away. In the real world she had to sit here nodding along. And there wasn't even spaghetti.

'I have a few ideas,' she said at last, channelling her inner Caractacus Potts. 'I'd, um, love to get some more outdoor seating happening.'

'Oh, I like the sound of that,' called Reba, stretching out her legs the way she always did when she'd finished her crossword. Her rainbow woven sandals flashed. 'These old gams could do with some sun.'

'Can you smell hamburgers?' interjected Frank, sniffing. 'I thought that burger joint down the road closed down.'

'Maybe you're having a stroke,' said Reba archly. 'What else, Adele?'

Adele closed her eyes, imagining all the things that Riffraff could be. 'Maybe a rotating exhibition of local artists' work on that far wall, with weekly pour and paint classes. And perhaps a Brews Clues trivia afternoon. And definitely some community groups, like the Shut Up and Write group I used to be a part of, and one for table reads for the local community. Oh, and a farmer's market!'

The excitement rang out in her voice – oh no, she was projecting. It was hard not to when you had years of performing under your belt. Your diaphragm wanted to get involved in everything.

Donny nodded slowly, the way you nodded when you *really* wanted to shake your head, but you were talking to a small child who was particularly insistent about the beneficence of the Easter Bunny.

'Well, if there's a business case for each of those, and the ROI is there, then I suppose . . .'

Adele stood there like a deer in headlights, wishing a car would hurry up and hit her. *Here Lies Adele*, her tombstone, bought on credit, would say. *Dead from Ignorance, and Better Off For It.*

Donny pulled out a card. 'I have a hard stop, but how about we talk about this over drinks? Pro bono real estate consulting is a personal interest of mine. They really stressed it at Harvard. Pick you up at seven on Thursday.'

Adele hesitated. She didn't particularly like the idea of being someone's charity case, but she *could* use some guidance on this whole running a business thing. Not to mention a free cocktail. One with a four different liqueurs and a fancy citrus peel garnish and a name that referenced Zelda Fitzgerald. (Or, if she were paying, a house vodka and soda.)

And she *was* flattered that he had come around to her charms. Even if it was belatedly.

'You don't know where I live,' she pointed out. Brooklyn wasn't exactly her town back home where you could figure it out based on the surnames written on the letterboxes. And the semaphore of terrible flags that flew proudly in the face of modernity.

Donny chuckled. 'That's my driver's number. Text him, and he'll come get you. Look sharp!'

Vachetta leather briefcase in hand, he slid off on his invisible Segway. As he neared the door, the elusive Ember reappeared, hissing as Donny tried to navigate around him.

'I'm allergic,' said Donny, with a shrug.

As Donny finally exited, Adele turned back to her work station. She jumped as she found herself facing Ben, who as usual had his muscular arms crossed. Although to be fair, if she had arms like that, she'd be crossing them all the time, too. Would it be wrong to squeeze them, just once? She could probably make it look like an accident: she'd once slipped on a fan's phone and had landed in the orchestra pit.

'You're not going out with that wanker, are you?' Ben had a smudge of dust on his face that Adele had to focus very hard on not brushing away. Apparently coffee roasting was sweaty, messy work . . .

'No!' protested Adele, blushing furiously at the debauched path her thoughts were coquettishly strolling down. 'We're going to talk about improvements to the business.'

'That tosspot wouldn't know business improvements if they bit him in the arse and rubbed tea tree oil in the wound. Let me guess: he mentioned Harvard.'

'Once,' admitted Adele. Once was reasonable, wasn't it?

'I'm just saying it's a bad look. How would you feel if I started dating every rando who walked in here?'

It was Adele's turn to fold her arms. 'I'd feel like it were none of my business.'

'Well then,' said Ben, smiling brightly at an attractive lacrosse player who'd strolled in. 'G'day, and welcome to Riffraff,' he said, slathering on his accent like Aussies did their Vegemite, weirdos that they were. 'What can I get for ya?'

Spilling the Beans

After awkwardly avoiding the retaliatorily flirtatious Ben for an hour or so, Adele excused herself from the shop, saying something about needing to get Doralee's personal effects in order. What precisely personal effects were, she didn't know. But she assumed it was a fancy word for *stuff*. And Doralee had incredible amounts of stuff.

Munching on a day-old cinnamon bun she'd snuck from the Riffraff fridge, Adele regarded her new living space. Not that there was room to do much living in here – or sleeping, as Adele had learned last night as she'd clung to one edge of the garment-strewn bed as though she were Kate Winslet gripping the *Titanic* door. In Adele's case, however, there definitely hadn't been room for another person to climb aboard.

Every horizontal surface in Doralee's apartment groaned and teetered with boxes, knickknacks and reusable shopping bags. And the vertical ones were draped with tinkly beaded curtains and tie-dyed canopies.

Bit by bit, like learning her lines. It didn't all have to be done today.

But *some* of it did. Because, thanks in part to Kyra's

excellent brownies and the even more delicious phở from Side-Part-Neighbour-Whose-Name-She'd-Forgotten, she hadn't got especially far with the whole decluttering goal last night. A couple of the other neighbours from the enclave of apartments – Tori and Bart? Terrance and Babs? – had rocked up shortly after with pizzas, and then someone else had waltzed in with a guitar. There'd been a lot of reminiscing, a lot of singing, and very little tidying. Although they had got as far as collectively deciding that there needed to be at least five clutter categories: the Keep, the Garbage, the Goodwill, the Yard Sale and the Find-the-Owner-of.

When Adele had finally come in, she'd simply moved a handful of the boxes on the bed into the bathroom and conked out until daybreak. Of course, this now meant that the shower was filled with old books and piles of records. But if she moved those boxes out of the bathroom, she wouldn't have anywhere to sleep. Similarly, if she wanted to sit, she had to move the button jars on the chair over to the bed, and . . .

Basically, it was the same Tower of Hanoi issue that Adele dealt with when transferring her credit card balances from one card to another. Shuffling things around worked for a while, but eventually you had to actually handle the situation.

Promising herself she'd deal with her credit cards at some acceptably distant future point, Adele grabbed a few of the lighter-looking boxes and dropped them on the bed. Pulling a Riffraff order pad from her pocket, she wrote a heading for each of the five decluttering categories and set them on the floor. Presumably this was how Richard designed his cast lists.

All right. It was Stanley knife time.

Adele cut open the first box, revealing several hand-painted vases and cups. Yard Sale. Turning them over, she saw they were all etched with the name *Ilona*. Cute. With archaeological consideration, Adele nudged the pottery items over so they sat between the Yard Sale and the Find-the-Owner columns. Next up was a box of wonky-looking rocks and crystals. Donate. Then a croaking frog door alarm. *Keep*, for Riffraff. The fourth box contained a bunch of shoes, including, to her delight, a pair of red sequinned slippers. *Wear*, thought Adele, popping them on her feet and giving her toes a waggle. Feeling like Dorothy stepping into Oz, she opened box after box, clapping happily as she unearthed one containing bundles of dried flowers – silvery eucalyptus, pom-pom craspedia, dried dogwoods like the ones her parents had in their backyard. Yard Sale, with a Keep for the dogwoods. Mom would love those.

They were also a sign that Adele *had* to give her parents a call tonight.

Hmm, what was that? Setting aside a box of mirror-studded Rajasthani elephant toys that would fetch a fortune on Etsy, Adele picked up a photo album with a macramé cover dotted with seashells. The thing was *huge*, and heavy. Meanwhile, all of Adele's photos lived somewhere in the cloud, which she assumed meant that they were floating above her head somewhere. Leafing through the album, she found herself smiling: every shot had that yellowy vintage tint that always made her think of California.

Here was Doralee with a band, each of them making peace signs at the camera. Doralee filming some sort of play on one of those old-school wind-up camcorders. Doralee with a raggedy group of people outside some sort of log cabin. Doralee in a sunflower field hugging a woman holding a baby in a striped romper, like a compressed Big Top.

Every photo seemed so casual, yet so impressive. Her great-aunt had lived such a big life.

Adele's phone flashed, distracting her from the extremely cute, extremely fat baby. *Missed call: Mom.*

Ack, the reception in this place was as lukewarm as the one at the last dress rehearsal she'd attended.

She still hadn't told her parents about this whole situation. And while it wasn't a surprise pregnancy, it wasn't something you randomly sprang on someone over Thanksgiving dinner. There was a window for these things. If you left it too long, it got weird, like you'd been avoiding telling them. Which Adele definitely hadn't been. It had been a busy few days.

But maybe you are *avoiding telling them, Adele.*

All right, maybe she was. A bit. Her parents had been relentlessly supportive of her less-than-conventional career goals – Dad even had a mug that said *Broadway Dad* – and here was Adele doing a full one-eighty on her dreams. But she'd given it her all for years. Maybe she deserved a break.

Maybe this break was her big break.

Pulling the purple door closed behind her, Adele went out into the plant-filled courtyard, waving her phone about like she was dowsing for phone reception. One bar. No signal. Emergency only. What had Kyra said? You had to go to the cemetery if you wanted decent reception.

Mindful that the sun was drooping in the sky, she tiptoed through the wrought-iron courtyard gates, and then down the street, spinning in slow circles as she waited for her phone to gather a decent number of bars. The most promising spot so far was next to the stained lamppost mattress with the milk jugs. No thanks. From here she could go left, towards the coffee shop, where Ben was probably hard at work on Secret Roasting Business, or right towards the cemetery. Sigh.

Adele took the right, which turned out to be an uphill trek that made her calves scream. If she wanted to maintain her conditioning she'd have to work some dancing and twirling into her days (and maybe take it easy on the croissants and chocolate-chip cookies).

The street became steeper, to the point that the pavement turned into a series of steps and the red-brick buildings seemed like they were sliding down the hill. What was this – San Francisco?

Murmuring up ahead: a group of goths descended the hill in a veil of black velvet and lace. With the sun at their backs, it looked like they were dragging the waning day down with them.

'Ugh, being a goth in summer *sucks*,' said one, detouring around Adele.

'"Bela Lugosi's dead",' muttered another, in a Peter Murphy monotone. 'Yeah, of the goddamn heat.'

Adele hid a smile. She checked her phone: two bars! A bit higher up, and she was at three. Wow, but the air was thin up here. It was like sitting in the mezzanine seats at the Gershwin Theatre.

Soon enough, the wonky houses gave way to a huge Gothic-style gate whose architect had a clear fascination with triangles. Through the street-straddling gate she could see an expanse of lawn, hundreds of lichen-dotted statues and tombstones, and some astonishingly involved mausoleums, all of which were larger than any apartment she'd inhabited during her time in the City. Like living on the Upper East Side, being dead took a lot of upkeep.

Finally, her phone was showing a legitimate number of bars. Maybe graves and 5G were a good combination. Perhaps all that stone amplified the signal, like the sunbathing reflectors from Doralee's Seventies photos.

Traipsing over some surprisingly lush grass – *don't think about that too hard, Adele* – she made her way to a stone bench seat with a plaque honouring someone called Fitzy Fring, who had apparently been both a writer and an itinerant gambler. *Read 'em and weep*, read the inscription in the stone. A crow ambled past, a twig in its mouth: even crows took smoke breaks.

She pulled up Mom's contact details and hit *call*.

After some fumbling, Mom's face appeared on the screen. Whoops, now Adele was looking at the ceiling. Now a foot . . . and now at Marple, her parents' ancient basset hound.

Ah. There they were: her beaming parents, both trying to squeeze themselves into the shot. Between Mom's painstaking blonde curls and Dad's prized beard, which had made it to the regional finals of the National Beard Competition, it was a tall order.

'Adele, sweetheart! Sorry about earlier: butt dial. Where are you? Is that Central Park? Is that a horse and carriage going by?'

A hearse, more likely. 'I'm in Brooklyn. I've moved.'

'But I thought you loved your apartment,' said Dad, who was chowing down on a bowl of Cheerios, sans milk. 'It reminded you of Meemaw's. Homely.'

Adele had always been strategic about the photos she'd shared of her last place. For example, none of them contained the kitchen shower curtain, or evidence of Lane's existence. When her parents had asked about the family in the photo frame by the bed, she'd explained that they were part of a cast she'd been working with.

'What was the reason? Were there bedbugs?' The phone showed a flashing glimpse of her parents' shaker-style kitchen cabinets as Mom added excitedly, 'Did you move in with a boy? Or a girl. That's fine, too. So long as there are grandbabies. But y'all can work that out among y'allselves.'

'Actually, it's Great-Aunt Doralee.'

'Doralee,' said Dad, crunching away. 'Now there's a name I haven't heard in years. Wasn't she your aunt in the City, Lorna?'

'She was. An absolute wild child, according to Ma. I wish I'd kept up with her, but who could? So what's that got to do with moving? Are you moving in with her?'

'Not exactly,' said Adele. Unless Doralee had come back as a ghost, of which there was a decent possibility, given how attached she seemed to be to her possessions. 'She passed.'

'. . . the Bar?' asked Dad, who always fully believed in everyone's ambitions, no matter how lofty. He was convinced it was a mere matter of days before Cousin Farley (who owned prodigious supplies of aluminium foil) would be recruited by the United States Space Force.

'. . . on from this world,' clarified Adele. 'She's dead.'

Mom and Dad conferred, going through the various possible causes of death and the lifestyle habits that might have led to them. This always seemed to happen upon a death: people played the 'what did her in?' game and then tried to rationalise it. Adele supposed it was a coping mechanism. If you could connect a heart attack with the habitual eating of seventeen packets of corn chips a day, you could protect against the same thing happening to you. Or at least come to terms with it, because let's face it: no one was giving up corn chips.

72

'Dear old Doralee!' said Mom, making an exaggerated moue. 'All that flax seed. It's bound to get you eventually.'

Having minutes ago sorted an entire box of bongs into the Garbage pile, Adele suspected that flax was the least of Doralee's questionable health decisions. 'Anyway, I got her apartment. And her coffee shop.'

Mom and Dad conferred again, excitedly this time. Marple popped into view, dragging a droopy ear over the screen.

'Oh, bless her heart,' said Mom.

This was the southern way of saying, *well, that's a bit silly, but it's none of my business.*

'But what about Broadway?' asked Dad, appearing over the top of Marple's fuzzy head in a bizarre melding of dog-human facial hair. Poor Marple received a dusting of Cheerios. 'You've put your whole life into that.'

'Exactly,' said Adele, her gaze sweeping over the gap-toothed rows of tombs. All these dead people with their dead dreams. But solid views. 'And I'm getting nowhere.'

'But you were that smiling girl in that one about the boat,' pressed Dad. 'And you had that role in *Grease*.'

'Teacher #3?' Adele grinned ruefully. Hers hadn't even been a real role: the theatre group had merely been extremely gracious about giving everyone who'd signed up *something* to do.

'Well, I say those three lines were worth the two hundred bucks in gas, *plus* the Nashville accommodation. And the money you spent on hair gel.'

'Thanks, Dad.' Adele blinked back tears. She felt like she was letting them both down: all those late-night pickups throughout her childhood. The endless hours they'd spent helping her memorise her dance routines – and the three times

Dad had thrown out his back performing lifts with her. She had to make the coffee shop work.

'I'll always be your biggest fan, baby girl.'

'But a coffee shop is a good, solid business,' said Mom. 'Everyone drinks coffee. Except for British people.'

'Hence the Revolution,' said Dad.

'Whereas you have to admit that musical theatre is more . . . niche. All that narrative through singing. It's not a very efficient way of telling a story, is it?' (Mom was a lifelong subscriber to *Reader's Digest*.)

'I'm just saying that you can do both,' said Dad. 'You wouldn't be the first performer to hold down a day job as well.'

Adele thought of all of her friends half-assing their nine-to-fives and casual work. *Holding down* was being generous. But she understood the sentiment.

'So!' said Mom. 'When can we come to visit? We have travel points, you know.'

Adele nodded, but distractedly. Her attention was on the billowing smoke coming from the direction of the Riffraff. How much coffee was Ben roasting down there?

What was he doing with it? Setting it on fire?

Oh shit.

'I gotta go. Love y'all.'

All Steamed Up

Adele raced back down the hill towards Riffraff, thankful for the ankle strength she'd developed from years of high kicks and spins on the stage. Her speed elicited a few cheers from a bunch of college-aged guys wearing ironic Eighties calisthenic outfits and carrying frisbees, a scowl from an old guy stooping to bag his Pekingese's doggy deposit, and a prolonged horn tooting from an e-bike delivery driver with an executive's dry cleaning balanced over his legs. Adele jumped, startled: no wonder Leonard Bernstein had called the horn section of the orchestra the 'hunky brutes'.

By the time Adele hurried across the weird intersection cornered by the coffee shop, the street was shrouded in smoke. The gang of goths she'd encountered on the way up to the cemetery lurked nearby, surreptitiously taking selfies as they posed not very surreptitiously in the manner of Siouxsie Sioux.

Riffraff's door was propped open with a brick. Ben was standing grumpily in the doorway, dressed in a Brando-esque white T-shirt and jeans, looking like he was about to howl *'Stella!'* into the endlessly changeable aural backdrop of the Brooklyn evening.

'What's going on?' she panted, out of breath from her hurried steeplechase across the neighbourhood. Was it wrong to swoon into his arms? She could blame the smoke inhalation.

'Just a bit of smoke.' Ben waved indifferently at the air. 'Nice kicks, Dorothy.'

Adele waggled her toes, watching the sequins flash. 'They have surprisingly good arch support.'

'I'll bear that in mind when I need to replace my Maseur Sandals.' Shooting a wary look at the selfie-taking goths, Ben leaned a shoulder against the doorframe, blocking the shop entrance. 'Everything's under control. Go back home and get some beauty sleep.'

'Some of us don't need beauty sleep,' said Adele. She stood on her tiptoes, trying to peer past Ben. Damn him for having such broad shoulders. 'What's with the smoke? Were you barbecuing in the shop or something?'

'Are you disparaging my sausage-sizzling prowess? I've seen what you lot call sausages. That's not food. It's a declaration of war. Criminal.'

'Criminally delicious.' Adele pushed past him, ignoring the delicious zap that ricocheted through her as her shoulder brushed his chest. She couldn't even blame the rubber shoes this time.

Ben cleared his throat – had he felt it, too?

'Really, it's nothing,' he said evenly. 'Front door was open and someone came in. Probably an unhoused person: happens all the time. They made themselves at home, and that's that.'

Adele frowned, surveying the shop for damage. Nothing seemed especially out of order: the chairs lounged upside down on the tables, the counters shone, and the crockery towered like the Manhattan skyline. The only thing that looked odd was the basement door, which hung open, its seven locks glimmering uneasily in the low light. A broom was propped next to it.

'Did they mess with the roaster?' she asked, peering down the dimly lit steps into the shadowy basement.

Ben grabbed the broom, using it as pretext to close the basement door. She'd never met anyone so protective of a basement. Even Pops, who famously had the most elaborate model train set-up in all of eastern Tennessee, had allowed a young Adele to frolic around in his. Maybe Ben was working on an embarrassing epic Lego scene and worried she'd take a photo that would go viral on Reddit.

Ben started sweeping with the intensity of a *STOMP* cast member. 'I dunno. Anyway, they're gone now.'

'I think they left their jacket.' Adele reached for a woman's puffer vest draped over one of the tables. Was that the Canada Goose logo? Wow, someone had been generous during last season's coat drive.

Ben hurried over to grab the vest, balling it up in his hands. 'I'll pop it in the Lost Property box. Anyway. I'll see you tomorrow.'

Adele felt faintly crushed. He was so desperate to kick her out. She didn't mind Lego, really. She could look past an obsession with plastic bricks. She'd looked past much worse, like the guy whom she'd learned during a supposedly romantic backroads drive was into roadkill taxidermy. And the one with a literal collection of red flags (he stole these from the club sandwiches he aways ordered at restaurants).

Was Ben still sore about Donny? Or was something else going on? Adele racked her brains, trying to remember what the attractive lacrosse player had been wearing. She hoped that all this smoke wasn't the result of a sexy candlelit scenario gone wrong.

'Will you be able to sleep?' she said at last. 'It's pretty smoky in here. You can always . . .'

A pause as she mulled over what she was about to offer. Ben raised an eyebrow, waiting patiently for her to incriminate herself.

'Open a window?' he said finally.

'Right,' said Adele, with a dash of relief. And also a dollop of disappointment.

'All good here?' came a voice that was half gravel, half squawk.

Adele jerked.

The voice had come from a guy with demonstrative eyebrows who had poked a beanie-topped head through the door. The beanie had a firefighter insignia on it; swatches of dark curly hair poked through its multitude of burn holes.

Adele hadn't known a firefighter could sneak up on someone like that. They weren't renowned for making a stealthy entrance. They were meant to arrive with sirens wailing and million-decibel horns blasting. And from what she'd seen on TV, they typically chopped down doors with an axe.

At the sight of yet another interloper, Ben swore under his breath. 'All good, mate. Burnt some toast. And the bacon.'

The firefighter's eyebrows leapt to give his beanie a double high five. 'Thought I smelled that. Haven't had bacon since I started on the job. Smells like human flesh, you know. And my cholesterol levels are through the roof. Which, if we're being honest, is the main thing.'

'Righto,' said Ben, who was looking a bit clammy. Must be

all that carbon monoxide. 'Well, no human flesh here. Just a burnt dinner.'

'Where's your truck?' asked Adele. The red strobing lights that came standard with a fire engine were nowhere to be seen. Ah, budget cuts.

'I'm coming home from my shift,' said Eyebrows. 'That's my Toyota by the hydrant.'

'Nice parking,' said Ben, drily.

To be fair, it was a good spot.

'What were you planning to do if there *had* been a fire?' Adele was baffled.

'Nothing. Couldn't legally help if I wanted to.' Eyebrows shrugged. 'I can call the department. Jimmy's sleeping, though. He might be pissed.'

The firefighter had roughly the same sense of civic engagement as the goths, who had gone off gently into the velvety night, bragging about how their smoky shop selfies would make the perfect album cover.

'Nah, we've got it,' said Ben. He reached across the counter, his white shirt riding up to reveal the bottom of a cursive tattoo that Adele didn't catch – a name? 'Here. Have a fully punched loyalty card, on the house. Night.'

'Thanks.' The firefighter held up the card to the light, as though verifying it wasn't a forgery. 'Maybe try oatmeal next time. Microwaved.'

'Righto, Goldilocks,' muttered Ben.

As the Toyota pulled out from its spot, it was immediately pulled over by a police cruiser. The red and blue lights bathed the interior of Riffraff in a first-responder-themed disco.

Adele couldn't resist humming the chorus to 'The Circle of Life'.

Ben didn't seem to find this funny. Which was a him problem, not a her problem. After stalking past her, he checked the windows, cracking open any that were closed. A teasing cross-breeze meandered through the room, bringing with it the thudding of a Celica's subwoofer, the angry refrains of a distant argument, and the smell of roasting garlic.

'Why'd you lie?' asked Adele absently, eyeing the puffer vest bulging out from the Lost Property box like a yeast starter gone mad. You weren't cooking bacon.'

Ben grunted as he hauled a window open. 'Because otherwise we'd be dealing with an investigation that would shut us down for at least a day, then a whole insurance thing. Sometimes, the less said, the better.'

Adele frowned: she'd got another flash of that tattoo. A woman's name: Lena? Lyra? And a date: 1994.

Before her brain managed to resolve the letters into a word, Ben hit the main light switch, swathing the shop in a darkness broken only by the glow from the streetlights and the Christmassy green and red LEDs of the coffee equipment. 'Sweet dreams.'

And . . . curtain, she thought, as she stepped offstage.

Trouble, Stirred

'Insurance papers, insurance papers,' muttered Adele, digging around in the drawers behind the counter. How could *every* drawer be a junk drawer? She'd never seen so many rubber bands and old matchbooks and mangy bundles of sage.

The day had flown by in a flurry of frappés, deep-fried mini doughnuts and food feuds between multiple sets of twin four-year-olds. At three, Ben had grabbed his bag and hurried out the door, evasively citing a standing commitment. Curious. But it gave Adele a handy-dandy window of time to poke into the business side of the, well, business. Because in theory that's what Riffraff was.

But something was off.

Ben's comment last night about avoiding an insurance claim together with Donny's dig about P&Ls (not a shampoo manufacturer, it turned out) had unearthed a few fossils of concern from the stratigraphy of Adele's consciousness. For one, Adele hadn't been paid yet, and the scrunched-up twenties she'd been finding around Doralee's apartment would only go so far. She had the sneaking suspicion that Riffraff was a not-for-profit – and not by choice. If so, she had to figure something out, and fast, before her windfall became her downfall.

The doorbell jingled. Adele stood, banging her head against the top of the counter. She hissed at the pain, an unimpressed audience of one judging her own slapstick comedy.

'Are you guys open? I'm fresh out of goat milk, and Oreo is starving.' It was Autumn, the goat yoga instructor from next door, complete with a black-and-white goat friend nibbling at a blue leash.

Maaah! screamed Oreo. Hissing, Ember sought higher ground.

The sign on the door, another of Frank's masterworks, read *Dammit Janet, we're closed*, which was hardly ambiguous. And got points for being a *Rocky Horror Picture Show* reference. But Adele supposed goats couldn't read. And who could say no to a goat, anyway?

'I can get it myself,' said Autumn blithely, as Oreo dragged her through the door with a determination unique to beasts of the cloven-footed variety.

Adele hadn't known yoga involved so much resistance training. Although she *was* beginning to see how someone could sneak into Riffraff and start a fire. Or worse, eat all the condensed milk. Maybe they'd have to revisit Doralee's unlocked door policy.

Oreo chomped on one of Kyra's planters, a terracotta sheep growing alfalfa 'fleece', as Autumn lifted the counter flap and made herself at home in the prep area. Bottles clinked and containers clattered as she hunted through the fridge.

'I don't know if we serve goat milk,' said Adele dazedly, rescuing Kyra's sheep from Oreo. Her head pounded from where she'd whacked it. What had she been doing again? That's right: the books. Where had Doralee kept all of her accounting stuff? *Had* she kept any accounting stuff, or was Adele going to have to ship off a tote bag full of receipts to the IRS?

Ember, sitting high on a bookshelf, was no help. His sharp gaze on her, he lifted a leg to begin his afternoon ablutions.

'Do you meow at your mother with that mouth?' Adele chastised him as she popped a Dusty Springfield CD into the janky boombox by the record player. She really needed to get that scratchy old thing fixed. Especially now that she'd carted several boxes of Doralee's records down to the shop. Frank had picked over them, nodding appreciatively at her great-aunt's taste in music. And chuckling at the memories.

'Remember the hill-rolling race?' he'd said, waggling the blue-sky cover of a Traffic album at Reba.

'Shut up, Frank,' Reba had snapped.

Frank had.

'Although I still laugh thinking about her chasing after that cheese wheel,' Reba had added, mostly to herself.

Adele could imagine it: a rainbow of laughing hippies tumbling towards a duck-filled lake in search of lost cheese.

Or lost goat milk, as was presently the case. Humming along with Dusty, Adele went over to help Autumn, who had emptied half the fridge.

'Doralee always keeps a stash of goat milk,' explained Autumn, with a whip-like flick of her goat-nibbled hair extensions. Adele barely ducked in time.

'Got it!' said Autumn, hefting a silvery thermos. GOAT-ARADE, said the raised label on its side. Puns that bad should be a jailable offence.

Excited by the promised feast, Oreo bounded across the room, bouncing off chairs and ottomans and a bar cart like a horned pinball. Not wanting any part of this, Ember disappeared through his basement cat flap.

After a few more fleet-footed jumps, Oreo leapt over the counter, headbutting the drawer labelled *Out of Sight, Out of Mind* that Ben had tapped a few days ago. The drawer burst open, and an array of envelopes sprang out like a possessed accordion. They were all cattle-branded with the same red stamp: *Past Due*.

Great. Doralee had hired Ulla Inga Hansen Benson Yansen Tallen Hallen Svaden Swansson Bloom to do her books. Which meant that Adele was going to have to get intimate with Doralee's chequebook tonight.

'I'm so sorry,' said Autumn, helping gather envelopes as Oreo sucked at the thermos like a possessed vacuum cleaner. 'Kids, am I right? Hey, I gotta get going – I have this drum circle thing – but you're always welcome to stop by for class. It's a great workout. Reba says it's the GOAT.'

Autumn and Oreo trip-trapped out of the shop, leaving Adele trying to muscle the drawer back into place. No luck. It was stuck. She wiggled it about, using the same finesse she'd used when attaching her eyelashes for her role as Backup Dancer #6 in *Hairspray*. No luck. Crouching, she saw a notebook was jammed between the drawer and the top of the cabinet. She tried to prise it out, but it was caught fast. How come there was never a knife around when you needed one? If only Ben were here. Being Australian, he probably had a whole knife block stowed inside the light, very well-fitting jacket he always slid on (weather permitting) before he checked out at three.

Adele grabbed a wooden coaster from one of the junk drawers and used that instead.

Finally the book yielded. She pulled it out and flipped

through its coffee-stained pages. It was not, as she'd hoped, an accounting ledger. It was a weird diary filled with dates and sketches of leaves and odd shorthand scribbles written in a purple, beetling script. Apparently Doralee had doodled when she was on the phone.

A rumble from somewhere beneath her made the whole building shiver. Was that her stomach? She'd been chowing down pretty consistently on baked goods, but those didn't really count as a proper meal. Which reminded her, she was meant to be meeting Donny tonight!

Their rendezvous had slipped her mind entirely, which was strange, because historically, she rarely forgot a date. Usually if she was interested in someone, she'd spend every spare moment brushing up on their favourite media while mentally choreographing a *Dirty Dancing*-esque performance to what would inevitably become *their* song.

She snatched up her bag, almost dropping the dog-eared copy of *Glengarry Glen Ross* she'd picked up from McNally Jackson's after Ben had supplied the answer to Reba's crossword puzzle.

'So what?' she told a judgemental Ember, who had cautiously emerged from the basement. 'I've been meaning to read Mamet for years. He's part of a well-rounded Broadway education. Even if there's no singing. But there *could* be. There's always room for singing.'

High up on its knoll, the pointy church overlooking the grassy hilltop cemetery sounded a single bell, marking half past six.

She gave Ember a quick stroke and backed out the front door. 'I'm out, but Ben will be back for you soon. Go cough up a hairball on his bed for me.'

Whack. Adele backed into a warm, solid figure – definitely not the lampposts and coffee table corners she usually bumped into, distracted by whatever *Chicago* lyric had popped into her head. It was Ben, of course. How was he always there?

'I live here,' he said, gently turning her around and answering her unspoken question. 'And work here. How's the Mamet?'

Dammit.

Hit Me with Your Best Shot

Adele sighed. The entire contents of the duffel bag she'd brought with her from her kitchen apartment was set out in wrinkled, slightly musty glory upon the cheerfully canopied bed. It all seemed so dull. The single item that showed any personality was Doralee's bedspread, which was a handmade patchwork of botanical glamour beneath an equally dramatic canopy.

Now she knew how Richard felt when he had to audition hundreds of starry-eyed, over-emoting hopefuls trying so hard to convince him of their *it* factor that they managed only to convince him of their *It* factor. And no one liked a clown. Not even Stephen King.

Adele sank down on the creaky bed, twisting a finger around one of the tie-dyed canopy sections and smiling as its lacework fringe tickled her forehead. According to the Riffraff regulars, Doralee had never sat around wondering what to wear. Armed with her sewing machine, she'd worked her magic on whatever piece of fabric was vaguely within arm's reach. Adele had heard the colourful stories, seen the bedazzled photo albums, tripped over the mounds of textiles.

She bit her lip as she regarded the hand-painted wardrobe and the stack of vintage suitcases against the wall. There had to be some gems in there.

Hand on the wardrobe's push-button latch, she sang an ode to the fashion gods in her best Freddie Mercury impersonation.

The wardrobe door swung open, and the lingering scent of incense and rosewater perfumed the air. A profusion of floaty dresses and kaftans wafted in the breeze that spilled in through the bedroom window. Everything was loose and patterned and floral. It was like staring at a rainbow pinwheel in the hands of a cartwheeling child. Adele could only begin to imagine the memories they carried.

She pulled out item after item, her senses overwhelmed by the colour and texture. Patchwork jumpsuits. Fringe vests. Paisley harem trousers. Batik shawls with jingling coins. They were all so lovingly made that it seemed wrong to keep them confined here in their dark wardrobe. At least Doralee had decoupaged its inside with cheerful fashion magazine cut-outs.

This was the one. A dotty yellow kaftan with huge painted poppies and sunflowers blooming up from the hem. Adele spun a circle, marvelling as the flowers danced and twirled like merry-go-round animals.

She fumbled in the back of the wardrobe for a clutch, frowning as her fingers closed around a metallic vessel. Pulling it out, she saw it was painted with mandalas and dots resembling paw prints. She twisted its lid off, coughing as a fine powder wafted from it. Why would Aunt Doralee hide a pepper grinder back there?

Holding her breath, she screwed the lid back on and popped the grinder on a windowsill, next to a set of nesting dolls, a green vase filled with feathers, some decorative rocks and a stack of vintage fashion magazines. (Doralee really had taken cluttercore to its maximal limit.)

A honk from outside. Was it seven already? She'd spent longer than she'd thought poking through all that gabardine and chambray. Such was the hypnotic nature of psychedelic clothing.

Dragging on a pair of low slingbacks, Adele hurried into the courtyard, digging in Doralee's Glomesh clutch for her keys. Which were not there. Nor was her wallet, now that she thought about it.

Well, she'd have to hope no one came barging into the apartment while she was gone. Although the incense and fragrant soaps were probably enough to keep most people away. Not to mention the karaoke-prone courtyard, which was a good burglar deterrent.

'Disavowing your keys, I see,' said Kyra, who was wheeling out a terrarium bursting with Venus flytraps and pitcher plants. 'Isn't it freeing? That's how I learned to hotwire cars back in the day.'

Adele blinked. These old hippies were full of surprises.

'I'm on Doralee's side,' Kyra went on, spritzing the Venus flytrap. 'What's the point in having a space if people aren't welcome? That's why Riffraff's called what it is. It's always been home to all the riffraff in the city. A community space.'

The horn again. A huge black beetle of a car sidled up to the courtyard entrance, like Gregor Samsa nervously waking from his slumber. The carnivorous plants eyed it hungrily.

'That's you?' Kyra thoughtfully tapped her secateurs against her face. 'Well, you look lovely. I hope you have the night that you're after.'

Adele hurried towards the hulking Cadillac, feeling like she was making the ill-advised decision to confront a bear. She pulled on the front passenger-side door. The driver shook his head, pointing to the back door. Adele grimaced, blushing. She couldn't even get private car etiquette right.

The driver took pity on her. Grinning, he leaned over to shove open the front door. A light strip cast a trail of glowing red skulls across the kerb.

'You're good. You can ride up front. But only because that dress is fire.' He tapped the gearstick, which was topped with a bronze skull. Adele was noticing a theme. 'The badly dressed ones I make ride in the trunk. Joking, joking. But there's room, is all I'm saying.'

Adele clambered in – the car was so high off the ground that she almost needed a safety harness. She was reminded of the time she'd ill-advisedly held her birthday party at the local rock-climbing gym. She'd required rescuing.

The driver held out a burly arm to help her up, gripping her hand in a Cheeto-dusted firefighter's grip. At least orange went well with her outfit.

'Federico.' The driver tapped the ID card pinned to the windscreen. 'You're looking bright. Big night?'

'I'm not sure,' admitted Adele. 'I haven't really had time to think about it.'

'Living in the moment, huh.' Federico peered in the skull-clad rear-view mirror as he twisted the steering wheel. The vehicle's enormous tyres crunched beneath them. 'I know these apartments. A bunch of hippie ladies used to host ragers there. My pa would go. Brought me once or twice, but I always ended up in this coffee shop up the road. That one.'

He pointed at Riffraff Coffee Co as they cruised past. The

lights in the main shop were dimmed, but from the glow coming from the glass basement tiles, Adele assumed Ben was roasting.

'That's my shop,' she said, adding, 'It's a recent development. Do you mind if we pull over for a second? I need to grab my wallet and keys.'

And if she happened to cross paths with Ben, all the better.

The indicator tick-tocked like an old clock as the car pulled over.

'Damn, the memories of this old joint,' mused Federico. 'You still got that record player?'

'Yep, although it's just a display table for now. I need to get someone in to fix it.'

So long as they'd accept payment in the form of gratitude.

Adele tumbled out of the car and hurried across the wonky pavers that framed the shop's tiled patio. Multiple pairs of rat eyes flashed green from their garbage can hideouts. There was no such thing as being alone in the City. There was always a human above or below you, and failing that, the local vermin population was happy to provide companionship.

Smoke poured from the ancient exhaust pipe poking out from the basement, tinging the air with the unmistakable aroma of roasting coffee beans. She wrinkled her nose – the smoke had an odd undertone to it, like barbecue.

It was probably from the nearby churrasco restaurant: their ventilation hood had been having issues. So Ben said, anyway, and he seemed to know the neighbourhood pretty well.

'Hello?' she called, pushing open the shop door.

The coffee shop felt odd at this time of night. Without the hum of the espresso machine and the murmur of the regulars' conversations, it seemed somehow ghostly. She clacked over to

91

the counter, scratching around for her wallet and keys. Not that she *really* needed them for tonight. Donny had made it clear he was going to pay, and she wouldn't be entirely distraught if someone broke in and stole half of Doralee's stuff. They'd be doing Adele a favour.

But she *definitely* wasn't here merely to show off her incredible outfit to a hot Australian barista.

Still, in case said hot barista happened to appear, she took a moment to reapply her lipstick in the distorted reflection of the La Marzocco. *Perfetto*.

Ben emerged from the basement, looking adorably grumpy and deliciously scruffy. He was grimy with coffee, and his forehead and neck were sheened with sweat.

'Thank fuck, it's just you,' he said. It was a statement that wouldn't ordinarily make Adele swoony. But the way he said it made her feel like she was his safe place. Her cheeks burnt at the thought.

Grabbing a tea towel, Ben wiped down his neck and dried off his hands. For the umpteenth time Adele wished to be reincarnated as a piece of decorative yet functional cloth. He gestured to the door. 'I heard footsteps.'

'Just me. I forgot my wallet.'

Ben nodded. He turned to her, his eyes widening as he took in her admittedly fabulous outfit.

'Great dress,' he said at last. 'You look . . .'

He trailed off, leaving Adele to fill his mouth with a million imaginary statements, all of them superlatives in the best way. Going over to the shelf bursting with Kyra's colourful arrangements, he gently drew a poppy from its uranium glass jar. 'Do you mind?' he asked, gesturing to her hair.

Adele nodded, holding her breath as he tucked it into the twist of curls behind her ear. He was close enough that if he bent his head slightly . . .

She shook away the thought. She was on her way to a date with someone else! And Mom always talked about how important it was to stick to your obligations: it was your punishment for making them in the first place.

'The butterflies are going to love me,' she joked, reaching up to touch the poppy. The butterflies in her own stomach had certainly taken flight.

'You betcha.' He almost whispered it.

Adele felt as electric as a third rail. Was it too late to send Federico away and spend the night helping Ben roast?

'Do you need any help?' she asked. 'I can tell the driver . . .'

Ben shook his head. 'Keep your commitment. Even if it's with a doofus.'

Ben and Mom would get along.

The ground rumbled, and Adele wobbled in her slingbacks. Ben steadied her, his hands warm against her bare arms. She flinched as his gaze met hers. Oh, but those eyes were unfair. So was the fact that she was his boss. Maybe they'd be perfect together. But if they weren't, and she had to spend the next year tiptoeing around him . . .

Defying all the laws of magnetism, she stepped back.

'I think we need to get a structural engineer in,' she quipped, her voice cracking from nerves. She'd never had stage fright in front of one person before.

Ember appeared at the top of the basement stairwell, leaping on to the counter with feline ease.

Mrow? He said to Ben, giving him a pointed headbutt.

'The subway,' Ben explained to Adele, as the floor quaked again. He pointed a regretful thumb over her shoulder. 'But I really have to . . .'

'Sure. Me too.'

They backed away from each other, each off to their respective obligations.

All Froth and No Substance

'So,' said Federico, as the massive vehicle stampeded through the neighbourhood towards Smith Street, eating up the roads like Godzilla as cyclists and skaters zipped around them like daredevil gnats. 'Are you and that coffee shop guy a thing?'

Adele shook her head, watching the dandelion lights of the street lamps flare through the car's tinted windows. 'That's kind of a no-go. We work together.'

'Ah. Been *there*,' he said knowingly.

'It didn't work out?' she said, hopefully. Maybe he'd regale her with a horrible tale of woe and put all thoughts of Ben out of her head once and for all.

Federico pulled down the driver's side visor and tapped a grainy photo of a laughing woman in a bikini holding a water pistol. 'We've been married twenty years this December. Well, this is you. Password is Poppycock.'

'Password?' Adele blinked. Had Donny signed them up for a couples' computer programming class?

Of course. A speakeasy. This part of Brooklyn was usually so far out of her price range that she'd blocked it out of her consciousness. If she allowed herself to ruminate on the

Grand Canyon–sized gap between price and her purchasing power, she'd spend her days regretting every life decision. Why hadn't she studied finance and become an investment banker? The Faustian bargain involved in exchanging ten years of your life for an early retirement didn't sound *that* bad. She'd exchanged ten years of hers for bunions and throat nodules, after all.

'Good luck. You want the badminton display in the general store.' Winking, Federico inched off into the night, his brake lights flashing as a group of guys in the universal tech-bro uniform of skinny jeans, puffer jackets and glossy boots drunkenly wove past on fat-wheeled unicycle skateboards.

Wishing Donny had picked a normal restaurant with signage and exterior windows, Adele awkwardly tiptoed into a small hipster general store sparsely decorated with shirts hanging like ghosts from a central hanging clothes rack and cubbies elegantly stacked with muted rainbows of ballet flats. A shop attendant glanced up pretentiously from a copy of *Infinite Jest*, then pointed towards a glass display case of vintage badminton rackets and shuttlecocks. Next to it was a vintage telephone in an eminently edible tone of mint green.

She picked up the receiver.

'Password?' muttered a bored voice.

'Poppycock,' said Adele in her best upper-crust British accent. It was a word that demanded it: Americans shouldn't legally be allowed to say *poppycock*. She smothered a smile as she imagined Ben's take on it, and how he'd inevitably manage to turn it into a swear.

'One moment.'

The badminton display swung out into the shop, revealing a set of stairs carpeted in Astroturf. Adele picked her way down the steps, holding on to a railing crafted from grip-side-up badminton rackets.

Pushing through a curtain of hanging shuttlecocks, she found herself in a green-floored room surrounded by neon-decorated plant walls against which a few students were surreptitiously taking selfies. Couples and small groups hunched over the retro tulip tables, while awkward business travellers scrolled their phones, wishing they'd had drinks at their hotel. One woman who had clearly imbibed something other than a cocktail was staring admiringly up at the enormous shuttlecock light fixture fashioned to look like a Murano glass chandelier.

It was a weird spot, but she did love the theatricality of it: it felt like if *Wicked* had a sports subplot. Maybe that was why Donny had chosen it. Perhaps he was more thoughtful than she'd given him credit for. And he *had* sent a car.

Speaking of Donny . . . he was nowhere to be seen.

A girl in a sequined badminton outfit and platform running shoes waltzed over. She looked familiar: another would-be Broadway starlet?

'For one?' she said, with a smile that didn't budge. Never mind the stage: she should audition for toothpaste commercials.

'Two. I hope,' said Adele shyly.

'Oh, of course,' said the waitress lightly. 'In that dress? It's a sure thing.'

She led Adele over to one of the tulip tables, passing Adele a painstakingly embossed and gilded menu that was staunch in its dedication both to badminton puns and esoteric liqueurs Adele had never heard of. That said, the Soft Serve sounded decent. And the Total Racket. And a Shuffle Cock did roll off the tongue, she thought, trying not to laugh at the visual.

Although there was not a price in sight, which made her think that perhaps a soda water was the way to go.

'I'll give you a minute,' said the waitress.

A phone dinged: Adele turned to see Donny sliding across the floor in her direction, texting the entire time. Clearly a few drinks in, he'd traded in the invisible Segway for something approaching a moonwalk. He *was* handsome, though, she had to admit. In a sort of *Wolf of Wall Street* way. Pressed and polished, with more brand logos than a *Vogue* photoshoot, he was the opposite of Ben's casual, scruffy handsome. Not that she was thinking about Ben right now.

She dropped her hand, which had been reaching for the poppy.

'Ah! There you are,' said Donny, with the careful articulation of someone trying to convince the world that they were in charge of their faculties. 'Business meeting before this. Too many Tom Collinses.'

'I think the plural is Toms Collins,' joked Adele.

'Doubtful.'

Donny held up a finger to get a waiter's attention, to Adele's dismay adding a click when no one appeared. She and Ben had commiserated over customers who did this, brainstorming all sorts of revenge fantasies. Nice ones, of course.

The waitress returned, her pasted-on smile betrayed by narrowed eyes.

'Sorry for the wait,' she said, in a tone that said, *If I killed you right now the jury would side with me*.

'He's a flamenco dancer,' Adele explained, apologetically.

Donny, distracted by his phone, didn't react. Typing away, he pronounced: 'I'll have an Old-Fashioned. And for her . . . champagne?'

So much for getting to say the phrase Shuffle Cock aloud.

'Why not,' said Adele, who never ordered champagne when out. If she was going to pay for an absurd markup on booze, there was going to be some mixing and shaking going on. For the cost of a Centre Orchestra ticket plus tip, she wanted theatrics. A character arc, even. Perhaps an ill-advised sequel.

'Fun bar,' said Adele, gesturing around at the decor. 'The turf is a nice touch.'

'I played Badminton at Harvard, so you can see the appeal.' Donny's mouth tightened as he looked her over. 'I should've told you where we were going. You must feel out of place in that.'

Adele looked down at her dress. She'd felt like a summery wildflower field until a second ago. Now she felt like a hydrangea bush that had been pruned back to nothingness by an overzealous amateur gardener. 'Oh.'

'It's fine. Mood lighting solves everything.' Donny hung a menu over their dim table lamp. 'See?'

The waitress stalked back up with their drinks balanced on a badminton racket, then set them down on coasters made out of sweatband fabric. She scooted an extra mini champagne bottle across the table to Adele.

'My gift,' she whispered.

Adele smiled in gratitude.

'So, how's the shop going?' asked Donny, sipping his Old-Fashioned and making a face. 'I hear it's a new endeavour for you. Have you run a business before?'

Wow, he really was a Harvard MBA. They hadn't even discussed the weather yet! Or the outside traffic conditions! Adele had a whole commentary on those one-wheeled scooters ready.

The champagne bubbles fizzed at her nose as she swigged. 'I've directed some amateur theatre productions. It's pretty similar.'

'Is it, though?' Donny turned the champagne bottle towards him, grimacing at its label. 'They could've done better than this year and region. Might as well be prosecco. So, what are your plans for improving footfall? I know you're limited with the zoning restrictions and the signage issue.'

'Um.'

Donny leaned back in his chair. 'I saw that look of fear. Don't worry: I've got you covered. I've been researching coffee shop trends and their ROI. According to the *HBR* and *Forbes* . . .'

Adele topped off her drink as Donny rattled on about market segmentation and brand elevation. He seemed to know what he was talking about, but was that because he was talking loudly? Confidence and competence didn't necessarily conflate, as she'd found out during a performance of *Moulin Rouge* where an enterprising pyrotechnician intern had set the theatre ablaze with an impromptu fireworks show.

'Baz Luhrmann would have appreciated my vision,' he'd sobbed, as the cops had led him away.

'But that's all right,' Donny was saying. His phone flashed on the table. 'Do you mind if I take this?'

'I'll just—' She pointed to the restrooms.

As Adele followed the white turf striping that led past the bar and to the bathrooms, the waitress caught her arm. 'Let me know if you need me to give you an out,' she whispered. 'We do it all the time for disastrous Tinder dates.'

'Oh, this isn't like that,' said Adele. She'd sworn off Tinder after the time she'd ended up at a roller rink with a former male porn actor who'd made it big with his line of dungeon attire.

He'd actually been lovely, but there were some incompatibilities. Mostly that he kept quoting *Frasier*.

'Sure.' The waitress passed Adele a card. 'Just in case. Theatre girls have to stick together.'

When Adele returned from the bathroom, Donny was chatting with two girls who cut familiar – and identical – figures.

'Adele!' purred Honour Nivola, ambitiously clad in what appeared to be a gold lamé handkerchief and a shoelace. Apparently badminton was clothing-optional. Her Shuffle Cock splashed Adele as she leaned in for a performative hug and a triple kiss. There was a Tonya Harding dangerousness to the move that made Adele lower her clutch protectively over her knees.

'You never told us that you knew Donny Parker,' added Gracie, who didn't sound entirely impressed by the fact. Hand on a silvery hip – she was in the pantsuit equivalent of her sister's ensemble – she pointed a Polaroid camera at the shuttlecock chandelier and its ardent admirer.

'He was telling us about your darling shop.' Honour took a swig from Adele's champagne bottle and made a face. 'What a fun portfolio diversification. Write off those losses like a boss, girl.'

Adele skulled the rest of her drink before Honour could. 'How do you . . . know each other?'

'We go way back,' Donny explained proudly, tapping the heavy class ring he wore. Presumably in case he had to fistfight someone from Yale. Or worse, Princeton.

'You should've seen him at Harvard,' cackled Honour.

'And your internship with our dad?' Gracie raised a shrewd eyebrow. (Her brow artist was an *artiste*.) 'You definitely made an impression.'

She would've gone on, but Donny clicked his fingers for the waitress again.

Honour wrapped a delicate arm around Adele, who felt like a Shetland pony tasked with keeping a flighty race horse company. 'Sly dog, moving and shaking behind the scenes! I love that for you. We miss you at the theatre.'

'Richard quit, by the way,' said Gracie absently, now pointing her camera at a couple Adele had seen a few times at the coffee shop.

'Something about not getting paid enough for this shit,' added Honour. 'He's going all in on his one-man bakery instead. Brave. I might do the same. Pursue my own dreams.'

'Pastries?' asked Adele, confused. Honour did not seem like the baked goods type.

Honour glanced at her nails, which were painted in a striped, abstract design. Probably by one of Rothko's heirs. 'Hollywood.'

Donny sipped at the Old-Fashioned that had appeared on a passing badminton racket. Was that his third? 'The twins were telling me you were up for their latest role. You must be proud to be working at their level. Almost at their level.'

'Almost,' agreed Adele. Her left eyelid twitched from the effort involved in mustering a smile.

'Are you coming to Trip's rooftop thing?' asked Honour, eyes wide with excitement. '*Everyone* will be there.'

Gracie was nervously adjusting her outfit, which had not held up well under the strains of Polaroid photography. 'Hon, did you bring that double-sided tape?'

Honour feigned dismay. 'You know I don't carry anything on a night out. Not even cards,' she added in a stage whisper.

This was evident.

'Here.' Adele reached into her clutch, pulling out the shawl she'd jammed in there in case the weather turned.

Gracie reverently pressed it to her throat, as though Adele had handed her Audrey Hepburn's Givenchy gown from *Sabrina*. Then she tied it around her waist, turning a wardrobe malfunction into an iconic fashion moment. Of course.

A camera flash went off behind them. 'Gracie! Can you turn this way, give us more shoulder? We're going to print this. Who's your bohemian friend with the poppy?'

'I'm Adele,' called Adele, a touch bubbly on champagne.

'Just Adele?' came a voice from somewhere behind an installation of badminton nets.

'Sure.'

'She owns a coffee shop,' said Gracie generously. 'An entrepreneur.'

'It's Riffraff,' added Adele, squinting off into the dim light. Who was she even talking to?

Donny stood, wrapping an arm around Adele, who stood awkwardly, not sure what to do with herself. Was he *claiming* her? And why now, after all the digs at her dress and the coffee shop?

'Here.' Donny pulled out a black credit card so thick you could use it as a guillotine. Maybe someone should. 'We should do this again. This was fun.'

Adele blinked. Had it been?

Look What You Made Me Brew

Adele made it into Riffraff before the clock hit double digits, which felt like an achievement after last night's champers and chagrin. The shop thrummed with mid-morning ambition: would-be authors pretending to write; yoga students who had communed with the gruff nanny goat at the goat yoga studio next door; a squeaky-voiced guy taking an interview over an expansive cream-topped drink; two awkward Gen Zers stumbling their way through an Italian session with a tutor whose dramatic gesticulations kept knocking things off the table. And of course, Reba and Frank, swaying along as Stevie Nicks and Lindsay Buckingham poured their respective hearts out on the CD player.

The coffee shop was the opposite of the bar from last night, and Adele couldn't be more relieved.

Ben folded his arms, looking faintly amused. He was in the middle of plating up a wobbly custardy dessert bookended with flaky pastry. 'Look what the cat dragged in.'

'I wish,' said Adele. 'Tell Ember he's asleep on the job. I had to walk.'

Ember, who was curled up on his favourite yellow armchair, opened an eye. Then shut it. Pesky humans.

'You made the paper.' Ben tapped a grainy image of Adele in Doralee's colourful floral dress. The photographer had cropped out Donny, but his arm was still visible around her waist. Adele was angled away from him like she was the Tower of Pisa and he was a plumb line.

'I didn't take you for someone who read gossip pages,' she retorted, scrutinising herself in the picture. It was a decent shot, actually. Maybe she'd send a copy back home to her parents.

'I don't even read the paper.' Ben dusted icing sugar over the plate. 'You happened to be wrapped around my fish and chips.'

'You had fish and chips for breakfast?'

He slid the custard concoction her way. 'Yeah. Didn't you?'

She never could tell when he was joking. *Was* that a standard Australian breakfast? Could you even get fish and chips in Brooklyn?

Adele regarded the dessert. It did smell fabulous, but she'd been tricked by Australians before. Vegemite was to Nutella what Velveeta was to Camembert. 'What weird Australian nonsense is this?'

Ben passed her a fork. 'You said you wanted to see some change around here. So here's my contribution.'

Adele tentatively tasted the dessert, catching a falling glob of custard with her free hand just in time. 'Okay, so that's actually pretty good.'

Ben nodded matter-of-factly. 'A snot block, known colloquially as a vanilla slice. Breakfast of champions. Second only to Weet-Bix. Or beer.'

'You are a strange people.'

'Strangely *impressive*,' he said, green eyes twinkling. 'I'm just saying, my gran won the Victorian Vanilla Slice Championships twice over.'

Adele handed an approaching customer some spare paper napkins. She was getting good at anticipating their needs based on their body language. 'There's no way that's a thing.'

'Wait till you hear about the Dunny Derby,' Ben said, deadpan as always. He *had* to be making this stuff up. There was no chance a single country could be that strange. And she came from a region that held the Fried Pickle Festival. Ben tapped the plate with his own fork. 'Anyway, if you want a game changer, I reckon this is it.'

Adele harrumphed. 'I've seen the *Out of Sight, Out of Mind* drawer. We're going to need more than a . . . what did you call it? Phlegm sandwich?'

Ben held up his tattooed hands. 'Don't ask me. I'm just the barista. Once my looks go and the tips dry up I'm moving back to a country with universal healthcare.'

'Well, I'd better get the books sorted out before that happens.' Adele took another bite of the vanilla slice. It *was* good. 'Still, put this thing on the menu. And feel free to cook for me anytime you want.'

'Is that a date?'

Adele raised a coy eyebrow. 'More the reality of living in an apartment where the kitchen is buried deeper than Atlantis.'

Ben grinned. 'At least I never had to worry about Doralee cooking for me.'

'Was she bad?'

Ben met Reba's eye as he tried to formulate a diplomatic response. 'She was . . . creative. Refused to be held back by the shackles of a menu. Or the taste limitations of tofu.'

'Rumour has it she was the Brooklyn poisoner,' called Reba.

106

'If you wanted to off someone, all you had to do was suggest that she make them a nice pot of mushroom soup.'

Adele smiled into her vanilla slice. 'I wish I could've known her. She sounds like a blast.'

'She was pretty great,' agreed Ben.

The shop door jingled. Adele looked up to see Kyra shouldering her way through the door with a garden cart and a few watering cans. Setting aside the vanilla slice for morning tea, Adele hurried over to hold the door.

'Plant lady's here!' cried Kyra, dressed head to toe in tropical palm prints. Twin palms swung in her long-suffering earlobes, and a frangipani clip held her hair in place.

'Kyra, darling!' Ditching her crossword, Reba jumped up to wrap Kyra in a hug. The two of them formed a kaleidoscope of decorative prints. Or a migraine aura, thought Adele, blinking. 'I've barely seen you these past weeks.'

'It's been *bu-sy*,' said Kyra, inspecting a succulent planter on a table claimed by a stern-looking woman with a chihuahua poking out of her shirt. 'Weddings, parties, funerals, ghost tours, the flower show. But who's complaining? I love seeing my babies get the love they deserve. Cute puppy.'

'Brutus says thanks.' The woman lifted her puppuccino up to her tiny dog's lolling tongue. Her knife-like fingernails gleamed as she rubbed a succulent leaf between thumb and finger. 'Is this you? Can I buy this planter?'

'Sure,' said Kyra. 'Scan the QR code on the tag and you're set. Go easy on the water and give it a sprinkle of the fertiliser in the pouch there every now and then. It's my own blend – uses the grounds right from this shop. I swear by it, and if you don't believe me, check out Audrey III up here.'

She pointed to the ever-expanding pothos vine, which

seemed to have stretched across another of the rainbow window panes since Adele had closed up yesterday. Sunlight twinkled in over its glossy green leaves, giving it a natural glow.

'Sold.' The woman pulled out her phone. Then she plonked the chihuahua in the planter and carried pup and succulent out by the planter's hammered copper handle.

'Pleasure doing business.' Bouncing up on her tiptoes, Kyra reached to check the pothos' leaves. 'Now this is one healthy plant. Always has been, although it's growing like a mother recently. Nice variegation.'

'That's what I tell myself when I look in the mirror.' Frank tugged on his salt-and-pepper ponytail.

Reba snorted. 'I can think of a few other choice things you should be telling yourself.'

Poor Frank, thought Adele, as she straightened the picture of the aurora borealis, which always seemed to be wonky. Frank seemed like a decent guy – he always had a smile and a kind word for everyone, and she'd even seen him wipe down a table after a harried mother of twins had urgently extricated herself from the shop after a double biting incident. Why was Reba so cruel to him?

Like Miss Tweed in *Something's Afoot*, this was a mystery Adele planned to solve.

Kyra pulled a stepladder away from the wall and unfolded it. 'Let's get these lower leaves up high so that they're out of reach of Ember. We don't want you eating those, kitty.'

Ember darted away from the plant, racing over to attack the trouser leg of an unimpressed business student. (You could always tell business students. They smelt like one-upmanship and dividend stocks.)

The student pushed his oversized glasses up his nose.

'Could we do something about this cat? There's kitty litter in my soy frappé.'

'Extra fibre,' said Ben, brandishing the portafilter. 'Keeps you regular.'

The student scoffed in disbelief. 'I'm so leaving a Yelp review.'

'Let's not do that,' said Adele, who had deleted her entire review history the day she'd inherited Riffraff. The other small business owners of the world would be happy to know that she'd vowed off drunken review-bombing for good. Except for that one place on the waterfront where the broey bartender had refused to give her a leg up so that she could reach the bar stool. They'd deserved every sweary word.

She picked up Ember, who yowled indignantly and kicked his back legs like a furious, if ineffectual, kangaroo. 'Unless it's "cheerful owner with a great singing voice risked cat scratch fever to make my dine-in experience a positive one. Five stars".'

She set down Ember on his favourite yellow velvet chair. The fluffy captive clawed at it with the relish of an Oregonian lumberjack felling a Doug fir.

Mollified, the student went back to fiddling around with his spreadsheet.

'Ben, whatever you're doing with your roast blends, keep it up.' Kyra pinched away a few leaves on the pothos. 'Everything is shooting up.'

Ben didn't reply: he was banging around on the espresso machine in the kind of time signature only known to jazz drummers. There he was, off in his head again. Adele couldn't figure him out. He was an Australian Jekyll and Hyde. Although hopefully less homicidal. Although he *did* vanish every afternoon at 3 p.m. sharp . . .

That's called 'leaving work', Adele. You and your Millennial productivity guilt complex.

Adele wrenched her eyes from Ben as a skinny guy in an impressive double denim outfit wandered in. Clad in blue from his shirt to his runners, he was a walking Levi-Strauss swatch department. And an excellent advertisement for lash extensions (the volume!). Blinking, the guy spun a slow circle on the spot, as though looking for someone. Maybe he was on a blind date. That would explain the easy-to-describe outfit.

Adele gave him a friendly wave as he poked at a Riffraff-branded coaster gift set. 'You're welcome to grab a seat if you're waiting for someone.'

The guy recoiled as though she'd threatened him.

'No thanks. I'm just browsing,' he said, tugging on the huge onyx earring in his left ear.

Strange response. But then Adele used that same line every time she wandered into a retail store whose price point turned out to be far beyond the wild dreams of her monthly budget. Maybe he'd do a lap and be on his way.

'Well, just let me know if you need anything.'

The guy nodded, then turned away. A second later he spun back, his whole demeanour showing he was about to jettison an emotional forklift load upon Adele. 'It's my boyfriend. Partner. We've been together for two years, and he's . . .' the guy flumped down in the seat next to Ember's throne '. . . *ghosted me.*'

Time to switch to therapist mode. 'Can I get you a drink? On the house.'

'I really shouldn't. I've been drinking my feelings, and it hasn't been pleasant. I've gone up a waist size. And I'm having these visual disturbances. I think it's anxiety. Or a tumour.' Crossing his legs, the guy adjusted a sock patterned with maple leaves. 'Maybe a hot water with lemon? And a drizzle of honey and two tablespoons of sugar. And maybe a pump of caramel. For Kai.'

The resulting drink was almost a solid block of sugar. It absorbed the water like Adele absorbed her critical reviews. She brought it over with a piece of Ben's vanilla slice and took a seat.

'So tell me what's going on.'

Kai pulled at a thread on his denim shirt, grimacing as a hem started to unravel. 'It's so out of the blue. Things have been good. We've been talking about living together and everything, getting a low-maintenance pet like a guinea pig. Maybe a turtle. I have the most adorable hutches saved in my Amazon wish list. But he *does* travel a lot for work. And I know he was saving up air miles.'

'You think he got on a plane and . . . left?'

'I think so. According to the *Find my iPhone* app he came here first, although after that, the trail . . .' Kai made a gesture like a magician disappearing a pair of doves. 'I need closure. And to know what's happening with our streaming services. I'm on Season 6 of *Lost*, so an interruption is out of the question.'

'Can I see what he looks like?'

Kai flipped his phone out from its leather case and pulled up an Instagram account filled with artsy photos as annoyingly cropped and chopped as the letters on a ransom note. Adele frowned. It was like pulling together a police sketch from Mr Potato Head pieces.

Kai zoomed in on a heavily filtered black-and-white shot

that showed half a man's face. 'You'd remember this face, right? It's not like this place is so busy that everyone blurs into each other, like Starbucks.'

Adele did not, in fact, remember the half-face she was looking at. But she *did* remember his topknot.

'He was probably wearing an ascot with a Hawaiian shirt? And riding a fixie. And talking about coffee roasting.'

Instant recognition. How could anyone forget the dulcet, patronising tones of Topknot Guy?

'Ben, can you come over here?' Leaning over to the bereft Kai, she explained: 'They had a roasting session. Maybe he can clue you in.'

Passing a cardboard carrier filled with oversized to-go cups to a young girl who trembled with Ad Agency Intern intensity, Ben came over. Adele blinked. It should be illegal to wear a white shirt when you were that buff. Also, *how* was he so buff? The portafilter wasn't *that* heavy. Although the bags of coffee were, she supposed, and apparently he hauled those up from the basement every evening.

Now there was a visual. A visual that Kai clearly shared.

'Oh.' Kai stared heartbroken at the towering Ben, who cut a figure that would've made Michelangelo's chisel hand tremble. 'Oh. I see what happened now.'

He slid his phone back into his pocket.

Ben was bewildered. 'What in the bloody hell did I do?'

'Bicep curls,' said Kai. 'Lot of them.'

He stood, decisively brushing down his distressed jeans. 'Well. That's that. I'm going to open up my own Netflix account. And fuck it. You know what? I'm going to get a guinea pig of my *own*.'

Reaching behind the counter, Adele popped the vanilla

slice into a box, adding a cookie for good measure. 'At least take this.'

Kai did. On his way out he turned, tears glistening in his lash extensions.

'Do you know where the nearest boba shop is?'

Hey, Big Tipper!

Much like Adele's diligent yet flawed attempts at the choreography for *Newsies*, the following few weeks were an experiment in trial and error. And an exercise in patience.

Stepping into a business that was collapsing was like looking at yourself in an aluminium nightclub mirror the night of a breakup. You couldn't quite pinpoint the one thing that was wrong in the distorted reflection looking back at you, so you decided to change everything about yourself. Starting with your bangs, courtesy of the nail scissors in your vintage Glomesh purse.

When she'd said this to Donny, he'd snorted and said that it was more like defusing a bomb: something you left to the experts.

Fair enough, she'd said (albeit still contemplating her bangs).

Like a motorcyclist staring down a 3 a.m. red light at an empty intersection, Donny had taken her response as an invitation to forge ahead. And so, Adele's phone constantly dinged with business recommendations written in bullet-point format, most of which were followed up by links to paywalled websites. It got to the point that she twitched when a message came in, and had to set her phone to silent. Still, it was sweet that he cared enough to put so much energy into helping her.

Even if his love languages were SMART Goals and Moving the Needle.

And at least every change or update felt like she was doing *something*.

First came the Bluetooth speaker system, which connected to something called Algorhythmix, which was a royalty-free generative AI music start-up platform. An early investor, Donny had excitedly explained how anyone sitting in the shop could log in and tweak the algorithm. (Arguably) best of all, it could analyse the sentiment of a room and share it back to the account owner as a star rating. *And*, if you upgraded to the premium tier, you'd get AI-generated, data-backed tips for improvement.

'It's collaborative music without the barrier to entry,' Donny had enthused, shoving the *No Wi-Fi* signs off the tables. 'The democratisation of creativity.'

'So like . . . a jam band without the band?' Frank had said, so witheringly that a whole arm of the pothos had browned on the spot. 'This is Brooklyn. Half the population are aspiring musicians, and the other half are failed ones. You couldn't give someone a guitar and five bucks?'

'Tell me you don't know anything about tech without telling me you don't know anything about tech.'

Donny's fingers had flown around on the iPad he'd hooked up to the speaker – and to the newly installed modem, which was glowing red-hot from the demands of a sudden influx of tech bros, who'd seen the open Wi-Fi signal and had clattered through the door with their GitHub-stickered laptops and cans of La Croix held high.

Frank had gone back to his book, muttering: 'The printing press. Now *that's* technology.'

The second Harvard MBA-approved business addition was a programmable sandwich board sign to replace the old chalkboard one that Doralee and Frank had painted together. It had been stolen within half an hour, and the hastily couriered replacement the hour after that. Although to be fair, that probably wasn't Donny's fault.

'Cost of doing business in this part of town,' he'd said with a shrug.

Weirdly, the cost of doing business was getting ever higher thanks to Donny's involvement. But as he said, you had to spend money to make money. Adele's high school best friend Yvette, a notorious shopaholic, had a similar mantra, which was that if you bought something on sale, you were technically saving money, not spending it. Ah, Yvette. She'd declared bankruptcy by the age of twenty-three and was now living in an undisclosed location in Central America. Presumably one close to a shopping centre.

'Don't say a word,' Adele had said to Ben, as she'd lugged the original sign back out to the patio area outside.

Ben's eyebrows had spoken volumes. A whole Library of Babel's worth.

The third addition to the business had been an online ordering thingamajig called EatMe. So far, that one had been a grudging success. Customers placed their orders from the comfort of their bed (or more likely, the bathroom), then sidled in to grab them when they got around to it (and hopefully having washed their hands). And for a truly mind-boggling extra fee, someone from a food delivery service would whizz by to pick up and drop off said coffee. Adele

116

was secretly delighted that there were so many people with such terrible time and money management skills that they'd spend twenty bucks on having a cookie delivered to their apartment.

Ben called them 'cashed-up bludgers' – whatever that meant.

Anyway. Today was the installation of the new POS. Which apparently, the long-suffering sales tech had informed Adele, stood for 'Point of Sale' and not 'Piece of Shit'. Who knew?

In full girlboss mode, Adele strode ambitiously into Riffraff, senses immediately assaulted by the warp and weft of the Algorhythmix soundtrack, and then soothed by the sight of Ben in a gloriously well-fitting shirt.

An eyebrow raised, Ben pointed to her waist. 'I know that belt. That belt means you're about to change something.'

Adele fiddled with the thin blue belt she always wore when she needed to feel strong and important. (Or to break up an especially piratey-looking outfit, as she had on her first day at Riffraff.) It was an Eighties Ferragamo piece she'd bought from Goodwill for $7.99 plus tax and a round-up-to-the-nearest-dollar donation to a charity she couldn't remember, and it always made her feel like she was wearing armour. Or at least shoulder pads and impenetrable hair.

'What's with the music?' she whispered. 'Has it been like this all day?'

Ben angled his head at a group of tech workers encircling the communal table, heads down and gazes affixed to their glowing laptops. They looked like they were participating in an ancient ritual. Ah yes, the Ceremony of Market Disruption through Evasion of Regulation.

'I'm game to chuck that whole system in the bin.'

'We have to keep it through the whole trial period,' she said, straightening the napkins. 'It's some data-training thing.'

Making a face, Ben pushed a flat white her way. 'Try that.'

She sipped, swishing the coffee around her mouth as pompously as possible.

'Nice. Very . . . coffee-ish.'

'Sophisticated palate you have there.' He sipped the espresso shot he'd just extracted. 'I'm giving a different roast profile a go. I know you found the last couple of roasts . . . sooty.'

'Sorry if "notes of crematorium" isn't my thing,' said Adele.

Clearing his throat, Ben whacked the portafilter against the knock box, dislodging a compressed puck of coffee grounds. 'I might have gone too dark with those last few. The roaster can be temperamental. Likes to do her own thing.'

'Nothing wrong with a woman who knows what she wants,' called Reba. 'Two down: a Eugène Ionesco play named for a piece of household furniture?'

'*The Chairs*,' replied Ben, not missing a beat. He turned back to Adele, who guiltily set aside the canister she'd been using to squirt whipped cream into her coffee.

'I'll take that.' He grabbed the canister.

Adele breathed deeply, trying to clear her mind of the image that had galloped into her mind with all the vividness of a technicolour dreamcoat. If the intrusive thoughts won now, it wouldn't be her fault. She could claim entrapment.

He set the canister beneath the counter. 'So. What's the big change for today? We're rebranding as a tapas bar?'

'Only in the evenings,' she quipped. To his credit, he chuckled at this. 'We're installing a new point of sale system,' she added.

'So we're finally replacing the old Piece of Shit, huh?'

'I figured we had to act when I saw that the official header on Doralee's Profit and Loss statement was "Hopes and Dreams".'

Ben patted the vintage cash register. 'Well, the old girl here has had a good innings. Will it be harder to steal from the till?'

Adele averted her eyes. She still hadn't figured out the getting paid thing, and taking money out of your own cash register wasn't a crime, was it?

The door jingled, and an anxious guy with stand-up comedian vibes hurried in, hefting a box branded with the tagline *I'm the biggest POS you'll ever meet.* He slapped it down on the counter, sparking a hissing fit from Ember, who slunk off to his velvet armchair.

'Who's the boss? You?' Pointing to Ben, who was busily frothing milk, the guy stationed himself behind the counter, where he shoved aside the carefully stacked cups and drink sleeves that Trix and her friends had spent a recent afternoon stamping and arranging.

'She's the brains.' Ben beckoned for Adele to come over. He slid a latte across the counter to a blushing woman with painstakingly curled hair. The till dinged as he took her payment and passed back her change. 'I'm merely the good looks.'

'I see it. My wife is both.' The POS guy tore open the box and scattered its guts all over the counter. 'You gonna get that dinosaur outta here?'

'We're doing this right this second?' Ben rinsed the portafilter. 'I'm in the middle of a shift.'

'I got another appointment after this. Hotdog stand. You can't work around me?'

Ben muttered something that Adele assumed was a prayer to the cricket gods.

'Righto, mate.' He cleared his throat. 'Drip coffee only for the next while,' he called out across the shop.

No one looked up from their phones: only Reba and Frank paused to give him a thumbs up.

Adele bit her lip. The shop's cosy vibe was starting to feel . . . off. Usually Riffraff was rich with murmured conversations and people happily sharing space. Now with everyone hiding behind a screen, it was all feeling a little *Invasion of the Body Snatchers*. But maybe it was simply teething pains. And besides, this was all in service of the elusive bottom line whose health directly influenced their ability to stay open.

As the POS guy fiddled around with the new system, Adele grabbed a cloth and wiped down the tables. The AI music responded to her movement, warping around her like a casual acquaintance going in for an ill-timed hug.

Ugh. It was like attempting to dance to the theremin in *Be More Chill*.

The door jingled, hefted open by a Stanley cup so large it could sustain a Death Valley hiker for a month. The cup's owner was a petite woman dressed in beige sportswear and sporting a face of equally beige contouring. No doubt her children played only with organic wooden toys and her bookshelves were arranged with spines faced in for visual uniformity.

In the woman's non-Stanley-cup hand (the one with the enormous diamond) was a sheaf of papers in a lime-green case decorated with smiley faces. She set the case down on the counter and pulled out a handful of pages.

'Um, hi. So . . .'

Here came the spiel. Growing up in the South, Adele had

heard it more times than the Pledge of Allegiance. The gentle chitchat followed by the inevitable invitation to a place of worship.

Adele pre-emptively pointed to the sign stuck by the front door. 'Sorry, but no soliciting.'

The woman flinched. Her beige mouth dropped open.

'Are you . . . calling me a prostitute? I'm here about my missing friend and you're calling me a . . .' The woman turned to the shop patrons for support. Having been trained by years of subway riding, they were stone-faced and disinterested. And also busy scrolling social media on the new Wi-Fi.

'Sex work is work,' pointed out Reba, glowering over her sparkling cats-eye glasses.

Adele felt like she'd fallen into a nightmare improv class. She held up her hands in an *I surrender* gesture. 'Let me make you a skinny caramel cappuccino with extra light whipped cream, and we'll start over.'

The woman put her hands on her Lycra-clad hips. 'How did you know my drink?'

'Lucky guess.'

It was the beigest thing on the menu.

The POS guy was blocking the spot in front of the La Marzocco, so Adele started up the machine at the kiddie table instead. She pulled the shot, frothed the milk, then squirted a generous blob of whipped cream from the canister Ben had hidden minutes before, once again hoping the thought police were otherwise occupied.

'Here you go.' Adele pushed the drink over, frowning as the counter rumbled. 'Sorry. Subway,' she said.

The woman frowned. 'Does the subway go past here?'

'Sure,' said Adele. 'And a fault line.'

'I don't think . . . anyway.' The woman took a deep breath, then gave the high-wattage smile of a zealot. 'Less correcting, more converting, my mother always said. But I'm not here about that. I'm here about Lexie.'

She pulled out a charmingly decorated MISSING PERSON poster.

'You've put some effort into that,' said Reba, coming up for a refill on her coffee. 'I like the flowers. Gouache?'

'Yes!' The woman beamed. 'I take folk art classes on my de-load weeks from goat yoga. I go next door. *Love* that place. Anyway, we're spin class frenemies, and she hasn't shown up for two weeks. No spin girl would ever miss *two weeks*. So either she's changed instructors without telling me, which is . . .' She gawped in disbelief. 'Or she's missing. Like actually missing.'

Adele had an odd sense of déjà vu. This was the second time someone had come into the shop searching for someone. Although in this case she was willing to bet that the missing person had simply blocked her friend's number.

'Anyway, I *do* know she comes here sometimes,' said the woman. 'I've seen your cups.'

Reba preened: she'd designed the distinctive flower power design on the to-go cups.

'Have you asked her family? Or other friends? Or coworkers?' asked Adele.

'What about a psychic?' added Reba. 'I see one called Willa Fjutcha, right up the road. If you need to connect with the spirit world, she's your gal. I use her to talk to Janis all the time.'

'Joplin?' asked Adele, confused.

'The dog. My dog,' clarified Reba. 'My no-longer-corporeal dog.'

Adele needed to steer this conversation back to normalcy. What was this? A scene from *His Girl Friday*? 'I haven't seen her, but I'll keep an eye out. Has she been active on social media?'

'She has a private account.' Stanley Cup huffed with frustration. 'With a very exclusive following to followers ratio. But look, all I'm asking is that you put up my poster. It doesn't have to be in the window. It could be back there near the menu board. Or even in the bathroom.'

'Good visibility,' added Frank. 'Everyone pees at a coffee shop.'

This, unfortunately, was true. Adele had learned the disgusting way why all the Starbucks bathrooms had codes. Maybe it was a good thing there were seven locks on the basement door.

'What about the police? Have you talked to them?' asked Donny, who'd sidled in with a group of baby-carrying dads. The polite professor-looking guy who'd unsuspectingly held the door for the first in the group was still holding it. He rubbed his shoulder sadly.

'Surprise, babe.' Dropping a swanky box of gold-wrapped chocolates on the counter, Donny kissed Adele on the cheek. The peppermint balm he always wore smudged across her skin. Smiling politely, she rubbed it off with the butt of her hand. Donny had a habit of showing up with no prior warning. Meanwhile, if she wanted to see him, she had to schedule an appointment through a calendar app. But he was doing his best to help her, and that was something. So he wasn't perfect. He was . . . fine.

Spoken like a woman madly in love, she could imagine Doralee saying.

'Why would I go to the police?' The woman's perfectly threaded eyebrows dove. 'Just because I look like a basic bitch . . .'

Adele sighed. Taking three of the woman's posters for good measure, she promised to keep an eye out for the missing friend. Even though Occam's razor said that the other woman simply *had* changed spin classes to get away from this bunny boiler of an individual.

'So, how's the POS?' asked Donny, once the frantic woman had wandered back outside to tuck missing posters into Citi Bike baskets and beneath Range Rover windscreen wipers. Oh God, now she'd let out one of the goats from the studio next door.

Adele smothered a cackle as a group of yoga students chased after the gallivanting Oreo, who was joyfully headbutting everything in sight.

Somehow immune to the delights of wayward goats, Donny was still waiting on her answer.

'It's being installed right now.' Adele nodded to where the technician was tapping away at an intimidatingly thick laptop slathered in intense red stickers.

Donny smirked. 'I meant the Australian.'

Lips thinning at the unwarranted jab, Adele glanced around. 'I guess he's downstairs. Coffee?'

'Macchiato. I figured he was roasting from the smoke out there. I'm surprised the city hasn't called you out on that. Maybe the permits are grandfathered in. Until they're not. You never know with a place like this.' Donny tapped the possessed light switch with the warning sign taped to it.

Pulling the shot, Adele took a quiet breath, trying not to think about the rabbit hole of permits and engineer's reports.

There was so much more to running a business than she'd ever imagined. It was just coffee! All they did was pass people drinks made out of hot water and a socially acceptable stimulant! How difficult did it need to be?

To make a macchiato simply mark the coffeeato . . . she whisper-sang as she daubed the espresso with a perfect circle of foamed milk. There. She pushed the drink across the counter towards Donny.

Donny pushed it back. 'Needs more milk.'

Adele repeated her sing-song mnemonic in her head. She'd got it right, hadn't she? Uncertain, she added a dash of milk, then another. Then another, until the drink in front of Donny resembled a cappuccino.

Donny took a sip and made a face. 'Bitter. Anyway, omakase for lunch. The waitlist is nine months long, but I know a guy. Ready?'

Adele gawped. 'I don't really . . .'

Ben appeared from downstairs, looking sooty and tousled from his latest roast. He had a bag hoisted over his shoulder like . . . Adele swallowed. Gosh it was humid in here.

'Shop's handled,' said Ben. 'Go on.'

'The stair-climbing dolly exists, you know,' said Donny, regarding the sweaty barista. 'I prefer to work smart.'

He checked his chunky gold watch – *chronograph*, rather, thought Adele, because when you spent the average annual salary on a watch, it wasn't just a watch – which reportedly kept near-perfect time. And yet, Donny was always late. Interesting how that worked.

'Lucky for blokes like you, there are some of us who prefer to work hard,' said Ben, his tone pleasant but with an undercurrent of four-letter words.

'We won't be long. I have an investor meeting after,' said Donny.

'Enjoy that,' said Ben cheerfully.

Adele could've sworn she heard him whisper *fuck knuckles* as they left.

I'll Have That to Go

Adele returned from her sushi lunch ravening, and with her mouth tingling from the second-hand fear of watching Donny insist on trying the pufferfish. Heading behind the coffee counter, she helped herself to the enormous cinnamon roll that Ben had set aside for her in a paper bag on which he'd scrawled *For Post-Sushi Snack Emergencies*.

She was unwinding its sticky guts when Ben returned to the counter with a full cart of dishes for washing.

'How was lunch with king dingus?'

'The usual. He tried the fugu.'

'Did he die?' Ben asked innocently, his green eyes crinkling at their corners.

Adele chuckled, covering her full mouth with her hand. 'No. Go on, he's not that bad.'

'Glad to hear you have such high standards.'

Letting Adele mull on that one, Ben started stacking the dishes into the dishwasher.

'How've things been going here? Did Reba bring her own mug today?' She nodded at the flamboyant parrot mug he was stacking on the top shelf.

'An old one of Doralee's. I've been using it upstairs. Fills a gap.' He tapped its handle, which was a twist of red ceramic feathers. It took a moment, but he shook himself free of the memory. 'Anyway, that POS is working pretty well. You'll be pleased to know that we lose money on every drink.'

'Much money?'

Ben closed the dishwasher door and started the cycle. 'The technical term is a fuckton.'

'Guess I have some homework,' said Adele. At least it would be a hot date with a spreadsheet instead of a handwritten ledger with some receipts stapled to it.

'Also, that Al Gore Rhythm Sticks music thing is, and I say this with love, absolute shite. This dishwasher here makes better music.' He slapped the machine, which was whooshing away like a wind gust at the intersection of Court and Montague.

Adele hid her grin behind another bite of cinnamon roll. 'It is bad, isn't it.'

'Frank and Reba made earplugs out of serviettes, and they're both half deaf from a lifetime for following the Grateful Dead around.' Ben nodded at three guys clustered around a BYO power strip squawking words like 'Repo' and 'Commit change' and 'monkey patching'. 'See that table of tech bros? They've been fiddling with the system all day. Carrying on like absolute pork chops. They reckon they've got the next billion-stream hit.'

Adele cocked her head. 'Is it . . . quacking?'

'It is quacking,' said Ben solemnly. 'There's a cowbell, too. And all for a mere three hundred bucks a month. Bargain.'

Adele winced. There had been so many pretty pie charts on the website, and who could pass up a pie chart? It was science, but dessert-shaped. Wow, marketers were *good*.

'You've also given it permission to record every sound in the coffee shop for potential sampling.'

'Every sound?' Adele hoped she hadn't spoken any of her intrusive thoughts aloud.

'Every sound,' said Ben.

'I suppose we should whisper then,' she whispered.

'I didn't know Americans could whisper,' he whispered back. 'You guys are so *loud*.'

Adele had reached the gooey heart of the roll, which she ate with extreme joy. 'Not sharing,' she said, licking her fingers. After a moment, she added, 'How long have you been here, anyway? I've heard you pronounce the occasional R.'

Ben seemed to stiffen. He was silent for a moment – the embodiment of a laconic Aussie – as he perused the breakdown of costs on the new POS. 'This thing's pretty decent. Here's your profit on each drink here. Well, the loss on each drink.'

He pointed to a line item in red. Actually, every line item was in red. Adele bit her lip.

'And every time you put an order through, it pulls the ingredients from your stock so you know what you have on hand.'

He flicked thoughtfully through a few screens. 'I was born here, actually.'

'You're one of us?' She put her heart over her chest, preparing to sing the national anthem.

He squirted her with a spray bottle. She shrieked.

'You can keep your nationalism, you weirdo.'

Handing her a paper napkin, he propped his palms against the counter, bracing himself for whatever he was about to say. When he spoke, he didn't make eye contact. 'My mum disappeared when I was six. My dad . . . he was Australian.'

Adele awkwardly fiddled with the cinnamon roll wrapper. Something in Ben's intonation suggested Ben had revised that sentence halfway through. It didn't sound like he was on good terms with his dad.

Ben drummed his fingers against the counter, gathering his thoughts. One of the teachers chose that moment to hurry up for a refill.

'Don't mind me,' she said, awkwardly topping up her cup, then quickly retreating to her table of colleagues – a slightly smaller crew than usual. Teacher attrition was no joke.

'I went to live with my gran after that,' said Ben at last, his words carrying the ache of decades. He rubbed at his forehead, as though trying to scrub away a memory. 'She lived in this tiny town out in the Mallee: nothing but red dirt and sheep and scrub. Moved to Melbourne for uni like everyone does, bludged my way through an arts degree, ate my way through Brunswick Street, drank my way down Gertrude Street. But then my gran passed. Doralee got in touch out of the blue – how she knew I'll never know – and said she needed me here.'

'Funny how Doralee knew these things,' said Adele, musing that Doralee had somehow known exactly what Adele had needed as well. She reached for the Baileys hidden under the counter and poured a splash into her favourite knobbly mug. Liquor licence be damned.

'She was special like that.' Ben grabbed the Baileys and toasted. 'A little legend.'

'If you're drinking on the job, we want in,' called one of the teachers.

As Ben went over to top off the teachers' drinks, the doorbell jingled. It was Trix, the theatre kid and part-time Riffraff helper.

It was odd to see her flying solo: Adele had assumed the girls were a package deal.

'Trix!' said Ben. 'How's it going?'

'Pretty good.' Trix ran a tongue uncertainly over her braces. 'Um, so I got some beans for my dad's birthday a few day's back.'

'Did he love them?' asked Adele enthusiastically.

'Mostly,' said Trix. 'Almost as much as the blazing sun pin I got him – he works for NASA, and he's really into all the sunspot activity that's going on right now. But, anyway, I found this in the bag. I thought you might want to know.'

She deposited a tooth on the counter.

Adele almost fell through the floor in fright.

'Oh that,' said Ben nonchalantly, coming back to put the Baileys away. 'That's from my necklace. Must've fallen off.'

Adele was agog. 'You keep a . . . tooth necklace?'

Ben nodded as though this were utterly normal. 'Shark teeth. Croc teeth when I can find them. It's an Aussie thing.'

Adele prodded the tooth with a teaspoon. It looked awfully like a molar. Was that a filling? 'That doesn't look like a shark tooth.'

Ben raised his eyebrows. 'You don't look like a dentist.'

Trix waved a distressed hand. 'Bickering triggers me. My parents have this really unhealthy relationship. It's majorly codependent. They do everything together. It's so weird.'

If Adele hadn't been so unnerved by the tooth, she would've laughed.

'I'm so sorry. We'll make it right, I promise.' She reached for a fresh bag of beans and plonked it on a counter. 'Here, take these. And a mug. And this set of agate coasters, handmade by one of Reba's friends. And um . . .' She looked around for something else. A cutting from the pothos?

'How's the theatre group going?' she asked finally, trying to change the subject.

'We're on hiatus.' Trix pulled at her oversized band T-shirt – a Soundgarden one with a picture of Savage Garden. (From where was she sourcing this amazing collection?) 'Our rehearsal space is being turned into a natural wine bar.'

'Well, Riffraff is free in the evenings,' said Adele slowly.

Ben stiffened. 'That's when I roast. The air quality's shit, and it's loud. And there's a whole safety component with minors around heavy machinery.'

'Not where I'm from,' said Adele. In Tennessee having a fight with a giant machine with the safety turned off was a rite of passage.

'Here.' Ben went over to a corkboard bristling with business cards and flyers and pulled one down. 'Try this place instead. It's on borrowed time, like everything that's not a VC-funded grift to siphon money away from labour and towards a tiny pool of billionaires. But they'll be happy to have you.'

He passed Trix a card for a place called the *Moving Parts Theatre*.

Adele chewed her bottom lip. First Mamet, now a surprise knowledge of the area's underground theatres.

Maybe she and Ben had more in common than coffee.

Rage Against the Espresso Machine

Adele groaned, groggy with the remnants of sleep and the brownies she'd shared with Kyra and the other neighbours at last night's impromptu courtyard pizza party. (The third this week.) What was that noise? Was that her alarm? No, it was too early for that nonsense. It couldn't be her phone: it didn't get signal here. But it was *a* phone.

Adele dug around in the endlessly cresting sea of Doralee's belongings, which night by night she was slowly sorting into piles. Alas, the Keep pile kept growing: Doralee had so many unique tchotchkes and mementos that it was hard to part with any of them. Maybe they could do a Doralee exhibition at the shop and charge for entry. That could help offset some of the drink losses . . .

The phone kept ringing. She felt like Audrey in *Little Shop* frantically singing 'Call Back in the Morning'. Except it was morning. To some, anyway.

Focus, Adele. Tossing aside a crocheted quilt, a dachshund shoe rack and a box of seashells, she finally unearthed the fuse-box-torching retro toucan handset she'd pondered the other day. It wasn't as remarkable a piece of design as a hamburger phone, but it was close.

Crossing her fingers she wasn't about to be electrocuted, she put the toucan to her ear. 'Hello?'

'Are you up?' It was Ben, and he sounded peeved. He must be, if he were calling. Only boomers, scammers and two-step verification services called these days.

'I'm at the gym,' she lied, banging her foot against the wall for verisimilitude.

'Get it girl!' yelled a neighbour.

'Adele. You need to get that all-singing, all-dancing arse up here right now.'

Well, this sounded promising. 'What's going on?'

Ben paused to shout at someone in the shop. 'A *farrago* of *fuckery* is what's going on.'

'Nice alliteration, Shakespeare.'

'It's Nick Cave.'

'Really?' Adele was only familiar with the duet he'd done with Kylie Minogue.

'No. Look, if you're not up here quick-fucking-smart, I'm walking into the East River with a novelty helium balloon that says: "this is Adele's fault".'

'Really? In this helium shortage?'

'Fuck off,' he said, in that way that only Australians can. *FAHK OHFF.*

He ended the call.

Shoving the toucan back on its perch, Adele flicked through her wardrobe. Everything she owned was wrinkled, sweaty, or covered in coconut oil from her attempts to make 'bulletproof coffee' for the bodybuilder type who stopped in at Riffraff on Wednesdays. Nothing passed the sniff test. Not even the Covid sniff test.

She'd been meaning to get to the laundromat, but she'd

been run off her feet with the shop and Donny's endless impromptu dinner dates. Donny never seemed to have an issue with unwashed clothing. He probably had an actual washer and dryer in the apartment she'd never been allowed to see. Or used an app. Or simply threw out his clothes and bought new ones.

More likely: his mom did his laundry.

Adele wrenched open Doralee's wardrobe and pulled out the first thing she touched: a floral maxi dress with ribbony bits around the neck. Done. No, wait, bra. No, no time for that. She kicked on a pair of clogs, thanking evolution for its role in helping humanity progress to a point where shoes no longer needed laces.

She ran out the door and across the courtyard, pulling her wayward curls into a ponytail as she hurried downhill towards Riffraff, apologetically shoving people out of her way left and right. Oh shit, had she kicked that poodle? No, it had been more of a nudge, and it was unintentional, so it didn't count. She checked the Swatch she'd borrowed from one of Doralee's jewellery boxes – a bright Memphis Group style design number. Why were there so many people pressing about on a residential street at seven in the morning? Had a rent-controlled apartment become available? Had there been a gas leak? Had C.H.U.D. crawled up from the sewers?

As Adele approached the corner that housed the coffee shop, she realised the hubbub had a purpose. All of these people were milling around *Riffraff*. What's more, they all had their phones out in front of them like metal detectors.

Please let there be treasure beneath the coffee shop. That would solve so many problems.

Adele slowed, trying to read over the shoulder of an older

135

guy who had his text zoom set to maximum. He had some sort of order screen loaded.

'There's a queue,' said a velvet-clad goth – one of the group Adele recognised from The Great Smoke Inhalation Incident a few weeks back. Her platform boots were so tall that Adele made a note to buy a pair for the next time she needed to reach the top shelf at the bodega.

'I'm not in line. I work here. What's all this for?'

'You do? Normies all look alike to me.' The goth flashed her coffin-shaped phone case at Adele; a glittery spider dangled threateningly from it. 'There's this deal through EatMe. Fifty per cent off every order, and a free cookie. Do you know if this place is *actually* gluten-free, or the pretend kind?'

As far as Adele knew, it wasn't either kind. She liked her gluten like she liked Bette Midler. In everything.

'Adele, Adele!' Ekaterina – her hair now turquoise – was leaning against a fire hydrant, arm in arm with Alejandro as usual. A chalk artist was creating some kind of elaborate optical illusion at their feet. Farther down, a violinist had his case open and was playing 'Some Enchanted Evening'. Was that Joshua Bell? Adele hadn't known he was a Rodgers and Hammerstein fan. But then, who wasn't?

'What are you doing here, *mija*?' asked Alejandro, whose eyeshadow was as always unfailingly perfect. 'And I'm loving this outfit. Very loosey-goosey.'

Adele hoped Alejandro meant the dress and not her boobs.

'This is my place. It's kind of a long story. A rags-to-riches thing. Well, rags to not-quite-as-raggy rags.'

'Sounds *loverly*, Eliza. Tell us everything when we finally get our coffees and cookies.'

'A cronut for me,' intoned Ekaterina.

'No substitutions, babe,' said Alejandro.

'Don't ask, don't get.'

Adele glanced around at the ever-growing crowd. The queues for *Hamilton* hadn't been this intense. 'How long have y'all been standing here?'

Alejandro gestured to their flawless eye makeup. 'See this? All done standing in line. We've been here for an hour. We saw the sunrise and everything. You know, I've never actually woken up to see the sunrise. Stayed up, sure. But *woken* up? A literal whole new horizon has opened up. I feel like Moana.'

'This discount is an *amazing* offer, by the way.' Ekaterina shook her phone like a tambourine. 'You're trending on EatMe. And there's someone here from Shipping Container Radio. They're walking around with an earpiece thing and that smug NPR face.'

'What cynical sis here is saying is that if they or the NBC Peacock car shows up, we're going to sing our guts out. Always be hustling!'

Adele smiled brightly in agreement. But even as she did, she realised that she hadn't thought about performing in weeks. She still approached the world in a musical way – there was rhythm to *everything*, especially the making of espresso drinks – but the endless rigour of perfecting lines, drilling turns and caking on makeup had faded into the background of her busy coffee shop days. And honestly . . . she was okay with that.

Besides, Riffraff was home to as much drama as musical theatre.

Alejandro's compact flashed in the morning sun as they dabbed their elegantly contoured nose with blotter paper. 'Why is this line not m-o-o-oving?'

Adele bit her lip as she remembered Ben's tone on the phone.

He must have been there since 5 a.m., pouring shot after shot on the La Marzocco with only Reba and Frank there to back him up. No wonder he'd sounded so grumpy.

'Have y'all worked an espresso machine before?'

'Does the Phantom of the Opera wear a funny mask?' Alejandro snorted. 'We're Broadway hopefuls. Of course we've worked in hospitality!'

'Under duress,' added Ekaterina.

'All work is under duress,' said the chalk artist. 'Capitalism is violence.'

'Well then.' Adele grabbed her friends' hands and pulled them through the crowd. 'Staff coming through. Staff!'

Getting to the front of the queue required the same kind of logistics as squeezing both a bathroom and drinks break into a thirty-minute intermission. Fortunately they were pros at that.

'About frigging time!' called Ben as he hammered two portafilters in unison against the knock box. The box – which sat over a huge receptacle beneath the counter – was mounded high with coffee grounds, like a gopher had dug its way under a lawn. 'Someone empty this into the compost before it becomes sentient.'

'On it,' said Alejandro, shamelessly giving Ben the once-over as they pulled out the puck-filled receptacle from beneath the counter. '*You sly slut!*' they mouthed at Adele, who bit back a grin and pointed to the back of the kitchen, where a door led out to the cramped area that housed the trash cans and a bunch of wooden pallets no one knew what to do with. Trix and her friends were stationed back there stamping insulator sleeves with the Riffraff logo and sliding them onto the shop's signature flower power to-go cups.

'Shouldn't you be in school?' asked Adele, frowning as an

endless curl of white tickets poured from the EatMe printer. It was like watching Jack Kerouac type *On the Road* on its infinite scroll.

'It's Sports Day,' said Trix, with a shuddery intonation that told Adele all she needed to know about Trix's relationship with sports.

'We're definitely not, like, missing anything,' said Chaya, who was wearing orange cat ears today. The colour suited her complexion.

Reba hurried by with an enormous stack of paper napkins under each arm. It was odd to see so much white on her otherwise colourful form.

'Need help, love?' asked Frank, who was putting together takeout boxes.

Reba slapped him with the napkins. 'Don't call me that.'

'Can we put those out after they've been used in an assault?' asked Frank, rubbing his cheek.

'Anything goes today,' said Ben, pouring the milk for half a dozen lattes in quick succession. He was deliciously sweaty from the espresso marathon he'd been running. 'Fucknuts – Donny – signed us up for some discount thing through EatMe.'

Adele had known right away who he'd meant. But she didn't want Ben to have the satisfaction of knowing that.

'He didn't mention anything,' said Adele, handing out the drinks with their accompanying cookies to a group of artsy makerspace people brandishing their phones. 'Thanks for being a Riffraff!'

Ekaterina was passing out cookies and croissants as she chowed down on a muffin. 'This pastry case looks like it's been ransacked by thieves. Who's your baker?'

'This old bohemian lady Doralee shared a flat with in Paris,' said Ben, over the hiss of the milk frother. He passed a cup to a guy in a well-loved Yankees hat. 'Me, if it's vanilla slices or mini doughnuts. But I've been flat-out keeping the hungry hordes at bay. And Etienne is probably out feeding the pigeons.'

Ekaterina pulled out her phone. 'I'm texting Richard.'

Adele balked. 'Casting director Richard?'

'Former casting director. You're not the only one taking a step back from the biz.'

She remembered now that the war of attrition that was Broadway had taken another victim. Perhaps Richard had run out of witty one-line rejections.

Ekaterina's witchy fingernails tapped away as she entered into what Adele assumed was a Faustian bargain with Richard. With Adele's soul at stake.

'He'll be here in twenty with a freezer worth of cookie dough. Does anyone know how to preheat an oven? We only did bagels at my old place.'

The last time Adele had been near an oven, she'd stored her shoes in it. And if Doralee's place had an oven, she hadn't found it yet.

With well-meaning but unhelpful commentary from Alejandro, who'd handed off the emptied grounds receptacle to Ben like a star relay runner, Ekaterina fiddled with the oven, turning dials back and forth like she was programming a time machine. She squealed as the gas caught.

'Thank goddess that wasn't a range. My *eyebrows*!' said Alejandro.

'They're painted on, babe,' pointed out Ekaterina.

'But *still*.' Alejandro smoothed them, just in case.

Meanwhile, the tiny EatMe printer gurgled, then spat out a new expanse of white tickets.

'At least I have my mummy costume for Halloween sorted,' noted Adele, scanning over the endless stream of orders.

'Are we done chin-wagging?' called Ben. The espresso machine hummed and spat as he slid four cups beneath the two group heads, splitting each shot. He angled his chin toward the kiddie-table machine. 'Adele, you can fire up the Babyspresso and handle the brewers. Your friend – Ekaterina? Is in charge of these.' He tapped the steamer on the La Marzocco and the manual frother in turn. 'And our mate who did such a good job with the bins is handling crowd control.'

'I *can* work a crowd,' said Alejandro proudly. They twirled off to ensure the queue remained orderly.

Ekaterina twisted the steamer knob on the side of the espresso maker, making the machine hiss. 'Hello, old friend.'

The group settled into a rhythm of pouring drinks, packaging snacks, and sending customers out the door. A jazz rhythm, but still a rhythm. Even if it was against the backdrop of the awful AI music which, thankfully, was mostly drowned out by the clamour of the marauding free coffee folks.

'Big group coming in,' called Alejandro.

'Milk's low,' added Ekaterina. 'And cookies.'

Ben paused to chug a glass of water, wiping his forehead with the back of his hand. Catching Adele watching him, he raised an eyebrow. Busted, again. She turned back to the coffee she was making.

'I'm heeeeere!' came a mellifluous voice. It took Adele a few seconds to place it, mostly because she'd never heard it say anything other than 'that was an interesting choice' or 'we're going in a different direction'. Richard.

Alejandro raced to hold the door for Richard, who was showboating in with a fringed scarf looped around his shoulders and a Radio Flyer wagon stacked with baking sheets in tow. A jar of macarons was tucked beneath the expanse of his puffed sleeve like the severed head of the proverbial horseman.

He flicked his overlong bangs. 'Call me Deus ex Machina, because I'm here to save the day.'

Adele was getting Ichabod Crane vibes, personally.

With noted local oven expert Ekaterina overseeing, Richard slid the baking sheets into the blazing oven, setting the vintage red egg timer that lived on the counter.

'In the meantime, we have the macarons,' said Adele, passing them off to Ekaterina, who catapulted them at the hungry customers.

'I'll squeeze in here . . .' Richard cleared off Trix and Co's table to make room for his basket of bags and labels. The teens gave him a majestic, unified look of disgust.

'*Love* the emotion,' he said, tidily lining up his labels. 'Adele, take notes.'

Adele picked up a label. '"You've eaten a bag full of Richards." Quite the tagline.'

'*Right?*' said Richard, delighted.

'Save the constructive feedback for a workshop,' said Ben, although Adele could see he was trying not to laugh. 'Half of bloody Brooklyn is banging on the door. It's like the hipster zombie apocalypse.'

'Coffee's a hell of a drug,' said Adele, handing over a coffee and éclair to a woman dressed entirely in pink. 'Here you go, Barbie. Bag of Dicks, on the house.'

'And . . . milk's out,' pronounced Ekaterina, slapping an empty carton on the counter.

142

Adele grimaced. There was no way she could get it delivered with the crowds outside. The courier would be crushed to death.

'Don't even think about leaving,' warned Ben. 'You got us into this mess.'

'I categorically did *not*.' She'd been asleep! No one blamed Sleeping Beauty for Maleficent's shenanigans.

The insistent scent of hemp hand cream suddenly overwhelmed the aroma of freshly brewed coffee and baking cookies. Reba had come up behind Adele in a swirl of tie-dye and insouciance.

'Milk situation is sorted,' she said, slapping down a receipt.

Behind her, Frank grunted as he unpacked crate after crate with Trix and Co's help. Was that . . . raw milk?

Adele gaped. 'When did you do that?'

'We snuck out the back and went to the farmer's market. It's the good stuff. Unfiltered. Unpasteurised.'

'Unscientific,' muttered Ben, coming in to grab a tower of stamped-and-sleeved cups. 'American quacks.'

It did look a touch green. But milk beggars couldn't be choosers. Adele slapped away a reaching hand trying to top off their own drink with the newly acquired milk. 'Hey!'

'ETA on the cookies is five minutes,' shouted Richard, with the intensity of someone with an invisible Gordon Ramsay sitting on his shoulder.

The EatMe machine was still printing. Determinedly humming along to *A Chorus Line's* 'I Can Do That', Adele grabbed a streamer's worth of orders and started pouring shots on the backup espresso machine, handing off the newly filled cups to Ekaterina, who was having a blast.

'The movement in here!' she exclaimed, lifting a leg over her head. As one did. 'I'm getting the most incredible choreography ideas.'

Adele held her portafilter beneath the grinder, which spat out a sad spray of grinds and then went still. She'd had a great-uncle who did similar: you had to carry an umbrella at all times around him.

Time to top up the hopper. Grabbing a scoop, Adele opened one of the enormous coffee tubs. The last one, she realised, glancing around the back-of-house area. 'Ben, can you do a roast?'

Ben closed his eyes and flitted off – Adele assumed – to his happy place. Which was presumably Bells Beach. Although he did seem tense. Was the surfing bad at Bells Beach today? It couldn't be as choppy as the bedlam in Riffraff.

'The roast won't have time to rest,' he pointed out, frowning at the slightly uneven rivers of coffee pouring from the La Marzocco. On a different day, he'd redo those shots. 'Ideally you want to give it time to de-gas and ripen into its taste profile.'

It was too early for these sorts of nerdy words. 'Save the science for our coffee-tasting event next week.'

Ben's hand froze on the espresso machine. 'You'd better be taking the piss.'

'I am absolutely not taking the piss. I'm dehydrated as all hell because someone dragged me out of bed at 7 a.m. with barely a minute to get dressed. Let alone drink my eight glasses of water.'

'You look good,' he snapped. 'Dehydration brings out the hazel in your eyes.'

Well, there was a compliment for the ages. Adele flushed as she handed over a coffee and a cookie to a grumpy-looking Karen.

'Soy,' said the Karen, waving a hand shackled with an impressively thick gold bracelet. Not a bad way to add some light resistance training to your day. 'I want soy.'

Adele checked the ticket. 'But your order says—'

'Soy,' repeated the Karen.

'All right. Give me a second . . .'

'Forty-five minutes,' snapped the woman, as Adele poured a drip coffee from the brewer and topped it off with soy. 'That's an entire episode of *Suits* I've been waiting.'

'We're kind of backed up today,' explained Adele apologetically. She started as she felt something warm and fuzzy wind around her feet. Not a pair of magically knitted socks: Ember.

'Next time I'm taking my business to Starbucks. There's a reason small businesses stay small.' The bracelet clinked as the Karen dropped an empty sugar packet in the tip jar. 'Also, I need your bathroom code.'

'There's no code,' said Adele, as sweetly as she could manage. 'It's open to everyone.'

The woman shuddered. No, wait, that was the floor rattling. A murmur went up among the madding crowd squeezed into the shop in defiance of the maximum-occupancy sign. Adele promised herself she'd pray a rosary to the FDNY.

'The subway,' explained Adele. That had been a big one, though. Did freight trains go through the underground?

Ember, who had been at Adele's feet, appeared on the counter in that silent way that cats do. It was like he had an invisible parachute guiding him on the last part of every landing.

'Mrow,' he said, golden eyes flashing as he stalked along the counter, his frizzled tail wafting against the angry boomer's face.

The Karen softened slightly. 'What a cute kitty. My Milo recently passed. He was twenty-one, a real mess by the end. But the sweetest baby. Quiet. Self-sufficient. So much nicer than my kids, yanno? Anyway. Bathroom. And I'm not using an all-gender one.'

Alejandro gave her a look so pointed it was a wonder she didn't keel over from the stab wound.

To Adele's relief, Ben stepped up. 'There's another dunny downstairs. You can use that. I'll show you.'

The woman twirled a strand of brittle hair around her finger. 'I like your accent,' she said, suddenly mollified. 'Very exotic.'

'I wouldn't describe regional Victoria as exotic, but it takes all types.' Ben guided her towards the basement, helping her down the stairs. Ember raced ahead of them, purring.

'That man's like a sexy bouncer,' noted Alejandro, as he and Adele watched Ben's well-built form disappear into the basement. 'How do you work in these conditions?'

'Distractedly,' admitted Adele, distractedly.

Ben was criminally good-looking, and funny as well. And he made a mean vanilla slice, made all the more delicious by the fact that he used his dear old gran's recipe. (Even if dear old gran had allegedly both drunk and sworn like a sailor.) But the whole employer-employee thing was a lawsuit waiting to happen. Not to mention the way Ben's mood shifted whenever roasting came up. She'd never known anyone so possessive of their creative space. And she'd done an arts elective in college.

'Delly!' came the self-satisfied tones of everyone's favourite meddler.

Donny, of course. The other thing that stood in the way of

a potential relationship with Ben. She'd forgotten about him in the chaos of the morning.

'Look at that tickertape! It's like the Stock Exchange in here. Except you have a pit bull instead of a bull out front. And everyone is badly dressed. And poor.'

Adele set her hands akimbo. 'Some warning would've been nice.'

Donny scoffed. 'You should be happy, babe. This is the most volume the shop's done since it opened.'

'We were booming during the blackouts of '77,' noted Reba.

'And the protests of '82,' added Frank. 'Those were the good ol' days.'

'You'll thank me when you see your takings for the day. Has the news been by?'

'They're probably still in line.' Adele handed a coffee and a cookie to the next person in line, a thin man who'd come from the pool. Or at least Adele assumed, given that he was wearing Speedos and a towel.

The ground rumbled once more, and the now-familiar smell of roasting coffee filled the air. An approving murmur went up around the room. The Algorhythmix sound system, which Donny had turned up using his phone, sucked it into its algorithm and started humming it back across the crowd.

'Oh, that smells so good,' muttered a mystical-looking guy with an enormous beard, like a hipster Rasputin.

'Where's that Australian? He left you alone to handle all of this?' Donny took the coffee out of Adele's hand and sipped at it. 'That's what you get for hiring a convict.'

'He's downstairs. And I'm not alone.' Adele pointed out her cluster of helpers, who looked up from their various stamping and packaging chores to wave. 'And there's a spare apron if you want it.'

Donny recoiled, as though she'd suggested a date at an outlet mall. 'That side of the counter is not for me. I'm a big-picture guy. A strategist. We all need to play to our strengths. Those of us who have them. I need to take this call. Okay if I take this?'

He'd picked up one of Richard's bags.

'Of course,' beamed Adele, thinking, *you are, at this moment, absolutely welcome to eat a bag of dicks.*

A Roast a Day Keeps the Grumpy Away

What seemed like an hour later, Ben set a huge tub of freshly roasted coffee down behind the counter. The roast smelled incredible: punchy and bold – almost . . . argumentative. No wonder he'd called this particular roast *The Last Word*.

'That should do it,' he said, running a hand through his perennially mussed hair. 'Won't be great for espresso – the roast is heaps too fresh, but it should be decent on the brewer. Chuck enough milk and sugar on top and no one's gonna know.'

'Are you okay? You're bleeding.' Adele reached into a drawer for the first-aid kit, which housed a magnificent array of novelty Band-Aids. 'Here, let me—'

Ben leapt back as though she'd insulted Samuel Beckett.

'It's nothing.' He rubbed his face with the coffee filter Adele had been about to pop into the brewer basket. 'Oil from the coffee beans.'

'Do they stain like that? I didn't know they were so juicy.'

'Oh yeah,' said Ben, not making eye contact. 'They're like mangosteens. A mouthful of food dye.'

'Maybe I should help out with a roast one day. See how the

whole bean-to-bag process works. We do that in the theatre. Try out every role so that we know how it all comes together.'

'Yeah, right,' said Ben distractedly. Well, it was more promising than a *yeah, nah*. 'How's the crowd?'

Adele scooped the new beans into the grinder they used for the brewer. 'It's slowing down. Richard is out there with a huge pot of cold brew and a basket full of—'

'I don't want to know,' said Ben.

'—desserts,' finished Adele. 'That's helping keep the numbers down in here.'

She checked the setting on the grinder, then waited as the machine thoughtfully spat out a measured mouthful of grounds. Halfway through, it sparked, then screeched.

Then the power went out. Adele hadn't realised how noisy the shop was until the endless humming and buzzing of the various pieces of equipment came to a standstill. At least the Algorhythmix sound system went down with it.

Wafting the smoke away from the grinder, Ben yanked its cord out from the power point.

'Shit. The thing's cactus,' he said, inspecting it. It smelled like melted plastic and fritzing electricals.

'What does that mean?'

'Dead.'

This ran counter to Adele's understanding of cacti as extremely hardy, virtually indestructible plants. But Australian slang rarely made sense.

She shook the portafilter she'd been directing the grounds into, wondering if the grinder had hit a rock or something similarly unyielding. A piece of brassy metal flashed up at her.

'Look at that – prospecting for gold,' she said, picking out the piece. Weird. It was mangled on either end, but it looked oddly like a . . . belly button ring. A blingy one.

'Sometimes things fall in from the farmers or during the packaging process,' said Ben, offhandedly. 'Feathers, shoelaces, beetles – I've found all sorts of things in my raw beans of the years.'

'But belly button rings?' Adele turned the scarred piece of jewellery over in her hand. 'Are they popular among coffee farmers?'

'I couldn't tell you much about the sartorial habits of coffee farmers.'

Nor could Adele, but none of the visuals she was conjuring made sense. She couldn't imagine someone bellyflopping into a coffee harvest. Or belly dancing above a vat of beans.

'We're not all getting cold brew, are we?' moaned someone from amidst the throng of people.

'We at least deserve double cookies after all this.'

Double cookies! Began the chant. *Double cookies!*

'Where's the fuse box?' asked Richard, who had been known to work the soundboards on occasion. 'The basement? A few quick flips and we'll be back in business.'

'NO!' shouted Ben, grabbing him in a rugby tackle. Or what Adele assumed was a rugby tackle. She knew very little about rugby other than it was seemingly played in reverse, like a contact-sport version of *Merrily We Roll Along*. Richard crumpled to the floor.

'It's a liability insurance thing,' explained Ben with an apologetic grin. 'I can't let you go down there if there's a safety hazard present.'

Strange, thought Adele: twenty minutes earlier he'd obligingly directed the Karen downstairs. Speaking of, the woman had left her drink on the counter! Rude.

'But I'm wearing blue and yellow,' pressed Richard. 'That practically makes me a Best Buy employee.'

Ben wasn't having it. 'Mate, how about you go eat some of your dicks, and I'll sort it out.'

'Some of my *whats?*' asked a happily scandalised Richard.

Ben went back downstairs – carefully closing the door after him. Momentarily the lights came back on, and the machines started to whir and buzz once more.

He came back up to a round of high fives, including an off-kilter left-handed one from Adele – whose right hand was in her pocket, wrapped around the mysterious belly button ring.

Something peculiar was going on. And handsome, affable Ben was at the centre of it all.

She *knew* he was too good-looking to be true.

Adele kept out of Ben's way for the remainder of the day. It wasn't so hard, not with the endless stream of orders that continued to pour from the EatMe printer. Her forearms were aching from the repetition of loading a portafilter, locking it in, then emptying it out after the shot had been pressed through it. Her head, on the other hand, ached from the etched-in frown she'd been carrying around ever since she'd found the heavy piece of jewellery in the roasted beans.

It was all too odd.

Finally, as though hearing the aches and pains of Adele's lesser-known muscles and tendons, the printer stopped spitting. The sun played over it through the stained-glass windows, giving it a halo. Of course, she thought, nothing like romanticising the grind.

She took a deep breath, and then projecting the way she did on stage, she yelled: 'That's it, y'all! That's a wrap.'

The crowd broke into scattered applause, then a rowdier show of appreciation. Alejandro grabbed Adele and Ekaterina by the hand and clambered up on to the counter.

'And you as well,' they said, gesturing at Frank and Reba, who were chatting quietly at the back of the kitchen, their rift temporarily bridged. Frank carefully climbed up to the counter, balancing hesitantly against the La Marzocco; Ben effortlessly lifted Reba up by the waist, planting her upon the tiled surface.

'Give us a twirl, lady!' called someone from the crowd.

Grabbing the ends of her fringed shawl, Reba gave a solid Stevie Nicks twirl, kicking paper napkins off the counter in true rock-star style.

Adele reached out a hand towards Trix and Co, but the teens shook their heads.

'We're, like, strictly backstage,' whispered Rivka, who was painting a fresh *closed* sign.

Adele beamed down at the captive crowd. Sure, it had been an absolute debacle – a *de-fucking-bah-cle* as Ben would say – but this was the biggest audience she'd ever played to.

'How about a song?' called someone from the audience.

Adele came dangerously close to breaking into 'Oh What a Night!' from *Jersey Boys*. But she was pretty sure that would be a breach of the Algorhythmix T&Cs.

'If we didn't get to y'all, we'll make it good next time,' she promised. 'Just bring in your receipts. Or slap it up on the suspended coffee board and pay it forward. In the meantime, help y'allselves to whatever's left in the cookie bowl.'

'If anyone needs a bag of Richards, my number's on there,'

added Richard, tossing his scarf over his shoulder as though he were about to climb into a biplane and fly off heroically into the sunset. 'I'm available for catering. And producing and directing. Any kind of above-the-line role.'

'Cheers,' added Ben, toasting with an espresso cup. 'Now fuck off.'

Adele marvelled as the milling crowd slowly trickled out the front door, navigating past the fallen napkins and overflowing trash cans and out onto the sunburnt streets.

'Imagine being hot enough that you can tell people to fuck off and they take it as a compliment,' murmured Alejandro, awestruck. 'I'd totally go into politics.'

Adele turned over the sign on the door, blinking at the chaotic state the shop had been left in. Despite their best efforts at keeping the space tidy, it looked like the aftermath of a Bryant Park concert. Cups were stacked all over, and someone had been bowling with the tiny takeout creamer packages. AirPods were scattered on the floor like expensive confetti. Kyra's plant-wall-for-purchase had been stripped bare, with only a few remaining air plants bobbing in their tiny vessels. At least Audrey III was safe and sound, although Adele *had* turned down multiple offers to buy it.

With a world-weary sigh, the exhausted team sank down onto the rubber-matted floor.

'We're done,' said Adele, passing around the Baileys. 'We did it.'

The adults toasted with their paper espresso cups; Trix and Co raised their bottles of San Pellegrino.

'Old fucknuts'll be proud,' said Ben, knocking back his drink. 'What happened to him, anyway? I thought I saw him make a cameo.'

Adele shrugged: in the chaos of the day she hadn't had time to think about Donny's whereabouts. 'He had a work call.'

Ben nodded. 'Hate that.'

Richard pulled out his phone and started tallying up his cookie orders, drumming his feet against the floor in delight at the number his calculator showed him.

Watching Richard typing away, Adele suddenly blurted, 'Speaking of calls, I'm sorry about my phone ringing. During my Belle audition. I hope it didn't affect anything.'

Richard didn't even look up from his phone. 'Oh, honey. You were never in the running for that role. Oops, gotta run! My Pekingese needs me.'

He trotted out the door. Adele stared after him, deep in thought. All this time she'd been wondering whether the call regarding Doralee's estate had cost her the gig she thought had been a shoo-in. She'd spent so many nights wondering whether she'd been in a *Sliding Doors* situation, where the coffee-free alternative path led to Broadway success. But it had never been in the cards in the first place.

'Everything good, Adele?' Ben looked concerned.

She shook off the cloud of her realisation. 'Absolutely!'

Taking off his apron – oh, how she loved this time of day – Ben tugged on the endless stream of paper that had spewed from the EatMe machine, then frowned at the timestamp on the last one.

'Oh, fuck me,' he said. He cracked open the machine and pulled out the roll of printer paper, replacing it with a fresh one. Seconds later, the device started printing again.

Adele reached up and knocked it off the counter.

'I didn't see a thing,' she said. 'Did y'all?'

The Crème de la Crema

It took the shop a solid few days to recover from the EatMe fiasco. The roaster smoked through the night as Ben tried to shore up their bean stores, Kyra had swung by to replenish her all-but-naked plant wall, and Trix and her friends skipped another sports day to help out with stamping and boxing. Adele herself had picked up enough order tickets off the floor to reach to the moon and back. It was the closest she'd been to snow in months.

Meanwhile, Ember had decided that the safest spot was beneath his yellow armchair. No amount of tuna could coax him out. Not even the *o-toro* Adele had snuck from Donny's sashimi lunch yesterday had tempted him.

Alas, if high-grade sashimi didn't work, then today's lunch certainly wouldn't. Adele had been part-way through making a batch of cold brew when Donny had texted her that his driver was en route to pick her up. She'd said something to Ben about having to run out to deal with some of Doralee's personal effects, hoping he hadn't seen her climb into the hulking Cadillac.

She wasn't sure why she'd lied. Probably because she didn't

want to seem like she was skiving off from work. That was definitely it, and not the Donny angle.

Anyway, here she was, picking with a pair of specialised tweezers at some sort of foamy concoction that was apparently a deconstructed salad. Deconstructed at the molecular level. Either that, or one of the dishwashers had mixed up the actual food with the sudsy plates. She couldn't take it back for Ember even if she wanted to.

She'd suggested a picnic, but Donny didn't eat outside. Actually, he seemed to be indoors-only as a rule. Especially if that indoor place had a bizarre novelty theme and bottled sparkling water that cost ten bucks a pop. Like the one that they were presently at, which was called *Laundry*. To be fair, this explained all the foam. And the way the wait staff all seemed to be dressed in togas made from fitted sheets.

Donny, always a sparkling conversationalist, quickly turned the discussion to business.

'It's called a loss leader,' Donny was saying as he chewed a mouthful of suds. 'People come in for the cheap stuff. Buy things they wouldn't otherwise. Keep coming back.'

'I think it's just a *loss*,' said Adele. Especially after she'd paid Richard for his cookies. Who knew a single gingersnap could cost seven dollars wholesale?

Donny swished his fancy reverse-osmosis water around his palate, then sipped his wine. A waiter darted in to top it off. 'These things take time. Amazon bled money for years.'

Oh yes, that tiny mom and pop shop. Adele swallowed at the prospect of bleeding out over multiple calendar periods. Not fun. Especially when Riffraff's bank accounts were notably iron-deficient.

'We're taking a multi-pronged approach. Ready? You're going to *love* this.'

Adele had her suspicions that she was, in fact, not going to love whatever Donny had to say.

'I had an NLP – that's Natural Language Processing – friend run an analysis on your mentions across the web. Overall: not great. But there's influencer interest.'

'Influencers,' repeated Adele, stirring her foam. 'You mean people posing butt-first on Instagram.'

Social media had never really been her jam, or even her marmalade. The whole point of theatre was sharing emotions and opinions with people in a room. It was alive: a conversation. Whereas social media was a broadcast. The audience was transient and changeable. You never even knew who you were reaching.

'Those butts have put a lot of third-tier cities on the map. So. An ad firm reached out to me—'

'Why would they reach out to you?' said Adele, distracted by a spindly daddy longlegs of a guy getting down on one knee to propose to a startled girlfriend. Oh no, friend. Don't propose at the foam place. '*I'm* the business owner.'

'Maybe I called them. Who called whom: irrelevant. The relevant thing is that calls were made. The news: some of these influencers want to use the shop to shoot.'

'To shoot what?' asked Adele, suspiciously.

'Their content.'

'Content.' Not one of Adele's favourite words. It was up there with *moist*.

'Content is the new creative. It's a great way to get the word out. Do you want to keep serving the same old regulars again and again? You'll be a desiccated old husk pouring coffee for those old hippies. Healthy businesses grow. They start with one location, then two, then one on every block, even if that's only to choke out the competition until they close and you go public with an eight-figure valuation. You gotta feed the machine. That's the beauty of capitalism.'

Adele had no interest in feeding the machine. She wanted to feed humans.

Unlike this restaurant, she thought, as she watched a waiter strut past with a plateful of dryer sheets.

'What if I only want to grow a bit?' she suggested. 'Enough to pay my bills and make sure my staff have health insurance.'

Donny snorted. 'I'd say that providing health insurance in a service business is the death knell to your bottom line. Hire healthy, fire fast if symptoms appear.'

This didn't seem either legal or ethical. Time to change the topic before he started talking about podcasters.

'So, what do I do with these influencers?'

'Let me call the rep.' He jabbed at his phone, then held up a finger. She had to give him credit: he was always impressively prepared. His Boy Scout badges had clearly been concentrated along the lines of Business Administration.

A beep, and then an asthmatic voice on the line. In the background came the quacking of what sounded like ten thousand ducks. (An Algorhythmix system, perhaps?) The newly betrothed couple, who were swooping their forks through a gratis foam dessert poured from a laundry detergent bottle, glared daggers at them.

'Maybe we should turn it down,' whispered Adele.

'Donny!' crackled the voice. 'Sorry about the water fowl. We're at a rooftop pool party photoshoot, and we thought the bird life would add some pizzazz. Who let that goose in here? The rider says *no geese*, Louise! Anyway. Adele, is it? Van Vanderbly, Chief Effervescence Officer of Vanderbubbly Productions. Let me tell you what we do. We capture and explode attention spans with targeted aspirational content that shapes shopping behaviour and drives purchasing intent.'

Adele wasn't sure what any of that meant, but he delivered it with such intensity that she was convinced. Adele was a sucker for a well-delivered line.

'I hear you have a hospitality-aligned space that could do with a few eyeballs and eardrums?'

Before Adele could say that, actually, what the space could do with was cold, hard cash, Van bulldozed on like her neighbours back home obliterating the trees that had the cheek to cast a dapple of shade over their chain-link fence.

'So, there are a few ways you can make it happen. You can either shut down the place for a day so that our influencers can shoot without civilians getting in the way. It's a *nightmare* when they're twenty-eight seconds into a flawless dance routine and then some uggo steps into the picture.'

'Yeah, I hate it when I do that,' said Adele.

'Or, and this is the super convenient option, they can come in before or after hours.'

Adele wasn't sure that a bunch of needy TikTokkers showing up out of hours *was* super convenient. But that still sounded better than the EatMe situation, which she was doing her best to block from her mind. That tickertape haunted her dreams: she recoiled every time she went to unspool the toilet paper.

'They'll bring their own makeup and lighting teams, which makes your job *so easy*,' wheezed Van. 'And if they need to move things, they can do that as well.'

Adele could just imagine the look on Ben's face. Not that she was thinking about Ben's face while she was out with Donny. Donny's face was perfectly fine, even if he was looking shiny today. Had he come from a Botox session?

'Earth to Delly.' Donny clicked his fingers in front of her. How did he have better nails than she did?

'I'm really not sure—'

'Look,' interrupted Donny. 'Do you want to be on the map? Or do you want to be a nobody? Because I've seen your accounts. And they're not great. Not great.'

He was right about this. The depths of hell were less in the red than Riffraff.

'It'll be the teensiest of interruptions,' barked Van over a background chorus of ducks. 'You'll barely even know they're there. Until the likes and shares start doing their work. That's the power of virality. We make ideas *contagious*.'

Adele was no marketing expert, but as someone who avoided contagion like the plague, that tagline needed some workshopping.

'But I'm going to need an answer soon, because my influencers are in high demand. Wait too long and they'll go to Zeit Ghast Coffee instead. And your potential customers will go with them.'

'It's a good idea,' said Donny. 'A great idea. Trust me.'

Always with the *trust me*s. But he did have a Harvard MBA and a subscription to the *Wall Street Journal*. And she had a novelty Grande Gulp Margarita Drinker certificate and quickly accruing business credit card debt.

'I'll send over our marketing packages,' said Vanderbly. 'They're *gorj*.'

'All right,' Adele said cautiously. Before work was out of the question, but maybe after. Ben would be out attending to his secret post-work business, so he wouldn't be around to huff and puff about it. She'd stick around to keep an eye on the place. 'Tomorrow afternoon. We close at three, so they can come by then.'

Beaming, Donny ended the call. He waved his fork in her direction. 'We'll make a businesswoman of you yet. And maybe even a business of that place.'

He threw his black card down on the table. 'Damn, I'm stuffed. Isn't this place great?'

Adele didn't answer. She was dreaming of the bagful of mini doughnuts she was going to devour the second she got back to Riffraff.

You're a Latte to Handle

Sugar-addled on home-fried doughnuts, Adele broached the upcoming influencer event to Ben, who was scowling at a woman in a polka-dot dress who'd ordered her coffee to go and was now sitting at a table sipping languidly from a paper cup. Ah, the old takeout bait and switch. Adele recognised the culprit: she was a life coach who worked from the shop a few days a week, mostly because she was going through a vicious divorce after she'd quit her well-paying corporate job to become a life coach.

'Abso-fucking-lutely not,' said Ben, as much to the life coach as to Adele. There it came, the sweary infix. (An eavesdropping linguistics major had educated her on this enlightening term and its prevalence in Australian slang. She'd also coyly asked Ben to be the subject of a research paper, an opportunity that Ben had swearily turned down.)

'It'll be good for business,' said Adele. Tongue poking out in concentration, she wobbled milk into a cup, trying to make a swan. The end result looked more like a fish skeleton. But the goths would love it. And the fishmongers.

'Where have I heard that before?' Ben jabbed a milk frother

at the locked cabinet that housed the EatMe printer whose electronic brains they'd bashed out with the metal milk jugs after finishing off the Baileys. Cathartic, even if there was no way the company would refund them the device now.

'The difference is that this time we don't have to do anything.' Adele dabbed at the swan-fish with the handle of a spoon, trying to rescue her latte art efforts.

'Ah, righto. The time-tested business strategy of getting rich by doing nothing. Is the Institute of Intergenerational Wealth coming in to do a talk?'

Adele snorted. 'I don't think there'll be much talking. Probably more posing. And dancing. Is this counter big enough for dancing? Should I tell them to wear non-slip shoes?'

'That's a health hazard. I worked hard for our A grade.' He nodded at the sign in the window. 'You should've seen this place before I took over. It was like a Haight Street footpath in here. No offence to Doralee,' he added.

Adele suspected that Doralee, wherever her spirit currently lurked, would take this as a compliment for the ages. She was growing to love her great-aunt and her ability to muscle in on any conversation through sheer unforgettability. Every customer in Riffraff had a story about her generosity (and kookiness) – the community garden fundraisers she'd run; the clothes she'd made for job interviews; the time she'd slapped soundproofing on the walls and turned the shop into a recording studio.

'Don't worry. They'll stay out of your way. They're booked for tomorrow afternoon, after we close.'

'I have something on.'

'I know. You have something on every afternoon. Anyway, I'll be here.'

Ben looked unconvinced – although whether by her latte or her words, Adele wasn't sure.

'No one goes in the basement. It's a food production area.'

'I know, I know. Liability stuff, except when someone has to pee.' Adele shot him the steeliest gaze she could manage. Maybe he was charging Karens for bathroom access. Was that a thing? It seemed like it could be a thing.

'I did a risk assessment. Reckon I'd rather get in trouble with the Department of Agriculture than a Karen. What the hell's that? A Rorschach cappuccino?' Shaking his head, Ben poured Adele's latte art efforts down the sink. At least it was good enough for the Ninja Turtles.

Adele pouted at the waste. 'Anyway, you're the only one with the key. Keys. I promise no one's going down there.'

When she turned back to Ben, she was facing a coffee cup, a small metal jug and a bottle of detergent. He nudged the cup towards her.

Oh no. It was lunch at Laundry all over again.

'That's for you. We're doing soapy lattes. If you're going to do latte art, it can't look like Jackson Pollock munted in a cup. Do it properly.'

'With detergent? Are we trying to appeal to coriander fans?'

Ben grinned in that way that did funny things to her knees. He needed to stop that, because her insurance was too miserly to cover a knee replacement. Or an X-ray. Or a quick wave at a passing doctor on the street. 'Soap's cheaper than milk, so it's good for practising with.'

He squirted detergent into the jug, then used the espresso machine wand to steam the water.

'Give it a try. We'll start with the rosetta. Here, angle the cup like this . . .'

Adele did, frowning as she nervously poured the frothy water into the espresso shot, making a sea of white waves. 'Ta-da!' she said.

'Nice onion,' said Ben.

'Oh, shut up.'

In the breaks between customers, they steamed and poured, with Adele's squiggles slowly coalescing into something resembling a heart, a wilted tulip, and then finally a demented peacock.

'There you go. You can almost send that out without feeling ashamed of yourself.'

'I'll give it a try,' called Frank bravely.

'Make sure you give him one with an extra squirt of detergent,' muttered Reba. 'Ben, how did Cormac McCarthy find the sunset? Seven letters.'

'Limited,' answered Adele, before Ben could chime in. He raised his eyebrows, impressed, but said nothing.

'He's from my neck of the woods,' said Adele with a nonchalant shrug that did not at all reflect her inner shriek of delight. 'We read all of his stuff in school. Before the book-banning set got to it, anyway.'

The door dinged, and a sneezy-looking girl with streaming eyes staggered into the room, an enormous arrangement of white lilies over one shoulder.

'For Adele?' Shoving aside a succulent planter, the girl dropped the lilies on the communal table at which Reba and Frank sat at opposite ends, each stealing glances at each other. 'They're from a Donny Parker.'

'Sorry for your loss,' said Ben, eyes twinkling as he took in the funereal bouquet.

'Hush,' said Adele.

'Sign here. I'm double-parked. Al*though*,' added the girl, drinking in Ben's good looks like he were a lemonade on a hot day, 'can I get a drip, to go?'

Apparently the urgency of being double-parked was lessened in the presence of a hot barista.

'To *go*, to-go?' clarified Ben. 'Or sit-in to-go?'

The life coach was too busy writing affirmations in her bullet journal to hear this dig.

Adele signed, blinking as a sneeze threatened to erupt from her throat. All right, so maybe Adele would have chosen gerberas – or poppies – but the lilies *were* pretty. Donny was definitely one for big gestures. Although she wouldn't mind if they were a touch more personal. Not that she was complaining.

'Oh hey, do you mind if I . . .' Pulling out a few notes, the delivery girl swapped them for some of the change in the tip jar.

Ben's eyebrows dove. The delivery girl had committed a unforgivable sin. Adele bit her lip, waiting for Ben to excoriate her for her misdeed.

'Don't let Kyra see those,' said Reba, carefully working through the last few clues on her crossword. 'Cut flowers break her heart.'

'And these ones are deadly to cats.' Slapping the delivery girl's coffee down on the counter, Ben shooed a curious Ember away. 'How about you get those home so that we don't have to worry about this little guy. I'll mind the shop.'

Deciding against adding to the formidable medley of stuff at Doralee's apartment, Adele lugged the fragrant bouquet of lilies up to the cemetery that evening, feeling like a leafcutter ant hauling its cargo through the Amazon.

'Happy birthday, friend,' she said, setting them down at the base of the stone bench honouring the long-departed Fitzy Fring. Checking the dates on Fitzy's plaque, she saw that she was a few months off, but she figured time flowed differently when you were dead. For good measure, she sang old Fitzy an upbeat version of the birthday song – the normal version was such a dirge. Although maybe more appropriate for this particular setting.

She was wrapping up her birthday claps when a familiar duo crossed her path: Kyra and Ben, with Ben pushing Kyra's wagon along for her.

'Hey, stranger.' Ben looked slightly uncomfortable, like he'd been caught doing something inappropriate. Peeing behind a grave, perhaps. Or accidentally summoning a demon by reading the Latin inscriptions on some of the older headstones.

Kyra, however, had no such reservations. She swept Adele up in a hug, then did the same to the statue. 'How do you know Mister Fring?' she asked, nudging the lilies with a sandal.

'Oh, we go way back,' said Adele.

'He's a good guy,' said Kyra approvingly. 'Not a big talker. I like that in a man. Oh shoot, I left my workbook back there. I'll see you two back at the courtyard? Leave the wagon with me – it's light now.'

'Sure!' said Adele, excited at the idea of having a spare minute with Ben outside Riffraff's extended opening hours.

'Maybe,' hedged Ben, much less enthusiastically. 'I need to roast.'

'No wonder you don't have a girlfriend. You're married to that thing.' Adele paused by a headstone carved with regal-looking lions. *Leo Leone still reigns*. Dramatic.

'She's a jealous mistress. But I could do worse. Like these

two. Dead on the same day? Suspicious as an empty subway car.' Strolling ahead of her, Ben pointed out a his-and-hers tombstone sculpted with birds and ferns. *Here lie Dolores and Dolph Rentgen, together to the end.*

'I think it's kind of sweet, going out together.'

'Depends on how they went.'

He had a point. He'd also expertly dodged the girlfriend topic.

'How did Doralee go?' asked Adele, presently. She rubbed the head of a bronze sculpture of a terrier that sat waiting by its owner's headstone. The dog's head was polished and glossy – Adele wasn't the only one who gave it a pat when she passed.

'In her sleep. But before that, kicking and screaming. Didn't much like being told what to do, especially by death. She always thought he was a tosspot.'

'Why can I imagine her saying that?' Glancing around as though the ghost of her great-aunt were staring over her shoulder, Adele realised she'd never visited Doralee's grave. 'Is she buried here?'

'Vermont. She wanted a natural burial. No embalming, no casket. Just heaps of singing and food and weed. And cats.'

Adele grinned. 'I heard about the cats. But wow, Vermont – quite the jaunt.'

'It was like a bloody music festival, let me tell you. Better than Big Day Out. Or the Woodstock reunion.'

'I bet.' Adele brushed a hand over the colourful floral puffs of a rhododendron bush, thinking. Initially she'd been sad to come into Doralee's life only after it had been over, but there was a certain special joy in seeing all the ways that Doralee lived on.

'Thanks for looking after her.'

Ben paused. 'It went both ways.'

They strolled quietly back through the cemetery, reading out some of the wittier epitaphs or the more unusual names. Soon enough they had a whole 'Would You Rather' tombstone game going. Ghastly, yes; hilarious, also yes. Adele had never laughed so much while being surrounded by the dead. Except the time she'd worked through the 'Thriller' choreography with Ekaterina.

'So if you weren't here to visit Doralee, what were you doing?' Adele asked, when her abs had recovered. 'Taking a phone call?'

Ben chuckled. 'I don't take phone calls. I was helping Kyra unload some grounds in the greenhouse.'

He gestured over to the huge greenhouse structure by the stone-faced administrative building. Adele hadn't known the greenhouse was open to the public: she'd assumed it was a strange crypt for a mid-century architect who liked their spaces sunlit and open plan.

'Speaking of, there she is.'

Kyra had looped around a different pathway, wagon out in front of her like a reverse chariot. Seeing them coming down the hill, she waved.

'Got distracted by plants,' she yelled, her voice carrying towards them at dead-waking volume by a sudden gust of wind.

Ben flinched as a sheet of paper ripped free from a huge sassafras tree and flapped towards them like a Hitchcockian bird. He caught it with a frown: one of the spin class stalker's missing posters. Crumpling it, he threw it in a nearby recycling bin.

'I never did see her again,' mused Adele. 'Do you think she's okay?'

'Probably found a new local. Or switched to day drinking.'

Ben seemed irritated – Adele supposed he didn't like to talk about work when he was off the clock. Her uncle was the same, although he worked at a slaughterhouse, so she kind of understood why he wasn't a fan of bringing work home.

'Are you joining us, Ben?' asked Kyra, as she caught up to them. 'I've been baking, and you know what that means.' She winked.

'You girls have fun. I'm gonna check on the shop.'

'More for us!' Kyra rubbed her hands together.

'I'll bring leftovers,' called Adele, as Ben stalked off into the evening, his shoulders tight with tension.

A Whole Lot of Brew-Haha

But Ben's attitude was nothing compared with that of the influencers who filed into Riffraff at 4 p.m. the following day. Well, their minders did, anyway – the influencers were safely ensconced in the custom Sprinter vans parked out on the street, in clear violation of the prolific parking signs.

'*Cute* shop,' said a guy in a striped jumpsuit and heeled boots. He wore a director's lanyard that said *Noel*, and spoke in a rapid-fire stream-of-consciousness that could equally be pinned upon enthusiasm or speed. (*¿Por qué no los dos?*)

'I *love* the crazy grandma vibe – and those hand-chalked signs? Amazing. We can so work them into a vid. So, I'm thinking this bit under the leadlights could be the performance area. If we move those chairs out of the way . . .'

Adele had been standing in front of him for three minutes and still hadn't found a break in the conversation long enough to introduce herself. She'd have better luck trying to somersault across a highway in peak hour.

'I heard there's a café cat?' drawled a silver-clad woman who apparently took her baths at the perfume section of Nordstrom. She swung a ring light around the room, testing for shadows and highlights, of which there were many. 'They're great for elder millennial engagement. Assuming it's photogenic.'

Ember appeared, golden eyes narrowed. He did not take well to having his looks disparaged.

'Oh, you're in a tux!' The woman made a swooning gesture. At least she'd brought her own smelling salts. 'Does he like to be picked up? I'm Darlena.'

'Not particularly.' Adele watched Ember's back stretch into an angry arch. His tail swished murderously, signalling he was looking for a foot to attack.

'That's probably good.' Noel tested the floor with a boot heel. 'We had that whole thing with PETA after the snakes.'

Darlena grimaced. 'Never work with children or snakes. Or with children *and* snakes.'

Adele was not about to ask. 'I'm Adele, by the way. The owner.'

Darlene nodded vaguely, looking past Adele as though she were incorporeal. 'It's just you? There was that barista on the clips we saw from that EatMe day you did. We thought maybe we could get him in a few clips.'

'He's off the clock.' And off wherever it was that he went with his mysterious notepad collection and pencil case filled with ballpoint pens.

'Do you think you could get him to come back? His whole look could really be good for our views. He has that cross-demographic appeal. Does he dance?'

The closest Ben had come to dancing in Adele's presence was when he'd stomped out the fire she'd caused by leaving a tea towel too close to the brewer. That had been quite the sight. One she'd happily revisit, even if it meant a possible arson investigation.

'He doesn't.'

'Sing?'

'I don't think so,' said Adele, who had wondered this as well. With all those tattoos and that swoopy hair, Ben *seemed* like the kind of guy who was secretly a multi-instrumentalist. But he'd never joined in with her ditties. Not even her really catchy one about expressing oneself through espresso.

'I do, though,' Adele added shyly. 'Well, I did, in a previous life.'

'He should,' said Darlena, as though Adele hadn't spoken. 'That face? He could be in the millions of followers like that.' Darlena carefully clicked her fingers, mindful of not accidentally slitting her wrists with her scythe-like pink nails.

'I don't think that's Ben's thing. He's more of a behind-the-scenes guy.'

'Like me. I get that,' said Darlena, who in her silvery nightgown with *Look at me!* hand-stitched on it, categorically did not.

The bells on the door jingled. Adele braced herself.

'Here come our influencers: Mazzy, Tiffany and Empatica. Mazzy dances; Tiffany is lifestyle; and Empatica is a travel vlogger. You know those "This isn't Rome; this is actually an alleyway in Boston," videos? She pioneered those. You're going to love them.'

The influencers strode into the shop like models on the catwalk, each pausing to scope out the space and the opportunities for advancement. The twin currents of narcissism and low self-esteem crackled in the air, and Adele was back in freshman psychology, both fascinated and appalled by the edge cases the human psyche could present.

Darlena waved much more emphatically than the situation

required. She and Noel attacked the girls with intolerably lavish cheek kisses, like peckish piranha trying not to ruin their appetites.

'Oh wow, I can really vibe to these tunes,' said Mazzy, giving the Algorhythmix muzak the thumbs up. She did a shuffly dance move that looked a lot like someone wearing Heelys being electrocuted. Seeing that Mazzy was indeed wearing Heelys, Adele quickly scanned the floor for a wayward electrical cable. Phew: everything was out of the way and properly taped down.

As Mazzy struck a *ta-da* pose, the other influencers applauded, then broke into a facsimile of the same dance.

'Oh, I love it when they riff off each other.' Darlena's nails carved the air as she gave a golf clap. 'Doubles the views. Even if Empatica is never sharp enough. But that's her brand. She's more of a swayer.'

'Did anyone get that?' Tiffany panted. 'We can go again.'

'Oh hey, I think you follow me?' Mazzy, who was unfairly tall, loomed over Adele in a floaty ensemble of terry cloth and jersey. It was the kind of casual *going-to-the-store-in-my-pjs* outfit that took a team hours to dial in. The kind of outfit that if Adele, at five-one, tried to pull off, she'd look like she'd come from robbing a Bed, Bath & Beyond.

'I don't think so.' Adele had been on a social media detox since she'd arrived in New York City. There was no need to compound the horrific sense of personal failure that came with trying to make it in one of the most competitive cities in the world by adding a bunch of tanned L.A. twenty-something millionaires to the mix.

'I have three hundred thousand followers, so maybe I'm mixing you up with someone else. But I swear I've seen your face in my mentions.' Mazzy pulled up a video of herself dancing atop a star on the Hollywood Walk of Fame. 'Does this place have a handle?'

'It's this one.' Tiffany flashed her phone. 'Ten followers. Wow. That's actually kind of impressive. Are any of them real? Dyer on the Mountain? Frankophone? Who comes up with these usernames?'

'Those two are definitely real.' Adele was flattered that Reba and Frank followed the shop, especially since it only had one post: a blurry shot of a grinning Doralee holding up a coffee carafe. She paused to zoom in on it, smiling herself at the fuzzy capture of her great-aunt. Doralee had made such an impact on so many people. 'So. What now?'

'We'll spend about an hour filming, and then we'll let you get on with the cleanup,' said Noel. 'Tiffany and Empatica are quick – they've got shoots after this. Mazzy, though, she's a perfectionist. An absolute workhorse. If it requires a thousand takes to get her vid just right, she'll do it.'

'But a touch erratic,' whispered Darlena. 'She's a very . . . creative personality.'

'Quick Q?' Empatica pursed purple lips. 'Is this place haunted? I'm doing a series on the most haunted places in Brooklyn, and this place has a *vibe*. I think it's all the crochet and plants. If you can't answer that for legal reasons, blink twice.'

Adele did, but mostly because Darlena's extremely perfumed self was hovering over her in an obnoxious, noxious cloud of pulverised roses. She sneezed.

'Is a sneeze code for a poltergeist?' Empatica held out her hands as though she were trying to commune with the spirit world. 'Spirit? Friends? If you can hear me, give me a sign.'

The floor rumbled ominously.

Empatica jumped, clapping her hands against the collar of her lacy, utterly see-through top. 'Oh. My. God. Let me pull up my Spirit Scanner app . . .'

'It's the subway,' said Adele.

Empatica flapped a hand thick with bangles. 'I've already done some subway content. I'm going to do the ghost thing. That stained glass over there is perfect.'

She ducked beneath the reaching tendrils of Audrey III, directing her crew to set up a tripod and ring light.

'Spookier,' she exhorted. 'Make it spookier.'

One of the crew members ran to switch off the lights.

'Not the one that says turn off at risk of death,' called Adele.

'I hear you roast on site?' interjected Darlena, speaking past Adele in an impressive display of disdain. 'Can we get access to that area?'

'All that hissing and churning and *burning*,' added Noel. 'That kind of thing is amazingly theatrical. We could have Mazzy dancing next to the machine as it roasts. Or *on* the machine.'

Ben would never forgive Adele if she let a bunch of influencers loose around his prized roaster. Never mind the flames coming out of the roaster: they'd be coming out of his ears.

'The basement is off limits,' said Adele firmly.

Mazzy rose up on her toes. The wheels set into her shoes spun sadly. 'An industrial backdrop would work really well with the routine I've been working on.'

'Our head barista is really protective of the roaster. Proprietary blends, hygiene, all of that stuff.' Not to mention the seven locks Ben had on the door, none of which Adele had the key to.

'Hmm.' Mazzy's tone said *we're not done here*. Adele had the feeling that she'd never heard *no* in her life. She'd been told it, sure. But she'd never heard it.

Adele went to the *Out of Sight, Out of Mind* drawer and pulled out the croaking frog door alarm she'd brought over from Doralee's. She set it in front of the basement. 'You trespass, he croaks. Got it?'

'Sure,' said Mazzy. 'But according to NYC codes, every room needs to have two methods of egress. So if I happen to find the other one . . .' She angled her head innocently. 'Can we set up the strobe? And the disco balls? We're losing light.'

Noel clapped, and a group of assistants dressed in theatre blacks appeared. Where had they come from? Maybe there were hundreds of them packed into the Sprinter vans like clowns in a clown car.

'What was all that about methods of egress?' asked Adele, watching the assistants drape the shop with string lights and twinkly beaded curtains.

'She has a master's degree in architecture,' said Darlena. 'She's the whole package.'

Mazzy climbed atop the counter, testing its surface with her wheeled Heelys. 'I can work with this,' she said, nailing a triple spin. 'Let's move some of the mugs closer. Those tie-dye ones.'

Adele watched Mazzy spin and whirl amid the rainbow beams of the disco lights they'd set up. She kind of admired the girl.

Darlena gave Mazzy an austere thumbs up. 'Trust me when I say that influencing pays better than designing buildings. Way better. I tell you, the whole college to workforce pipeline is old hat.'

'You don't need to tell me,' said Adele, whose student loans

178

had ballooned so much they could take Phileas Fogg on a trip around the world.

'And they can always pivot into something more staid when they need to. Like you.'

Adele cocked her head.

'You were an up-and-comer on Broadway, so I hear. Richard Cuttle speaks fondly of you.'

'Does he?' Adele bit back a smile. Perhaps she'd made an impression after all. She gestured across the coffee shop. 'I perform for a more intimate audience these days. I'm more about providing a space that lets people express themselves.'

For better or worse, she thought, watching Mazzy perform a dangerously acrobatic dance routine on the tiled counter. Ember was pressed up against one corner, hissing.

'Good for you. That's so admirable,' said Noel. 'I love people who think of others instead of their own financial enrichment. Speaking of which, let's talk payment. We're flexible; so any way you want to do it is fine by us, although our terms are day-of. And US dollars. Although I'll accept Bitcoin for a fee.'

Adele blinked. 'Wait. I'm *paying* you?'

Noel stiffened as abruptly as if he'd been struck by lightning. 'How did you think this all worked?'

'I thought this was like . . . a studio shoot, where you hire the space for a set amount of time?'

Darlena cackled at this apparently hilarious statement.

'Or maybe,' Adele went on, desperately trying to save the situation, 'a sort of mutually beneficial thing where you feature Riffraff, and I give you access to a space that helps you with your . . . content creation.'

She might as well have suggested walking the red carpet in a repeat outfit.

'Girls, we're done here,' snapped Noel.

Fortunately, Tiffany and Empatica were already outside, Tiffany chugging some sort of pop-top sparkling water while Empatica sucked on a vape like it was a precious source of oxygen and not, well, the opposite of oxygen. Only Mazzy was still spinning and gyrating, unaware that she was generously donating her time.

'How about an annual coffee subscription?' offered Adele. 'Or a lifetime's supply of beans? Our Blood and Bone roast is really popular.'

Noel huffed. Adele felt like a toddler whose macaroni art had fallen extremely short in its efforts to win over an imperious child-free second cousin.

'I can write a cheque.' She scrabbled the drawers behind the counter looking for something resembling a chequebook. Aha! No, just an artsy book of IOUs.

'Cashier's only,' said Noel, who had run an imaginary pull on Adele's credit and didn't trust her to write a personal cheque that wouldn't bounce like an over-pumped basketball.

The door dinged, and Ben stepped in carrying an armload of books.

'What in the name of the Moomba boat race is going on here?' he demanded, discombobulated by what the influencers had done to the shop. He set down the books on the communal table, which had been shoved over against a wall.

'It's the hot barista!' Mazzy leapt down from the counter, skidding on her wheeled heels just enough that Ben had to catch her. 'Nice reflexes.'

The corner of Ben's mouth twitched. He set the unruly influencer down, then folded his arms. It was a pose that said, *there will be no more catching*.

A tiny part of Adele's soul bubbled happily at the thought of Ben turning down this extremely attractive, semi-famous individual. Another part reminded her that she had no right to Ben's attentions. After all, she kept saying yes to Donny's invitations, didn't she? Even if that was mostly out of inertia. It was hard to stop something when it was already moving. Just ask Newton, who apparently knew all about going along with someone simply to save them from getting hurt.

Sigh.

We hope you can join us tonight for a special evening of Angel on My Shoulder and the Devil on My Shoulder together in conversation!

'I need to get to the bank before it closes,' said Adele, mostly as a way to shut up the voices in her head. 'Can you help out Mazzy while she finishes up?'

'I have all night if you do,' purred Mazzy, eyeing Ben as though she might eat him. 'I'm *dying* to see this basement.'

Ben frowned as the floor rumbled. 'I don't think—'

'Good luck!' said Adele, as Noel ushered her out the door and towards the bank.

Excuse Me While I Kiss the Chai

But the line does not go 'all's well that spends well'. Adele's professional woes were compounding like the unread Reddit threads Donny – who had not responded to her lengthy voicemail about the whole pay-to-play element of the influencer 'opportunity' – kept sending her. Currently her life was the opposite of the plot *How to Succeed in Business Without Really Trying*, for which she'd auditioned for the role of Hedy LaRue, but had been told that the company had been looking for someone who was, looks-wise, more convincing.

It was with a world-weary sigh and a barely solvent business bank account that a drenched Adele entered the shop the next morning. The weather gods had laughed in the face of her difficulties, reasoning that what didn't kill you only made you stronger, so it was worth going in for round two.

Oh yeah? Give this a try! They'd gleefully shouted, upending buckets of rain on her freshly styled hair. Adele supposed it was her own fault for tempting fate by getting out her curler.

At least the tables and chairs had been pushed back into place – in a slightly updated formation, actually. A good move:

it opened up the space, and hid some of the more dramatic dips and bumps in the hardwood floors.

'Adele! Did you see this? We're famous!' exclaimed Reba, who today was surrounded not by crosswords, but by an army of plush ghosts made from tie-dyed cloth. 'Oh this? I'm getting ready for Tie Dyepalooza. Enough about me. Look!'

She showed Adele a glitzy video of Empatica in which the influencer, her face shadowy beneath a cobwebby filter, spoke scathingly of Riffraff's too-dark coffee and lack of supernatural energy against a knock-off version of the *Halloween* theme tune.

'In conclusion, Riffraff Coffee Co goes on my list of Brooklyn's most *un*haunted buildings. The tuxedo cat says it all: every witch knows that the only appropriate familiar is a feline of the properly black variety. For ghosts, murders, and overall heebie-jeebies, give it a skip—' here she clutched the counter as the floor rumbled beneath her '—and get your coffee opposite the church on 9th Street instead. Rumour has it that the church bells ring every time a soul is taken. And all ingredients are locally and ethically sourced. See you next time, babes!'

Adele sighed. Obviously the sad cheque she'd wheedled the bank into giving her hadn't lived up to the influencers' expectations.

'Well, she's wrong,' said Reba, searching around for the angry-face emoji. 'If you ask me, this place has excellent haunting energy. Look at that borealis photo! Riffraff survived an electromagnetic storm, you know.'

'Doralee was always a stickler for local and ethical sourcing, too,' added Frank. 'We had only non-dairy milks for the longest time.'

'The milk comes from free-range cows upstate,' called Ben, who was steaming the milk for a cappuccino. 'Certified organic. They're even smiling on the bottles. Happy as Larry.'

'Oh yes, that's definitely what a cow looks like,' retorted Adele, who had grown up near a large dairy farm conglomerate with similarly cheerful branding. Alas, the business had shut down after it had turned out they were diluting their milk with water from the local swimming hole. (The swimming hole had simultaneously been shut down due to waste-water runoff from the dairy farm.)

'Well, some of us grew up in sheep-farming land.'

'What about the beans?' asked an eavesdropping customer whose backpack pins indicated he ran a niche podcast and had made his fortune in cryptocurrency.

'It depends.' Ben handed over the cup to a woman in voluminous culottes. You could smuggle children in those things. 'The house blend is mostly a Brazilian base. The rest depends on . . . availability.'

'Riffraff should grow its own beans,' said Frank. 'Brooklyn Beans. Has a ring to it. How hard could it be? Kyra could help.'

Ben carried a French press and a plate of pastries over to the group of teachers at the communal table, who were blinking back despairing tears as they marked papers. To their collective relief, he popped the ever-present bottle of Baileys in the middle of the table for them. 'Deadset? Pretty bloody hard. Coffee plants like a hot and humid climate—'

'We've got that going for us.' Frank pulled at his Hawaiian shirt, which was sticky with sweat.

'I've got a technician coming for the AC,' said Adele. 'Or you're welcome to run around in the rain to cool off.'

'But New York winters are a killer. We'd need a greenhouse or something. A big one.'

A killer, a killer, a big one, a big one! sang the Algorhythmix system, sampling his words back at him.

'My fault. Sorry.' The podcaster tapping furiously at his keyboard. 'Wanted to give it a try.'

'Kraftwerk did it better.' Frank scowled at the Bluetooth speaker.

Cats-eye glasses perched on the tip of her nose, Reba was still scrolling on her phone.

'This Tiffany girl did a video on your secret menu items. All the things you can order even if they're not actually on the menu.' She winked, flashing a colourful eyelid. 'Like my afternoon nightcap coffees.'

'Every bloody drink these boofheads order is a secret menu item,' muttered Ben, coming by with a tray of dirty dishes. Adele tried to ignore the delicious shiver that spilled down her spine as he brushed past her.

'What about Mazzy Stevens?' asked Adele. 'The dancer. She has those shoes with the wheels. And kind of an . . . insistent personality.'

Ben slammed down the dishes on the counter and started stacking the dishwasher with an aggressiveness that made Adele wonder whether the influencer had applied her insistent personality to the hot barista. A tiny prickle of jealousy needled beneath her skin as she imagined Ben giving the architect-turned-dancer a VIP tour of the out-of-bounds basement.

Reba tapped away on her phone, which had the text size scaled up so much you could use it as a teleprompter. 'She hasn't posted since last week. She must be cooking up something big. Or she's pivoting.'

'I heard she's in rehab,' said one of the teachers. 'If an influencer stops posting, it's always rehab. It's the only way you can extricate them from their phones.'

'Wish we could do the same with the students,' added her colleague.

The door jingled, and a group of kids in novelty onesies came in, saturated from the rain, but pulling it off far better than Adele had. Oh, to be young and comfortable walking around in a sopping head-to-toe frog outfit.

One of them passed a decorative sheet of paper to Ben.

'What's this?'

'We heard you have a secret menu. Can we have one of everything on this list? No straws – we brought our own.' The theatre kid unzipped a pencil case filled with reusable bendy straws.

Ben dangled the sheet from his fingers as one might a piece of used toilet paper collected from one's shoe. 'Did you write this in Wingdings? Adele, can you get up here?'

Adele left Reba to her TikTok scrolling and hurried up to the counter. 'Welcome to Riffraff, y'all!' she declared in her best theatre voice.

The onesie menagerie eyed her, unimpressed.

'We've got some blended drinks nonsense to prepare. A uni-bloody-corn latte indeed.' Ben looked as though he'd been sentenced to a lifetime of cruel and unusual punishment. 'You're on ice-crushing.'

'Deal.'

Adele threw several trays of ice into the crusher and set it to pulse. The machine's blades made short work of the ice, grinding it up like Adele's teeth on a night she'd been especially stressed over an audition. With the added hum of the espresso machine and the hiss of the steamer, the sound behind the counter became cacophonous.

'It's like Drums and Space back there,' shouted Reba, making twin peace signs with her ring-smothered fingers.

Adele had no idea what she meant, but at the same time . . . she sort of did.

'Never did mind industrial music,' yelled Frank, drumming on the table with his teaspoon.

As Adele dialled up the ice crusher again, something blew.

The Algorhythmix music system crackled and spurted, like it was delivering a pronouncement from the moon. Then it shut off entirely.

A groan went up from a huddle of tech bros, who had been animatedly discussing the benefits of disrupting music by removing musicians and instruments from the equation. And something about the blockchain.

Everyone else looked faintly relieved.

'But we need *some* music,' muttered an exhausted-looking woman in hospital scrubs.

'I don't leave my house just to be alone with my own thoughts!' groused a pet psychologist regular who had some *thoughts* about Ember's attachment to the yellow velvet armchair.

'That's not a unicorn latte,' said the kid despondently. 'Where's the rainbow?'

Adele reached into her handbag and pulled out a jar of Alejandro's body glitter. She spooned out a generous portion and stirred it into the latte, which glowed with the power of a thousand My Little Ponies.

'I'm pretty sure it's edible,' she told a horrified Ben as she stuck an upside-down waffle cone into the drink.

'Here's your unicorn bullshit,' said Ben. He slid the cryptic drinks menu over to Adele. 'Here. Hope you're better at chemistry than I am. I'll go check the breaker.'

Humming as she worked, Adele started chopping up a

dozen mini doughnuts to top off some sort of coconut iced coffee confection that Ben had got halfway through preparing.

When a coconut meets a do-co-nut . . . she sang as she worked. She pushed the elaborate orders across the counter, proud at how they'd turned out. Her latte art could almost go in a gallery! A preschool gallery, but still a gallery.

Cleaning up, she spied a guitar case lurking beneath a table. The guitar's owner was nowhere to be seen: she was either vaping in the rain, or vaping in the bathroom. Hopefully not that one, because the Riffraff bank account was not in a position to pay a fine.

'I saw that look, honey,' called Reba. 'Pull that thing out and get yourself up on stage.'

'Wish she'd say that to me,' whispered Frank.

There wasn't officially a stage at Riffraff – to the chagrin of yesterday's influencers – but Noel had been right when he'd said that the spot beneath Audrey III and the stained-glass windows worked perfectly. All you had to do was add some fairy lights, and you'd have the perfect setting for a wedding. Not that Adele was thinking about weddings, she told herself. Unless it was for her customers.

Adele unlatched the sticker-smothered guitar case and pulled out the guitar, a glowing old Martin with stars painted on it. Looping the strap over her neck, she perched on a stool that Frank had dragged over.

'This one's called "Somewhere Over the Rainbow".'

Adele's fingers plucked nervously at the strings, feeling out the guitar and waiting for that moment that everything clicked. She could feel the attention of everyone on her – but especially the green eyes of one person in particular who had taken up his spot behind the counter.

There. The song started to spill up through her, warm and sweet, like ambrosia of the soul. It had been weeks since she'd performed in front of anyone other than her reflection in the mirror, but it was all coming back. She could hear the smile in her own voice as she sang, hear the weight of the attention of the cosy room. All these people who were here for not just *her*, but for the environment she was helping to create.

It wasn't Broadway, but it was special in its own way: the kind of intimate, no-strings performance that people would buy their five-dollar-plus-tip ticket to every single day, sitting there for as long as they could between the demands of their lives, murmuring during the intermission, clapping during movements, and standing on ovation as their friends and loved ones shuffled in and out.

No wonder the shop had endured longer than *The Phantom of the Opera*.

Outside, the thundering sound of the rain halted. Then a gasp went up from everyone in the shop. Reba was standing in her chair like a tie-dyed phoenix arising from colourful ashes. Her bangles jingled as she pointed to the stained glass above Adele's head.

'Look, love. You summoned your very own rainbow.'

Turning, Adele broke into a grin so broad her cheeks ached.

'Bra-fucking-va,' whispered Ben as Adele handed over the guitar and went back to the La Marzocco.

Adele was working through her closing duties when Frank sidled up to the counter. He snuck her a fiver – for the cookies Reba had filched over the course of the day before heading out to prepare for Tie Dyepalooza, which was reportedly the area's pre-eminent tie-dye event (but only the fifth biggest in the nation).

'Reba can never go past an oatmeal raisin,' he admitted ruefully. 'Or those ones that Ben makes? The ANZAC cookie things.'

'Those *are* good.' Adele had eaten three for dinner last night, washing them down with steamed milk and Baileys like a Santa Claus in a Raymond Chandler movie.

She popped the money in the till, figuring she'd wrestle with the POS later. She still hadn't figured out all the quirks, and quietly wished they could revert back to Doralee's system of envelopes and tote bags. At least they still had the vintage till with its sing-song creaks and dings. Adele would love to write a song that accompanied its cheerful ditties.

'She loves those vanilla slices of Ben's, too. The ones he calls the "snot blocks". Aussies, they're a different kind of people, aren't they.' Frank tugged thoughtfully on his ponytail. It wasn't like him to chitchat, which meant he was working up the nerve to ask a question.

Adele cocked her head. 'Go for it, Frank. What's on your mind?'

'Your record player. I'm a handy guy, and I think we can fix it. It'd be a shame to see that thing go to the dump or be used as furniture. It's beautiful. It's real. You can play actual music on it. And let's face it, as we've all seen these past few weeks, this place needs actual music.'

Something inside Adele brightened as he said this. She didn't know much about business, but she *did* know about music, and she'd always felt the Algorhythmix idea was a bad one. But how were you meant to argue with someone with so much confidence and a *Harvard Business Review* loyalty card?

'Did that boyfriend of yours put you up to that? The digital soundscape stuff?' Frank pushed the record player out from the wall, frowning as he poked about at its innards like a coroner.

Adele nodded, although calling Donny her boyfriend seemed like a stretch. Even if he did keep coming by with gifts, something that wasn't helping with her decluttering efforts. 'It was worth a try.'

'Everything's worth a try,' said Frank. 'But you don't have to keep it up beyond that. Do you keep a tool bag around here?'

'We do!' Adele had had Ben lug it up from the basement so she wouldn't trip down the stairs and jab herself tie the eye with a screwdriver. Which was an unlikely thing to happen, sure, but her fear of having a fan fall upon her had been realised during a school camp one year. She'd survived (obviously), but she'd spent the better part of a night having her head stitched up. You never could be too careful where mechanical things were involved.

She hauled it over to Frank like a grandparent walking with a toddler standing on their feet.

Frank held up a screwdriver with a painted handle. 'Doralee's been here, I see.'

Adele chuckled. 'Her legacy endures.'

With a grunt and the snap, crackle, pop of an ageing pair of knees, Frank descended to where the guts of the record player lived. He effortlessly popped out the front panel, then started fiddling with the wiring inside.

'I do love a strong woman. As I suppose you know by now.' He gestured to Reba's chair, which his cookie-clutching wife had vacated slightly earlier than usual, citing Tie Dyepalooza responsibilities.

'So how do we get you and Reba back together?' Adele asked.

Frank regarded his screwdriver thoughtfully. 'What I did, Adele. She's right never to forgive me.'

'Come on. It can't be *that* bad, can it?' Although after the song and dance he'd made about it, she almost hoped it was. Dear old hippie Frank! What shenanigans had he been up to?

'Our dog,' said Frank at last. 'I lost our dog. Our dear girl Janis. She was a sausage dog, a real kielbasa of a thing with the stompiest legs you've ever seen. We had her for fifteen years. She was the smartest girl. She'd fetch my keys for me when I needed them, tap on her food bag when she was ready to eat, even roll out the newspaper for Reebs.'

Adele smiled gently. 'She sounds perfect. Did she get out?'

Frank twisted together two lengths of wire. 'No, no, she was already dead when I lost her.'

Adele blinked. Was there some sort of taxidermy thing going on here? Or a ghostly possession situation?

'Her ashes,' explained Frank. 'Reba had ordered a special urn from one of her artist friends, and we were going to do a celebration of life with a community walk past all of Janis's favourite sniff spots.'

'That sounds lovely,' said Adele. And it did. It was much better than the commemorative vinyl decals people would put on their cars back home. She was always astonished that any of the drivers could see out their rear windows. Especially since they were all busy looking at their phones.

'It was quite the night. All the neighbourhood dogs came out. But at the end of it all, the urn had vanished. And Reba had placed me expressly in charge of it.'

'Oh.' That *was* a predicament. 'Are you in the habit of losing things?' From Adele's experience, every relationship had a Loser and a Finder, and the Finder bore some of the responsibility if they were to entrust something important to the Loser.

'Never,' said Frank. 'I'm the responsible one. I still pay all the bills. And file the taxes. And pick up her medications. I honestly don't know what happened. Poor Janis. And poor Reba. It broke her heart.'

He plugged in the record player and nodded as the Bakelite platter spun hesitantly. Browsing the nearby shelf bristling with a striation of records, he pulled out a well-worn sleeve, reverently drawing a record from it.

'Here we go.'

He set the record down on the Bakelite and carefully set the needle in place.

Momentarily, the gentle notes of 'Landslide' poured from the tweed-covered speakers, warming the coffee shop like a wintertime fire. Even the pothos seemed to turn towards it. Adele jumped up to wrap Frank in a hug.

'You did it!'

Unused to praise, Frank ducked his head.

'Reba's favourite,' he said, cautiously twisting the volume knob. 'Well, this and the October '74 version of the Dead's "Morning Dew". We'll put that on next.'

'Let me grab some snacks.' As Fleetwood Mac faded out and Jerry Garcia's wavering vocals filled the air, Adele warmed some croissants and pulled a few espresso shots, adding some perfectly frothed milk – look at that finesse! She was humming along by the time she came back.

'This is a great song,' she said.

'Isn't it? I love a song that tells a story. I suppose you do too, with your background.'

'Ah, that,' said Adele. She had a better chance of bringing

Janis back to life than she did of reviving her musical theatre career. But that was okay. Maybe the car decal lovers from her hometown were right: sometimes you had to put things in the rear window. Lots of things. In the most illegible font you could find.

The bells by the front door tinkled, and Ben came in, looking harried. He carried a huge stack of books and documents that he dropped down on the first table with a sigh.

'Are you doing my paperwork for me?' called Adele.

'Yeah, nah. I don't get paid enough for that. Nice tunes, though. Your handiwork, Frank?'

Frank flipped his glasses back up to the top of his head, signalling that his work for the evening was over. 'I was just the supervisor. Anyway, I'll leave you two to it. Thanks for the croissants and the therapy session, Adele.'

'Any time, Frank. See you tomorrow. We'll have Reba's cookies ready and waiting.'

'Ah, see? That's why I love this place. And the coffee, of course. You're on a roll with your new blends, Ben. This Flat Tyre one is a killer.' Frank sipped the cup Adele had poured for him.

'It'll have you bright-eyed and bushy-tailed, as my gran would say,' agreed Ben. Then, with a frown: 'Would've said.'

Without thinking, Adele laid a hand on his.

Frank smacked his lips. 'There's a note I can't put my finger on. It's rich . . . almost meaty.'

Ben pulled his hand away. 'I'm changing up my roast profiles.'

'Well, I love it. Lingers on the palate. Nice earthy taste to it. Keep it up.'

Getting to his feet with the sound of popping candy, Frank shuffled out the door. 'Don't stay up too late, kids!'

'We won't,' said Adele and Ben simultaneously.

They lapsed into a comfortable silence as they worked alongside each other to finish up the day's-end duties – something that seemed simple but in reality took hours.

Adele was stacking the espresso cups when the floor rumbled, more insistently than usual. The crockery clattered like the teeth of someone in the refrigerated section of a supermarket. Stumbling, she grabbed at Ben, whose hands caught her shoulders in time to prevent her from falling.

'Thanks,' she whispered. She wanted to kiss him more desperately than she'd wanted anything in her life.

But. But! There were so many buts, dammit.

Not least being that the door jingled, as it always seemed to.

A familiar figure in an impeccably tailored suit slid across the floor. Designer glasses flashed like the knife in the *Psycho* shower scene.

'Delly, babe!' Donny called, tapping a watch (a different one) valued at approximately the total GDP of Adele's hometown. 'We have a reservation in twenty. Let's do this!'

Adele took a step back, her shoulders burning with the memory of Ben's touch.

'See you tomorrow,' she said brightly.

He didn't respond: he was frowning in the direction of the basement.

Take Some Time to Smell the Coffee

The following day at Riffraff was as strained as Meemaw's overcooked pasta. Things didn't improve when Adele reminded Ben that the coffee-tasting event was that evening, and that there was no cancelling it because they'd sold out on EventBrite.

'I'm busy,' he said, keeping his distance, presumably in case Adele fell into his arms again. That hadn't been her fault! She had excellent balance.

'It's not till seven,' Adele pointed out over the whir of the grinder. 'You're usually back from your Freemason's gathering or wherever you disappear to by then.'

'They're asking me to perform some extra sacrifices this week.'

'Hilarious. Well, I suppose *I* can host it. I know plenty about coffee by now. Look, I'm even making cold brew!' She poured the ground beans into a nut-milk bag and started filling a Takeya tub with water. 'And Donny can help with the tasting notes and stuff. It can't be too different from wine. Besides, a food critic from *718 Plates* is coming.'

Ben's eyes widened in alarm, and not because he'd witnessed

a customer pull a squeezy bottle of honey from their bag. Adele hadn't known he was so sensitive to criticism.

'They'll love your work. How could they not?'

Ben stammered out a few *um*s and *ah*s as he awkwardly protested. The man had received no media training.

'It's a bad idea, Adele. Horrible. Shithouse. You don't understand.'

The customer was still squeezing honey into their coffee.

'Oh, you're too hard on yourself.' Adele hoisted the batch of cold brew into the fridge to steep. 'It'll be great!'

Ben let out the most ragged breath Adele had ever heard. And she'd tried going for a run in Denver, a city built a hypoxic mile above sea level. 'I'll cut my thing short.'

And so he did, hurrying in the door with a solid hour before the event participants were due to show up.

'So what do we call this event?' chirped Adele, excited, as Ben stomped back up from the basement with several bags of beans slung over his shoulder. 'Taste testing? Coffee prix fixe? Flight . . . of coffee fancies?'

'It's called a cupping.' Ben threw down the bags and locked the basement door, as always. After cutting open the bags, he grabbed a few beans from each, frowning.

'I still reckon this is a shitty idea. That critic . . .'

'But people have bought tickets!' exclaimed Adele, feeling that old musical theatre thrill that came with a sold-out show. 'We might actually make money.'

'I dunno if my recent roasts are going to stand up to scrutiny. There've been a few quakers recently.'

'Quakers? As in the religious group?

'As in wonky beans.' He picked one such bean out and showed it to her. It looked like . . . a bean. 'Ones that were picked too early and don't have the sugars they need to caramelise during the roasting process. A couple are all right. More than that, and your roast tastes ashy and dry.'

'Like chewing on a corpse.' Adele folded her arms, amused.

'Absolutely not like that,' snapped Ben, surprisingly testily. Perhaps a close family member had been gnawed on by a cannibal. His brow furrowed beneath the dark flop of his hair. 'How do you . . .'

'I hear it's kind of a porky taste. According to a friend of a friend of a friend.'

'Were they a Uruguayan rugby player stranded in the Andes?'

This was an oddly specific description. 'I don't think we're talking about the same friend.'

Ben shook his head. 'You're a unique individual, Adele Forrest.'

'If only casting directors felt that way. Small-town girls are a dime a dozen on Broadway.'

Ben pulled out a small hand-grinder from beneath the counter. 'And yet you've made it in the City for years. The work's never wasted.'

Reba, who'd volunteered to help as a break from her Tie Dyepalooza preparation, zoomed in to sneak a cookie. 'He's right. Maybe all that hard work was to get you where you're meant to be. Every decision you've ever made has led you here.'

Well yes, but the logic broke down depending on whose life you applied it to. Every decision Jack the Ripper's victims had made had led them to being chopped into pieces. Adele shook her head. Why did she have corpses on the brain today?

Maybe it was that she'd fielded a surprising number of missing people queries these past few weeks. People were coming up to her asking where their loved ones were almost as often as they were asking if they'd left their umbrella or AirPods behind. But then that was life in the City. Not everyone stayed – not everyone *could*. Most people had a set timeline in which they had to make it. They were in a race against the clock of dwindling finances and bedbug infestations: a clock that determined whether they would cling on to life in the City long enough to claim an exalted 212 area code, or head back to their hometown with tales of windowless apartments and subway streakers.

'Off with the fairies there?' asked Ben, writing out labels for the bowls of coffee beans Reba was placing along the shop's central communal table. He had tidy, practised handwriting – Adele had seen him scribbling away at a secret notebook here and there. Was he a poet? A stenographer? An obsessive chronicler of overheard conversations?

Adele blinked, taking the labels he'd handed her. 'Maybe. What am I doing with these?'

'They go clockwise.' Ben thoughtfully tapped one of the handmade bowls, running a finger over it. 'Where'd you get these?'

'Doralee's,' said Adele. 'I thought they were cute.'

'They are. Now let's set up the brew methods . . .'

Adele placed the notecards. *Flat Tyre. Early Riser. Spun Up. Button Chewer.*

'I don't know how you come up with these roast names,' she said, chuckling.

Now Ben was setting out glasses of distilled water for each guest. 'Each roast has its own personality. A lot goes into every one. I reckon it's only respectful to give them names. Can you do the water?'

He was back to his usual, affable self. Adele couldn't figure him out. Every time she talked about beans or roasting his entire personality went through more changes than Sandy in *Grease*. Which was an issue, given that beans and roasting were his entire job.

Reba swooped in with a jug, ensuring that every seat had a full glass of distilled H_2O in its place. Goodness, this was all quite scientific.

'They're coming!' called Frank, putting on a Dizzy Gillespie album. The smooth sounds of Dizzy's bent trumpet softened the air, twining around Audrey III and mingling with the ever-present aroma of coffee and baked goods.

'Decent choice, Frank,' said Ben, approvingly.

'This is from his South American tour in '56.' Frank played a few notes of air trumpet. Wait 'til "Vida Mia" comes on. Tears will stream. Beautiful.'

The doorbell jingled, and guests started filing in. There were a few faces that Adele recognised: the day-drinking teachers and the swim instructor, and some she didn't: an ancient-looking guy carrying a knobbly cane and a girl in a striped romper hugging a handmade notebook with pressed flowers on the cover. And Ekaterina and Alejandro! Adele hurried up to give them both a hug. Finally, a snooty guy who walked with his nose thrust upward strode through the door, casting judgement everywhere he looked.

The critic.

Ben eyed him uneasily.

'That's Clarence Festerbaum,' he muttered to Adele. 'He's going to tear us to shreds.'

'Water off a duck's back,' responded Adele, directing the group towards the communal table. 'Take a seat wherever y'all like, but no hiding at the back of the classroom. Unless y'all really hate coffee and don't want to try any.'

A light titter went up among the group of coffee tasters as everyone took their seats.

'These are the comfiest ones,' she whispered to her theatre friends as they plonked themselves down on twin vinyl chairs. 'Not a wobble between them. Loving the new hair, Ekaterina.'

Ekaterina's hair had been freshly dyed the same shade of magnificent purple that united Prince, Jimi Hendrix and Disney's Aladdin.

'Wobble-free chairs? For *us*, dahling?' Alejandro exclaimed, going full Scarlett O'Hara. 'Why, I've never felt so special!'

Adele grinned. 'Y'all always get front-row seats at my events.'

'All the coffee shop's a stage,' quoted Ekaterina. 'Except the table. That's gauche.'

'We've already dealt with counter-dancing. It won't happen again.'

Ekaterina crossed herself.

'That's right, your influencers!' Alejandro inspected the spoon Ben had placed at their setting, giving it a ringing tap against the table. 'Ooh, like a tuning fork.'

'Middle F,' agreed Ekaterina, who – damn her – had perfect pitch.

Alejandro experimented with Ekaterina's spoon, nodding excitedly as it gave off a slightly different pitch. 'So sad about Mazzy. What a mess. I heard that girl had problems.' Alejandro meaningfully tapped the side of their nose with the spoon.

Walking past with a gooseneck kettle, Ben cleared his throat. He did a lot of that these days – it must be a hay fever thing.

The cars and bikes outside were covered in yellow pollen. And if Adele's last five apartments had been anything to go by, there were definitely some mould spores floating around.

'So, the first thing I'm noticing is that these beans are *dark*. Like, beyond French and almost over to burnt,' said Clarence, who had a permanent expression of disgust on his face, as if the wind had changed while he'd been sniffing something scatological. He poked distastefully at the coffee samplers with the end of a spoon.

'No, that's definitely a French roast,' replied Ben, with an inaudible *fuckwit* at the end.

Clarence ran a bean between thumb and forefinger, unconvinced.

'I do the occasional medium roast,' added Ben. 'But darker works better for our espresso drinks, and for our audience's palate overall.'

The door jingled again: to the delight of every pair of eyes of the room, in came Gracie Nivola, looking as though she'd stepped out of a Bloomingdale's display window.

Adele blinked. Why was a Nivola gracing them with her presence? She desperately hoped Gracie didn't expect payment for her appearance.

'Sorry I'm late,' Gracie whispered, zooming in for a series of double-cheek air kisses with the precision of a military bomber. She flashed her camera at Adele. 'Richard forwarded the EventBrite listing. All right if I take photos?'

Clarence sniffed, not impressed by the competition. 'Do you have a press affiliation?'

'I'm just a hobbyist,' said Gracie smoothly.

Clarence nodded knowingly. 'We all start somewhere.'

Adele suspected everyone in the room would've killed to

have started where Gracie had: in an enormous Fifth Avenue abode orbited by a Who's Who of the brazenly influential and unremittingly successful. It was hard for the stars not to align when you were surrounded by them. Still, she was flattered that Gracie had decided to spend the evening at Riffraff rather than playing croquet with State senators at Gramercy Park, or whatever it was that wealthy people did with their spare time.

Ben rubbed his hands together, as though preparing to step into a role. He exhaled. 'Righto. Let's get started. Welcome to Riffraff, home to Brooklyn's riffraff for thirty years.'

Ben gestured around the shop. With its wonky floor, mismatching chairs, succulent planters, ancient record player, and the half-stripped wall that Adele was working to turn into a miniature art gallery, Riffraff was aptly named.

'. . . and home to our new owner, Adele, for, what, a good two months now?'

Adele blinked. She hadn't expected the shout-out. She waved shyly.

A few light whoops went up among the crowd. Definitely Frank's doing.

'As you can see, we do things differently here. Especially Reba.' He gestured to Reba, who had sat down with the Irish coffee she'd snuck from behind the counter.

'You heard him,' said Reba, toasting with her glass.

Ben shook his head. 'Exactly. Anyway, we also *roast* differently. Everything you're tasting tonight, or that you've ever tasted in Riffraff, was roasted in-house, downstairs, by me.'

'No wonder it's so hot in here,' said Ekaterina, fanning herself with her shirt.

'He can roast me anytime,' whispered a woman in a power

suit with folds so crisp she risked cutting herself any time she moved.

'Careful, or he'll take you up on that,' chuckled Donny, who'd slid into the room without Adele noticing. She flushed. She'd been so fixated on Ben she hadn't even heard the doorbells tinkle. 'This one has a reputation.'

'As a great barista,' interjected Frank smoothly. 'And an animal lover.'

Oooh. This got some approving nods from the group.

'And doesn't give a shit about dollar signs,' murmured Reba, sipping her drink.

Donny went to add something, but Adele grabbed his arm and seated him at the spare bench seat at the end of the table.

'Are you drunk?' Adele admonished.

Donny adjusted his glasses. 'What? No. I had a business meeting before this. They broke out the Macallan. Who's going to say no to that? Anyway, I thought you'd want me to come and support you.'

Adele smiled tightly, aware that everyone was pretending not to watch. 'You're right. It's really sweet of you.'

'Are we good to proceed?' said Ben, smiling genially, but with a subtext of *don't fuck with me, mate*. 'Righto. As you can see, we've got five roasts here. First we're going to observe the aromas. Take a bowl, give it a shake to agitate those smells, and let me know what fragrances come to mind.'

'Easy,' said Donny. 'As a connoisseur of wine and cologne, I have the olfactory sense of a god. And the body of one.'

Ben raised an eyebrow at Adele. No, nope. She was not engaging with that.

'There are no wrong answers. Say what comes to mind.'

'Um, chocolate?' suggested one of the teachers.

'Camphor,' pronounced the old guy.

'Definitely caramel,' said Alejandro. 'But the good dulce de leche kind, like in an alfajores. Not, you know.' They pointed in the direction of the scuzzy diner down the road.

'I'm getting notes of medjool dates,' said the girl in the romper. 'I'm vegan,' she added.

At the word 'vegan', Ekaterina snapped her fingers at Alejandro, who handed over a twenty-dollar bill.

'Over-roasted,' said Clarence flatly.

'One-dimensional,' added Donny competitively.

Ben's jaw tightened. 'Huh. Reckon there is a wrong answer after all.'

'I think it's . . . full-bodied,' offered Adele placatingly.

Ben set down the French press he'd been carrying over from the counter. 'Give me a tick, Donny. I've got one just for you. Roasted it today, in fact.'

'What kind of roaster?' Clarence was taking notes so viciously that his pen almost scored through the page.

'A 1930s Probat,' said Ben. 'Doralee found it in some tiny European town while backpacking in the Sixties; had it shipped back. It was installed during the Seventies, with some retrofitting done since then.'

'Interesting choice.'

Apparently Clarence had attended the same School of Understated Yet Brutal Criticism as Richard.

As the other guests passed around the bowls, jotting down their thoughts about the fragrances, Ben disappeared downstairs, returning momentarily with a canister. He opened it, letting the rich scent of freshly roasted beans infuse the air.

'God, that smells *so* good,' moaned Ekaterina. 'Don't you want to bury your face in it and eat it up?'

'Yes I do,' said Alejandro, shamelessly eyeing Ben, who was handing the coffee canister to Donny.

'I call this one the Market of Bull,' said Ben.

'Bull market,' corrected Donny. 'That's what we call a thriving market.'

'Oh, right. We don't have Harvard in Australia.'

'And that's why you'll never be a superpower. That and the spiders.' Donny swirled the canister, planting his face so deep into his opening that he almost lost his glasses. 'I'm getting notes of . . . rust. Pennies, but the older sort. And Brioni suit.'

'Not bad,' said Ben, arms folded. 'How about we brew it up for you, and you can give it a taste?'

'Go on, then.' Donny leaned back on the bench seat with glee – and a lot of confidence in his core strength, thought Adele, who absolutely would've tumbled to the floor. He made a *when you're ready* gesture that seemed like a challenge.

Adele frowned. What was going on? It was like watching two roosters scratch around in the dirt.

'May I?' Clarence gave the canister a deep sniff before making a face (a different, equally awful one). 'I'm finding this one quite forward. Is that . . . burnt hair? And a touch of melted button?'

Adele blinked. Were these normal things to smell in coffee? Perhaps he was being sardonic. Or he'd had a recent near-death experience while ironing his clothes.

'It ain't Kentucky bourbon, guy,' said Frank with a snort.

Reba rolled her eyes and reached for a cookie.

The kiddie-table grinder whirred as Ben ran the beans through it, tipping the grounds into a bowl he placed before Donny. He then used the normal grinder to grind beans for everyone else, passing them around the table. The group collectively inhaled the aroma of the freshly pulverised beans, happily writing down their thoughts in their notebooks.

'Now we pour. This takes a minute.' Ben tilted the gooseneck kettle, letting water trickle over the coffee grounds in the handmade cup sitting in front of each person.

'Like sand through the hourglass,' intoned Alejandro. 'So are the days of our lives.'

'We're brewing our coffee to a ratio of one to seventeen. One gram of coffee to seventeen millilitres of water. I don't know what that is in American. Don't ask.'

Everyone dropped their hands.

'Not one to sixteen?' asked Clarence, making a note in red. 'Zeit Ghast swears by that ratio.'

'It depends,' said Ben, again with the silent *that's not a knife: THAT'S a knife*. 'There are always variables. Right. Ordinarily we use a finer grind and a filter system – either the paper cones for the pour-over, or mesh for the espresso machine and French press. But for cupping, it's just water and grounds. One quick drizzle to let the grounds bloom, and then we're off to the Melbourne Cup. Chat amongst yourselves for four minutes.'

'I'll do the countdown,' said Reba excitedly. Grabbing the red egg timer from the counter, she set it on the table, where it ticked away like a cheerful bomb.

The group chatted awkwardly over their cookies as everyone waited for the timer to wind down. Reba broke the ice with a few off-colour jokes, bless her. Gracie wandered off, snapping pictures of the shop: the acid-tab-decorated tabletop always claimed by students; the infinite tendrils of Audrey III; the in-progress chess game in one of the nooks.

Adele watched Ben tense as Gracie got too close to the

basement door – but relaxed as she stepped back at the last minute.

'This is fun,' said Adele, watching the group ease into the event. Sometimes Riffraff felt like if Xanax were a place.

'It's not fun,' snapped Donny, staring intently at the bowl in front of him. 'It's a blood sport.'

Clarence nodded in agreement, his pen gouging his notepad.

'I meant to tell you!' Alejandro leaned forward, propping their elbows on the table. They glanced over at Gracie, who was distracted by Ember's fuzzy belly, seeing whether it was safe to spill the beans. 'Honour pulled out of the show. A scheduling commitment in LA. She's trying to break into Hollywood.'

Adele swallowed. The role could have been hers, if she'd hung in there a little longer . . .

But there was a line, she thought. A line where you stopped being an aspiring actress and became a failed one. Either you chose when to draw it, or life drew it for you. So she'd drawn it.

Oh, honey, echoed Richard's voice in her head. *It was never going to be you.*

'Hollywood, schmollywood,' whispered Reba. 'What do they have that we don't?'

'Great weather. And access to experimental anti-ageing drugs,' said Ekaterina.

Fair.

'Righto,' said Ben, his soft drawl reaching through Adele's thoughts. 'Does everyone have a spoon? We're going to break the crust on the coffee like we're digging into a crème brûlée. Keep it superficial. You're not Murray River carp, so don't go digging around in the mud stirring up the grounds.'

'That's offensive to carp,' muttered the vegan in the romper, dipping her spoon into her coffee.

'Oops!' cackled Reba, who'd whacked her spoon into her coffee, splashing liquid all over.

Donny and Clarence tapped at their coffees with equal distaste.

'Now it's time to get your nose right up close to the coffee,' said Ben. 'What do you smell? Write it down.'

Reba wiped the coffee from her nose. 'I'm a step ahead of you, babe.'

Frank grinned at her with so much love that Adele's heart swelled. It was hard to believe the two had separated over such a silly reason. Although it probably didn't feel silly to them. She wished she could help: the world would be a better, brighter place if they got back together.

'Now, we're skimming any crema that's settled on the coffee,' said Ben. 'Discard that. Dip your spoon in and slurp away. The more slurping, the more your whole palate can experience the coffee. We're gonna do that for every roast on the table. Give your spoon and mouth a rinse between tastings.'

'Gladly,' said Clarence, chugging his water.

Everyone slurped and swished away as though they were gargling mouthwash. Self-conscious giggles arose initially, but those gave way to excited chitchat as the guests started discussing the flavours they were experiencing.

'You're meant to slurp it,' said Ben to Donny.

'I don't slurp.'

'Sounds like you're bearish on coffee.'

A look of challenge in his eyes, Donny picked up his cup of coffee like it was a bowl of miso soup. He drained it thoroughly, grounds and all, then smacked his lips.

'Notes of Italian leather. Charcoal. A hint of scorched rubber,' said Donny.

'Not bad,' said Ben.

Adele frowned as she sipped at her own coffee, searching for notes of Goodyear tyres and designer wallets, or whatever it was she was meant to be tasting. If Clarence and Donny had both mentioned it – and Ben hadn't laughed in their faces – those flavours *had* to be there. No wonder triple caramel lattes sold so much better than espressos.

Over the next hour or so, everyone worked through their coffees, asking questions of Ben and selecting bags to take home with them. Adele made sure they all left with a loyalty punchcard and a hug.

'Thanks for that,' said Ekaterina, looping in Adele for a group embrace. 'From now on, I'm slurping all of my coffee.'

'I have a whole makeup look inspired by "notes of melted buttons",' added Alejandro. 'Think *Coraline* meets *House of Wax*.'

As Adele emerged from the hug, she spotted Gracie, who was popping a roll of film into its canister. Old-school. 'I got some great shots. Thanks for having me.'

'Thanks for coming out. It was a pleasant surprise.' Actually, it had been. Adele had expected Gracie to behave like the influencers, but she'd been very sweet – she'd spent most of the evening chatting about vintage cameras with Frank. 'Sorry about Honour. The role.'

'Oh, I don't care about that. The only reason I act at all is for Hon. I prefer to be on this side of the camera. Night!' With a waggle of her fingers, Gracie stepped out the door, where she was immediately swooped away by a waiting car. Off into the night it went, an industrious metal owl hooting balefully at anything that deigned to block its way.

'Interesting evening,' said Clarence haughtily, turning over a bag of *Flat Tyre* beans and tapping the roast date thoughtfully. 'My write-up will be in Friday's edition.'

The remaining group members tromped out into the street, which rang loudly with the laughter of a nearby block party and the falsetto wail of sirens. Adele turned over the sign on the door.

'You're a good teacher,' she said to Ben, impressed. 'Have you ever considered—'

'Abso-fucking-lutely *not* doing that again?' Brow so furrowed you could swipe a credit card through it, Ben yanked off his apron and tossed it at the cloisonné hook on the wall. 'I'm going to bed. Goodnight.'

He stomped up the stairs to his apartment, slamming the door behind him.

'Finally,' said Donny, skimming minty balm over his lips from a golden tub. 'Thought the guy would never leave. Delly. That was the worst coffee I've ever tasted. I don't trust that guy at all. He's trying to sabotage your shop. Take it from me. I can always tell a guy with bad intentions.'

Trouble Brewing

Adele kept a close watch on Ben the following few days (this was not a particularly difficult sacrifice), but despite Donny's words of warning, nothing seemed especially off-kilter. Sure, Ben was familiarly curt with anyone who broke the coffee shop rules of propriety by snatching the wrong drink off the counter or using Starbucks sizing in their order, but he didn't seem to be actively trying to burn the shop down.

Not even when the latest edition of *718 Plates* landed on Riffraff's well-worn doorstep.

'I'll take that,' he said, intercepting Adele's efforts to sneak it into the recycling bin.

He scanned the magazine for Clarence's inevitably scathing review, giving the page a good old sabre rattle when he found it. 'Ready? Gritty blends . . . improper ratios . . . strange social dynamics. I'll have to cut this out and put it on the fridge.'

'At least he says you look the part,' said Adele generously, peering around him to read.

'Yeah, right after the bit where he says our coffee has the qualities of a pistachio with halitosis and that I should intern at Zeit Ghast. And that you need to stop with the singing, because the coffee alone is enough to make you grind your teeth.'

'Where? Give me that.' Adele grabbed the magazine from him. 'What a c—'

'Cruel man?' suggested Ben innocently.

Adele ripped up the magazine and chucked the slivers of paper on the composing grinds where Ember liked to do his business.

'There,' she said, slamming the door that led to what her theatre friends called Riffraff's back-of-back-of-house. 'Some bathroom reading for Ember this evening.'

'Evening?' Ben glanced up at the clock on the wall, which had stopped. It did this more often than peak-hour traffic over the George Washington Bridge. 'Shit,' he said. 'I'm gonna be late. Can you close up? I'll handle the breakdown when I get back.'

Grabbing his book bag, he hurried out the door, giving Adele a wave goodbye.

Adele gave a merry one back, delighted to realise that in his haste, Ben had left behind something *very* important.

His keys.

Here was Adele's chance to sneak a peek at the mysterious roaster.

'And . . . closed!' shouted Adele, ushering the remaining stragglers out of the shop. Just the teachers and a monacled guy today, at least. Even Frank and Reba had headed out early – the Tie Dyepalooza preparations clearly required quite the time investment.

Adele turned over the '*Come in, petal*' flower power open sign on the door. That would buy her at least a few minutes if Ben came back while she was snooping. Although, to be fair, she had a *right* to snoop! She owned the basement and everything that was down there!

Should she lock it, though? No, that was taking things a step too far. She didn't want to disappoint the spirit of Doralee, who'd already done so much for her.

Adele took a deep breath, all the way into her diaphragm, like when she warmed up before a performance. She felt a pang. And not from a collapsed lung. She just . . . missed performing. It was all very well and good to declare one part of your life over and done with, but was it actually possible to make clean breaks like that? She'd stepped away from musical theatre, and yet she was finding music in everything she did. She'd fled Tennessee, and now Broadway. And she'd drawn a line where she and Ben were involved, but all she could think about was the way he grinned whenever she entered a room.

All lines were permeable, she supposed. Like waterproof mascara.

Steeling herself, Adele slipped behind the counter, navigating around the racks of dishes and bags of beans. Then she pulled out Ben's extremely heavy keychain and began unlocking the seven locks in turn.

The basement door swung open, revealing a vast, dimly lit space lurking at the base of the steepest set of spiral wooden stairs Adele had ever seen. How did Ben lug the bags of coffee upstairs? Was there a dumbwaiter down here or something? No wonder he was so buff.

Adele stretched out a foot, gently testing her weight on the top step. She knew she was being silly – Ben weighed close to twice what she did, and he went up and down here all the time. In truth, she was anxious about what she might find below.

Like armchairs made out of human skin. Or a shrine to a football team.

She tiptoed down the stairs, cringing as a rat slithered over her foot – at least she'd switched to close-toed shoes. The rat squeaked. So did Adele. Where was Ember when you needed him?

After a brief beat to squeeze her disgust down into a digestible size, she continued, relieved when her shoe met solid ground. Squinting, she tried to take in the basement, but the sad single schoolhouse light fixture and the trickle of sun from the glass bricks set into the streetscape above meant there was more shadow than light.

The air down here smelled rich with roasted beans and the inescapable earthiness of basement damp. There was another scent that made Adele wrinkle her nose: the stench of burnt hair, like when she got too ambitious with her curling wand. Her Spidey sense started tingling. Had Ben been bringing girls down here?

Adele turned on her phone flashlight, shining it into each corner of the basement – in case evil clowns lurked there – before turning it around the room. Most of the space was taken up by the huge roaster Ben was so obsessed with. A weird, dusty-looking thing welded together with rust and curses, it definitely had unearthed-from-a-haunted-town-in-Europe vibes. The bulk of it was a massive cast-iron body that hunched above an enormous dish, like a witch stooped over a cauldron. To one side was a sort of funnel that Adele assumed was for pouring beans into. Beneath that was a switchbox bristling with buttons and levers. It was a wonder that it worked, although now all the thudding and rumbling made sense.

Next to the roaster was a striped love seat strewn with items

215

of clothing. And not all of it men's, Adele realised in dismay. Ben wasn't just stripping off those extra layers that got to be too much when the roaster was cranked up. He was stripping extra layers off *other people*. He was a sex addict! Look, there! The polka-dot dress from the life coach. And one of those perky oversized caps that the Pastels-Only Moms Club wore as part of their uniform. And the too-large T-shirt Topknot Guy had been wearing. And one of Mazzy Stevens' Heelys!

Adele desperately tried to give Ben the benefit of the doubt. Maybe this sordid collection was a Lost and Found, like the Lucky Dip bucket Adele kept behind the counter for forgotten umbrellas and sunglasses. Ben had his apartment upstairs, after all, which made more logistical sense where canoodling was involved. Unless the coffee shop ceiling also needed the assistance of a structural engineer.

And let's face it, the basement didn't exactly scream sex dungeon. All right, maybe the dungeon bit. Especially with that creepy roaster lurking around like a flasher behind a bush.

As Adele's flashlight played over the coffee roaster, the ground rumbled. The subway. Or fracking. Was fracking common in Brooklyn?

The bulb in the schoolhouse light jittered and fizzed.

Adele grimaced, thinking about Donny's comments about engineers and their costs. If there was something *that* wrong, she'd definitely sell when the year was up.

Another rumble. Definitely not the subway. Or fracking. It seemed like it was coming from the coffee roaster. Maybe Ben had left it turned on, although Adele wasn't sure how to tell. There weren't any lights or helpful displays. Avoiding the lever with a label over it that said DO NOT TOUCH, she thwacked her palm against the largest button on the console panel. The roaster shook like a dog waking up from a nap. A metallic stench filled the air. Ugh, Ben needed to oil his machine.

Adele poked at another button. The roaster seemed to move from first to second gear. It was vibrating like the clothes dryer that Meemaw bragged about having had since the Seventies. The one that moved so much it had beaten a Roomba in her hometown's one-hundred-yard Appliance Sprint.

This was not going well.

Then, to make things worse, a creaking sound came from above. Was the coffee shop settling in the summer heat? Or was someone up there?

Ember meowed, wrapping his tuxedoed fluffball self around Adele's legs as Adele turned back to the inscrutable panel with its buttons and levers. The cat's needle-like teeth tattooed her ankle.

'Ow! Ember, what the fuck?' Stumbling against the love seat, she knocked a few items of designer clothing to the floor. A Ralph Lauren glove floated slowly to the ground like a piece of performance art.

The roaster coughed – or something like it. But Adele was too preoccupied with avoiding Ember's fangs to pay much attention.

She froze as she heard another thud overhead. Definitely a footfall this time.

Leaving the roaster rumbling and thudding – that was a Ben problem – Adele raced up the steps with Ember in her wake. When she reached the kitchen, she slammed the basement door closed, locking it firmly behind her. Ben would know she'd been down there. And for all she knew, she'd even broken the machine. But she'd deal with that later.

217

'Delly?' came a voice from over the counter.

Oh thank goodness. It was just Donny.

Adele scowled, even though Donny wasn't the one in the wrong here, not really. He'd wanted to see her. Unlike Ben, who apparently kept a harem of women and topknotted dudes downstairs. So much for his *I-keep-to-myself* act! All this time he'd been doing goodness knows what down there. He might not be keeping up with the roaster's servicing schedule, but he'd been servicing human beings damn well enough.

'What are you doing here? You scared the ever-loving song out of me.' Her tone was sharp, and she wished she could use the same one on Ben. How *dare* he!

Although you're the one seeing Donny, she reminded herself. *You're the hypocrite in this situation.*

Whatever happened down there between two or more consenting adults and a coffee roasting machine was none of her business. Except maybe that burnt-hair-stench thing. She'd have to implement a no-hair-straighteners-on-the-premises rule before the whole place caught fire.

'The door was unlocked,' said Donny. He perched on one of the bar stools – he refused any of the regular seats, as they made him lose a few inches of height. Adele couldn't judge him for it. Personally, she refused to perch up high, as it showed her all the spots she hadn't dusted. Short-person ignorance was bliss. Except when you were trying to reach something off the top shelf.

'Quiet day, huh,' he said in commiseration, although with that head cock that said *tell me about it. Let me fix it.*

'The usual.' Grabbing a cookie and the bottle of Baileys they used for Reba's afternoon Irish coffee – Donny curled his lip when she offered – Adele sank down on a chair, propping her feet up on an ottoman the way Frank always did. Frank was right: that *was* a weight off.

'You look like you just opened someone's closet to find more skeletons than the Paris Catacombs. Have you been? You should. Anyway. Anything you want to share?'

Adele had no intention of revisiting the basement. Especially not with Donny.

'Why isn't this working?' she asked eventually.

Donny seemed surprised at the question. He even put his phone down. 'You and me? I mean, we're from different worlds, like the lady and the tramp. Except I'm the lady and . . . You know what I mean.'

Adele liked Donny a lot better when he didn't talk. He was a decent movie date. Or a Formula One date. Or a Heston Blumenthal blindfolded silent dining date. But he was an awful companion when you actually had to listen to him. Adele always found herself filling the silence for the edification of her own poor ears.

'I mean the *shop*. I've tried a bunch of different things.'

'My suggestions, or yours?'

Adele shot him a look. 'Both. Some of it I can *see* that people hate. Like that Algorhythmix thing and the surge pricing – which only lasted five minutes. There are other things that people respond really well to. But we have all these people I'll see once, but who never come in again. Is it *me*?'

Donny frowned at the *No Wi-Fi* sign that Ben had jubilantly replaced after the algorithmic music system had gone on the fritz. 'Not you. That barista. He's got that arrogant swaggery Australian thing going on. It's off-putting.'

'But I can't fire him. He came with the business.'

And also, I like looking at him.

Donny propped his elbows up on the counter, flashing his expensive cufflinks. 'But why? Don't you think that's weird? There must be something janky in his past for your aunt to say you *can't* fire him. What did the background check say?'

Adele blinked. 'I . . . didn't do one.'

'Why not? I did one on you. Pulled your credit and everything. Joking,' he added. Although . . . was he? Donny had a very specific sense of humour that Adele didn't always get. But then he was a city guy, and she was a starry-eyed girl from rural Tennessee. As he liked to remind her.

And besides, he'd helped her so much, and without asking for anything in return. As he'd reminded her, his consulting fees on a project like this would run into the tens of thousands, maybe hundreds of thousands.

Adele frowned. 'That all seems a bit . . . over the top. I try to approach the world with kindness. Assume the best in people.'

Donny guffawed so hard he almost fell off his stool. To be fair, it was a wonky one. Adele had propped it up with a stack of cardboard coasters. 'Spoken like someone who'll never be rich.'

'I don't want to be rich. Just . . . happy. I want to create a place that people feel at home in. I feel like I owe that to Doralee.'

'Kid, if you want to make it in the City, you can't go around thinking like that. That's how you end up owning a money pit like this instead of an income-generating multi-family development geared for maximum tax rebates.'

Was he speaking in tongues?

'Donny . . . I think I need to be alone right now. It's been a long day, and I have to be back here at five in the morning.'

Part of her wanted him to protest, but only a small part. It was nice to be wined and dined by Donny, but he was exhausting.

'I hear you. That's when I do my affirmations. And then hit the gym. Another time. Later, Delly.'

Setting the bottle of Baileys back on its shelf, Adele waited until he left, then headed out.

Actually, you know what?

She went back to get the Baileys. She was going to enjoy this night on her own terms.

Livin' la Vida Mocha

All that Baileys and the continued challenge of navigating Doralee's apartment had motivated Adele to hit the fast-forward button on her yard sale idea, and she'd spent the night on Doralee's toucan phone calling up all the vaguely creative people she knew. And the pizza shop.

But not Ben. Even in her tipsy state, she'd exercised some restraint.

The end result of all those calls was the Riffraff Hoarderfest, which was taking place this weekend in the front courtyard area of the shop. And also the sidewalk. And wherever else they could until the City came by to complain.

It was one of those perfect summer days, and Adele felt like a sunflower bobbing in a field as she waltzed around outside Riffraff setting up the milk crate displays and metal clothes racks for the yard sale. Brightly patterned clothes and dried pampas grass bouquets wafted in the gentle breeze, and vibrant pottery and jewellery gleamed under the sun's playful touch.

Adele and her theatre friends had spent all morning lugging

the items from Doralee's cosy – and now oddly empty – apartment to the shop using a wagon that Ekaterina had 'borrowed' from the props department of the theatre for which she was moonlighting as a choreographer.

A handful of other vendors had set up as well, hiding from the sun beneath the decorated awnings of their tents. Richard was excitedly stacking trays of everything-free baked goods next to a powder blue ornamental Vespa. This was in celebration of the new delivery arm of his business, which had the tagline *Ride a Richard*.

At least he was consistent with his branding.

Gracie Nivola – who'd come solo, as Honour was still on the West Coast fighting off offers of representation – had set up a photo booth using some of Doralee's more dramatic items of furniture, and was standing by with her Polaroid camera at the ready. A line of twine swung under the weight of dozens of clothes pegs from which a couple of shots of early-bird shoppers swung.

'We'll make a gallery wall of these when the day's over,' said Gracie. 'They'll look great on that alcove wall to the right of where you come into the shop.'

'You're not a fan of the crying clown statue with the plants growing out of his pants?' asked Adele, pretending to be shocked.

'You mean Penis-wise the Clown? I dreamt about that thing last night,' called Reba from within the psychedelic depths of her own vendor tent. 'And not even a good dream.'

Reba's massive tent was three walls of eye-wateringly bright tie-dyed fabric ornamented with tasselled fringes and ties. *Dyer on the Mountain* was painted in ballooning retro script along the front, and a profusion of rugs, clothing, and upholstered seating bristled from it.

'This is a preview of what I do at Tie Dyepalooza,' she explained.

'It's like looking at a Magic Eye,' said Ekaterina.

'It's like if Alexander the Great was tripping balls while travelling through the desert,' said Alejandro reverently. 'And I mean that as the greatest compliment, Reba.'

'Tripping balls is the aesthetic I strive to embody,' said Reba proudly. 'You know, I have a kaftan that would go perfectly with your eye makeup . . .'

She produced a kaftan so colourful you needed the all-seeing eyes of a mantis shrimp to truly appreciate it and helped Alejandro put it on.

'It's perfect!' Alejandro twirled like the Colour Wheel in motion, admiring themself in the shell-studded mirror that Reba had set up in her booth. 'Can I keep it?'

'It's all yours. You're being a walking advertisement for me, and a good one.'

'Look at me, being an influencer.' Alejandro winked at Adele, who shook her head, still scarred by her own disastrous influencer day.

'Goddess, look at all this stuff.' Ekaterina was flipping through a box of batik scarves, coughing at the overpowering scent of incense that the box had exhaled after years of holding its breath.

A woman with a to-go cup in hand emerged from the coffee shop, whereupon she was pounced on by Reba.

'You know what would go well with that cup? Tie-dye.' Reba held a scarf up, flapping it in the air like an Uruk-Hai holding a scalped head.

'I'm kind of more . . . minimalist.'

'Oh, bah to that! You're too young to be complicit in the capitalist drabification of the world.'

The woman looked down at her monochromatic outfit. 'Technically it's ecru.'

'Houses, clothes, food – everything is stripped of its individuality to make it easier to sell at scale. Colour is a form of protest, my love.'

'Aren't you . . . selling these, though?' asked the woman. 'Doesn't that seem—'

Reba thrust the scarf at her. 'Take it. I don't need the money. I have everything I need. Except Janis. She's gone forever. Thanks to *him*.' She scowled at poor Frank, who was making his way out of the shop with a cream-topped iced latte and a stack of cookies in hand. Frank seemed to shrink a foot under Reba's gaze.

'I'll just . . .' The woman dropped a twenty-dollar bill in Reba's lap and hurried off before she found herself in the middle of a scene.

'We'll be here all day,' yelled Reba. 'Tell your friends! See you at Tie Dyepalooza!'

The woman raised her coffee cup in acknowledgement as she raced down the street.

'What's all this ruckus?' Ben poked his head out from Riffraff, blinking in the bright sunlight. 'Reebs, are you scaring off our customers again?'

'I am *enticing* them, Benjamin. You know all about my wiles.' Reba gave a suggestive tie-dyed waggle.

Ben chuckled. 'I do indeed. Anyone need an iced coffee? We don't want you melting out here.'

'Relax,' said Reba. 'We have an ozone layer in this part of the world.'

Ben went around the lot in any case, pouring iced coffees for the vendors and the handful of shoppers browsing through the magnificent plurality of hippie artefacts from Adele's carefully selected Sell pile. 'Take it from someone from the skin cancer capital of the world: wear a hat.'

'I hear hats protect against drop bears,' teased Frank.

'Smart move,' said Ben, eyes twinkling.

'What are drop bears?' Adele asked Frank, setting out a stack of decorative tea towels next to the display of glittery ornaments she'd unpacked. She was still finding it hard to meet Ben's eyes after her basement discovery the other night. It wasn't that he'd done anything *wrong*. It was just . . . she'd had a certain perception of him that had been dashed on the shores of her own wishful thinking.

She felt silly. And there was nothing worse than feeling silly. Except maybe feeling a slimy bit in the salad you were eating.

'You're brave to even ask,' said Ben. 'Smudge some Vegemite under your eyes and you'll be set.'

'Why would . . .' Her desire to flirt overriding her self-pity, Adele whacked Ben with a starburst tea towel. 'I get it. Taking the piss.'

Ben raised his hands in defeat and retreated, in doing so stepping over the decorative ribbons that marked the boundary of Gracie's photo booth. She waggled her camera at him.

'You've done it now. It's time to pay the camera tax. Scoot over there.'

With the no-nonsense attitude of a kindergarten teacher escorting a group of kids on a school trip, she directed Ben towards one of the peacock chairs she'd set up against the shop's red-brick exterior.

'Hot, but we're missing something. Adele!'

Adele hid behind the tea towel. Oh, no. Not this.

Gracie grabbed her by the arm and marched her over to the wall. 'You two are the heart and soul of this place. Well, and these two.' She gestured at Frank and Reba, who puffed with delight (Frank) and huffed with annoyance (Reba). 'But I'll get them in a second.'

'You will not,' groused Reba, pouncing on a cheerful Pomeranian with a rainbow doggie jacket. 'Oh, look at him! He loves it! And a tie-dyed collar . . . I have tie-dyed booties, too, for when the pavement gets too hot for those little paws . . .'

'Oh, he doesn't actually walk,' said the Pomeranian's owner, gesturing at the dog's Ibiyaya dog pram.

'Even better. They'll last forever.'

Ben and Adele shared a grin as Reba shamelessly harangued the dog's owner into buying a complete tie-dyed wardrobe. With flawless timing, Gracie's camera clicked. The Polaroid whirred out from it, slowly coalescing into an image as she carefully held it between outstretched fingers.

'That's a keeper,' said Frank, peering over Gracie's shoulder.

Blushing, Adele rushed away under the auspices of helping a shopper with the pricing on a selection of pottery she'd stacked up on one of the rickety tables.

'Do we know who Ilona is?' asked the shopper, a heavily pierced girl challenging the upper bounds of her ear cartilage.

Ben started, sloshing coffee all over the shag rug that Gracie had set up in the photo area.

'My mum.' Ben pulled up his shirt to reveal the cursive tattoo that Adele had misread. 'Ilona was my mum.'

Adele blinked. *Ben* was the cute fat baby in Doralee's photo album?

Things were starting to come together now.

'Those are display only!' she said quickly. 'Not for sale.'

The shopper drifted away, presumably to test out the metal detectors at JFK.

'Speaking of moms,' came a familiar voice from behind her. Turning, Adele let out a shriek at the upper end of Mariah Carey's vocal range.

'Mom? Dad? What are you doing here?' Adele gaped as two familiar, extremely touristy individuals darkened the door of Doralee's tent. Well, not *darkened*, given that Dad was wearing a bright orange Tennessee Vols sweater and that Mom was in patterned leggings – definitely a guilt purchase from a friend who'd succumbed to an MLM – and a surfeit of rhinestones (possibly also a guilt MLM purchase).

'We thought we'd surprise you. You've got a lot going on, and we wanted to be here for it. And Spirit had cheap flights today. Fit all the essentials in my handbag.' Mom clapped her enormous handbag, in which presumably both she and Dad intended to sleep tonight.

'We were going to try for next week, but the prices are nuts,' added Dad. 'Something about sunspot activity messing with the air traffic controls.'

That's right: Trix had mentioned something about sunspots.

'I'm sure it's nothing,' said Mom. 'So long as we don't have to fly in one of those planes that have been on the news.'

'Look at this sunny duo,' purred Reba approvingly, sending away a customer with a stack of fabrics as bright and decadent as a seven-layer dip. 'I'm Reba, purveyor of tie-dye and neighbourhood gossip. And that's Frank. Ignore him.'

Frank was covertly stuffing a voluminous dress into a Strand tote bag.

Adele raised an eyebrow – a gift for Reba, or himself? They

both had the legs for it, she supposed. And Frank's support socks added some extra pizazz.

'Lorna and Cade,' said Mom, giving the two-fer introduction that couples always do. 'Good luck ignoring him.'

Somehow in the interim ten seconds, Dad had draped himself in a green fringed shawl and had popped two painted river pebbles over his eyes. He was pretending to swim around the market, making Mom roll her eyes good-naturedly.

Gracie tiptoed over with her Polaroid camera, snapping a photo of Dad at his apogee of ridiculousness.

'There's one for Meemaw's album,' giggled Mom.

Dad removed the river pebbles and gave a pleased grin. 'Here to entertain,' he said.

'I see where Adele gets it from.' Switching out the carafe of coffee to his other hand, Ben held out a hand for her parents to shake. 'G'day.'

Adele's mom gasped in delight. 'You must be Adele's boyfriend. My *word*, Adele.'

Ben raised an eyebrow at Adele.

Adele felt her cheeks turning the colour of a red velvet cupcake. 'No, this is Ben. He works with me. My boyfriend is Donny. He said he was going to stop by for the market sometime today. He's probably in a meeting.'

'Oh, one of those flashy types.' Dad was enthusiastically browsing Reba's tie-dyed shirts. 'Does he have a business card? Lorna, what do you think?'

Dad held up an oversized shirt with a swirl of neon green on it.

'He does.' Adele produced it from her wallet.

'You look like a Romanesco broccoli,' said Mom.

Frank snorted.

Pulling on the shirt, Dad took the card. He held it up to the light like he was checking a potentially counterfeit hundred-dollar bill. 'Huh,' he said.

'Look at that subtle off-white colouring,' said Ben, pretending to be mesmerised. 'The tasteful thickness of it.'

Adele cocked her head at Ben. 'Are you quoting *American Psycho*?'

'Would I do that? Coffee?' Ben poured Adele's parents an iced coffee each, balancing a chocolate-chip cookie on the top of each glass.

'I've always wanted to go to England,' said Mom, munching on the cookie.

'Nice place,' said Ben. 'Wet. Terrible cricket team.'

'Ben's Australian,' explained Adele.

'Oh. Well, your English is very good,' said Dad, clapping Ben on the back.

'Thanks. I try,' said Ben, as drily as a Mallee summer. (At least according to what he'd said before about Mallee summers.)

'So, where's your hotel?' asked Adele. There were a few cute boutique spots in the area, most of them snuggled into one-time factories. Or there was all of Manhattan, but she wasn't sure if her parents had the whole subway situation figured out. Tennessee wasn't famed for its public transportation. Unless hitching a ride in the back of your cousin's clapped-out van counted.

'We thought . . . we'd stay with you,' said Mom, frowning. 'It was all a touch last minute. Is that all right?'

Adele wasn't sure how to explain to her parents that acreage was not a normal state of being in the City. Nor was having more than one bedroom. Or even having something that properly counted as a bedroom.

'Um,' she said. 'I don't really have the space, unless you want to sleep on a box of Doralee's trinkets.'

'We're fine with that,' said Dad. 'This old back has been through worse things.'

This was true: Dad often bragged about a youth spent sleeping in the bed of a truck in the winding foothills of Starr Mountain. And then there was the extremely ambitious deadlift competition – something that could not be blamed on the folly of youth – that had put him on the couch a few years ago.

Reba was braiding a scarf into the ankle-length hair of a twenty-something Rapunzel who was reading a book as she worked. 'I'd give you the run of my spot, but we've got the fumigators in. And you don't want to stay with Frank in the garage. Snores louder than the incoming traffic at LaGuardia combined. I know: I've measured it.'

'I've got those breathing strips now, just so you know. Neighbours haven't complained in months.' Frank jabbed a thumb at the cosy, plant-smothered façade of Riffraff. 'What about here? There's plenty of room in the coffee shop. Plus snacks. We could bring in an air mattress and get you all set up.'

Ben's eyes widened in alarm. 'Your parents aren't sleeping on the floor, Adele. Besides, I'll be roasting, and it gets noisy. Not to mention the smoke.'

'I've got my trusty puffer.' Dad slapped at the fanny pack he wore slung over his hips.

Reba had finished braiding the girl's hair (an effort that had taken three scarves, and a flower-topped headband thrown in as a special gift). As the girl twirled in front of the mirror, thwacking everything within a six-foot radius with her hair, Reba gave Ben a calculating look.

'I can text Donny,' said Adele hastily.

Ben closed his eyes, as if preparing for what was coming next.

'Adele, how about your parents take Doralee's place and you take mine. *I'll* sleep downstairs.'

Reba nodded like a wise teacher whose student has finally provided the right answer to a challenging question.

'Well, look at that,' said Dad, giving Adele a hug. 'It's like a game of musical chairs, but we figured it out.'

Adele flushed again at the thought of finally sneaking a peek at Ben's secret apartment. And not just sneaking a peek, but being surrounded by his things. Showering in his bathroom. Sleeping in his bed.

At least they'd have a flight of steps between them, she thought anxiously, avoiding Ben's eyes. Was it hot out here? Gosh, the day had warmed up. She needed some sunscreen before the heatstroke got her . . .

She turned, bumping into Ben, who caught her before she knocked Reba's entire tie-dyed set-up to the ground. Rainbow sheets and kaftans flapped from the tent, creating a vibrant backdrop to Adele's anxiety, which heightened logarithmically the longer Ben's hands were on her waist.

Gracie swooped in with her camera. 'Say Perlagrigia truffle cheese!'

Make Mine a Doppio

Adele turned the sign over on the door. (*So fucking closed*, it read, the perfect counterpoint to the *So fucking open* sign that had hung there all day.) The day had been the right amount of busy – somewhere between EatMe and Algorhythmix levels – and Hoarderfest had been a surprising success. All day she'd been fielding interest from vendors who were happy to pay actual money to be part of the next one.

Her phone buzzed: *Can't, babe. Work stuff.*

'Donny can't make it,' said Adele, not *entirely* disappointed.

'Well that's all right,' said Dad, who was playing Connect Four against himself. 'He sounds very important. He probably has business things to do. This is the city that never sleeps, after all.'

'The *big apple*,' agreed Mom, basking in the rainbow light of the stained-glass windows. 'So where would *you* like to go out, Adele? Our special treat?'

'But you came all the way from Tennessee!' protested Adele. 'It's . . . Ben, what's your weird term for it?'

'Your shout,' said Ben, who was in the middle of backflushing the La Marzocco.

'Shouting, huh? No noise ordinances in Australia, I see,' said Dad. 'Not like Meemaw's HOA . . .'

'Hard to have those when the birds screech up a storm every morning,' said Ben. 'They're what I'm most homesick for. And money you can tell apart.'

'So, hon?' nudged Dad, pumping the air as he made a diagonal line of red tokens. 'What about one of your Broadway shows?'

'I'm not in anything right now,' said Adele, trying to keep the whiff of failure out of her voice.

'But your friends must be.' Dad re-set his game. 'Who were the ones from Nashville? Alejandro and that girl with the orange hair? Has MTV picked her up yet? They should.'

'It's purple these days,' said Adele. 'And you're right: they should.'

'I might be able to get tickets to something. If you don't mind it being more . . . low-key,' offered Ben in a voice so quiet it was almost drowned out by the gurgling espresso machine. Was he . . . shy? Ben, collector of phone numbers and hearts and apparel memorabilia?

'Perfect!' Mom poked curiously at one of Kyra's succulents, a gesture that reminded Adele that she still had those dried dogwoods set aside. 'How about we do that, and then we grab some food to eat back here. Food always tastes better in takeout containers, don't you think?'

'Don't tell Clarence from *718 Plates*,' said Adele wryly. Although Mom had a point. Maybe she associated food in boxes with fun nights out with friends – and lazy ones in with her parents.

'I gotta run, but I'll be back with those tickets.' Looking faintly regretful that he'd made the offer, Ben wiped his hands with a kitchen cloth. 'Go explore in the meantime.'

As soon as he disappeared, Mom produced two pairs of decorative sandals, which she'd bought from Reba's booth when Adele hadn't been looking. Even the soles were tie-dye. *Thanks for that, Reba.*

'It's time for the Shoe Shoot!'

This was a Forrest family tradition. Every time they travelled anywhere, Mom broke out the matching shoes for photo-documentation purposes. Adele suspected this was mostly because Mom hated showing her face in photos, even though she personally thought Mom, with her crinkly blue eyes and upturned lips, had a lovely face.

Glad Ben wasn't around to see her in open-toed shoes, Adele changed into the sandals – all right, so the peace sign buckle was cute – and posed as Mom snapped a picture of their feet kicking up in front of the pothos. This involved a lot of jostling; Dad lent an arm for Mom to balance on.

'Got it! We should get a pedicure while we're here. Your toenails are a disaster.'

'Have you been letting subway rats chew on them?' joked Dad, smiling broadly as Mom turned her phone camera on him.

'Ninety-nine per cent of our reason for visiting is so that he can see the rats,' explained Mom. 'So, where are we off to?'

Adele took her parents on a tour of the neighbourhood, introducing them to the novelty sunglasses shop, the artisanal mayonnaise stand, the primal screaming therapy booth, the boombox roller skater guy down at the basketball courts, and the local parkour group, who were currently sprinting down the street and hurdling over fire hydrants and sandwich board signs. One, in a move straight out of the New York City Ballet, leapt gracefully over a mid-sized dog. The dog's tongue lolled as it panted away, oblivious to what had happened.

'I can see why Doralee loved this place,' said Mom, laden with several jars of spiced mayo and an elaborate terrarium. 'I wish I'd spent more time with the old gal. She was a hoot. The stories Meemaw has . . . like the Full Moon Nights!'

'Do tell,' said Adele, who was placing a substantial order for dips and pita at a tiny Lebanese restaurant with a shopfront of decorative tiles and hanging metallic lanterns. These cast a stippled light across the dimming evening sidewalk.

'It's all a bit . . . bacchanal,' said Mom, adding two huge containers of tabbouleh and kebabs to the load she was carrying. 'Basically, any weather event, any turn of the moon, she held these outdoor, semi-clothed . . . what would you call that religion, Cade?'

'Pagan, I think.'

'There was a lot of drumming, and . . .' Mom dropped her voice. 'Mushrooms.'

'And we're not talking morels.' Dad grabbed the rest of the order with the reverence of someone accepting their first communion. To be fair, this restaurant's food *was* a religious experience.

Adele smothered a grin. She wasn't about to incriminate herself by commenting on that.

'Remember the one during the solar storm?' asked Mom. 'Things got *weird*, according to Meemaw. A bad trip. September 6, '94 – I remember, because it was the day of Annie Barnes-Greer's birthday party, where she got drunk on schnapps and tried to bleach her own hair. The whole lot fell out. The girls do an anniversary celebration at the hairdresser every year.'

Adele's eyes widened. She knew Mom had a standing salon appointment with her friends every September, but she'd never known the provenance of it. No wonder Mom always came home sporting a bob or some bold highlights. It was the Doralee influence!

'I suppose I have more memories of old Doralee than I thought I did,' mused Mom.

'Seems to be a common theme,' said Adele, thinking of all the customers who'd shared their Doralee anecdotes with her. Sometimes it seemed that Doralee's generosity and kookiness had touched the entire borough of Brooklyn.

Ben was coming down from his upstairs apartment when they arrived back at Riffraff. He had a fresh shirt on and smelled of plain soap and dryer sheets – there was a simplicity to the scent that made Adele's heart skip. Especially when compared to the olfactory lasagne of Donny's multi-layered designer scents.

'That came for you while you were out,' he said, directing them to an enormous bouquet of daffodils sitting on the counter in an elaborate box tied with trailing ribbon.

'Nice shoes,' he added, as Adele reached for the card on the flowers. 'Did Reba put you up to that?'

'I did,' said Mom proudly, as she hefted the containers of takeout up on the counter. 'I hope you're hungry. I think we own shares in that restaurant now.'

Adele peeked at the card attached to the flowers. *To A. – D.* How . . . personal.

Brevity might be the soul of wit, but it was shitty at romance.

'Look at that!' Dad measured a line between the top of his head and the top of the bouquet. 'Tall enough to get the likes on those dating apps of yours.'

Ben raised an eyebrow.

'*Dad*,' warned Adele.

'Aren't those poisonous to cats?' asked Mom with a frown.

'Classic Donny,' said Ben. 'I'll keep Ember out of the way while you're out.'

Mom sagged in disappointment. 'You're not coming with us?'

Ben almost dropped the flowers. He looked like a deer caught in a hedgerow.

'We're only here tonight and tomorrow. Go on. Humour an old girl from Tennessee.' Mom clutched her hands to her heart in stereotypical Southern belle fashion.

There was enough tension between Adele and Ben already. She didn't need to throw the parentals in the midst of it. 'You don't have to. I'm sure you have a roast . . .'

'Adele, are you making this young man work when he's meant to be off the clock?' Dad put his hands on his hips. 'I thought this was a pro-union state.'

'*Honey*,' wheedled Mom.

'Do you promise to get me an introduction to Dolly?' said Ben, faux sternly.

'Why, of course,' said Mom in an exaggerated drawl. She batted her eyelashes.

Adele hid her face behind the daffodils. Her parents were quite the force of shamelessness to be reckoned with.

'Let me put these somewhere safe,' she said, 'and we'll get going.'

'This is it?' asked Adele warily. She'd been tricked by seemingly innocent entrances before. What kind of nightmare speakeasy scenario awaited behind this elaborately arched, highly ornamented metal door? It looked like the skeleton of a trilobite, but fancy.

Moving Parts Theatre, read the hand-lettered sign over the semi-circular awning. The same words flapped on a sad flag unfurling from the upstairs window. It was the place Ben had directed Trix to a while back.

'Oh wow, this is like *real* New York. I feel like I'm in *Taxi Driver*,' said Dad excitedly. He glanced around like he was hoping to get jumped.

Adele bit back a chuckle. To Dad, the notion of any city was *Taxi Driver*.

The ornate doors opened into a once-opulent space to which a red-and-gold threadbare carpet was hanging on for dear life. A handful of art deco couches, so deep they could swallow you up, were squished together like a losing game of Tetris. Umbrella-shaped lamps cast shaded light across a series of framed posters and playbills that clung gamely to the walls with failing tape. One was a handprinted poster with a forlorn message: *Demolition scheduled. See us before we're dust*, it said. The image on it showed a grainy picture of the theatre with a hand-drawn wrecking ball superimposed over the top.

Adele felt a pang as she took it in: the entire borough was evolving into luxury apartments. Darwin had been right when he'd theorised that evolution didn't have a point. It just . . . was.

'Benny boy!' A long-haired guy with serial-killer glasses and a *Peaky Blinders* accent clapped Ben on the back.

'Tommo, your Aussie accent is pure shite.'

'I'm working on it,' said the guy, in his regular American one. 'It's a running joke,' he told Adele. 'I test out different accents and pretend I'm trying to be Australian.'

Ben shook his head. 'He's just really bad at Australian accents.'

'Crikey!' added Dad, in a decent impersonation of the late, great Steve Irwin.

'They know you by name here,' noted Adele to Ben, now brimming with curiosity. Ben's uncanny ability to solve Reba's theatre-related crossword clues was starting to make sense. But how exactly did he fit into the picture?

Ben shrugged. 'I'm a memorable bloke.'

Adele was not about to argue.

'Is this your girl? And the folks! Must be serious!' Tommo gave a twirling bow. 'Ben never tells us anything about his life. I assume he retreats into his lamp the second he walks outside these doors.'

Adele grinned. She'd thought the same: that outside his work at Riffraff, Ben ceased to exist. Spotting him out and about was like seeing your grade-two teacher at the supermarket: it upended your whole solipsistic world.

'My boss,' corrected Ben. 'But she's taken, so don't get any thoughts.'

Tommo tore their tickets with a knowing nod. 'Refreshments are in the cooler behind the lion's head table – on the honour system. Toilet's busted, but we've got a hookup in the apartments across the road if you're desperate.'

Mom and Dad exchanged a delighted look. *This* was the New York experience that the television of the 1980s had promised them.

'Look, Lorna! Sticky floors!' Dad did a dance on the chewing-gummed carpet to demonstrate.

'Adele, get your toe in this shot too, will you?' Mom snapped a photo of the family's collective feet. 'Oh, that's a good one for Facebook,' she exclaimed.

Ben led them through a grimy hallway smothered with

framed posters and playbills. Here and there a few fashion-forward individuals leaned against the walls in what appeared to be *Ghostbusters* attire. A girl dressed in head-to-toe white waggled her fingers at Ben.

'Break a leg, Saphira,' he called.

Was that a real name? Definitely not.

Dropping a note in the cash box by the refreshments stand, Dad pulled out a dewy Coke from the cooler, holding it up like he'd yanked out Excalibur.

'Look, Lorna! Mexican Coke! With actual sugar!' He tapped at the label on the tall bottle, then popped off the lid with the key to the backyard shed (Adele would know that key anywhere).

Mom watched him chug the drink in three gulps, stiffening in anticipation of the inevitable burp. 'Don't forget about the bathroom situation, Cade.'

Dad waved her off. When you were a guy, there was always a place to pee. This explained why the plants closest to any doorway were always in such a sorry state.

To his credit, he held in the burp.

'I'm on my Big-City Best Behaviour,' he whispered to Adele.

'In we go!' said Mom, with the reverence of someone about to step onto Mars.

The theatre space was tiny, with maybe thirty seats divided into a strange zigzag, as though the furniture movers a hundred years ago had dropped them off in that don't-give-a-shit hour before a much-needed lunch break. Glossy wooden panelling formed an acoustic skin over the red-brick guts, and lights recoiled from the walls. Air conditioning ducts wove a black spine overhead. Adele, whose nose had become accustomed to coffee shop aromas and now expected them everywhere, was mildly startled by the sensory assault of cheap beer, weed, and pre-show anxiety.

'Wow, smells like San Francisco,' said Dad, who had never been to San Francisco.

A handful of people were already seated in hipster Twister style, legs slung over the backs of the chairs in front of them and arms dangling from the backs of their own chairs. They murmured amongst themselves as they passed around a bottle of vodka.

'They're in our seats,' whispered Mom anxiously, glancing at her ticket.

'She'll be right,' said Ben, gesturing to an open row of seats. 'I've never seen a full house in this joint. Pick whatever seat speaks to you.'

'First in, best dressed. Like on our flight,' said Dad, taking an aisle seat in case the Coke kicked in. 'Although that did get kind of gladiatorial.'

A few others trickled in: a trio holding hands; a guy in a kilt and an oversized trucker cap; girl in head-to-toe houndstooth; and a lumberjack. At least according to Dad.

'I chop wood, too!' he called, as Adele tried to disappear into her seat.

Behind Lumberjack came someone carrying an enormous length of Toblerone like a ceremonial sword.

'Toblerone?' offered the one wielding the chocolate. It was approximately two-thirds of an Adele long. Whatever that was in Australian, she thought wryly.

'I'd love some!' said Mom. 'Just a little . . . oh, okay, well, a lot is fine, too.'

She now had a chocolate triangle the size of half a sandwich to eat.

'Adele, do you want some? Adele?'

Adele absently took the hunk of chocolate Mom was waving in front of her face. She'd been distracted by a conversation being had by the seat loungers, who were somehow draping themselves in ever more spidery ways over the seating.

'They're saying it could be a serial killer,' whispered one.

'But what about the bodies? It's not a murder unless there's a body.'

'Well, the bodies have to be *somewhere*.'

Ben squirmed in his seat, which Adele understood: they *were* uncomfortable.

'Yeah, probably back on a train home to the Midwest. Or chained to their desk on Wall Street. If there's a killer, it's capitalism.'

'All I'm saying is that my brother-in-law is on the force—'

'And all I'm saying is that if capitalism isn't the killer, it's probably the cops. Man, it's going to suck seeing this place turned into apartments.'

The lights dimmed.

'Shh!' said Dad, the way he always did. He leaned over Mom, who was still working on her Toblerone, to whisper to Ben: 'I love doing that. The power!'

'That was fun,' said Mom after. 'You know what it needed, though? A musical number. Imagine the job you could've done in that funeral scene, Adele! You would've jazzed it right up.'

Adele grinned. Her parents weren't wrong. Nearly everything could be improved with a song-and-dance routine.

'Remember that dance we learned with you when you were first starting out?' Dad gave a wobbly spin. Uh-oh. Here it came. 'Sparkle fingers! Sparkle toes! Sparkle in our eyes and nose!'

243

'I'm glad you enjoyed it,' said Ben. 'I know it's a low-key spot, but I like it here. And as a bonus, the best pizza in Brooklyn is two doors down. Make sure you leave room for your Lebanese.'

A few minutes later, the group strolled out of the pizza spot awkwardly folding giant triangles of cheese and pepperoni.

'You look like you're playing the trumpet.' Adele laughed as Dad pinched his together into the world's oiliest funnel.

'At least it's not deep dish,' pointed out Mom. 'You'd be wearing it.'

'Well, I *am* a fashionable kind of guy.' Dad looked back longingly at the pizza shop. 'Back in a sec. Deep dish calls.'

Ben watched their antics as he neatly ate a much more restrained pizza – a rustic-looking thing with blubs of mozzarella and basil. And . . . anchovies?

'Bite?' he offered.

Adele waved him off with an exaggerated gag. 'It's you. *You're* the serial killer. Anchovies! What else? Pineapple?'

Ben coughed – he must have choked on one of his horrible toppings. 'What's wrong with pineapple on pizza? Or beetroot on a burger?'

'No wonder our customers are dropping like flies,' she said.

Ben picked off an anchovy and devoured it like a monster. 'They are, though, aren't they. I mean, I s'pose it's not my place, but some of these changes are a bit out there.'

'But there's a business case for all of them,' said Adele. 'Donny's been consulting. For free and everything.'

'It's the *and everything* that bothers me.' Ben wiped down his hands with a napkin.

'Oh, so you're jealous.'

'No, it's not—'

244

'Are we talking about Donny?' asked Mom, looping her arm through Adele's. 'I hope we get to meet him. Foot shot!'

Adele and Ben's tiff was put on hold as Mom paused to take a shot of their tie-dyed sandals against a decorative grate. By the time Mom was done filtering her photos and posting them to Facebook with a caption she had to edit three times, any animosity between them was gone.

'Nice night,' said Ben, after they'd dropped Lorna and Cade off at Doralee's apartment, where they'd been pounced upon by Kyra and the other neighbours. Fortunately they'd come bearing a restaurant's worth of Lebanese food, so they fit in right away.

The tortured strains of courtyard karaoke followed them back to Riffraff, where Ember waited with an indignant expression. To be fair, this was his normal expression.

'Your parents are cute,' said Ben, stooping to give Ember a scratch. 'They're like the American version of my extended family back home.'

'Sorry about all the crocodile questions,' said Adele. 'And for Dad's demonstration of the crocodile roll. That was . . .'

'A solid indicator of where you got your love of the performing arts.'

'They're definitely my parents,' said Adele with a rueful grin.

'Lucky thing,' said Ben. 'I mean it. I miss my mum every day.' He tapped at the spot where his mum's name was so elegantly written.

Adele couldn't even begin to imagine what it would feel like to lose her parents – and then the person who had taken you under their wing for so long.

'Let me run up to grab some blankets, and then the flat's all yours.'

'I can stay downstairs,' said Adele. 'I don't mind, really.'

'Nah, it's my job to protect you from the roaster,' Ben said lightly.

Of course, the precious roaster.

Adele put a hand on her hip. 'More like you're trying to protect the roaster from me, the way you baby that thing.'

Adele's phone buzzed: Donny.

You can stay at mine. But I'll be out. Business.

'All good?' asked Ben.

'Just Mom saying goodnight,' said Adele, hoping Ben wasn't going to quiz her on the phone signal situation at Doralee's.

Leaving the text on unread, Adele made her way up to the apartment, trying not to react as she brushed past Ben on the stairs.

Wake Me Up Before You Cocoa

There she was. Adele was almost too anxious to breathe. She was in Ben's space, the space she'd been trying not to think about since the very first time she'd realised that Ben was not, in fact, a tuxedo cat, but an unfairly handsome Australian with a ridiculous jawline and a sense of humour she secretly adored. Not to mention the generosity of heart to explain what a cortado was before she'd humiliated herself in front of a customer by replying with *gesundheit*.

Speaking of – a sneeze below. The walls were crepe-paper thin.

Mindful that Ben was probably clocking her every move, Adele stood on the spot as she took it all in. The apartment was all she'd hoped for: as simple and rustic as the pizza he'd ordered, but hold the anchovies. Clothing hung neatly from wall-mounted hooks and racks. A comfortable-looking plaid couch (sans throw pillows, because this *was* a guy's apartment) was pushed up against the tall sash windows. Mounds of books formed a brickwork pattern along a series of shelves bolted into the bare walls. Any space that wasn't stacked high with books was claimed by framed prints, all of them posters for plays –

and not one of them a musical. *A Long Day's Journey into Night. Accidental Death of an Anarchist. Who's Afraid of Virginia Woolf?*

Well, no one was perfect.

Spying a narrow desk stacked high with paper and . . . a typewriter? Really? Strangely charmed by this, Adele tiptoed over. An unframed photo with a weird greeny-purple tinge – from age, perhaps – wobbled in the toothy bite of a clip-style holder. Adele recognised Ilona from Doralee's photo album, although she was a few years older in this picture. Her mouth was tight, and her brow was furrowed: she had none of the carefree expression from the other photo. Baby Ben was a little boy in this one, smiling gap-toothed from beneath a glossy bowl cut and clutching a stuffed dog to his striped T-shirt. Imagine being that cute!

Frowning, Adele ran a thumb over the slightly crooked edge of the photo. Someone had been excised from the picture – not by the photographer, but by a pair of scissors. Squinting, she could make out a smudge of denim and the faded blue of a button-up shirt. A man.

What was the story here?

Had Ben cut him out? Or Ilona? Or even Doralee?

Or maybe he had cut himself out. This was pre-Facetune, after all. Analogue photos were like perms: if you looked bad you had to deal with it. And grimace every time your relatives passed around photographic evidence of your most disastrous haircuts and makeup choices during a family get-together. Which was their primary hobby.

Adele pushed the desk chair back out. Oops – she'd almost knocked over the guitar lurking by the desk. She caught it by the fretboard, grimacing as its strings let out a discordant hum. It needed tuning.

Pulling the guitar into her lap, she strummed a few gentle chords, adjusting the machine heads until the strings sang. It was a lovely-sounding instrument: vocal and full-bodied, with a warm tone befitting of its coffee shop home.

She sang softly along with it, making up a tune to go with the poem scrawled on a piece of torn notepaper sitting on the desk. The metre was a touch off, but she could make it work. It wasn't for nothing that Adele had a reputation as the girl who could sing a chocolate cake recipe.

As she set the guitar back down, the headstock nudged the cover page of a document written in Courier. It wafted to the floor. Well, now, she *had* to look if she was going to put it back.

It was a play entitled *The Girl Downstairs*.

As she set the sheet very carefully back atop the rest of the stack, Adele couldn't resist the extremely silly grin that clowned across her face.

Roast Me

The next morning, Adele packed off her parents with a list of all the TV shows that were filming and where, handwritten directions for taking the Subway, and a stern admonishment to walk at an NYC pace, not a rural Tennessee one.

Among the approximately gajillion texts that Mom sent throughout the day documenting their (touristically slow) progress throughout Manhattan was one saying that they were three drinks deep at a Tim Burton–themed restaurant and couldn't be held responsible for their availability or Facebook posts in the coming hours. Adele was a touch relieved that this meant they wouldn't be joining her at dinner with Donny tonight, partly because pretension wasn't their thing, and partly because she could already foresee a battle between Dad and Donny over who was going to pay. And Dad had a pretty good grappling technique.

Anyway, there Donny was, elbows on his Vachetta leather briefcase, tapping busily on his phone. 'Reservations don't wait forever, Delly.'

'*Delly* indeed. Have some respect, Donny,' whispered Reba

indignantly from over her crossword, her reward for a long day of Tie Dyepalooza preparation.

Adele privately agreed with Reba's thoughts about the nickname, but she wasn't about to say that to Donny. Besides, it was really more of a delivery thing than a name thing. On the lips of a New Yorker, Delly sounded like a cramped place you hastily ordered a pastrami sandwich from a harried guy wielding a butter knife and an endless commentary about his in-laws.

But in another accent, it had the potential to sound . . . *enticing*. In, say, an accent like Ben's. Not that she spent her off hours imagining Ben saying her name.

Where was Ben, anyway? He'd ordinarily be back from running his afternoon theatre workshop – for that's what it turned out he'd been doing all these months. No wonder he was always on edge: he was a theatre kid! It explained so much.

Adele checked the Felix the Cat clock above the front door. She'd put fresh batteries in, so she was fairly certain it was keeping time. Well, if Ben was going fluff-arse (his term), *he* could clean the bathroom. And mop the floors and put up the chairs. That seemed like a reasonable division of labour.

'I need to flush the La Marzocco, and then we're done.' Adele was somewhat flushed herself at the thought of Ben easily flipping over the coffee shop chairs like . . . No, *nope*. She wasn't going to go there. That was an HR incident waiting to happen, and *she* was HR. Which reminded her, she still had to read the handbook. Or maybe write it.

Shaking off all thoughts of bad behaviour, she added a blind filter to a portafilter and popped in a cleaning tablet, losing herself in the ritual of putting the espresso maker to bed. She'd come to love the huge silvery machine. The hissing and whirring involved made her feel like she was casting spells. Delicious, caffeinated spells.

Donny glanced up as she locked the portafilter in place, pushing his rimless glasses up on his nose. 'The way you baby that thing. Makes me worried about your intentions.'

Adele playfully wrapped an arm around the gleaming machine. 'It's tall, dark, handsome, and Italian. Can you blame me?'

'Keeps us up all night, too,' said Reba from over her crossword. Purple eyeshadow flashed as she winked.

'Very funny.' Phone in his hand as though it had been surgically grafted there, Donny made his way to the bathroom. 'Well, it's keeping us from our tasting menu. And Italian *wine*. Back in a sec.'

As the bathroom lock clicked, Adele felt an odd sense of relief. There was something about Donny that made her feel like she was always *on*. Like he was a critic writing a career-dousing review designed to go viral.

'Missed one.' Setting her crossword down, Reba pounced upon Donny's mug in a swoop of shawls and tie-dye, knocking his briefcase off the table. Papers skittered about. Reba hastily gathered them together and plopped them back on the table in a crumpled stack.

'We'll just ignore that,' she said, passing Adele the mug. 'Paperwork is for rubes, anyway.'

Adele groaned as she shook a chewed piece of gum from the mug. She'd have to restart the dishwasher. But that was fine! Everything was fine! She was definitely, absolutely looking forward to this dinner. Even though she was sweaty from a day behind the counter and hadn't had time to research the dishes on the spherification-heavy menu to find something that might actually be edible.

There were two chocolate-chip cookies left in the display cabinet. Munching on one – it always paid to pregame before fine dining – she popped its twin into a paper bag and scooted it over the counter to Reba. 'As a thanks.'

Reba waggled the bag like it was a tambourine in a jam band set. 'Perfect for powering through tonight's dyeing session. Only a week to go!'

'I'll have a cheesy croissant and spiced cappuccino ready to go by six. Or Ben will, anyway.'

'I bet. Men aren't really my thing, but he's a good one. He's jump-started my van three times now. And even pet-sat my parrot once. Helped it unlearn some swear words. Anyway. Reba has left the building.' False teeth squirrelling at her cookie, Reba pranced out the door in a cloud of patchouli and chocolate chip.

Adele smiled as she watched the old hippie go. Maybe switching out sheet music for milk steamers wasn't such a bad thing career-wise. The coffee shop drew the same creative, devil-may-care kind of people as musical theatre, but without the stress of dress rehearsals and synchronised jump turns. And it wasn't like she wasn't allowed to sing. This wasn't *The Little Mermaid*.

'Ember! You shit!'

All right, so the shop had its own stresses.

A sheaf of Donny's Very Important Papers clutched between his jaws, Ember made a jingling beeline for the stairway behind the counter that led to the vehemently out-of-bounds basement. His crispy tail wagged knowingly as he strutted through the cat flap.

How was Adele going to get to him now? She doubted Ben had left his keys behind a second time. And she only had moments before Donny emerged from the bathroom to find that his documents had become a cat's plaything.

Hang on, the Lost and Found! Adele grabbed out the kit that an unlicensed dentist had left behind a few weeks earlier and, worryingly, had never shown up to collect. It took some jabbing and prodding and the lock-picking equivalent of a root canal, but she managed to pop a couple of the locks. Then, snatching up the pair of extra-long tongs she used for seizing items off the top shelves, she reached an arm through the cat flap, stretching to reach the remaining locks.

Done, and with the stretchy elegance of Eugene Tooms in her second-favourite episode of the *X-Files*, which had taken a young Adele a solid year to recover from.

The door swung open.

Down she went, chasing after Ember as he circled the huge coffee roaster that some enterprising yet clearly mad scientist had Frankensteined out of washing machine guts, stovepipe tubing and rivets. It seemed even creepier than the last time she'd been down here. Had it grown? Couldn't have. The light was probably playing tricks on her.

'Gotcha!' Cornering Ember at the bottom of the stairs, Adele prised the papers from the cat's needle-like teeth. The light was dim, but she caught the words *multi-family luxury development*. And then . . . hang on.

She moved closer to the striped schoolhouse light that hung above the roaster. The address listed for the development was Riffraff's address. That couldn't be right. Donny had made it very clear what he thought about Bridge and Tunnel people. In his eyes, Brooklyn was a smidge above Jersey City, which was a smidge above Bumfuck, Alabama. It pained him to step foot outside Manhattan: even the badminton bar had been a stretch.

'Delly? Where'd you go? You're not trying to get a jump on the appetisers, are you?'

'Down here.' She sucked her finger – she'd cut it on one of the pages.

'In the *basement*?' Adele should have known Donny did not deign to enter basements. Anything below ground was for Pizza Rats and squatters and subway commuters.

Donny's glasses glinted as he poked his head over the threshold.

A mechanical hum came from the roaster. Adele needed to get someone in to upgrade that fuse box. It sounded like a bunch of Gregorian monks were chanting back there.

'Doing some urgent reading,' she snapped. 'In preparation for you turning this place into some Scandi-inspired wood-veneer bullshit with wafer walls and a stupid artisanal gelato cart and a fake grass "woof garden" amenity that costs an extra grand a month.'

Donny's leather-soled shoes clomped down the steps. One of his laces was loose, Adele noted triumphantly. No amount of money could protect against untied laces. Maybe he'd trip, the jerk.

'Delly, babe. It's a proposal. Some brainstorming. I needed to put a few ideas forward. You know how it is.' He reached out a hand like a parent trying to soothe a furious toddler.

The hum intensified. Now it was punctuated with a mild clanking, as if the Gregorian monks had found some cowbells. And a weird rattle, like the one on Adele's first car right before it had broken down in the turning lane in Nashville's peak-hour traffic as she'd been racing to make an audition. Bad times.

Adele turned to face Donny, the papers tucked behind her back. 'I don't, actually. What ideas?'

'Just ideas. Delly. They're confidential. Why don't you pass them back so we don't have to go through the whole rigmarole of NDAs and all that.' Donny pressed forward, breaking the socially agreed upon zone of personal space and beginning that strange dance people do where one person moves forward as the other creeps back. Like tango, but horrible.

Her back pressed up against the roaster, which was warm. Had Ben left it on?

'Why are you even here? Is this all some big grift? Get the girl to hand over her coffee shop by plying her with foie gras and fromagerie?'

'Do I look like someone who'd do that?' he pleaded.

Actually, with his crisp suit and groomed facial hair, he looked *exactly* like someone who'd do that. Adele gave him the deathly scowl that had prompted her third-grade teacher to send a concerned note home.

She didn't scowl often, but when she did, she *really* did.

'It's all a big coincidence,' wheedled Donny. 'I swear, on the soul of the S&P 500. I was looking at this place – to tear it down, sure, because let's face it, it's a shithole – and then I met you.' He paused, cocking his head. 'Did you hear that?'

'I only hear the sounds of a liar desperately trying to convince me.'

'*I'm* the desperate one?' Donny's eyes narrowed, and his jaw tensed. 'If you had half a brain you'd be begging me to take this place off your hands.'

There it was. The quick turn to anger that men were renowned for in the face of rejection.

Donny darted forward, grabbing for the papers. His hand

closed around Adele's wrist, twisting the skin like a childhood bully.

'Ow!' Adele's instincts kicked in, and she kicked him in the shin with her Doc Martens, suddenly glad she'd suffered through those months of blisters breaking them in. Now *there* was a photo for Mom's shoe album.

Donny stumbled forwards, grabbing the huge loading hopper on the roaster for balance. The machine rumbled a warning.

'What the bloody hell's going on?' Ben leapt down the stairs in practised threes, yanking Donny around and making a fist around his shirt. Buttons clacked across the cement floor.

'Did this smarmy wanker hurt you, Adele?'

The roaster chugged like a redneck truck left idling. The thick silver blades of the cooling tray spun ominously. The stench of a thousand pennies filled the air.

'Get your grimy hands off me. Although I'm sure you'd rather have them on *her*,' Donny said snidely. He twisted away, tripping over Ember, who'd twined his way down the stairs in the dark.

'Come *on*, Donny,' retorted Adele. 'Your moral high ground just suffocated in a landslide.'

Donny always had the last word. But not this time. No amount of Orangetheory training could help him maintain his balance. It didn't help that Ember was determinedly headbutting him.

'Delly!' bellowed Donny. 'Pull the safety!'

But there was no safety switch on a machine cobbled together out of spare parts and insanity. The lights on the roaster's control panel blinked from green to red. Air whistled through its exhaust, as though it was sucking in an excited breath. The machine whirred and churned, and the floor seemed alive beneath their feet. And Donny—

'Get back!' Ben yanked Adele away from the roaster, pulling her in so that her face was pressed up to his chest, muffling Donny's anguished cries and the roar of the monstrous machine.

Ben felt exactly as she'd imagined: warm and strong through his thick shirt, smelling of a day's hard work at the coffee shop. She wanted to stay there forever, listening to the confident thrum of his heart, feeling the heat of his breath on the top of her head, ignoring the chaotic scene mere feet away . . .

No. Not now. How *dare* he do this to her now?

'Get off me.' Shoving Ben's tattooed arms aside, she hurried over to the roaster's cooling tray, where a single cufflink twirled among the dark, oily beans. The machine's huge central drum spun and spun, thumping like a washing machine overloaded with towels. Inside, something trickled and squelched. And then the roaster . . . belched.

It was a stinky belch that smelt like a butcher's at the end of the day.

Adele's stomach twisted, and she clapped her hands over her mouth, trying not to vomit. She turned on Ben. 'What's going on? Where's Donny?'

Even as she said it, she was fixated upon Donny's rimless glasses gleaming on the floor.

Ben gestured diffidently at the roaster, which had switched itself back to its standby position. 'He's . . . in there.'

'Well let's get him out! Is there a door or something? An escape hatch!'

'Adele, that thing roasts beans to an internal temperature of 250 degrees Celsius. I don't know what that is in American.

Heaps.' Ben sank down on a milk crate, running his hands through his wavy hair. 'This isn't *Charlie and the Chocolate Factory*. There's no juicing him or putting him back together. He's dead. As a donkey.'

'Dead! That thing *ate* him!'

Ben nodded slowly. 'Yeah.'

Adele backed up towards the stairs. She was in that horrible backwards tango dance again, only now it was a dark realisation that was chasing her.

'And you knew it was going to! That that's what it *does*!' Adele's hand trembled as she pointed at the now-still machine. 'You *feed* it, don't you! That's why we're always low on beans even though you're always roasting.'

She eyed Ben warily, willing her stomach to settle. Ben said nothing.

'And that's where . . .'

She clutched the banister in awful comprehension.

'Holy shit! Topknot guy! Spin class Lexie! Mazzy Stevens! Transphobic Karen!'

She backed up as she named each victim.

'That *whole gaggle of soccer moms*!' she howled.

'They kept bagsing all the street parking.' Ben looked fretful, but also relieved at being able to share his dark secret with someone. 'It's not like I want this bit of the job. I'm a barista, not a bloody director of sacrificial services. But you don't understand. It has to feed on *someone*. And it's getting hungrier every frigging day! So excuse me for giving it shitty people instead of the good ones.'

Adele scoffed. 'And you're the person to make that call!'

Ben's green eyes stared her down. 'I reckon I'm a pretty good judge of character.'

259

'Well, apparently *I'm* not, because I thought you were decent. And not someone with a Satanic feeder fetish or whatever the fuck this is! Holy shit, everything from Australia really does try to kill you.' She swallowed. 'Tell me you've at least been throwing out the corpse roasts and not . . .'

Ben stared down at the blood-stained floor. 'Do you have any idea what green coffee beans cost? If I did that we'd be bankrupt in a week.'

Adele covered her mouth with a hand. Oh God, she'd drunk *so much* coffee over the past few months. Her blood type was *House of 1000 Corpses*.

She reached out a trembling hand to Ember. 'Ember, are you coming?'

Mrow, said Ember, noncommittally.

'He's with me,' said Ben, with a touch of apology.

Yellow eyes flashed as the tuxedo cat elegantly leapt to the top of the roaster and languidly started licking his own butt.

'Of course. Of *course* the cat's in on it.'

Adele's stomach churned as uncomfortably as the discount ice-cream maker she'd worked to the bone during college. It was all too horrible. Murder! No, *worse* than murder! Premeditated, serial, liquid cannibalism!

How could Ben *do* this? How could the (allegedly) sweet Aunt Doralee have put her in this situation? And how could Adele possibly face the churrasco place she'd angrily called up multiple times, complaining about their malfunctioning vent hood?

No wonder no one lasted in the City. You had to move back home to hide the fact that you were an unwitting, dim-witted accessory to a crime!

Betrayed, boyfriendless, and facing microwaved two-minute

noodles for dinner, Adele clomped up the last few steps, wincing as her Docs reopened the blister on her heel. At the threshold, she paused. How were you meant to end an interaction like this? What did you do after you watched a coffee roaster chow down up on your sort-of boyfriend while the guy you actually liked looked on?

She had no answers for any of it, but Reba's voice echoed in her head: *Sleep on it, love. Don't make any rash decisions until you've slept on it. Or with it.*

And then, just for funsies, the Third Stipulation of the Riffraff Coffee Shop deed came roaring back. *And you have to keep Ben on. No matter what.*

Fine, Doralee. She wouldn't call the cops or burn the place down or God forbid, *fire* Ben. Yet.

Instead, she made do with yelling the most hurtful thing she could think of.

'As of tomorrow, you're paying rent!'

See Ya Later, Percolator

Adele had a sleepless night. And not only because the artisanal coffee roaster that Ben spent so much quality time with had chewed up Donny into tomorrow's French roast. Well, largely because of that. And also because the neighbours in Apartment B were apparently having some sort of sex party, or were at least playing a highly competitive Dungeons & Dragons campaign. But *most especially* because Ben had been hiding a serious proclivity for slaughter this entire time.

Like the third-act reveal in *Dirty Rotten Scoundrels*, it suddenly all made sense.

The dwindling assortment of annoying regulars and those who had broken the unspoken coffee shop rules of engagement. The rattling and rumbling under the shop that Adele's frantic Brooklyn Library research trip just now had revealed were not in fact from a subway line or an overzealous dryer. The souvenir tooth and the bellybutton jewellery. The sturdy locks on the door under the guise of a stringent adherence to OSHA.

Not to mention Ben's joke about sleeping downstairs to protect her from the roaster.

All right, so that was sweet in a slightly psychotic way.

No, nope! No way, José. She was not thinking like that. Her high school days of entertaining any human being who showed the smallest degree of interest in her were over.

That never turned out well. Look at what had happened to Donny!

Ugh, she'd been so foolishly naïve to trust a man who owned seventeen pairs of Prada loafers. But how was she supposed to have known that a real estate speculator was only interested in her for her multi-million-dollar property and not her excellent sense of humour and ability to wear pastels without looking washed out?

It all made sense, but in the guesstimation-heavy way that Adele's algebra homework had at school.

She chowed down on one of Kyra's special brownies, thinking.

Ben had been hurling people into the roaster like they were haybales at the Highland Games. But he hadn't done it willingly. Well, maybe with the exception of Topknot Guy. Like tapeworms and the capitalist engine Donny had loved so much, the machine had to be fed. And according to Ben – and corroborated by Riffraff's gas and electricity bills and the growing objections from the neighbours – it was getting ever more ravenous. If it kept up like this, soon half of Brooklyn would be flavouring the double espressos being drunk by the remaining half of Brooklyn. And her recent application for Green Energy Certification tax credits would *definitely* be denied.

Ugh, why did all roads always lead to *Cannibal! The Musical*?

Wrapping Doralee's batik comforter around herself as a form of psychic protection, Adele stumbled out of bed for a cider to wash down the brownie. As she did, she tripped over the banker's box where she'd stuffed the overflow from Doralee's *Out of Sight, Out of Mind* drawer.

The two of them really were alike, she thought ruefully, as she realised she'd neglected to pay the business liability insurance. Although did that really matter, when it was fairly likely that her coverage didn't include multiple homicides caused by a murderous coffee roaster.

Although Doralee *had* kept that weird book of doodles. Maybe there was something in the marbled, glittery notebook that could help Adele understand this whole situation – and how to deal with it.

She rummaged through the box, but the notebook was gone.

Shit. Hoarderfest.

Best case, she'd sold it. Worst case, it was living a new life at the bottom of a skip as the religious tome of choice of the local pizza rats.

Double shit. Speaking of pizza rats, she owed her parents a goodbye breakfast.

The sky had cracked open like an egg and was pouring its contents all over Brooklyn. Adele would have raided the umbrella basket at Riffraff, but she'd demanded the place close its doors, effective immediately, until she figured out what to do about the whole human-flavoured coffee situation.

Instead, she'd grabbed a few of Doralee's shawls from the wardrobe to share with Mom. Dad, looking pleased with himself, had unfurled a plastic poncho from a keyring he'd picked up at a bodega.

'MacGyver walks among us,' he said, draping it over himself

like a trash bag. He rustled down the street with the ethereal silliness of the plastic bag in *American Beauty*.

'Sweetie, your makeup is running,' said Mom apologetically, smudging at Adele's undereye area.

Definitely the rain, and not the lingering visual of her fake boyfriend being woodchipped by the guy she wished she were her boyfriend. It was the worst love triangle in history. Well, love *line* now, she supposed, given that a whole participant had abruptly stepped out of the geometrical arrangement.

'That's better. We can't have you looking like a panda on our last day here!'

'That's right,' said Dad. 'You'll attract other pandas.'

'*Cade*,' scolded Mom.

Adele averted her eyes as she led her parents past the badminton speakeasy Donny had taken her to on their first date. This breakfast spot had seemed like a good suggestion a day or so ago. Now it was a series of reminders. Adele blinked back tears . . .

'Look, Lorna! A trash can rat! Like in the movies!' Dad stopped to snap a photo of a fat rat surfing atop a precarious stack of waxed sandwich wrappers. His poncho billowed in the breeze. 'The thing's as big as an opossum.'

Mom clucked from her hiding place beneath a deli awning. 'He's going to have a whole album of rat snaps to go with his armadillo sightings.'

'It's not normal to have armadillos in Tennessee! I'm tracking their migration! Besides, you can't talk with all your dance routines. She learns them off that clock app.'

'My latest is the shuffle. Ready?' Mom started kicking her legs as though fire ants were crawling up them. A vast loaf of bread in hand, the owner of the awning shook his head judgementally. *Tourists.*

'That's . . . quite something.' Adele gave a golf clap.

'My favourite girl has gone dark, though. Mazzy Stevens? She used to post every day, but for the past few weeks, not a single video. I've sent her dozens of laughing emojis, but no response. Rumour has it—' Mom looked around, in case a paparazzo was hiding somewhere in the sheeting rain '—that she's in *rehab*.'

'Fame isn't all it's cracked up to be.' Adele bit her lip at the thought of the Wheely she'd found in the basement. And the blend Ben had called On Your Skates.

And how Mazzy had mentioned she'd seen Adele's face before – *of course*: on Mom's social media user pic. Talk about six degrees of Kevin Bacon.

Although she really didn't want to think about bacon right now.

'This is us.' Wringing the excess water from her shawl, Adele guided her parents through the door of Nothing Up Top, a sleek breakfast spot with a glorious rooftop patio that zigzagged with industrial steel beams and Edison bulbs. Modern and metallic, it was the opposite of Riffraff, and precisely what she needed today.

As the elevator took them to the rooftop, Mom touched up her own mascara, which she applied with the generous hand of a palette knife painter. She gave Adele one of those spidery-lashed, assessing looks that only moms were allowed to.

'Are you all right, sweets? You look tired.'

'Oh, I'm fine,' said Adele, although her reflection in the elevator's mirrored panel said otherwise. Her hair looked like something out of *Weird Science*. 'It's been a busy few months. The business, moving. Doralee.'

Not to mention concealing a few dozen murders. Including that of her sort-of boyfriend.

'It's such a shame we didn't get to meet your Donny,' said Mom, as the elevator dinged. 'It's so exciting to encounter a mover and shaker like that. Although I suppose that's everyone in New York City. I tried the number on his card again, but no luck. He must be busy with work.'

'If he even exists,' said Dad, with a cheeky grin.

Adele swallowed. Donny existed. As a bag of coffee beans.

'There's a forty-minute wait. Is that all right?' The hostess pointed to a thronging group of hungry people sipping on mimosas while they side-eyed the brunchers taking too long over their microgreens-topped avocado toast.

'Forty minutes!' Shaking out his poncho like a matador in the Running of the Bulls, Dad looked scandalised, but happily so. He was going to tell all of his friends back home about the wait time. It was a war story for someone who'd never seen combat.

'We have a reservation,' Adele assured her parents. 'Forrest.'

'Well, in that case!' the hostess led them over to a four-top overlooking a coworking space. A few sad workers bounced on yoga balls, mainlining La Croix as they spent their Saturday morning Making the World Better Through Tech™.

'Sorry about the hungry onlookers.' The hostess waved at the ravening crowds milling about, their Apple watches flashing from their frequent checking. 'Our boss signed us up for this EatMe thing and didn't tell us.'

Adele chuckled as she unfolded her napkin. 'My tip: unplug the machine. It'll be better for everyone.'

'What did you say Donny does again?' Mom pulled out the card Adele had given her.

Adele choked at the sight of it. She sipped at her iced water to hide her anguish.

'His card says: "transforming skylines",' added Mom.

'Maybe he flies hot air balloons.' Dad took the card from Mom, turning it this way and that, as though that would help it give up its secrets.

'He's in property development,' said Adele tightly. 'He takes perfectly good properties and fleeces their owners so he can turn them into heinously expensive luxury apartments that no one can afford.'

'Like those ones down there?' Dad waved at one of the coworking hipsters, who nervously shuffled his yoga ball across the room and out of sight.

'Worse.' Was it all right to speak ill of the dead if they'd been ill-intentioned towards you? Having chugged her own drink, Adele moved on to Mom's glass of water, wishing it were a mojito. A dead boyfriend, a murderous coffee roaster, an aiding-and-abetting employee/cat duo, and departing parents. This was all too much for a Saturday morning.

'Well, that's city living for you.' Mom browsed the menu, pausing on the listing for the everything bagel. 'It's our last day. Gotta have a bagel, with lox.'

'I mean, if you have to have a bagel with *hair*,' chuckled Dad, who was hungrily eyeing the pancakes. Adele smiled, despite herself. She was going to miss having her starry-eyed parents around. She ordered on their behalf when the waiter stalked over, tapping away on a touchscreen. His ironic mullet belied an unironic expression.

'Anyway, he sounds smart,' Mom went on, frowning as the waiter stalked off – not angry, Adele reassured her. Just busy. 'Harvard's a good school. Not a football school, but a good school. And if he looks anything like that South African boy of yours . . .'

'Australian,' corrected Adele.

'Oh they all sound alike. Although I think I can pick out New Zealand. *Fush and chups*. Is that right?'

A guy in an All-Blacks hat glared daggers at them from the next table.

'Nice guy,' added Dad. 'Are those tattoos real? They can't be, can they?'

'I'm pretty sure they're temporary,' said Adele.

Their food arrived almost instantly, the waiter hurling the plates down on the table like he was participating in a Greek wedding.

'No rush, but there's a party waiting,' he said. A hungry-looking group of teenagers circled like sharks staring at the anglerfish glow of their phones.

'We'll be quick. We've got a flight to catch. Forks in!' Having drowned his pancakes in maple syrup, Dad attacked them with his fork. Maple blood splashed everywhere.

Then the bloodbath was staunched by a horrifying realisation. 'Hang on . . . are these . . . gluten-free?'

Never in the history of the world had there been a more devastated man.

Mom bit into her bagel, grimacing as she picked out a visible grain. 'I thought rye would be more . . . y'know. Whisky forward.'

'When's y'all's flight back?' asked Adele. She both desperately wanted her parents to leave so she could get to the bottom of the coffee roaster (not literally – she'd seen those flashing blades), and stridently wanted them to stay. They were such warm, gentle folk, and there was such a comfort to the way

269

they marvelled over day-to-day things like the street vendors and the subway turnstiles, as though by living in the City Adele were doing something huge with her life, even though she'd made an absolute hash of it so far.

'It's at four,' said Mom. 'I've got seven reminders set on my phone, just in case. You don't have to come with us to the airport. I know you've got a lot on, sweetie. Is your Australian managing well without you?'

'Austrian,' corrected Dad.

'I think so,' said Adele, forcing herself not to check her own phone. Ben was on his own today. She wasn't sure how she could face him. What would she even say?

'Reba had nice things to say about him,' added Mom. 'He had a hard time after he moved back after his gran died. Doralee took him in and looked after him like he was the son she'd never had.'

Adele gawped. How had Mom learned as much about Ben in the space of two days as Adele had over two months?

'He also runs an afternoon theatre group for kids who've . . . got off to a bad start,' said Dad.

Adele sipped her orange juice – no coffee for her today.

'Maybe he could write you a lead role.' Dad took a bite of the breakfast burrito she'd barely touched. His eyes immediately started watering at the Cholula hot sauce it had marinated in. 'Let you test out those pipes. Did you tell him you were a finalist in the Chattanooga Singer-Songwriter competition?'

Adele shook her head. 'I don't know that means much here.'

'Why not? It's a big deal.' Dad dabbed at his eyes with a napkin. 'Holy moly, I think they put napalm in that burrito. Look – even your eyes are watering, and you've barely touched your breakfast.'

Adele smiled through her tears. She had too many emotions to compute today. Donny's death. Ben's secret-keeping. Her parents leaving. The homicidal coffee roaster . . . shit, what was she going to do about that?

'No rush, but there's your bill.'

Adele grabbed it away from Dad, who was already reaching into his jeans for his Costco card.

'My shout,' she said, grabbing a few crumpled notes from Doralee's Glomesh purse.

But First, Coffee

It wasn't until Adele collapsed on to Doralee's enormously flamboyant bed that she saw she had multiple missed calls from Alejandro. Her mind, primed for the worst after the past few days, immediately went into overdrive. Had Ekaterina died doing the backbends in 'Turkey Lurkey Time'? Had the person who'd ordered the unicorn latte wound up at hospital with a case of glitter poisoning?

No signal. And the toucan telephone had sparked when she lifted the receiver.

The two closest options with solid reception were Riffraff and the cemetery. One of these sounded less full of dead people than the other. And less full of Bens.

Adele made the trek up the supersized hill, pantingly accepting that her fitness was going out the window now that she was spending her days pulling espresso shots and not rehearsing dance choreography. Although her triceps were looking pretty good from those long shifts behind the La Marzocco.

Parking herself on Fitzy Fring's stone bench – Donny's lilies were long gone, she saw – she pulled out her phone.

Alejandro answered immediately. 'Babe, I got you an audition at The Factory, 8 a.m. sharp. Which is like . . . now. Oh hey, I gotta go. If I leave this face mask on too long my skin will come off with it. But you know I live dangerously.'

They rang off, leaving Adele gawping at her phone. An audition! The Adele of a few months ago would've done a barefooted clog dance across broken glass to make it happen. She'd worked so hard on embracing her new life – but look where that had got her.

Had she wound up right back where she'd started? *Could* she even start over?

'What do you think, Julep?' she asked a grave with an elaborate statue of a woman stomping on bluebells. 'Should I do it?'

Well, you don't have anything better to do. Clearly.

This was a good point. The alternative was to head to Riffraff, and she wasn't ready for that yet. Oh gosh, the thought of all those people drinking corpse coffee that whole time . . .

And Kyra feeding the grounds to her plants! There were corpses everywhere! Every plant in Brooklyn was a corpse flower! Even Audrey III! Although that one made a gory kind of sense now.

But the pothos had been growing in the shop for decades. Which meant . . . had Kyra and even Doralee known about the murderous roaster? Adele frowned. She had so many questions that she didn't especially want answered. Which was how she'd approached her classes at school.

Hang on. Was there movement in the greenhouse? Adele shaded her eyes with her hand, squinting up at the heavily patinaed structure, with its charming domes and warped brass fretwork. Perhaps Kyra was at work. Maybe she could go see her and get the horticulturalist's perspective on this whole situation. But a second silhouette caught her eye. A familiarly broad-shouldered, well-shaped one with – yep, there was the swoop of the hand through a thick tousle of hair.

What was Ben doing here?

Maybe she'd guessed wrong about the cemetery corpse : Ben ratio.

Julep was staring imperiously down at Adele. The statue was right. She'd hotfoot it down to the audition. In all her years of chasing her Broadway dreams, she'd never, ever turned down an audition. It was a point of pride, so much so that for a while there she'd become known as 'Audition Adele'. Even if the role involved no more than spinning across the stage in theatre blacks, she was there for it. That's what a career in musical theatre took: your whole-hearted involvement. Even when your heart wasn't in it at all.

The greenhouse door swung; Adele could hear snatches of a conversation coming her way.

But Adele wasn't ready to face Ben yet. Nor Kyra.

Dusting her butt off, she hurried down the stone pathway, muttering quick hellos to the more forlorn-looking graves she passed along the way. She hoped it wasn't patronising to pat a tombstone on the head. Where else were you meant to pat?

On the way to the subway, Adele paused by a narrow shop called Dark Knight Coffee. Decorated entirely in shades of grey, it was the sort of space a house flipper would design.

Grey is the colour of real estate speculation, she remembered Ben saying. But after the events of the previous night, his opinion on interior design was dead to her.

Adele poked her head inside. It was a Donny wonderland:

the AI music system, the EatMe printer firing off orders that a Smartwool-clad bicycle courier was stoically packing into a pannier.

'A flat white, please,' she said cautiously.

The barista, wearing some sort of oversized sock on his head, like he was stretching it for a giant, squinted through glasses so large they had to be hurting his ears. 'A latte?'

Adele shook her head. 'They're different things. A flat white has a layer of microfoam on the top.'

'Sure.' He pulled the shot, then foamed the milk. The cup he slid over was a latte by any definition of the word. The foam climbed the sides of the cup.

Well, not everyone could be a hot Australian barista.

'We don't take cash,' said the barista, eyeing her jumbled handful of ones with disdain. 'Only card. Or Tezos. Or Bored Ape NFTs.'

Adele handed over her bent debit card, which had been taped back together twice over. The poor thing had been through some painful experiences.

As the barista rang up her order, helping himself to a sizeable tip, she regarded the silvery bags of beans arranged neatly on a sterile display. She flipped one over. Not a whit of a roast date stamped on it.

'Do you roast in-house?' she asked. The bag was so futuristic-looking it might have popped right out of *The Jetsons*.

'Nah,' said the guy offhandedly. 'We have a roaster somewhere upstate.'

'Oh.'

'We're not really a *coffee shop* coffee shop. That's kinda . . .' He drove his hand towards the ground, making a *that's beneath me* gesture. 'We're part of an incubator. You know the coworking space across the road from Nothing Up Top? They're our backers. Basically, we live and work on-site designing technologies to disrupt and delight. This shop is an opportunity to pitch our concepts to the public, see what the reception is like. It's kind of an updated take on lean start-up principles.'

'That sounds . . .' Like the worst idea she'd ever heard in her life. 'Cool.'

'There's a button you can press if you think an idea has legs. It's a sort of a conceptual round robin. We pit ideas against each other, and the ones with the most public support get to pitch in front of VCs. It's all about OPM these days.'

'Opium?' Sedatives and productivity bros didn't seem to go together.

'Other People's Money. Anyway, that one's mine. If you like it, give it a vote. We livestream all the live pitching. It's on the cup.'

Adele's latte was looking less and less appealing.

Adele tapped the thumbs down button and gave the guy a wave. 'Thanks for the latte!'

Which she chucked into the nearest trash can.

There she was, in an echoey open-plan building overlooking the Columbia Street waterfront in whose lobby clusters of people wearing Fashion with a capital F held stand-up meetings beneath deconstructed hot air balloon sculptures, while a guy dressed like Where's Wally crouched to snap a picture of a whisky bottle using the largest telephoto lens she'd ever seen. The space smelled bright and sugary, like they'd recently held a sherbet potluck.

'Can I help you?' asked a prim-looking guy with a tablet and a stylus adorned with handlebar streamers. 'I'm the roving receptionist,' he explained. 'Oh, *hey*, I know you! Riffraff! With the hot barista. My boyfriend brought home some of your *Flat Tyre* blend from the tasting night the other day. It was *so* good. Almost . . . muscular in taste?'

Adele swallowed. 'I'm glad you liked it. I'm actually here for an audition.'

'Ohhh, heavenly!' The guy scribbled effusively on his tablet.

'I hope so,' said Adele. Clearly this guy had never auditioned.

'Third floor. There's an elevator over there, or stairs if you're trying to get your steps in.'

Not wanting to arrive winded, Adele took the elevator. This maybe wasn't the best decision, as the elevator turned out to be a glass-walled contraption with a disco ball installation on the ceiling.

Hi! You're being recorded, so dance like everyone's watching! :) proclaimed a sign that displayed a QR code to the building's social media account.

Adele was no shrinking violet – she was ordinarily more like one of those bobbing sunflowers you sit on the dashboard of a car – but she'd never been one for a disco ambush. The lights flashed and flared as the elevator carried her up to the third floor. She waved awkwardly back at the people on each landing who offered some sample dance moves she could try.

Finally, the elevator pulled to a jarring halt, and Adele escaped out into a brightly coloured, if otherwise boring, landing. Bursting hungrily from the wall was a hand-crafted design made from scrunched burger wrappers that resembled a Dale Chihuly glass sculpture (Persian era), and which were hopefully the subject of a cease and desist lawsuit. Squinting, Adele deciphered the sign as spelling out the word *Heavenli*.

So that was what the greeter guy had meant.

It was amazing how many things made sense in retrospect.

A woman in a designer boxy cap and flowy purple shirt with audaciously large sleeves greeted Adele as she wandered over to where a few other perfectly coiffed souls sat awkwardly in beanbag chairs, praying they wouldn't be asked to spring to their feet with any sort of alacrity.

Adele waved as she recognised the waitress from the badminton-themed speakeasy.

'You're here for the bite and sming audition?' The woman's sleeves flapped in the air conditioning, like an airport wind sock. Her nametag beamingly introduced her as Madison. Of course.

Adele could imagine Ben's response to Madison's outfit: *How many knots can we expect today? Do we need to lower the sun umbrellas?*

'Bite and . . . sming?' Adele's mind raced to figure out what *sming* could possibly mean. Was it Zoomer slang? An acronym?

'It's a portmanteau.'

'Ohhh.' Adele felt more in the dark than Tennessee's Pickett-Pogue Park night sky viewing area.

'Well, usually the job involves taking a bite of food and smiling. It's really technical, you know. Involves some awareness of your jaw mechanics and so on. But this gig takes things up a notch, with a bite and smile *and* singing. Which is why we're tapping into the musical theatre demo. And it looks like you haven't worked in a while, so we figured you'd be hungry for the work.' Pointing at the logo behind her, Madison pantomimed munching on a Heavenli sprouted grains burger.

'I've had a career pivot,' said Adele. And a career tumble.

'Well good for you! Anyway, get up there and sing for your supper. We're going for edgy, but stopping short of psychotic. And the line is: *I'd murder my man for a Heavenli burger*.'

Adele spluttered. She reached for her water, buying herself a moment to regain her composure.

'You can change the gender if you prefer,' said Madison. 'I know it's kind of heteronormative. Also, we did have a full-on Heimlich sitch with someone who tried to add some tap dancing to their audition, so while we want you to make it your own, maybe don't play it *too* loose. Anyway. This is yours.' Handing Adele a lukewarm hamburger carton, Madison directed her towards an electrical tape cross on the vinyl planking.

Adele withdrew the burger from the carton, grimacing as shredded lettuce flopped out and on to the floor. Oops, there went a slice of tomato. And now the sauce was oozing down her hand.

Her nightmarish audition for *Dance of the Vampires* came back to her.

What would Reba do?

I'd murder my man for a Heavenli burger.

Donny's last moments flashed through her memory. The betrayal. The way he'd tried to play it off. Then the way he'd turned on her – and Ben.

Taking a deep breath, Adele slurped the sauce off her wrist, then took the biggest bite she could manage without dislocating her jaw (the job didn't pay enough for that). Grinning with the burger shoved into her cheeks like a chipmunk, she sang *I'd murder my man for this burger* in tones as sweet and chipper as Ann-Margret.

'Wow, some really interesting choices there.' Madison rose to her feet, clapping slowly. She seemed impressed, but also a touch unnerved.

'Thanks so much! You can take home what you didn't eat,' she added, reaching for a hand-held vacuum cleaner. Dropping her voice, she added conspiratorially – and extremely super-ciliously, 'I had my share of bagel years when I first moved here, too.'

'I'm sure,' said Adele, who was certain that Madison had never eaten anything less exorbitant than a Dominique Ansel cronut in her life.

Stepping out from the audition room, Adele tossed the burger remains in the bin. As she did, two familiar sets of never-ending legs (and one set of tiny chihuahua trotters) strode into view.

'Adele!' Honour ducked to give Adele a fluttery air kiss on the cheek.

'You're auditioning?' said Adele, who suddenly had a vague sense that she might actually want this job.

'Just Honour,' said Gracie, reaching in with an effusive hug. 'She's back from L.A. for the week. Good luck, sis.'

'Luck taken.' Honour snatched a handful of imaginary providence from the air.

As her sister strode into the casting room ahead of the other hopefuls sitting in the hallway, Gracie pulled out a folder from her voluminous handbag. It always struck Adele as odd that someone so rich needed a large handbag. Didn't they have people to carry their things? And what things did you need to carry anyway when you could pop into a shop and buy whatever you needed in the moment?

'I took this of you and Ben.' Gracie handed Adele the Polaroid photo she'd taken at Riffraff's Hoarderfest. 'I thought you might like it. I know that you and Donny are . . .'

'Donny's out of the picture,' said Adele shortly.

Gracie's grey eyes widened. 'Really? Not to be rude, but I'm kind of glad. He has a . . . reputation.'

Adele thought back over their endlessly disastrous dates. 'I'm sure.'

'Not in romance, I mean. But in business. He plays dirty. I always thought you were a strange match. You're too good for him.'

Adele pretended to peruse the photograph. Donny had turned out to be an absolute shit, but Adele had been at least partly responsible for his murder. *Too good* was definitely up for debate.

I'd murder my mom for this burger, Honour was singing in the background. Huh. That certainly revealed something deeply Oedipal about the Nivola twins.

Gracie winced. 'I don't miss these auditions, I have to say. Honour's determined to make it big, whereas . . . I think my place is more behind the scenes.'

Only someone as gorgeous as Gracie got to make that choice. Normal people had it made for them.

'Anyway. I mean it when I say that you and Ben, you two are the perfect pair. You know those old hippies at your shop? You're them, just a few decades younger.'

Adele swallowed, tracing a finger over the print. It had only been a few hours, but she already felt unmoored away from the shop. She missed its warmth and its casual, sociable charm. She missed counting the new leaves Audrey III had grown overnight and scooping the dregs of condensed milk directly from the can. She missed watching the shop's regulars settle into their mornings over a book or a newspaper, sipping at a drink she'd made and nibbling the mini doughnuts she'd fried. Most of all, she missed how the shop brought people from all walks together. Frank and Reba. Ember and pizza rats. Adele and Ben.

'It's a great shot.' Adele smiled at the way it showed Ben leaning into her, and how her head was tilted so unselfconsciously towards his, her lips wry, like the two of them were sharing a joke. And they probably had been: something sweary and rude about a terrible customer or one of Donny's awful business ideas. The awfulness of which she now realised had been entirely deliberate. And she'd gone along with them!

All right, so murdering Donny was a bit over the top – she could've got rid of him just as quickly by asking him from which part of the chicken caviar was produced, or if there was a prosecco region of France – but he'd been doing his best to run Riffraff into the ground so that he could buy it up and take it over.

Now it was time for some of *Adele's* ideas.

'Everyone loved the Hoarderfest photo wall, by the way. Have you thought about exhibiting? Formally, I mean,' said Adele.

Gracie's already huge eyes widened, then relaxed. 'Oh, you mean my photography, not my body.' A pause before she added, 'That was a joke.'

Adele smiled. 'Right. It's just . . . I'm starting a proper gallery wall at Riffraff, for local artists. And your photos would be perfect. We could mat them, add some annotations, price them . . . You could do a launch, if you'd like.'

Gracie sucked on her bottom lip. 'Sold. But let's skip the launch. I'm over the spotlight. I'm in my Paris Hilton restoring-vintage-radios-on-the-down-low phase.'

'Noted,' said Adele. 'Well, how about you bring by your best prints and we'll get your wall set up. Is it . . . all right if I hang on to this one? For sizing purposes?'

'I'd love that.' Gracie beamed. 'Oh, and I've been meaning to return this . . .'

She pulled the shawl she'd borrowed at the badminton speakeasy from her bag and passed it to Adele.

Adele was wrapping it around her shoulders when Honour strode out of the room, looking pleased with herself.

'The director loved it. She asked me to do this thing where I licked my arm and gave her a psychotic stare. Wild. I would never have gone with that direction. You're still here, Adele?'

'I'm on my way back to the coffee shop,' she said, hugging Gracie's picture to her chest. 'Lots to do. Congrats on the gig, Honour.'

'Hey, how about I come with you? I can check out the gallery wall space.' Gracie grimaced. 'But let's take the stairs.'

The Mug Life Chose Me

Adele felt strange being back at Riffraff: the whole shop sat differently in her mind now. Instead of a cosy, safe space for people to gather and chat, sip and think, hide and dream, it held a threat. But she was the only one who seemed to know it.

In apparent defiance of her order that Riffraff close to business, the place was thriving. Of course: she'd told Ben the shop had to *shut* its doors – but she hadn't said anything about locking them.

A ganglion of bicycles bristled beneath the well-fed exterior planter with its floral fireworks of asters and daisies. Companiable couples lounged separately over the tie-dyed chairs that Adele had commissioned Reba to reupholster for her. A raggedy professor swung in the self-standing hammock, a book open over his face. That was going to leave a distinctive tan line.

A departing customer held the shop door for her, somehow managing to balance their coffee and bagel between chin and chest. Adele held her breath as she stepped inside, the creaky floors welcoming her in. All the regulars were there: Frank, the Italian tutor, the exhausted group of teachers, Autumn from next door (sadly, sans goats). Very slowly, Adle tracked her gaze to the counter, ready to meet Ben's bright gaze.

Instead, Reba's cats-eye glasses and enormous dangly earrings flashed back at her.

Adele stiffened. What was going on? Where was Ben? Had he quit? Had he been ground up into fodder for the La Marzocco?

The door at the back of the kitchen opened, and a familiarly mussed head of hair poked through.

'Adele!' Ben had never looked so relieved to see her.

Despite herself, Adele was flattered – although only until she realised Ben was entertaining a man dressed in head-to-toe blue. And not because he was a member of the Blue Man Group.

He gestured for her to follow him. Hoisting her folio of photos higher on her shoulder, Gracie looped an arm easily through Adele's.

'In case you need backup,' she whispered, as she followed Adele through the kitchen and out into the back-of-back-of-house area.

'What's going on?' Adele couldn't hide the quaver in her voice.

'This is what happens when you give the library's Sunday budget to the fuzz,' Reba snapped over her kaftan-covered shoulder, angrily pulling an espresso shot for good measure. 'Small-time coffee shops get shaken down.'

'That's really not why I'm here,' said the officer.

Eyes narrowed, Reba spat in the cup with a vehemence that made Gracie jump.

Wow. Reba really had stuck to her anti-authoritarian roots all these years.

'I'm Adele Forrest.' Channelling her decades of acting experience, Adele reached out a hand to the officer, willing it not to shake. Well, *to shake*, but in a volitional kind of way. 'I'm the owner of Riffraff.'

'Officer Ortiz. I have a few questions.' Ortiz sipped his – oh thank the theatre gods, it was a green tea.

'Don't worry,' said Ben. 'I made it, not Reba. It's spit-free.'

Given the whole human-beings-as-beans situation, Adele wasn't sure whether this was an improvement.

'And I'm Gracie Nivola,' said Gracie, reaching over Adele. 'Of the Nivola Nivolas.'

Officer Ortiz brightened measurably at this. '*Love* your work. Huge Broadway fan. Huge fan of everything you do.'

'Even bite and sming campaigns? Because my sister is working on something unmissable.'

'I'll check it out on YouTube.' He jotted down a reminder in his notepad. 'So, I'm here about a Donald Parker. I hear the two of you were involved.' Ortiz raised an eyebrow – possibly a judgemental one – at Adele.

'If you can be involved with someone that self-involved,' muttered Ben.

'We went out a few times,' said Adele cautiously.

Ortiz nodded slowly, as though preparing to reveal terrible news. 'We have reason to believe—' he sipped his tea '—that he's fled the country.'

'Oh!' said Adele, perhaps a touch too excitedly. 'Oh, well, that's . . .'

'Tannins in this are strong. Very astringent.' Wiping his tongue with a handkerchief, Ortiz glanced at Ben. 'Where do you source your leaves?'

'Local supplier,' said Ben coolly.

Oh shit, please don't let the tea be grated human skin, thought Adele.

Ortiz smacked his lips, the way you probably would if you'd drunk a tincture of human skin. Which hopefully he had not. 'Did Donny mention upcoming travel plans? Specifically to anywhere without an extradition treaty?'

Adele thought back to the dinner during which Donny had showed off his passport in its Hermès holder. With the excitement of a private school child comparing holiday travel destinations, he'd excitedly matched his passport stamps to the restaurant wine list.

'He mentioned the Maldives? And Morocco, I think.'

'Doesn't surprise me,' said Gracie heavily. 'After the whole midterms scandal at Harvard and then the way my father had to cut him loose from his internship. I saw it firsthand. The lies. The deception. The cruffin thefts. He doesn't even have a sense of taste or smell. Covid,' she added weightily.

Ortiz regarded his pen, a novelty showgirl one that probably should have stayed in Vegas. 'Hmm. Good to know.'

Adele was aghast. None of this was, in fact, good to know. Embezzlement and theft aside, she'd endured all those awful molecular gastronomy meals, and he hadn't even been able to taste them? Not to mention the cupping event! If Ben hadn't already fed Donny to the roaster, she might have done it herself.

Gracie grabbed Ortiz's notepad and pen and started scribbling away. 'If you're looking for major purchases on his cards, he's probably using an alias. And by that I mean stolen cards. We didn't want to press charges, but . . . you know.'

Adele swallowed. Was Gracie Nivola . . . saving her ass? Never had she been more grateful for a nepotism baby.

'There's a whole pattern of behaviour we're looking

into,' said Ortiz, squinting over Gracie's willowy shoulder. 'Misrepresentation of intent to unwitting property owners, questionable funding sources.'

'Oh,' said Adele, head whirling. So it wasn't just Riffraff he'd been after. She wasn't even special enough for that. She was merely another mark in a con man's world.

'Sorry you had to learn about Donny like this,' said Ortiz. 'Must be difficult. You think you know someone, then realise it's a front for criminal behaviour.'

Adele choked back a hysterical giggle. 'I really do know how to pick them,' she said, glaring pointed daggers at Ben.

'Yeah well, this city, huh.' Ortiz took back the notepad, which Gracie had thoughtfully autographed for him. 'If you don't watch your back, it chews you up and spits you out.'

Ben burst into a coughing fit, and probably not from Adele's caustic stare.

'Sorry,' he said. 'Something went down the wrong way.'

'Maybe you sipped from my tea.' Ortiz tapped his cup with his showgirl pen. 'Anyway, thanks for the intel. And Gracie, I'll see you on Broadway, huh?'

Gracie reached into her folio and pulled out a card. 'I'm actually in talks about my first photography exhibit. But if you call this number they'll have will-call tickets waiting for you.'

'Photos! I like it. And my ma will get a kick out of the tix.' Setting his tea down in front of Adele, he added, 'If your boy turns up, give me a call, but it's safe to say he's gone.'

'Thank you,' said Adele to Gracie. 'That was . . . terrifying. How are you so comfortable talking to the police?'

Every time Adele so much as saw a cop car she worried

she'd get pulled over for running a red light at speed while smuggling counterfeit handbags and swilling zinfandel from the bottle. Even if she wasn't behind the wheel of a car. And had never done any of those things. Especially the zinfandel, which was a variety she loathed even more than chardonnay.

'My dad,' said Gracie with a lithe shrug. 'And I mean, there are some perks to—' she waved a hand vaguely '—all of this.'

Adele didn't doubt it. But she was hardly going to say anything. Here she was, owner of a coffee shop that had been chowing down on its clientele for goodness knows how long. Not to mention the accomplice in a murder. And now in the covering up of said murder.

'I knew that Donny was a bad egg,' said Reba. 'I don't trust anyone who buys their clothes new. But at least you didn't talk. Never talk. It only creates problems.'

'You're telling me,' said Frank, who had come up for a top-off of his decaf.

Reba held the pot away from him. 'With you, talk is only half the problem. The rest of the problem is you.'

'Reebs,' warned Ben, extricating the pot from her ring-smothered fingers. 'If you're behind the counter, you're nice to Frank.'

He topped up Frank's cup. Adele winced, hoping the coffee hadn't been brewed with corpse beans. But she wasn't about to bring that up in front of a whole room of regulars. Anyway, maybe it was healthier to wean them off the tainted coffee than force them to go cold turkey.

Mom was right: you really could justify anything if you tried hard enough.

'But it hurts to be nice to Frank,' pouted Reba. 'Anyway, I

mean it. You want Celia Fjutcha on your side if you're going to blab. Willa's also good if you're looking for temporal or celestial guidance.'

Frank passed Reba a cookie and popped a ten-dollar bill in the tip jar.

'For you,' he said.

'Bah,' snapped Reba, taking a generous bite from the cookie.

Leaving the two old hippies to bicker, Adele steered Gracie over to the recessed wall area currently guarded by a bright orange wing chair and a few vintage music posters. 'So, for your exhibition, I'm thinking here.'

Gracie did a Disney princess jump. 'Oh, I love it.'

'You can decide whether you want to sell the pieces, or have them on display. We're fine either way.'

Gracie pulled a tiny tape measure from her portfolio and started measuring. As she did, Adele shot a look back at Ben, who'd returned to his spot behind the counter and was busily pouring a flat white. An actual flat white, not three lattes in a trench coat.

'You. Me. Later,' she mouthed.

'Abso-fucking-lutely,' he mouthed back.

By Any Beans Necessary

'So,' said Adele as she turned over the sign on the door to read *Back Later, Loves*. 'I think we have some things to talk about.'

In the way that had become second nature, she gathered all the remaining dishes from the tables and packed them into the dishwasher, which thankfully was one of the few appliances in the shop that worked as it should.

When she'd started the load, Ben passed her a chocolatey square in a paper napkin. 'You're right. Made you this. It's a hedgehog slice. Doesn't contain hedgehogs: those are illegal in the boroughs.'

Adele squinted at it. 'What about people?'

'People can't be illegal,' he said, rolling his eyes good-naturedly. 'Come on. We're going to the cemetery.'

He pulled a light jacket on – nicely structured, definitely vintage – and held the door for her.

'I see we're at the point where we can laugh about this,' said Adele, shrugging into a cardigan as she finished off the hedgehog slice. (Dammit, it was delicious.) 'You work through the stages of grief really quickly.'

'Jeez, Adele. Makes sense that someone so sunny would be full of burns.'

Adele folded her arms, trying to pretend that she hadn't smeared chocolate all over her cardigan sleeves. 'You're Australian. You should know the dangers of the sun.'

Ben guided her past a gathering of trash bags heaped into a mound that resembled a family of pongy snowmen. Pizza Rat blew Adele a kiss.

'I'm trying to fix this, you know,' said Ben.

'How? You can't un-grind and un-roast someone. It's basic chemistry.'

Basic chemistry. Like the way she got zapped every time she brushed past him. Or just now, when their arms grazed as they both stepped to avoid an unsavoury sidewalk installation painted in stomach acid and carrots. Why were there always carrots?

'Okay, so you're trying to fix this. By . . . going to the cemetery. Do you need to make a phone call?'

'Reception's still shit at Doralee's, huh.' Ben was hustling easily up the hill, which in the late summer had become a jumbling profusion of wildflowers and overgrown bushes. Sparrows and squirrels darted about in their strange, freeze-frame way.

It must be nice to have long legs, thought Adele, clocking two steps for his every one. He was even squishing twice the number of invasive spotted lanternflies she was doing her best to wipe out. (Ordinarily Adele didn't squish things, but these were an exception.)

'Yeah, and the toucan's on its last legs. The cemetery's also . . . kind of a nice place to think.' Panting, Adele frowned in sudden memory. 'Did I see you here earlier today? With Kyra?'

'I *knew* that was you fleeing down the embankment.' Ben

paused, waiting for her to catch up. 'We've been working on something.'

They'd passed through the enormous Gothic gates and were hurrying along the neat pathways with their thoughtful stone edging. Mournful stone statues and mossy graves wove between the newer polished headstones with their built-in vases bursting with flowers and pinwheels. Here and there, wizened widows and widowers shared the day's stories with their loved one; in other spots people picnicked or flipped through the pages of intriguing hardcovers.

Ben led her over to the greenhouse, which Adele had never dared enter. It seemed so strange: an entire conservatory built to hold the remains of some dead guy. All it needed was its own model train set, like the Biltmore greenhouse in Asheville, North Carolina.

'I think it's nice,' Ben said, when she expressed this. 'The tombstones and mausoleums are just markers. Whereas this is a place of renewal.'

As Ben pushed open the door for her, the humidity of the greenhouse hit them the way the air in the bathroom does after you've taken a long, feeling-sorry-for-yourself shower without remembering to turn on the fan.

Adele swallowed, feeling fretful: she hated not being able to breathe. It was the flipside of her typical anxiety dream: showing up to an audition, opening her mouth and . . . nothing.

The greenhouse was a profusion of glossy leaves and an explosion of summer flowers glistening under the hydration of the endless misters. This didn't bode well for her hair: she'd be a poodle in minutes. But who didn't love a poodle?

She reached out to touch a huge pom-pom of a dahlia. 'The grounds are working well,' she said.

'That's not what I want you to see. Look.'

Fingertips pressed gently against the small of her back, Ben guided her through the greenhouse. Adele held out a languid hand, idly brushing against the hot-pink bougainvillea and the dangling yellow flowers of angel's trumpets. To Adele's delight, a vivid white admiral butterfly landed on her outstretched fingers, its wings slowly flapping. She emitted a happy squeak.

'You'd better make a wish,' said Ben as the butterfly floated off again.

'Already done,' said Adele, eyes scrunched closed with the hope of the wish she held tightly in her heart. Not a wish so much as a vision of a possible future.

'Here.' The pressure of Ben's fingertips directed her gently to the left and into a room lush with rows and rows of trees from which cheerful strings of reddish-green berries dangled. They reminded Adele of a miniaturised version of the decorative plastic grapes at Meemaw's house. Something about the shape of the leaves and berries rang a bell.

She reached for a hair tie, pinning her curls in a messy loop.

As she did, a gentle, citrusy aroma twined around her, playing around her neck and kissing her cheeks, the way—

Not now, Adele. They had the small complication of mass murder to work through first. And the larger complication of the whole secrecy around said mass murders. Which actually felt like the greater crime.

Ben perched on a wrought-iron garden seat. He plucked a berry from one of the trees and rolled it around in the palm of his hand. After a weighty silence, he looked up at her, taking in her stony expression. His whole demeanour was one of regret.

'I'm so bloody sorry about all this, Adele. It was shitty to keep you in the dark. It's your business, after all. Your . . . *life*.

I just wanted to protect you. I reckoned I'd be able to figure something out, but it kept getting worse.'

With a sigh, Adele sat down next to him, pulling up her feet and wrapping her hands around her knees. She hadn't forgiven him, not yet, but she was starting to understand. In her efforts to save the shop she'd been careening from worse to worst herself. And she'd made every decision without consulting Ben.

'How long has it been like this?' she asked. 'With the roaster.'

'I don't really know.' Ben picked the skin off the berry he was holding, revealing pale green innards. 'Doralee handled it. She never really let me down there, not until she was sick. And then she made me promise I wouldn't leave it.'

Adele nodded. 'It was in her will. That you stay on at the shop.'

'Not that I have any choice. No one's lining up to interview for a job where your responsibilities involve feeding a murderous roaster for tips.'

Adele wasn't so sure about that. The job *did* come with free rent.

'You're not . . . thinking of leaving?' she said. Sacrificial obligations aside, was life at Riffraff so bad that Ben wanted to run off back to the Antipodes? Making coffee and poking fun at Adele couldn't be worse than a whole day in transit, could it?

'It's hard to get excited about a job when you know you're gonna woodchip the next person who orders a lemonade mixed with a shot of espresso. It's like a shit version of Shirley Jackson's *The Lottery*.'

Adele reached forward to pick a berry of her own, thinking over what Ben had said about things with the machine getting worse. Was it getting hungrier? If so, *why*? And why *now*, when Doralee had presumably been able to keep it under control for years? She wished she had some kind of timeline that would help her figure it all out, the way she relied on her song lists to help dig deep into the characters she played on stage.

As she poked her berry with a nail, she realised where she'd seen these before. Doralee's book! 'These are coffee beans. Off coffee trees!'

Ben raised his eyebrows, impressed. 'Gold star for you. They're rooted into the plots below. I'm hoping . . .'

Adele's stomach did a triple pike that barely stuck the landing. A cemetery greenhouse. Kyra's coffee grounds. 'Corpse beans. You're hoping they'll be enough to satisfy the roaster.'

Ben looked relieved that she approved.

'Well, let's test them out!' Tossing her berry aside, Adele leapt to her feet, pulling Ben with her. 'So what do we do? Throw the coffee fruit into the roaster and hope?'

Ben's horrified expression suggested she'd committed a horrific coffee faux pas.

'I mean, it eats *bodies*,' she added. 'Are you sure it's that finicky about what you put into it?'

Ben shuddered as though she'd suggested NFL were superior to Aussie Rules. ('Why is it called football if all you do is throw the bloody thing?')

'You'd never put raw berries into a roaster.' *You monster.* 'Ordinarily there are two ways of processing coffee so that it's ready to roast. Washed and natural. Washed, you float the fruit in water, then use a machine to process away the flesh. Natural, you let it dry in the sun until the flesh melts away.'

Adele thought that maybe she was a tea drinker after all. 'Which one's the fastest?'

'The one that involves grabbing a bunch of beans and running them through a clothes dryer.'

And that was how they ended up at The Mean Sheets of Brooklyn with two enormous red-stained bags.

'It's not blood,' said Ben to a guy lounging on the bench seating wearing merely a pair of Wonder Woman undies – Wondies? 'It's coffee fruit.'

'I don't give a *shit*,' said the guy with a shrug. 'Mine's blood. One tough *stain*.'

He had a weirdly poetic way of emphasising every fifth syllable, like he'd been fed metrical feet as a child. If that wasn't a Gerber flavour, it should be, given that your little one needed to show that they were Ivy League potential as soon as possible. Ugh, now she was thinking about Harvard, and by extension, Donny.

Making sure the bags were tied off, Adele helped Ben jam them into the dryer, which she fed with coins she'd filched from the tip jar. Was this the first time she'd officially paid herself from her work at the shop? What a milestone!

'What are you grinning at?' asked Ben as he started up the dryer. The machine thudded away like a meat tenderiser.

'My first barista paycheque,' she replied, flashing a fistful of coins.

'Look at all that shrapnel. It's like the Detectorists Gone Wild.'

She popped a coin in his shirt pocket. 'That's to make you shut up.'

Ben pulled it back out and folded it gently back into her hand. 'It'll take more than the Tennessee minimum wage.'

'This guy, he's in *love*. You two, you are *cute*.' After grabbing an IKEA-yellow shirt and matching stovepipes out of the dryer, the guy pulled them on, spinning on the spot so effortlessly that Adele almost gave him Richard's number.

Shame he was out of the biz these days. 'How'd I do? Clean? *Tight?*'

'You look great,' said Adele cheerfully.

'Good. I got me a *date*. Good luck with those *beans*,' said the guy. Then, under his breath as he strolled out of the door: 'Hippies.'

The shop was shivering like a wet dog by the time Adele and Ben returned with their newly dried haul of corpse beans. It had taken multiple loads and all of Adele's quarters, but finally they had something resembling the fat, dried lentils that unroasted coffee was meant to look like.

'Mm, notes of dryer sheets,' joked Adele, lifting a handful of beans to her nose.

'Better than notes of the dry cleaner.' Ben's mouth quirked. 'That bloody cupping night. I thought you were on to me and that you were taking the piss.'

'I'd never take the piss. It's unsanitary.'

Mrow, agreed Ember, who had just come from his litter box. He snaked around their legs, yellow eyes wide as he nervously sniffed their bounty. The shop shook again, almost knocking Adele off her feet. The roaster was starved.

'When was the last time you fed it?' whispered Adele.

'Donny,' said Ben, with a brief but not entirely sincere pause in remembrance of the dead. 'Righto. Help me lug these down the stairs.'

The two of them awkwardly manoeuvred the bags of dried beans down the death-trap stairs, muttering and swearing in turn as they stubbed toes and fought gravity's best efforts. The rumbling and grumbling of the roaster didn't help: the floor was having a seismic experience.

The roaster's red lights flashed as they reached solid ground, and with a hiss and a roar, its drum began to turn. The blades of the cooling vat spun menacingly, flashing as they caught the wan beam of the solitary schoolhouse light.

'Let's give this a try.' Ben's voice was tight. His hand trembled as he scooped the beans into the roaster's hopper, spilling a few across the floor. The machine roared furiously.

'C'mon, mate. They're nice and corpsey. Grown in the remains of Brooklyn's best; fed on the remains of Brooklyn's rest.'

'You have the heart of a poet.'

'So the reviews say. Some of them. All right, here goes.' Ben yanked the lever and stepped back, his hand finding Adele's as the roaster clattered and boomed, a thunderstorm inside the small space. The exhaust system sucked and hissed like a desperate smoker wheeled outside a hospital ward for one last ciggie. *Ah, that's the stuff.*

Adele was torn between the delight of feeling Ben's fingers entwined with hers and the sheer horror of reliving the experience of watching Donny being devoured right in front of her.

The rich, smoky aroma of roasting beans filled the room, the way the stench from Donny's Vachetta leather case had. Adele swallowed, her fingers tightening around Ben's.

She jumped as the beans inside crackled like freshly doused Rice Bubbles. Flames leapt and licked.

'First crack,' Ben reassured her. 'It's the water vaporising inside. Nothing too scary. We're going to take this one through second crack all the way over to French. This one's for you, Clarence.'

Adele chewed her lip. 'He's not . . .'

'He's alive and cranking out his bullshit reviews,' promised Ben.

The crackling reached fever pitch, then slowed. The air grew thicker and smokier, searing Adele's lungs.

Ben pulled his shirt up over his mouth, coughing. 'I reckon there's something wrong with the ventilation system. Let me go up and—'

Adele grabbed him and pulled him back to her. 'Are you serious right now! What if the machine eats me?'

Ben looked askance at her. 'If it was going to do that, it already would have.'

Well that was heartening. Adele flapped away the smoke curling around her face, trying to breathe as shallowly as possible. What if the fire department came again?

'At least let me open the door,' she said.

'We're almost there. Can you hear that? Second crack.'

There was more crackling, although lighter this time. Then, finally, the roaring and thrumming lessened, and the cooling tray spun into action, its blades swooping and chopping at the beans.

The machine belched, then settled. The striped schoolhouse light, which had been swinging like a manic four-year-old, slowly came to a rest. Its flickering bulb buzzed and moaned, slowly returning to full brightness.

'Did we do it?' whispered Adele, staring at the machine.

'I don't know.' Ben stepped forward gingerly, as though anticipating that the machine might tilt forward and suck him in. The machine gurgled, but stopped short of any homicidal moves.

Ember gave a huff, then leapt lightly up on the top of the roaster, curling up on its warm drum.

'Well, someone's happy with the results,' said Adele.

Ben grunted: he was busy doing his usual assessment of his roast. Having scooped a spoonful of beans from the cooling tray, he bit down on a bean, chewing thoughtfully. Then he grabbed the pen hanging from the leather strap glued to the desk and scrawled his tasting notes into the template printed on the page, leaning back to check the weight being shown on the scale.

'Not bad,' he said, reviewing his notes. 'I mean, it's no Topknot Guy, but it's a quality roast. And the local beans are a selling point.'

'You're really thorough about this stuff, aren't you,' said Adele, watching with one eyebrow raised. He was shading ovals and circling terms with the diligence of a kid being paid to take someone else's college exam.

'I log every roast, like Doralee taught me.'

Adele peered over his shoulder, admiring his neat script. 'How far does that logbook go back?'

Ben flipped the book back to its first page. 'This one? A couple of months. But Doralee's went back years. Back to the very first roast, I reckon.'

'And they all look like this?'

'Hers have worse handwriting. And glittery purple ink. But otherwise, not far off.' Ben set down the pen, hesitating as he gathered the strength to ask her something.

But Adele was already hurrying up the creaky steps. She was going to find Doralee's purple doodle books if it meant emptying the entire apartment out into the courtyard.

'There's something I need to do at Doralee's. Stay here; don't get eaten.'

'That's the goal,' said Ben, taking a step away from the roaster.

Déjà Brew

Adele turned the apartment upside down (not that it looked any different from before) looking for Doralee's roasting annals. Of *course* that was what the marbled, glittery notebook had been. Not doodles or geographical coordinates or lottery numbers.

Ouch. Something poked at her finger, giving her a papercut. Sucking on her finger, she grabbed at the vicious stationery item: a sparkly loyalty card adorned with a stylised hand with a watchful eye in the middle. *Willa Fjutcha. Psychic*.

It was the one Celia had given her the day she'd learned about the inheritance.

Huh. Where'd that come from?

As she turned the card over, a knock at the door made Adele jump. She spun around, expecting Kyra with a box of brownies and a bottle of rosé, but instead, a skinny woman dressed in a sequinned bodysuit stood there, sparkling like a disco ball in the glow cast by the fairy lights draped around the courtyard. In her hands was a familiar cloth-covered book.

Adele blinked. Minus the ferret and the chain-smoking, the woman bore an uncanny resemblance to Celia Fjutcha. She glanced down at the shimmery card in her hand. Was it the light (and the wine she was sipping as she worked) or had one of the fingers in the image curled over? Had she . . . summoned Willa?

'Serendipity,' said Willa, in the same sharp accent as Celia. Adele was having a hard time believing that they were separate people. Had they ever been seen in the same place? Or was this a *Parent Trap* situation?

'I was on my way to grab some hot chips and vinegar. Before my cemetery tour,' said Willa, as though this explained things. Her earrings swung hypnotically from her effusive gesticulation. 'I remembered that Doralee's apartment was in the neighbourhood. Thought you might want this. It found its way to me after the yard sale you had at the shop.'

As Adele took the book, Willa stiffened abruptly, the way psychics always did in the movies before they started talking in tongues. Or in a pseudo-British accent. Adele drew in a breath. Something strange was happening.

'I feel something . . .' said the psychic, her purply eyebrows diving. 'There's a spirit here with us.'

'Doralee?' whispered Adele. Her great-aunt's presence loomed so large that it seemed impossible her spirit wasn't circling around them.

'No. Someone . . . with a powerful name. A musical name. Someone whose resting place is not where it's supposed to be. Someone . . . furry.'

Adele blinked. 'A furry?' This was a very unusual game of *Guess Who?*

'No, no, they're two doors down. A zebra.' Willa huffed a breath out of the side of her mouth. 'This is someone of the . . . canine persuasion.'

Adele could only think of one individual who matched this description.

'With the name . . . Janis?'

'Yes! Janis!' barked Willa. She grabbed at the strand of orange beads around her neck, tugging at them as though a deceased sausage dog were speaking through her. Now *there* was the speaking in tongues.

A slender finger pointed at the paw print-stippled vessel that Adele had found in the back of Doralee's wardrobe and which now had pride of place on the windowsill.

Adele glanced up at it, eyes wide. All this time she'd thought the brass container was a pepper grinder. But this explained the picture on the front. Maybe Sausage Doggone wasn't a brand of spice after all.

Oh shit, she thought. Mom had mentioned using it to season her Lebanese takeout. Adele was as bad as Ben! Worse! Eating doggy ashes was even worse than eating ground-up human gizzards!

'You look like you've seen a ghost,' said Willa.

'A . . . bit,' said Adele, slightly baffled by this entire encounter. It all seemed bizarrely fortuitous. 'How did you do that?'

Willa waggled her beads. 'Eh, I saw the urn up there on your shelf. I can spot a doggy cremation vessel a mile away. Especially a doggy I knew personally. Here. Want me to tell your fortune, kid?'

Magnificent nails flashing in the dim light, Willa wrapped her hands around Adele's, flipping them over so that Adele's palms faced up. Apparently in addition to telling futures she also practised karate.

'Ah. Ah! You've got a lotta love in your life, huh? See this line here?' She traced one of the creases on Adele's palm. 'There's

304

someone who loves you in ways they're not willing to admit. But they'll show it. In their own way.'

'What about the clamminess?' joked Adele, who had a desperate urge to wipe her hands on her jeans.

Willa chuckled. 'That's because of the sunspot activity. There's going to be another flare, mark my words.'

That's right – hadn't Trix said something about that? Her dad had a PhD in astrophysics from MIT, so he was probably trustworthy when it came to this stuff.

'And with that flare will come big changes. *Big* changes. Time to shed the worries of the past and usher in the new.' Willa set down Adele's hands and took a sip of Adele's wine like she was performing a strange sacrament.

'Like a celestial spring cleaning.' Adele had never considered herself one for what Dad called the *woo-woo world*, but then she'd never found herself embroiled in a murder mystery involving a homicidal coffee roaster.

'Yeah, sure.' Having polished off Adele's wine, Willa grabbed one of Doralee's mirrored resin elephants, hefting it as though trying to communicate with the spirit of Dumbo. 'I'm taking this. Anyway, I gotta go. The ghost hunters are waiting for me. But read the book. The answers you seek, as the saying goes, are in there.'

The Riffraff doorbell gave a world-weary tinkle, as though it had grown tired of working overtime and was considering unionising. Sliding a bookmark into the Ionesco collection he was reading, Ben stood.

'What have you got there?' he asked, confused. Although maybe that was a residual Ionesco thing.

'Present for Frank.' Adele set down the urn, which she'd

305

dressed up in a sparkly gift bag with purple tissue paper. 'It's a secret. But! I have something else.'

She slapped down Doralee's roasting notes on the communal table.

'Groovy. This thing's retro as. Did it come with a mood ring?'

Adele waggled her index finger, which was indeed bejewelled with a mood ring – a gift from Willa on the way out. According to its colour, she was feeling productive. And also a few other emotions she wasn't about to say aloud, in case the Algorhythmix machine was still listening. 'There are other volumes, but I think this one is where our troubles begin.' She flipped the book open and spun it over towards Ben.

'The sixth of September, 1994,' he said. 'That's the last time I saw . . .'

'I know.' Adele thought back to the photo sitting on Ben's desk upstairs: his grinning face and glossy bowl cut. Ilona's loving but haunted expression. The reversed date that suggested the photo had been taken with an Australian camera – Ben's Dad's.

It was all connected somehow, but how?

Ben turned his face away for a moment, trying to compose himself. 'Sorry. Grief is one of those things that moves the opposite of linearly.'

Adele's heart ached for him. All she wanted to do was wrap him up in a hug, but the front door had something to say about that.

A jingle, then Frank's familiar shuffling footsteps.

'I left my damn reading glasses behind,' the old hippie explained, patting his front pocket. 'Usually I have a spare pair, but those *were* my spare pair. And I'm up to the good bit in *On the Beach*.'

306

'All of that's the good bit,' said Ben.

Adele hadn't read it, but she was inclined to agree: she liked beaches.

'Roasting log, huh?' Frank squinted at the heavily orna-mented book, holding it at arm's length as he tried to bring Doralee's handwriting into focus. 'I remember that day. It was during that blasted electromagnetic storm. Fried my record player. Blacked out the whole neighbourhood. We should've stuck with roasting on the popcorn maker.'

Adele smiled at the thought of Doralee holding a foil-covered pan over an open flame. Old-school.

'Do you know what happened?' Ben added quietly. 'To my mum, I mean. It was the one thing Doralee never told me.'

Frank hesitated, then sank down in a seat with a relieved groan. He waggled his toes in his Birkenstocks. 'It was a strange day. It wasn't just the electronics that went weird. People did, too. All that energy in the air – it had to go somewhere, I guess.'

Looking for something to do with his hands, Ben went over to the Lost and Found box, sifting through it in search of Frank's glasses. He lined up six pairs on the communal table for Frank to select from.

Frank poked through them, thinking. 'I don't know the details – we were out on the street watching the borealis. And there were a lot of mushrooms involved. But I remember that your mom was helping Doralee fix something on the roaster, and that your dad wouldn't leave her alone. He was determined to take you back to Australia with him. We could hear your parents fighting all the way out in the courtyard. But then the aurora hit – man, what a sight – and they stopped. There was this huge power surge, and then the lights went out across the borough. All that remained was the borealis. It was beautiful. You can see it there on that picture on the wall.'

A pair of purple glasses propped on his nose, Frank gestured at the framed picture Adele had noticed on her first day. The green tinge in the background of the portrait of Ben and Ilona finally made sense. It wasn't sun-faded: it was the borealis. And now Adele knew who had been cut from the photo.

A set of novelty sunglasses snapped in Ben's hands. He set them aside, muttering something about the quality of 'servo sunnies'. 'What happened after that?'

'At first I hoped that maybe your parents worked it all out under the beauty of the aurora. But I suppose there are some things even nature can't fix.' Frank toyed with a pair of glasses with frames shaped like daisies. Reba would like those. 'I always figured your parents went their separate ways. That your mom took you somewhere with her.'

Ben sagged. No: he'd been put alone on a flight to regional Victoria.

'You never asked?' Adele whispered to Frank, trying to keep the disbelief from her voice.

'In these kinds of situations, it's better not to ask too many questions. Information is danger.'

Hell hath no fury like an abusive man, thought Adele.

There was a pained silence cut only by Ember's rumbling purrs. The cat leapt up, determinedly headbutting a pair of glasses off the table.

Adele reached for the wayward pair, which were ambitiously rhinestone-studded. 'Do you … think the roaster had something to do with it?'

'What would a roaster have to do with anything? Machines

are machines.' Frank peered through the daisy glasses, his eyes enormous through the thick lenses. 'I think these are the ones. They're full of flower power. Anyway. I'd better leave you kids to it.'

Judging from the look on Ben's face, the kids had a lot to ponder.

'Before you go.' With a small smile, Adele set down the gift bag containing the pepper shaker urn on the table.

Frank peeked inside, suddenly overcome with emotion. Pulling out the mandala-studded vessel, he slowly turned it in his weathered hand. Dust bloomed from it – ugh, it wasn't airtight. 'Janis. You found Janis.'

'She was under our noses all along.' And in Mom's takeout, but Adele wasn't going to mention that.

Frank dabbed tears from his eyes, his thick skull-shaped wedding ring flashing in the soft light. 'I can't wait to show this to Reba. Maybe she'll finally forgive me. Maybe she'll finally love me again.'

Having emerged from his memories, Ben whacked Frank with the roasting book, which, well, fair enough.

'Frank, you nong. I can't think of anyone in the world who loves you more than Reebs. You know she's been making me put almond milk in your drinks all these years. For someone who hates you, she's dead-set worried about your cholesterol.'

Frank couldn't argue with that. Raising the urn in thanks, he let himself out.

'So,' said Ben, his green eyes looking at her appraisingly.

'So,' said Adele, her own hazel ones surely looking positively lascivious.

Beneath them, the floor rumbled. Ben sighed.

'Well, I s'pose we have our answer on the cemetery beans. You should head home, just in case.'

'It's probably a good thing,' said Adele. 'I didn't bring pyjamas.'

'Who wears pyjamas these days?'

Mugs and Kisses

It was 5 a.m.

Adele's phone alarm looked at her as if to say, *what the fuck?* So too did her phone's facial recognition technology, which insultingly made her type in her passcode after laughing at her dishevelled morning self. Still, she'd done it: she'd trained herself to get out of bed at this inhumane hour of the day. Even if that was because she had a good-looking, Australian incentive to do so.

After a rummage through Doralee's wardrobe and a shower that was slightly wasteful in length – Ben would disapprove, she thought, thinking back to the time he'd told her about Melbourne's water restrictions and the egg timer he kept in the shower caddy – she was looking somewhat more shevelled.

She emerged out into a souvlaki breakfast gathering that was either getting started or in the midst of winding down – she couldn't tell.

'Morning, Adele!' came the tipsy refrain.

Grabbing the plump, tzatziki-heavy souvlaki that was generously offered to her, Adele hurried down the street towards Riffraff, which from the outside still appeared to be slumbering. This was the time of day that deliveries were made, garbage was picked up, and caffeine-seeking early birds were turned away. At least they were only after coffee. This sort of behaviour had been a lot more depressing the time Adele had worked in a bar with a noon open.

The door was unlocked as usual, but the shop was quiet. Adele's heart immediately started thrumming like a bassline from *Hair*.

'Ben?' she called. No answer.

'Ben?' she repeated, a tremble in her voice.

'Right here.'

As she spun, almost tripping over the wooden steamer trunk that had gashed her shins a few times – that damn table! – strong arms caught her. There it was, as always: that frisson of electricity that coursed up her like she was the Bride of Frankenstein. A very hot Frankenstein.

'I thought the roaster had chopped you up into pieces,' she chastised.

'Well, this is a nice plot twist, then, isn't it?'

'I suppose it is.' Adele stared up at him. It was worth every bit of the neckache to drink him in like he was a caramel latte with extra cream.

The door swung open with the kind of violence only seen from parents during Little League games.

'Fire safety,' called a brawny guy with an insufferably punchable face. Or maybe it was a normal face and Adele was projecting. 'We heard there was an issue with your smoke suppression system.'

'Fucken oath,' whispered Ben, scowling. 'It's always *something*!'

Adele nodded in the direction of the murderous roaster. 'I mean . . . it could be worse.'

While Ben was poking around at the ventilation system with the fire safety guy, Adele took up her now-familiar position behind the counter and began pouring the morning crowd's orders with a finesse that surprised even herself.

'Look at you go,' said Gracie Nivola, who'd strutted in with the leggy confidence of a prize-winning filly. She sipped at her long black as she rearranged the photos in the nook that had become her exhibition space, letting out a squeal of delight when she saw the red *sold* stickers sitting like stop signs on half of the pictures.

'That cop came by again.' Adele tapped the photos Ortiz had bought. 'The others were shop regulars with excellent taste.'

'Honestly, if I could, I'd buy this one.' Gracie pointed to the framed photo of the aurora that had always fascinated Adele – and which Frank had brought up just last night. 'There's so much movement in it. If you get up really close, you can see these figures dancing around this huge machine. Hey look.'

Lifting a finger to her lips, Gracie nodded towards the carved table where the Italian tutor was running her usual morning lesson with two students who had had a clear crush on each other.

'Today our lesson is about how to talk about your relationship status in Italian,' said the Italian tutor, as the tutees squirmed in the love seat they were crammed into, doing their best not to touch each other. 'Who wants to go first? Clara, *hai un ragazzo?*'

313

'Um . . .' Clara sipped her drink, trying to figure out how to answer this without bearing her heart on her sleeve.

'All right. Niko, *hai una ragazza?*'

Now it was Niko's turn to test the depths of the chair's cushioning. 'Um . . .'

Hurrying over to the counter, Adele swooped in with a plate of treats. '*Biscotto?*' she offered, breaking the tension between the poor students.

Gracie's camera clicked.

Just then, there was a commotion outside. Adele turned to squint out the window, where two bright hippies were jostling each other for the right to be the first through the door. She grinned broadly: it looked as though Janis's ashes had worked their magic.

The doorbell jingled, and Frank and Reba burst through the door in a surfeit of colour and colourful language.

'Everyone!' exclaimed Reba, jumping up on the steamer trunk in a swirl of shawls. Her beaded yin-yang earrings swung in her silvery hair. 'Frank and I have some news. Get up here, you old bastard.'

Using a standing lamp for balance, Frank hauled himself up on the steamer trunk, which gave an indignant groan. And fair enough: it had gone into retirement a hundred years earlier.

Ember jumped up with them, purring self-importantly.

'You will be delighted to learn,' began Reba, 'that we've overcome our previously irreconcilable differences.'

A few cheers went up around the room. The Italian students grinned shyly at each other. Even the disillusioned teachers seemed vaguely pleased.

'About bloody time, you silly sausages,' called Ben.

'On account of the fact that Frank finally found our dog. Which he lost.'

This garnered some mixed applause.

'Our dead dog,' added Frank. 'And I didn't lose her. She was misplaced.'

Only one confused person was applauding now. Adele finally appreciated those between-movements clappers.

Ben caught Adele's eye and winked.

Adele responded in kind.

'So in light of that, we're ready for a fresh start.' Reba beamed. 'Which means that we're renewing our vows, suckers! And we're doing it right here at Riffraff, the place that's been our second home for decades.'

'Our first home is being fumigated,' added Frank. 'Not my fault. I've been living in the garage.'

Alas, Adele knew from her parents' decades of quarrelling that this probably wasn't sufficient defence.

'Ben! Adele!' Reba slung twin coasters at them, earning a murmur of approval from the ultimate frisbee team at the back of the room. 'When can we do this thing? We're old. And impatient.'

'And our backs hurt from standing on this steamer trunk.' Frank was knuckling his lower back.

'Are you free tomorrow afternoon?' suggested Adele. Ben nodded heartily.

'Done and done! The day before Tie Dyepalooza – we can do that as our honeymoon, Frank. You're all invited. No gifts. Coffee's on me,' said Reba, which meant the coffee was on Frank. Who didn't seem to mind – he was already reaching for his wallet, a tie-dyed Reba special.

Adele grabbed the stick of chalk by the blackboard and

scrawled in the upcoming events column, as neatly as she could, *Frank and Reba's wedding.*

'Look at that, hon,' said Frank proudly, reaching for Reba's hand. 'It's official.'

'Oh, stop it.' Out of habit, Reba snatched her hand away. But then she relented. She twined her arm through Frank's, helping him step down from the steamer trunk.

'Watch your shins,' called Adele.

'Why do you think I wear layers?' retorted Reba. 'It's aesthetic *and* protective.'

'All right, everyone.' Frank pulled out a paperback from his back pocket and waggled it. 'Enough gawping. Back to it. I've got a date with my book, and Reba is dyeing. Dyeing with an E.'

A relieved murmur went around.

Arms twined like a human challah, Frank and Reba took their seats next to each other at the communal table. Adele would never risk Reba's ire by saying it, but the colourful hippie looked as happy as she'd ever seen her.

'What have you got there?' Adele asked Ben as she bussed back a clattery stack of plates and cups.

'A dessert for the lovers,' said Ben, dusting chocolate over the top of a huge cream-filled bowl. He held out a spoon. 'Want a taste?'

Adele nibbled at the offered dessert, suddenly shy. She held a hand over her mouth as she savoured the decadent combination of coffee, chocolate and mascarpone. 'Oh, that's good. Here. I'll take it out to them.'

Her insides asparkle, Adele carried out tiramisù to Frank and Reba, who were deep in discussion over whether the tie-dyed scarves Reba had pulled from her bag needed an additional whirl of pink.

'Compliments of the Australian,' Adele said with a grin.

'Coffee. Bringing people together forever,' said the Italian tutor, toasting with her espresso cup.

Emboldened by this, Clara finally chimed in with a response to the tutor's earlier question. '*Non ho un ragazzo*,' she whispered. 'But there's someone I like.'

Me too, thought Adele, watching Ben as he carefully poured a perfect latte art rose.

I Love You a Latte

Love was in the air, and on the menu for today.

Adele, Ben and the shop's growing assortment of theatre friends had spent all night – and much of the morning – preparing the coffee shop for Frank and Reba's nuptials. They'd enlisted the help of every prop master and set designer they knew, and the result was a bohemian wonderland of rhapsodic proportions. Wildflowers and peacock feathers burst from each table, and tiny tea candles bobbed in Ilona's beautiful pots and vessels. Ben had strung fairy lights across the stained-glass feature window and over Audrey III, giving the shop an ethereal effect. Even Ember grumpily sported a daisy-chain collar. A yellow Kombi van pulled up front.

'Here she comes!' said Trix, clapping over the sound of Oreo the goat bleating a welcome from the studio next door. The gang of theatre teens hurried to the windows, trying to catch a glimpse of Reba.

Ben set down the needle on the newly refurbished record player, and the Grateful Dead's 'If I Had the World to Give' played quietly, the pang of Jerry Garcia's guitar making tears well in

Adele's eyes. She dabbed at them with a fingertip, her thoughts wandering to the songs she might play at her own wedding.

Ben raised an eyebrow. She wrenched her gaze away, her cheeks hot.

The coffee shop doorbell jingled, saving Adele from her embarrassment. Stroking the potato-wielding ferret on her shoulder, Celia Fjutcha pulled it open.

'Wouldn't miss this for the world,' she said. 'Although I gotta bounce at three – the horses are running.'

'Make sure you get some cake,' said Richard, who'd pulled an all-nighter in the kitchen. 'It contains an entire bottle of brandy.'

At this, Alejandro and Ekaterina – who were helping out behind the counter – exchanged a look of delight.

As the beaming Reba stepped over the shop's threshold, a gasp went up among the crew of regulars. Reba was a vision in a white lace dress dotted with hand-embroidered flowers and an ombré hem that transitioned through every colour in the rainbow – the very dress Frank had snuck away with during Riffraff's Hoarderfest. Her ears and wrists glimmered with mother-of-pearl, and she carried the bouquet of the dried flowers that Adele, after much deliberation, had fortuitously set into the Keep pile weeks earlier.

Frank, standing beneath the lush swoop of Audrey III in a purple suit with flared legs and a magnificent striped shirt he'd topped off with a Stealie bolo tie, dabbed a tear with a paisley handkerchief. His ponytail gleamed: he'd graciously allowed Alejandro to work their conditioning magic.

'It's your dress,' he whispered, his voice cracking as he regarded Reba. 'From our first go around.'

'And your suit,' Reba teased, as she approached lightly in

her painted moccasins. 'From every Saturday night from 1970 through to 1990.'

'Ekaterina let out the seams for me.' Frank spun, revealing the patterned panels Ekaterina had added so his trousers weren't at risk of pulling a Full Monty when he sat down – or carried Reba out of the shop after too many Irish coffees.

'It's perfect,' said Reba, in a rare moment of vulnerability.

'You're perfect,' whispered Frank.

'Oh shut up.'

Reba turned her head. Was she blinking back tears? It turned out that she could emote with the best of them.

Ben stepped forward, looking painfully handsome in jeans and a white shirt whose sleeves he'd rolled up to reveal his colourful arms. He had something tucked into his shirt pocket: the origami swan Adele had folded on her first day.

Catching her sparkling gaze, he tapped the swan, shooting her one of those grins that made her feel all melty inside.

'G'day everyone. I'm Ben, and I'll be helping these two retie the knot.'

'Not retie,' said Frank. 'Tighten.'

'Good catch. *Tighten* the knot. I've known Frank and Reebs since . . . Jeez, how long has it been? A lifetime, really, but with a restart when Doralee took me in a decade and a half ago. Fifteen years is a long time to watch a couple who are perfect for each other bicker and whinge, let me tell you. But they've finally seen the light.'

'She has,' said Frank. 'I've known all along.'

Reba winked. 'Maybe I wanted a few nights of not being woken up by your snoring.'

'I've fixed that, you know.' Frank tapped his nose. 'Nasal strips.'

'I'm gonna stop you there before another fifteen years passes.' Ben held up a finger. 'Anyway. I s'pose the moral of the story is to not let a small misunderstanding or a wayward appliance get in the way of true love.'

Ben winked at Adele, who blushingly knelt to stroke Ember.

'Hear, hear,' came the murmur from the crowd. The Italian students shared a careful yet passionate kiss.

'Spoken like a playwright,' said Reba, her eyes crinkling knowingly. 'Let's get on with it. I'm coming off a fifteen-year drought here.'

At this, Frank burst into a coughing fit. Ben clapped him on the back to help him out of it.

'I won't keep you kids too long,' Ben promised. 'Frank, finisher of crosswords, repairer of record players, sneaky purchaser of biscuits, do you promise to celebrate your one-and-only throughout this life and the next?'

'And the next, and the next, all the way down,' added Frank, taking Reba's hands in his. 'I damn well do.'

'And do you, Reebs, dyer of outfits, feeder of cats, saviour of coffee shops, promise to celebrate this old hippie and keep him out of trouble throughout this life and the next?'

Out of habit, Reba went to say something impertinent, but then she checked herself.

'Too damn right,' she whispered. Her cats-eye glasses glimmered as she tilted her face up towards Frank's.

Ben was fighting a smile – everyone was. 'By the power vested in me by Jerry Garcia and Phil Lesh, I pronounce the two of you a force to be reckoned with.'

Frank swooped in, lifting Reba off her feet. The train of her dress swept the floor in a colourful rainbow, sending Ember skittering away. Reba shrieked in surprise, then burst into giggles.

The joy was contagious: unable to help herself, Adele whooped. This set off a chain reaction, and soon the coffee shop rumbled with the hollers and cheers and feet stamping of the crowd of regulars and friends who'd gathered there to celebrate Frank and Reba.

'You'll always be my eight across,' said Reba, arms wrapped around Frank's shoulders. 'The clue I always go to first.'

The two kissed so ardently that Adele gestured at Trix and her friends to look away.

'Hold it!' cried Gracie, her camera shutter clicking.

'This old back only has one lift in it,' said Frank, setting Reba back on her feet. 'But these lips are full of kisses.'

As the two old hippies embraced again, Adele felt a strong hand on the small of her back. She glanced up, blushing furiously as Ben's green eyes – serious, thoughtful – met hers.

'May I?' he asked, a finger under her chin. Tilting her face towards his, he ducked down, his lips grazing hers. Sparks coursed through her, and this time it was absolutely not the fault of rubber-soled shoes.

Ben retreated slightly, suddenly shy as he realised that dozens of people were watching. Adele, with all of her years on stage, had no such qualms.

'If you're going to do it, do it properly.' Adele pulled him back in, knotting her hands into his hair, and swooning as his strong, sure hands found her shoulders, then her waist.

The kiss was the product of months of tension and promises and interruptions: hungry, exhilarating, oh-so-electric. It was the opposite of an out-of-body experience. It was the kind of experience that grounded you wholly inside yourself, because you wanted to let every molecule of your body, every facet of your soul, be part of it. Adele had never felt so certain that she was meant to be in this particular place in this particular moment with this particular human.

'About freakin' time!' called Reba, who was snuggled up against Frank. Adele and Ben broke apart, each grinning sheepishly.

'Bloody hell,' said Ben, appreciatively.

Bloody hell indeed.

'You two are as stubborn as my bride here,' added Frank, kissing the top of Reba's head.

'Now let's eat cake!' called Reba. Like a Musketeer, she brandished the decorative knife Adele had retrieved from Doralee's apartment.

Everyone pressed in, eager to try the extremely boozy and gorgeously rustic tiered fruit cake. Simple and elegant, the cake was a perfect fit for the newlyweds – or oldlyweds, Adele supposed. White icing held the otherwise bare layers together, and dried sprigs of lavender and pampas grass encircled each tier.

Each with a hand on the knife, Frank and Reba sliced into the cake, rousing another set of cheers from the crowd. Scooping a crumbling piece of cake into her mouth and chewing away, Reba cut as Frank plated, ensuring no one went without.

'I'll handle the music,' said Ben, as the extended version of 'Dark Star' petered out. It was time for something danceable – and not the whirling, swaying, disconnected-from-anything-actually-happening-in-the-music Grateful Dead version of danceable. The languid rhythms of The String Cheese Incident's 'This Must Be the Place' crackled from the record player, to approving cheers from Reba and Frank.

'All right, so *this* is a bop,' said Kyra approvingly, her palm-print dress flaring as she grabbed Richard and pulled him, protesting, into a dance. Hand in hand, the theatre kids formed a circle around one of the tables and started spinning around it, like cheerful witches.

'I'm on the Irish coffees,' said Adele, hurrying over to the counter, where thanks to Ekaterina, two freshly brewed pots of coffee awaited her new-found mixology skills. Stirring in a generous portion of Baileys and sugar, she squirted cream atop each cup, then added a sprinkle of grated chocolate.

'So, you and the Australian, huh?' Ekaterina raised an eyebrow as she popped open a prosecco from the crate of *Hairspray* branded bottles that Gracie had brought over. 'Definitely saw that coming.'

'If you hadn't, we would've,' added Alejandro, sucking cream from their finger. 'He is . . . *mm-mm*. Even if you can't understand half of what he's saying.'

'It still sounds good,' averred Ekaterina. 'Like he's about to throw down with a crocodile for you as proof of his manliness. All that mud and sweat . . .'

'I'm not sure crocodile wrestling is Ben's thing,' said Adele. 'He's more . . . creative. A playwright.'

'He's that good-looking *and* he's an *artiste*?' Ekaterina made a flashing *danger* signal with her hands. 'If I were you I'd never let him out of this shop. He'll get eaten right up.'

If only they knew, thought Adele.

'Speaking of danger,' added Alejandro, nodding at the space the crowd had cleared to create an impromptu dance floor. 'Did anyone know Richard was classically trained?'

Richard had pulled away from Kyra and was pirouetting like a pro. He had better lines than an architecture student. Maybe that was a bad comparison, thought Adele, thinking guiltily of Mazzy Stevens.

The ground rumbled, making Richard fumble his landing.

'My *ankle*,' he complained, clutching at his calf.

'Just a subwoofer on a Subaru,' called Ben.

'It could be, like, a *daikaiju*,' said Trix.

Her cat-eared friend clapped her hands in excitement. 'Finally,' she said. 'Nothing ever happens around here.'

Adele exercised astonishing self-control by not rolling her eyes. Nothing ever happened . . . in the famously ho-hum, middle-of-nowhere borough of Brooklyn? Maybe they should pay rural Tennessee a visit. Although to be fair, *lots* of things happened there. Just not things you wanted to share in polite company.

The ground rumbled again.

'Oh no, you don't,' muttered Ben, folding his arms. 'We fed you last night.'

And they had: another batch of the graveyard coffee beans, which Ben had dubbed *The Plot Thickens*. The machine had grumblingly roasted and ground them, but much like Oliver Twist with his watery gruel, Adele could tell it wasn't satisfied.

Please, sir, I want some more! it had yelled in her dreams. Before launching into a rendition of 'Food, Glorious Food'.

Adele now understood why people took pills to sleep.

'Is the door locked?' she whispered. 'With all the locks?'

'All the locks,' said Ben. 'This is Ben and Reba's day. Nothing is going to take that away from them. We'll figure out the roaster another time.' He held out a vibrant arm. 'Dance?'

'Parking officer!' shouted Trix, who was perched by the shop windows with a high-tech pair of binoculars stamped with an Orion's Belt logo. 'Quick! Move it!'

'Look at those lenses,' marvelled Gracie. 'The Hubble is jealous.'

'There's meant to be a geomagnetic storm tonight,' explained Trix. 'My dad says the last one this strong hit back in 1994.'

'It knocked out the fax line at my dad's work,' reminisced Ekaterina. 'I was devastated – I'd been sending scans of my middle finger to his contacts. Those were the days.'

'You should unplug everything just in case.' Richard tapped the lion emblem on the La Marzocco. 'Imagine the damage an electrical storm could do to the equipment.'

Adele didn't have a chance to respond: Frank and Reba were barrelling past in a cloud of tie-dye and joy (and carefully rolled joints).

'Exeunt, pursued by a bear!' cried Frank, as Reba yanked him out of Riffraff.

Following behind them in a colourful knot, the crowd formed a semicircle around the van, throwing dried petals and grabbing last-minute kisses and hugs with everyone's favourite old hippies.

'Hang on,' said the parking officer, pausing halfway through writing a ticket. 'You two are back together? You sorted out the dog situation?'

'Did we ever.' Frank pulled Janis's canister from his pocket and gave it a waggle. 'Now if you don't mind, we've got some ashes to scatter.'

'And some clothes to shed.' Reba winked lasciviously. 'Not necessarily in that order.'

'Ah, who am I to stand in the way of true love?' The parking officer shredded the ticket, letting it scatter in the wind with the flower petal confetti. 'Just don't block the fire hydrant.'

'I only block traffic when a tree's life is at stake,' said Reba archly, picking up her colourful hem and climbing into the van. 'Or a duck's. Or when an SUV cuts me off.'

'Before we go . . .' Frank turned to Adele and Ben, wrapping them in a bear hug so strong that Adele could hear the seams on his suit strain.

'Watch the stitching!' warned Ekaterina.

'Ah, it doesn't matter,' said Alejandro. 'Have you seen the way Reba's looking at him? Those are coming off in five minutes anyway.'

'Ew,' said Trix, distinctly unimpressed by this concept.

'Thank you both,' Frank said, blinking back tears as he pulled back to regard them. 'The two of you have been here through the good and the bad and the very best.'

'That's what we do, mate,' said Ben. 'The two of you are family. We love ya, Frank.'

'We love you too, Benny boy. And Adele – lovely Adele. I'm so glad the two of you have finally found each other.'

'That's Riffraff for you,' said Adele. 'It brings people together.'

'Exactly like Doralee intended.' Frank blew a kiss towards the cheerful red-brick form of Riffraff, which today was even more profuse with flowers than usual.

'Frank! What's the hold-up? Am I doing this consummation thing alone?'

'Coming, my love,' called Frank. 'Well, that's me. Over and out.'

He climbed into the Kombi van, putting it into gear with a worrying crunching noise that sounded like the garbage disposal at Adele's parents' house. The vehicle clattered off, tin cans rattling behind it. At least Adele assumed that noise was the tin cans: it could also have been the vehicle's exhaust, which like the rest of the van appeared to be held in place with one of Reba's colourful scrunchies.

'All right,' shouted Ben. 'You lot are welcome to come back in to polish off the rest of the plonk and goodies. And anyone who stays back to clean up gets ten bucks and a photo on Gracie's wall.'

'Let's do this!' Stubbing out a cigarette in her champagne coupe, Celia Fjutcha clapped her clawlike hands and waltzed back into Riffraff. The cheerful posse of wedding guests and coffee shop regulars followed after her, glasses raised as high as their spirits.

What followed was a coffee shop party that laughed in the face of the local noise ordinances. It was like the EatMe event all over again, but to a background of communal joy and Fleetwood Mac, and only the occasional dropped glass. Adele's cheeks ached from the smiling – and her throat from singing along with the endless selection of classic music that the guests kept rotating on the newly refurbished record player.

Mercifully, the roaster stayed quiet throughout the festivities and the subsequent cleanup. Perhaps it was getting used to its new low-calorie corpse bean diet.

At long last, the Riffraff bells went silent: the final guests had headed out the door with their plates of cake and promises to catch up soon. But for the gentle purring of a dreaming Ember on his favourite velvet chair and the soothing warble of the turned-down record player, the shop was quiet and still.

But Adele's heart had never felt so full. Even if she were presently sorting silverware and scraping plates into the kitchen bins. Today she'd had a glimpse of how important the shop was to the community – and her own place, her own *future*, in it. Not to mention more than a glimpse of Ben in that spectacularly well-fitting shirt.

Speak of the devil.

'So,' said Ben, from behind her. He looped his arms around Adele's waist and rested his chin on her head. It was the most comforting feeling in the world.

'So,' said Adele, turning to face him.

'One second.' Ben flipped the sign on the coffee shop door over to read *Shenanigans underway. Come back tomorrow.*

'Nice sign,' said Adele.

Ben grinned. 'Doralee won't mind if we lock this door just this once, right?'

Arm in arm, they headed upstairs.

Take Life One Cup at a Time

Adele's phone was ringing. But how? She didn't get reception in her apartment, and she'd set the toucan phone outside after it had shown up in her dreams for the third time, like a tropical bird Bloody Mary. Wait. She wasn't in Doralee's place. She was upstairs in Ben's cosy apartment, with its plaid couch and its scratched coffee table and its wallpaper of framed theatre posters. And Ben, of course. A naked, sleeping Ben.

She glanced at the glowing analogue clock on the wall. 1:45 a.m. Not even her theatre friends called at this time. Was it her parents? Was everything all right? Had the solar flare hit and was messing with the line?

But it was Reba's photo flashing on the phone. She and Frank had probably had a big night of Irish coffees and Kyra's special brownies. Today only, Reba got a pass for calling at this hour.

'How are my favourite newlyweds?' Adele teased as the call connected. 'Do you need me to bring over some more cake so you're all sugared up for Tie Dyepalooza?'

There was an unsettling pause on the other end of the line.

'It's Frank.' Reba's voice caught. 'He's gone.'

Adele dropped the phone. She scrabbled to pick it up, catching a splinter beneath her nail. In her worry, she barely noticed it. 'What do you mean gone? Is it dementia? He's not here at the coffee shop, is he?'

She listened for the now-familiar rumble of the roaster, but all she could hear was the whir of the fan by the bed.

'No. He's right here next to me.' A rustling sound as Reba presumably shook Frank.

Ben stirred among the cotton sheets. He sat up, trying to orient himself. 'Adele? What's going on?'

'Something's wrong with Frank.' Reba's voice trembled with hurt and fear.

Ben hauled himself out of bed, throwing on yesterday's jeans and a T-shirt. 'We're on our way, Reebs. Sit tight.'

The two of them hurried downstairs into the slumbering coffee shop. They'd done a good job tidying, Adele thought, her breath catching in her throat. It was like the wedding had never happened. Only the fairy lights on the stained-glass window and the boxed-up pieces of wedding cake on the counter reminded them of the previous day's festivities.

Ember's eyes flashed as he unspooled himself from his place on his velvet armchair. His singed tail wagged lightly from side as he twirled figure eights around Ben's legs, curious about his plans for the morning.

'Ember, you're in charge of the shop,' said Ben, stroking the enormous cat. 'We might be late today.'

Ben led Adele through the coffee shop kitchen door to the tiny area that housed the trash cans and the fixed-gear bike that Adele vaguely remembered belonging to Topknot Guy. Rats scattered as they approached.

'Hop up on the back.'

Standing on the bolts of the rear wheel, Adele wrapped her arms around Ben's waist, holding him close. Nothing could make her let go right now. What if she did, and Ben disappeared from her life, the way Frank had from Reba's?

'She sounded so scared,' whispered Adele. 'I've never heard Reba sound scared before.'

And without even a warning, she thought angrily. It wasn't like he'd been visibly sick, or a daredevil, or a fan of gas station sushi, or had any of those factors that meant you'd sort of already come to terms with someone's death. No, just out of the blue: dead.

Like all the people who had disappeared into the coffee roaster, she thought with a pang.

'It's scary to lose someone you love,' said Ben, waiting for a late-night limo to pull past a stop sign. The passengers inside rolled down a window, gesturing and shouting wildly as they passed.

Adele bit her lip: it seemed wrong that someone could be having the best night of their lives while someone else had their worst.

As though he'd read her mind, Ben reached back to touch her cheek. 'Reebs has us.'

Ben took the back streets, avoiding the busy thoroughfares that even at this hour bustled with students and young professionals doing everything they could to prolong the night. A few midnight joggers plodded past, miners' lamps flashing on their foreheads – although they hardly needed them tonight: the moon seemed huge, and the sky bright. Somewhere, an owl played Marco Polo.

They pulled up outside an arched, charming brownstone with colourful mosaic pieces pressed into the steps and planter box ornaments whose legs whirled with every restless sigh the city took. It was the exact type of home that Adele had pinned to her vision board upon arriving in the City (but which Lane had made her remove from the fridge, saying that aspirational decor was unseemly). It seemed unthinkable that anything bad could happen in a building as beautiful as this: those ornate railings and decorative scrollwork had to be an insulating factor.

Reba was seated on the steps, wrapped in a tie-dyed dressing gown that somehow seemed muted in the drapery of night. An upside-down L of yellow light peeked out from the front door, which she'd left ajar in her haste.

The bike dropped to the sidewalk with a clatter as Ben and Adele clambered off. Its back wheel spun lazily in the nocturnal breeze, like a roulette wheel coming up unlucky. They hurried up to Reba, who embraced them both in a rainbow cloud of grief.

'It's not right,' whispered Reba. She still wore yesterday's makeup, which had smeared beneath her eyes in an anxious bruise of purply glitter. Her hair was a storm cloud of mats and knots.

'Have you called an ambulance?' asked Ben, when Reba finally released her viciously tight grip.

Reba shook her head. 'It's too late for that. I've called the funeral home instead. Can you help me . . . move him?'

Adele and Ben followed Reba inside the building, the ancient floor groaning beneath them as they navigated the labyrinth of the house. A handful of moving boxes lined one hallway, each marked *Frank* in thick text.

The bedroom door was closed.

Reba sank to the floor. 'He should be in his chair,' she said, pointing to a tan and brown floral armchair with a sagging middle. 'He loved that chair. For fifteen years he's been talking about listening to his records in his chair. And I kept him out of it. And all because I'm stubborn.'

Adele sat down beside Reba, taking her heartbroken friend's hand in her own.

'I haven't known you fifteen years,' she said quietly. 'But from what I've seen, you and Frank spend every single day together. Frank's chair is the chair at the coffee shop. He's always right by you, watching you, putting on your favourite songs, paying for the cookies you're always taking. Maybe you weren't living together, and maybe you weren't wearing your rings, but you've spent all those days in each other's orbit.'

'Like you and Ben.' Reba dabbed at her eyes behind her cats-eye glasses. 'I should've known something was wrong. Ember knew. He was always sidling up to Frank, giving him extra attention. Animals always know.'

Adele swallowed, thinking about the times Reba had used the canned tuna to tempt Ember away from Frank. She'd wondered a few times if Reba had known about the roaster, but maybe there was a different motivation behind her actions entirely.

Ben put a hand on the bedroom door, hesitating as his fingers found the doorknob.

'Adele, why don't you make Reba a coffee,' he said. 'I've got this.'

Pressed For Time

Topknot Guy's bike gave it a valiant shot, but wasn't up to carrying three people, especially when those three people were taking turns to burst into tears. Next up, the trio attempted to flag down a cab, but the taxi gods were not smiling upon them. (Not that they had a history of doing this where Adele was concerned – after all, being splashed by a cab was how she'd first met Donny. Somewhere, in a parallel life, there was an Adele who'd gone out for rooftop pizza following that inauspicious Belle audition, and was now living a quiet life free of death and drama.)

'Something's in the air,' called one cabbie, rolling down a window. 'Too many weirdos tonight. Not worth the risk.'

'We'll just use our legs,' said Adele. 'It's only a few blocks.'

Shouting at someone on his phone in a full chest voice, the cab driver veered off into the strangely bright night. Adele squinted as they hurried along, wondering if a nightclub were to blame. She'd initially put the vivid skies down to the full moon, but it was currently nestled behind a shrug of cloud, so that couldn't be it.

'Sorry about the Kombi situation,' sniffed Reba, dabbing

her eyes with her fractal-patterned handkerchief. 'If we'd known it was going to be towed from the fairgrounds we would've scattered Janis's ashes from the window. She loved riding with her head like that.'

Ben wrapped Reba up in a hug. 'Don't you dare apologise for anything, Reebs. Here we go. Sparrow & Sons.'

Adele blinked. 'That was quick.' In Tennessee she'd still be backing down her driveway.

'I love urban density,' said Reba weepily.

The funeral home was an ambitiously ginger-breaded black building with a flashing marquee sign that shouted existentially into the night: *perceive me!* A black awning stretched out towards the street like an elongated umbrella; dark tulips bloomed in glossy planters that could well have been Kyra's work. The planters smelled of stale urine and the stale chips that some enterprising urban farmer had stuffed into the soil in the hopes of growing potatoes.

'Wouldn't want to miss it, I guess.' Adele shaded her eyes as the gaudy sign cycled through its light show. Maybe this was why the night seemed bright: light pollution.

To be fair, the funeral home *was* wedged between a boutique ice-cream shop and an art gallery brimming with expensive balloon dog sculptures, so it needed to do its bit to stand out.

'Sparrow's good,' said Ben. 'He did Doralee's funeral, and never balked once. Not even at her request for the Macawchestra. Orchestra of macaws,' he explained to Adele, who probably could've gone without the explanation.

'Are we going in?' It was as business-like as Adele had ever seen Reba, which was how she could tell she was hurting beyond comprehension. She hadn't even asked to look at the balloon dogs.

Wrapping her black-and-white tie-dyed gown around herself – it was as close to a mourning outfit as she had – Reba squared her shoulders and shoved open the door.

Arm in arm, Ben and Adele walked on either side of her down the dramatically carpeted hallway. Between the floral carpet and the textured fleur-de-lys wallpaper, the whole place looked like a giant had stripped off his dress duds. A giant who'd had a thing for floral boutonniere, given all the cloying arrangements lurking like petaled gargoyles upon the marble-topped tables and podiums.

Adele swallowed as they passed an entire feature wall lined with coffins extolling the virtues of various finishes and hardware. Ordinarily she didn't mind how people arranged their bookshelves, but she drew the line at caskets.

Opposite the feature wall was an office crowned with stained glass: Morty Sparrow's, according to its nameplate.

The door was open, revealing Morty to be a thin man with a face like an unironed linen shirt and eyebrows the size and hirsuteness of house caterpillars. He sipped a coffee so dark it probably had its own event horizon.

'Young Ben,' he said. 'Sorry to see you here again. Sad to say, but it's been one of those years. There's something in the air, and not just this electrical storm thing. But I like to stay busy. So.'

He gestured for the trio to take a seat on one of the plastic-covered chairs. Morty seemingly used the same interior decorator as Celia Fjutcha. Minus the ashtrays, at least.

'Dad? Why are you up? These are the haunting hours.' A familiar monotone voice floated over Adele's shoulder. Surprised, Adele turned to see Lane munching on a whole bell pepper. 'Hey, Adele.'

'Lane? What are you doing here?'

Lane shrugged. 'Quit my job, moved back in with my dad. I'm thinking about going to embalming school.'

'She's a natural,' said Morty. 'She helps out with the funeral playlists, too. We get great feedback on our sound. Might even change the business name. Sparrow & Daughter. So. What do we know about Frank's last wishes?' Morty pulled a slim green package from his pocket. 'Gum?'

No takers.

'Bell Pepper?' Lane offered around her half-eaten bell pepper, which she was eating, seeds and all.

Ditto.

Reba prodded listlessly at the striped candies in the jar on Morty's huge leather-topped desk. 'He has a will with Celia Fjutcha. But there's no pre-need documentation. Just stuff about what happens with the Tiny Transistors trust.'

'Wait, *that* Tiny Transistors?' Adele blinked. She wasn't a tech person, but the company had famously kickstarted the first Silicon Valley gold rush.

'How do you think we got to spend all those years following the Grateful Dead around?' said Reba, spinning a candy on the table. 'Tie-dye certainly didn't pay for it. Well, it paid for the drugs. It helped that Frank's transistors were used in the Wall of Sound. Got us backstage with the band a ton.'

This explained so much. Including Frank's ease with reworking the coffee shop's record player. Adele had assumed he was a tinkerer. Not a multi-millionaire on the down-low. No wonder he so happily paid for people's drinks at the shop. And Reba's endless appetite for cookies.

'He was a good one.' Morty slid forward a dog-eared album replete with thumbprints. How many grieving families had sat here over the years, choosing between this coffin and that, that

338

bouquet or this? Adele blinked back tears, knowing that this day was coming for her family, too.

'You and me, between us, we'll give him the right kind of send-off. Flowers, finger sandwiches, guest performances – whatever you got in mind for a celebration of life.' He gestured to Ben. 'Even if that's in Vermont.'

Reba slapped the album closed. 'Bah. None of that. I just want to take Frank to all of our places around the city.'

Morty scribbled a note. 'And in what form would you like Frank to be when you do that?'

'Not a corpse. This isn't *Weekend at Bernie's*. His ashes – that's what he wanted. Like what we did for our girl Janis tonight.'

'Joplin?' asked Morty, deeply confused. And maybe ready to call the police.

'Our dog. Although the other Janis and I always got along like a house on fire.' Reba wiped her eyes. 'I did backup vocals for her once.'

Morty looked relieved, but then his expression clouded. He leaned back in his chair, spinning his elegiac Montblanc like a slow-motion baton twirler.

'I should warn you: the crematorium's on the blink.'

'Not my fault,' added Lane around her bell pepper, too hastily for this to be the truth.

'We can keep the body on ice, but I don't know when we'll be back up and running.' Morty tapped the folder again. 'You're definitely a no on the burial?'

Reba opened one of the candies and jammed it in her mouth. 'Frank didn't want to be mummified and stuck in the ground. He wanted his ashes to traverse every part of Brooklyn. And most of San Francisco. To relive every memory we had together. Even the bits where we blacked out.'

Morty drew in a breath through one corner of his mouth. 'Well, that's a problem. We're the only cremation provider in this neck of the woods. Unless you got a serious fireplace at home, you're gonna have to wait. And that means embalming.'

'Frank doesn't want all that,' said Reba around her candy, which had stuck her teeth together. 'No one's filling him up with poison.'

Morty sighed: the living were such a pain in the ass. 'I hate to say it, but you'd better figure out something fast.'

Ben and Adele exchanged a look.

'Reba,' said Ben. 'Can we talk to Morty for a moment?'

For once, Reba didn't put up a fight. 'Only because I have to pee. Where am I headed?'

'Down the hall, first door on the left.'

Reba shuffled off, doing her best to hold her head high.

'Morty,' said Adele, 'we've got a proposition for you.'

The neighbourhood church bonged four as Adele and Ben huddled on the steps to Frank and Reba's brownstone. Poor Reba had long since gone to bed, exhausted after the trauma of the long night.

'I'll face it when the sun's ready to,' she'd said. 'Until then, I've got Kyra's brownies to put me to bed.'

No one was going to argue with her. At least she'd been gracious enough to share a square of brownie with Adele and Ben, who weren't having the best night themselves. The whole city seemed to be out and about – why was it so busy? This was the city that never slept, sure, but that didn't mean that *everyone* was partying at 4 a.m.

The final church bong was draping itself over the streets when a hulking black Cadillac pulled up, its hazards flashing.

The bleating of an alarm; and the car's huge trunk arced up into the sky, revealing an enormously roomy space perfect for disposing of dead bodies. Adele tried to focus on the bronze skull-patterned upholstery instead.

'Tarp first,' said Morty, who'd come back with them for supervisory purposes. 'There can be juices. But I can't have my vehicles associated with . . .' he waved a hand vaguely, as if suggesting that devilry were all around them '. . . this.'

Adele threw a weatherised tarp into the back of the car, stretching it out so it covered the whole trunk area. Huh, she thought, finding a hobby horse with a tenderly braided mane wedged down one side of the trunk. It took all types.

'Sorry in advance, Frank,' said Ben to their dearly departed friend, who'd never been shy about his loathing of gas guzzlers – Yank tanks, in Ben's parlance. 'I'll plant a tree to make up for the emissions we're about to spew.'

Ben and Morty shuffled Frank, now wrapped in the half a dozen hessian coffee bags Ben had taken from Reba's craft room, into the trunk, groaning from the effort.

'These corpses, they never get lighter,' mused Morty. 'Well, not at this stage of decomposition.'

'I'm . . . gonna hop in the car,' said Adele.

'I see you two finally got it together,' said Federico, as Adele clicked her seatbelt in place. 'Sorry about Donny. I heard he skipped town. Doesn't surprise me. He was always squirrely about money. But wasn't I right about the trunk space? Cheeto?'

'I'm good.' Adele grimaced as the car bumped and jostled as Ben and Morty tried to hoist Frank into the trunk. 'Not much of an appetite right now.'

And yet everyone had discovered their inner Sicilian nonna and was trying to feed her.

'The whole body-in-a-bag thing, huh. Yeah, that's gross. But I've seen worse.'

Adele almost asked out of politeness, then stopped herself. She absolutely didn't need to know what awful things Federico had seen in his travails around the city. It was probably darker than the plot twist in *Sweeney Todd*.

Which, now that she thought about it, was not so far from her own plot twist.

'Righto. We're good,' said Ben, climbing into the back seat. He reached forward to squeeze Adele's shoulder. But it was hard to be comforted when all she could think about was the hessian-wrapped body of Frank in the trunk. Not to mention what they were about to do to said body.

'Good to properly meet you. Cheeto?' offered Federico.

'Ta, mate. Got a lolly,' said Ben, around the candy he'd filched from Morty's desk. 'We put down a tarp.'

'It's okay. I learned from one client how to get stains out.'

Federico pulled the car away from the brownstone and away from poor Reba, who would never again sleep next to her beloved Frank.

Blinking back tears, Adele turned her gaze out the window.

'It's busy out,' she observed, as the truck squeezed through the packed streets, which were filled with people staring up at the sky. Some had telescopes set up on the nature strips, while others were camped out on picnic rugs on the sidewalks. Phones were being held up all over like lighters at a concert.

'Everyone is aurora watching,' said Federico. 'From the geomagnetic storm. It should be a good one. Most of the country should be able to see it.'

'I've never seen the northern lights before,' said Adele.

'I have,' said Ben, quietly. His brow furrowed as though he

342

were working through one of Reba's crossword clues. Adele caught a glimpse of herself in the side mirror: she was doing the same thing.

Their eyes met.

Adele swallowed, thinking of the quarrel that Frank had recounted and the shadowy figures that Gracie had pointed out in the aurora picture. They hadn't been dancing. They'd been fighting. Falling. Right as the storm peaked. Right as the power blew and drenched the neighbourhood in darkness. Right as a dark magic had wound through the city – and the roaster.

'Doralee took me upstairs,' Ben whispered. 'That's why I don't remember.'

They rode in silence until Federico pulled up outside Riffraff. 'This is you. By the way, whatever you're gonna do, be careful. My wife says that crazy shit's about to go down, and she knows this stuff. Radio says you got about an hour before the electromagnetic energy peaks.'

He rapped a knuckle against the gold-rimmed stereo system.

Adele squinted up at the sky: she'd been right before. It *was* tinged purple, with a cape of green swinging down through the night. Like in the photo of Ben and his mum. The snapshot of one of her very last moments.

'Better through your phone,' said Federico, flashing his camera app. Purples, greens, and pinks all flashed and swirled, like a Nineties friendship bracelet on an acid trip.

The car trunk cawed as it lifted up like a crow's wing. Adele and Ben reconvened awkwardly at the back of the car.

'Fancy seeing you here,' said Ben, with forced lightness. To be fair, this wasn't really how Adele had imagined their first date would play out. She'd anticipated a romantic stroll along the waterfront eating a bowl of sorbetto as big as her head, not a furtive excursion to roast the corpse of a dear friend.

'Have you ever . . . cooked . . . an already dead body before?' whispered Adele, as she regarded poor Frank in his shroud of hessian. 'Do you think the roaster will take it? Or does it only take fresh blood?'

'There's only one way to find out. Again, sorry, Frank.' Steeling himself, he grabbed at what Adele assumed were Frank's shoulders. 'You take the feet. Let's see those portafilter-honed muscles at work.'

Taking the kind of deep breath that would usually power her through a solo, Adele slid her hands under Frank's calves.

'Need help?' asked Federico, who seemed rather blasé about this whole situation. Adele had a feeling that if Officer Ortiz interrogated him, they might solve a few missing persons cases.

'Get home to your wife,' said Adele, trying to forget that she was clutching a dead man's legs. Although Frank did have great calves. 'But, uh, maybe don't mention our cargo. Or our discussion.'

'A driver never talks. But I'll stop by for a coffee sometime. Do you do a macchiato?'

'She makes the best one in the borough,' said Ben.

Adele blushed.

'Let's do this,' she said.

As she shuffled Frank's alarmingly heavy legs out from the trunk, a business-casual, entirely hairless guy holding a clipboard emerged like a new-born rat from some shadowy corner. Adele wanted to scream.

It was 4 a.m.! The shop didn't normally open until 5:30. There was absolutely no reason for another human to be back here right now. Even noted caffeine addict Adele wasn't loitering behind buildings in the wee hours of the morning looking for her next fix.

'Are you the owner?' The guy's tone was worryingly combative. Was he from the IRS? Small claims court? The Algorhythmix customer care team? Maybe he'd flown in and got his time zones mixed up.

'I am,' said Adele, hefting a hessian-covered foot over her shoulder.

'Got him, Adele?' asked Ben, slowly climbing out from the huge void of the back of the Cadillac. The giant car bobbed like a buoy as Ben landed back on the ground.

'Him?' asked Clipboard, frowning at the hessian sacks.

'Um, yeah. Coffee beans are traditionally gendered male,' said Ben easily. All of those improv lessons he'd taken over the years had paid off.

'The things you learn,' said Clipboard. He didn't so much produce a badge as punch the air with it. 'I'm with the health department. Here to do a routine surprise inspection.'

'At this time of night?' asked Adele. He had the surprise bit down pat.

Clipboard shrugged. 'Just got done shutting down a nightclub. Anyway, we've had some tip-offs about some potential quality control issues.'

'Is this about the belly button ring?' Adele swallowed. 'Because that was . . . mine.'

'It's not.' Clipboard peered intently in the direction of Adele's belly button, which thankfully was obscured beneath one of Doralee's multi-layered shirts. 'But I'll make a note of that. So now's a good time?'

'It's not the best.' Adele shuffled her weight under the leaden heft of Frank's feet. How could a pair of legs be so heavy? 'How about tomorrow? During regular business hours.'

'It wasn't a question. I want to knock this out before the aurora peaks.' Clipboard smiled, a *ghastly* smile with a tinge of green to it. It was as if his mouth were a cheese cellar. 'Also, if you say no, I figure you have something to hide.'

'Nope, nothing to hide,' said Adele, as cheerfully as she could muster with a dead man's feet in her hands. 'At Riffraff, what you see is what you get. Let us pop Frank inside, and we'll show you around.'

'Frank?' Clipboard peered intently at the hessian sacks.

Oh shit.

'Frank's the name we've given this particular blend,' said Ben smoothly. Look at him go. He should've been a lawyer. 'We're calling it *Frank's Ashes*. It's a cricket reference.'

Clipboard followed them as they lugged Frank past the trash cans and through the back door into the kitchen area.

'Cricket, huh?'

'It's a great game for when you need something slower than baseball,' said Adele, grunting from exertion.

'Baseball's a perfect game.' Pulling on a pair of gloves, the inspector strolled about, sticking his thermometer into the various buckets and appliances, and wiping every surface. It was like watching a CSI team work. Adele tried not to think what a team like that would find. If they got out the black lights the whole shop would light up like a Griswold family Christmas.

'Do you mind if we take Frank – the beans – downstairs?' she asked. Her legs were buckling under Frank's weight. 'That's where we roast.'

'Downstairs?' Clipboard frowned as he counted the locks on the basement door. He pulled out a multi-colour clicky pen and set it to red. 'Are you set up with proper ventilation? Humidification? The proper methods of egress?'

Of course we're not! Adele wanted to yell. *Shut us down already so we can get to work!*

In reality, she said nothing. Pretending she was playing a non-speaking walk-on role, she merely gave her best high-wattage smile, hoping it would work its magic on this worryingly intense individual.

Mrow. Ember's eyes flashed in the aurora-tinged light, because of course they did. You had to hand it to cats: like toddlers, they knew how to make an entrance at precisely the wrong time. And at the wrong volume. And usually with something revolting in their mouths.

'Is that . . . a cat?'

Adele winced, hoping the inspector wouldn't ask to see Ember's coffee ground litter tray. Or his preferred path across the room, which involved putting his paws on every single food-preparation surface.

'I'm a cat rescuer.' Clipboard knelt to scratch Ember's fuzzy black-and-white chest. 'So any friend of a cat is a friend of mine.'

'Oh thank fucking God for that,' whispered Ben, who'd been struggling to keep up his nonchalant persona with the quickly decomposing body of one of the shop's most loyal customers hoisted upon his shoulder.

Clipboard sniffed. Still kneeling, he turned a slow circle on the spot like a Cossack dancer whose knees had seen better days. 'Do you smell that? Something faintly ripe. Like . . . compost.'

Adele tightened the hessian bags around Frank's legs. 'Deliveries for the farmer's market.'

'It might be someone's snacks for the aurora viewing,' added Ben. 'There's nothing like a tropical fruit salad.'

The hygiene inspector wrinkled his nose. 'Maybe. But it smells . . . where have I smelled that before . . .'

'Bin juice,' said Ben. 'It's always bin juice.'

'But you rinse your trash cans, correct?' The inspector poked around the coffee shop, taking measurements and making notes.

Ben nodded. 'Always. We earned our "A" rating.'

'Hmm.' Clipboard regarded the record player, poking judgementally at the Dave Brubeck record still in there. 'Is that . . . whipped cream?'

Adele flushed deeply. 'We hosted a wedding the day before yesterday.'

It was technically the truth. Just not the full truth. Which was quite a bit more fun than a hippie wedding, which to be fair, had been *quite* fun.

'Still cleaning up?' The inspector clicked his pen to red. Another mark.

'We were closed yesterday,' said Ben. 'We had a death.'

'In the family,' added Adele. 'Not in the shop. We've never had a death in the shop. At least that I know of.'

At least in the upstairs portion of the shop. And even the downstairs portion of the shops, well, technically they'd been murders, not deaths.

Mrow. Ember was winding circles around the inspector's legs, pulling him towards the basement.

'He wants to show me your roaster,' said Clipboard, flashing Stilton-esque teeth.

The ground rumbled. Please let that be a herd of stampeding escapee elephants, thought Adele.

'Abso-fucking-lutely not,' said Ben. 'Roaster's off limits.'

'It's a trade secret,' explained Adele. 'Our roaster is proprietary. And so is our recipe.'

'Just a quick look,' said the inspector. 'You roast your . . . Frankenbeans, was it? You won't even know I'm here. Of course you can say no, but I'll have to put that in my report. And it won't look good, will it. I've shut down six businesses this week. Actually, the nightclub was number seven.'

'Jeez Louise, what did the restaurant business ever do to you?' muttered Ben.

'Poisoned my mother,' snapped the health inspector, his lashless eyes narrowing. 'This is a career of retribution. And if anything goes wrong, I've got a backup on standby. So don't even think about it.'

'No worries,' said Ben calmly.

In contrast, Adele was all worries.

Sweeping aside Kyra's planters, they set Frank down as gently as they could on the communal table. Adele fought a sob as she carefully adjusted the hessian around his feet.

'You treat those beans like they're a baby,' observed Clipboard. 'Never did like babies. We ready?'

Ben's hands shook as he unlatched the seven different locks on the basement door.

'Down here, mate.'

Ember led the way, his frizzled tail directing the health inspector down the creaky steps.

The schoolhouse light cast its indifferent glow across the otherwise dark basement, picking out the canisters of stored beans, flared metal edges of the roaster and the ancient wooden roof beams.

'Unusual machine. European?' The health inspector walked

349

a circle around the hulking roaster. 'Who'd you bribe from the codes department to get this cursed thing approved?'

'It's grandfathered in,' said Ben.

Well, statistically speaking there were probably some grandfathers in it.

The roaster rumbled. Curious, Clipboard nudged a few buttons and levers.

Outside, the light filtering down through the glass bricks in the sidewalk was recreating the cover of the Pink Floyd album Reba had seriously considered as a wedding dance option. The solar storm had reached its zenith: it was almost time for the aurora to peak.

'It's on a timer,' explained Adele. 'It warms up this time every day.'

While the inspector's back was turned, Ben quietly scooped up a handful of Kyra's cemetery beans and dropped them in the hopper. The machine happily hissed and smoked.

Adele crossed her fingers.

'A few rust stains here.' Clipboard nudged the red spot on the floor left by Donny's untimely death. 'Might need a plumbing upgrade.'

Please don't look closer at the stain. 'We've got a guy on it,' she said.

Clipboard stood up on his toes, peering into the machine's hulking hopper. 'You can get started on your roast. Don't let me stop you.'

'She'll be right,' said Ben. 'We'll wait till you're on your way. It's a . . . proprietary process.'

The machine rumbled once more.

'Sounds like she's all fired up.' The inspector slapped the roaster. The sound echoed around the basement, bouncing off the walls like a game of Pong. 'Well, I've seen all I need to see. That's a pass.'

Ben and Adele exhaled a simultaneous breath.

They'd passed the inspection. What's more: no one had died.

Now all they had to do was roast poor Frank's body before Reba got wind that they'd stolen his corpse from the funeral home. Not stolen. Borrowed.

'Corpse flower!' cried the inspector, heading back up the creaky stairs. 'That's where I've smelled that stink before. The corpse flower at the Botanic Gardens. I knew I'd think of it!'

With the inspector gone, Ben and Adele set to work. The aurora was spangling the sky purple and green: crowds gathered on the sidewalk with their special glasses and high-end photo lenses. The light through the glass bricks started to shimmer and wobble, like the reflection of a pool's surface on a breezy day.

'How are we going to get him down the stairs?' asked Ben. 'I don't want to drop the poor bugger.'

'Hang on.' Adele fetched the stair-climbing dolly she'd ordered a few days ago. Finally, one of Donny's ideas had turned out to be decently useful.

'Thanks, Donny,' she whispered to the air, imagining him responding with ghostly finger guns.

You got it, Delly.

With a grunt of exertion, Ben tilted the dolly and carted poor Frank down the creaking basement steps. Adele walked backwards in front of the dolly, making sure Frank's feet weren't bumping along the splintery wood.

'Are we sure this is going to work?' she asked.

'I don't know,' said Ben. 'If feeding the machine a body during a geomagnetic storm created the machine, hopefully doing the same thing will put a stop to it.'

Well, at least testing the theory didn't involve additional murder. She hoped.

'I wonder if Mum . . .'

Did it on purpose, he didn't say. But the words hung in the air.

'There are some shit men out there,' said Adele quietly. 'And when the world doesn't believe women, sometimes they have to take things into their own hands.'

The room was turning purple, and the hair on Adele's arms raised, as though with static. There was an electrical crackle to the room, and not all of it because she was standing so close to Ben.

'If a roast takes fifteen minutes . . .' she said.

'We'd better get bloody moving.'

Ben grunted as he hefted Frank's body up out of the dolly and towards the feeder for the roaster. The machine rumbled happily.

Overhead, the light from the glass bricks danced and flickered. Adele could hear the excited shouts of the onlookers as they took in the rare sight of the Northern Lights at this surprisingly low latitude. Even in here the phenomenon was beautiful – and electrifying. Pinks and purples swept over the walls like the inside of Reba's dye vats. It seemed somehow fitting, Frank going out like this, amidst a swirl of colour and the happy murmuring of thousands.

'Love ya, Frank,' murmured Ben as he gently guided Frank's body into the machine. 'Thanks for all the memories. And for being like a dad to me. A good one.'

Tears welling, Adele poured a bag of the cemetery beans into the hopper.

Then she looped her arm through Ben's, lending support the only way she could manage right now.

'Let's send him off,' she whispered.

As cheers went up outside – the aurora was peaking – Ben pulled the lever on the coffee roaster. The machine rumbled and roared as it got up to temperature, smoking and shaking as it sucked in Frank's body. Adele closed her eyes, pressing her face against Ben's chest as the machine worked. She hummed to herself, trying not to think of her dear friend being charred into a million pieces, but rather floating free and unfettered over the city he loved so much.

The room turned an astonishing purple – the magical purple of bath bombs and unicorns and limited-edition Doc Martens – that made Adele gasp. It was a beauty almost impossible to comprehend. The schoolhouse light buzzed and hummed. Adele's phone grew hot in her pocket; she pulled it out and set it down on the nearby love seat. It flashed with a heat warning, then switched off.

The whole time, the roaster thrummed and roared. The beans inside crackled like bubble wrap as they reached first crack, and the smell of churrasco barbecue filled the air. At least, that was what Adele told herself that smell was.

'Almost there,' said Ben, his voice hoarse.

As the roaster clattered and chugged, it seemed to suck up all the available electricity in the air. Behind them, the fuses on the switchboard smoked, and the lights from upstairs flickered and popped. This was better than the effects for *Moulin Rouge*, which Lane had laboured over for weeks.

'Blackout!' came the cry from overhead.

'My reception's out!' shouted someone else.

All around, security alarms bleated and whistled, like after a particularly strident 4th of July display.

The roaster reached fever pitch, shaking and trembling like Adele's first car in fifth gear. When the entire machine looked set to explode, it suddenly slumped, as though it had stalled out. A pale chartreuse light poured from it, merging with the purple tinge of the room to form a parade of faces and forms – an endless stream of spirits auditioning for the role of coffee shop ghost. Some of them she recognised: Topknot Guy, Mazzy Stevens, the customers who'd committed unforgivable ordering faux pas over the past few months. But as the ghosts poured out of the machine in a strange reverse timelapse, like Rocky going backwards down the steps of the Capitol, the haircuts and outfits became less familiar: shoulder pads, mullets, horizontal stripes, oversized shirts. And then, finally, the woman Adele had seen in Doralee's photo album and in Ben's photo upstairs. A camera around her neck on a strap, she wrestled with a long-haired guy whose handsome face was a twisted sneer.

'Mum and Dad,' whispered Ben. 'She killed him to protect me. She *died* to protect me.'

Adele squinted in the ethereal light, the reality of the machine and its lore hitting home. The coffee roaster wasn't a source of hate. It had received its powers through an act of love: Ben's mum sacrificing herself to keep her child safe. And now, it was the recipient of another act of love – their determination to carry out Frank's last wishes. Both times, the aurora had imbued it with magic, like the crystals and glasses of water that Kyra left out overnight so that they could charge under the moon's rays.

This time it was imbued with a magic of finality.

'I love you, Mum,' whispered Ben. 'I promise we'll meet in the aurora someday.'

The machine rumbled and rattled, but without conviction. The memories it had stored for the past decades had escaped from its bowels, and had fled out through the ventilation system Topknot Guy had so derided.

Above their heads, someone on the sidewalk outside shrieked, yelling something about bats.

As the world turned and the more familiar yellows and oranges of day slowly trickled into the room, the coffee roaster seemed changed. It was less hulking and more streamlined, and seemed to take up less space in the basement. Its twisted, tilted hopper sat flush, the way it was meant to, and the blades on the cooling tray were no longer blades – just the gleaming chrome arms you'd expect.

Its dark magic had dissipated into the summery Brooklyn air, joining the endless scents and memories of a city that always had a story to tell.

Adele leaned into Ben, running a hand over his back as he fought the emotions that came with the loss of the roaster – and the realisation of how his mum had died.

'I think it's all over,' she whispered.

Ben shook his head. 'No. It's a new beginning.'

Straightening, he used the brass scoop sitting by the machine to sift gently through the beans in the cooling tray.

The roast smelled perfect: warm and chocolatey, with a hint of herbs.

Frank would love it.

The Perfect Blend

A familiar tuxedo-clad cat greeted Adele and Ben as they arrived at Reba's brownstone. Adele held Frank's freshly ground remains in one of Ilona's beautiful lidded vessels.

'What are you doing here, Embs?' Ben stooped to stroke the cat's profuse fur.

Adele frowned: had Ember's tail grown out slightly in the last couple of hours? No, it must be a trick of the borealis-infused light.

'Must've caught a ride with the postie,' added Ben.

The front door opened. Reba, clad in the brightest outfit Adele had ever seen her wear, greeted them with an unending hug so strong that Adele worried she might drop the ash-filled vessel.

When Reba pulled back, Adele could see her friend's eyes were bright with tears behind the familiar cats-eye glasses and the layers of sparkling makeup.

For a moment, no one spoke. What was there to say that the others weren't already feeling all the way into the depths of their bones?

Gently, silently, Adele passed Frank's ashes to Reba, who

held them with a peace she'd never before seen in the famously snarky hippie. Reba's heavily ringed fingers wrapped around the vessel, as though she were trying to hug Frank one last time. Ben clasped his fingers over Reba's, and Adele added hers atop Ben's.

Suddenly, Reba snorted with laughter.

'I'm sorry,' she said, both mortified and mirthful. 'But isn't life a funny thing. It's all one big, tie-dyed circle.'

Adele smiled up at Ben, whose tender gaze lingered on hers. It was, wasn't it. Everything came around in its own strange, colourful way.

'So where are you going to take him first?' asked Ben.

Reba pretended to ponder. 'To Tie Dyepalooza, for a few minutes. Then out for ice-cream. Then to the reading room at the library so he can browse his ratty paperbacks while I do my crossword. And then the shelter to adopt another sausage dog. And tonight, one of Kyra's ghost tours.'

'It sounds like a busy day,' said Adele.

Reba chuckled. 'Oh, love. I have a whole lifetime of joy planned.'

Ben kissed Adele's forehead. 'It's a good way to be.'

Coffee is the New Theatre Black

'On the count of *now*.'

Adele dropped her end of the tie-dyed sheet that had been covering the sign Frank had so painstakingly painted for the shop over the past few weeks. Reba had discovered it while she was moving the last of Frank's things back into her Brownstone. The sign hadn't been finished, but Trix had helped touch up the lettering.

'Such a team player,' said Ben, belatedly dropping his end. 'Reckon I know why Richard refused to work with you.'

Reba scuttled forward to catch the floating sheet, draping it over her shoulders as though she were about to command a Roman legion, something that Adele suspected Reba had done rather successfully in a past life.

Riffraff Coffee + Theatre Co, proclaimed the new sign.

'He did a beautiful job,' said Adele, tracing the thoughtfully drawn letters.

'No, love,' said Reba. 'You did. He'd be so proud. And so would Doralee.'

As Ben and Adele stepped down from their respective

stepladders, Reba lassoed them with the fitted sheet and embraced them both in a vibrant, colourful hug.

'There's always a new chapter in life,' she said. 'Those pages just keep turning.'

Speaking of pages, Riffraff was veritably flicking through them. Like Frank with his books, it had got to the good bit. Although really, thought Adele, it had all been the good bit. Murdery bits aside. Thank goodness human memories were good at repressing that sort of thing.

'Welcome to the new Dramaturgy room!' announced Ben to the crowd that had gathered in a caffeinated, highly sugared knot. It was *quite* the crowd, thought Adele proudly, as she hurried off to find a pair of scissors for the ribbon cutting.

Ben pushed aside the door to reveal the newly painted steps down to the basement. Inspired by a photo found in one of Doralee's albums, Trix and her friends had held a working bee to channel the vibrant, floral art that so perfectly encapsulated Adele's great-aunt – and the lives she'd changed with her community shop.

'Now that we're no longer roasting on site, we've converted the basement into a performance space. Anyone from the community is welcome to rehearse, create or perform down here. We've got a stage, a sound board, and basic lighting controls.'

He led the way down into the cheery space, where the schoolhouse lamp's nervous glow was now backed up by hundreds of strings of delicate fairy lights.

'And a huge prop box, thanks to Doralee and Frank.' Adele patted the wardrobe she and Ben had lugged over from Doralee's apartment – which, now that Adele had moved upstairs with Ben, was inhabited by an aspiring theatre performer from Nashville. Gratis, of course, because Adele knew how hard it was to make it in the city without help. And if she had nepotism on her side, she was going to use it to help others, not just herself.

'I'd say we have the largest collection of Seventies ephemera in the city,' said Ben.

'What's that?' whispered shy Rivka, pointing to the bulb that glowed softly in the back corner of the room, where a black curtain on tracks could be pulled aside to create a backstage area.

'It's a ghost light,' said Ben. 'To keep away the spirits.'

'Just in case,' said Adele. After all, you never knew what might happen during an electromagnetic storm.

'I'd always wanted to come down here,' said Chaya, her sparkly cat ears bobbing on her headband. 'But Ember would never let me.'

'That's how you know he liked you,' said Ben.

Chaya beamed. 'Cats are the best people. They're so good at setting boundaries. Where is he, anyway?'

'He lives with me now,' said Reba from the top of the stairs. Like an Aldi shopper who'd forgotten their reusable bags, she held Janis's pepper shaker jar under one arm – and Frank's vessel under the other. 'He's going through my tuna like no tomorrow.'

As Reba reached the bottom of the stairs, the entire crowd took turns hugging her.

'Frank would want to see the theatre,' she said, waggling the vessel at Adele. 'You've all worked so hard on it.'

'Not to mention the play,' said Adele, shooting a grin at Ben.

'Technically it's a musical,' said Ben.

He gestured to the seating they'd rescued from the Moving Parts Theatre before its untimely demise. Everyone sat, waving hellos to Adele from their chosen seats: her theatre friends; Kyra and the courtyard neighbours; the girl from the badminton bar; the ever-stressed teachers. Everyone except Honour Nivola, who was there in spirit. If by spirit you meant the box of branded merchandise she'd FedExed from her set in L.A., where after a few tough weeks of partying with beautiful people in Santa Monica she'd been discovered by a rep and had landed a recurring role on a respectable dramedy. (Their dads had gone to Harvard together.)

'So,' said Ben, mostly to Clarence, who'd been promoted from food reviewer to entertainment editor, '*The Girl Downstairs* is a departure from my usual work. But I couldn't resist incorporating Adele's ditties. Every time I wrote a line, she'd start singing it.'

'And every time I sang a line, he'd write it down,' added Adele.

'I promise this one is *unforgettable*,' said Richard, passing around a plate of . . . hang on, was that hedgehog slice? 'Amazing cast. Courtesy of yours truly. It's nice to be back.'

'And makeup courtesy of me,' said Alejandro, batting rainbow eyelashes.

'Choreography by me.' Ekaterina did a chair dance.

'Set design and lighting by us,' said Trix, pointing to her group of friends.

Lane paused from eating a raw zucchini long enough to add: 'Sound design here.'

'And I'm in charge of the goats,' said Autumn, as Oreo gave an alarming bleat.

Adele could barely keep from jumping up and down. They'd done it. It was exactly as Doralee had wanted: a place for the community riffraff to gather and thrive. If only . . .

'Excuse us, y'all,' came a voice Adele would know anywhere. 'Coming through.'

Adele blinked. It couldn't be, could it? She hadn't even finished her thought!

'Hang on,' said Ben. 'I forgot: plot twist.'

'Mom! Dad!' cried Adele, leaping off her seat and racing up to greet the two cheerful, familiar individuals who had appeared at the top of the stairs. Was Dad clutching an oversized Toblerone with a bow on it?

'Theatre tradition,' said Dad, giving her a gentle bop on the head with the chocolate.

'Ooh, steep,' said Mom. 'Quick, Adele, let's do a shoe shoot before I . . . break a leg.'

The dads in the audience clapped.

Adele glanced down at her shoes – her matching shoes. 'How did you know what shoes I'd be wearing?' she asked suspiciously.

Ben winked. 'I might've given them a heads-up.'

'They've even got a spot to stay this time,' said Reba, looping her arms around Adele's parents' waists. 'Ember will love the company.'

'I can't believe everyone's here,' said Adele, her voice cracking as she cast her gaze over the sea of coffee shop regulars. 'That you've all come out to support us.'

'You can't? My years as a theatre dad tell me y'all call this a "production number",' said Dad, setting up to perform his epically awful interpretation of the Lawnmower dance move, which he always followed with an even worse Sprinkler. 'Everyone's here, and ready to dance.'

From the top of the stairs, a Polaroid camera clicked and snapped. Gracie Nivola waved as everyone turned to see what the commotion was about.

'All right, everyone, say: *cool beans!*'

'*Cool beans!*' shouted the crowd.

Gracie grinned, giving the crowd a thumbs up as the image slowly materialised on the photo paper. 'That's one for the photo wall. And maybe the *Times*.'

'Question. What happened to the roaster?' Clarence nodded at the raised stage that had been installed where the roaster had been.

'We found a good home for it,' said Ben. The funeral home had taken it off their hands, with Lane's dad thoroughly impressed by the temperatures that the machine got up to. Lane had tried to hide it, but Adele could tell she was itching to sample the machine's grunts and gurgles into a soundscape.

'They don't make machines like this anymore,' Morty Sparrow had said, as Ben had helped him load the machine into a gleaming Sprinter van. 'Some retrofitting, and this thing will be perfect for our needs. Thanks, kid. You've helped us out of a tight place.'

'Same here,' Ben had responded. 'We're doing less roasting, more toasting these days.'

And they were: they'd even applied for an actual liquor licence.

'What are you munching on there?' Adele asked, as she showed her parents to their seats.

'Chocolate-covered coffee beans,' replied a teacher, who

was crunching away. 'Kyra grows them and Richard does the chocolate coating. They definitely give you a pick-me-up – and we teachers need them at this time of year. These were harvested during the electromagnetic storm.'

The teacher scratched at the skin behind her ear, which looked a tiny bit green-tinged. Then at her eyes, which looked a tiny bit jaundiced. Wait a minute, thought Adele. Wasn't this the geography teacher who'd mysteriously disappeared during one of her first weeks at the coffee shop? She gulped, trying to ignore the ringing in her ears. Cemetery beans, harvested during an electromagnetic storm . . .

But before she could think about it further, Ben clapped his hands.

'All right, everyone! Take your places,' he called. 'It's our time to shine. Adele, you're up.'

Adele took a deep breath and gave her sunniest smile.

She'd finally made it.

Roasting Notes

This book has been a labour of love and laughs, and though most of it was written squintingly early in the mornings over espresso, it was never a solo project. Is anything? So many people go into the making and finessing of any book, and I am profoundly grateful to those who helped give sweet, lovely Adele her time in the spotlight.

To Wes, love of my life, maker of coffees, human IMDB, diligent Deadhead and cheerleader without rival, I don't know how you do it, but I'm glad that you do. And sometimes even with a smile. To my darling little Leo, this book has too much swearing in it for you to read just yet, but the time will come when we can swear like sailors like we do everything else: together. And to Samson, the little dude, the very good boy, the lover of long walkies: thank you for being by my side during the writing of yet another book. How many is this together? I can't even count.

To my lovely agent Joanna Rasheed, thank you for indulging me as I gambol about across genres and formats. You are a star, and I wish I had even a touch of your New Yorker cool and sass. Pizza Rat is my gift to you.

Enormous thanks to Raphaella Demetris, for shepherding this project along and generously laughing at my jokes, and to Amy Mae Baxter for stepping in with aplomb and the suggestion of added goats (good choice). Francesca Tuzzeo, thank you for being the behind-the-scenes force keeping it all moving. Thanks too to Helena Newton for ensuring that narrative time did not flow backwards or sideways (oops), and for bringing my Australianisms under control, and to Anne O'Brien for carefully proofreading my tyops (stet). Any residual mistakes are mine alone!

To Toby James, what a cover! It's no easy feat to mash up three different genres into a clear, memorable design, and I dare anyone to walk past this book on a shelf without doing a double take. Thanks as well to our typesetting team: there's something special about seeing that first typeset version that makes this whole process feel 'real'. And to Maddie Dunne-Kirby and Jessie Whitehead, thank you for shouting about this book and getting it into the hands of the extremely clever and good-looking person who is reading it right now.

To Grandma, thank you for your excellent vanilla slices, and for the little snippets of my Mallee memories that flavoured Ben's character. To my parents, thank you for being as supportive as Adele's. To my writing friends – Kate Farrell, Svani Parekh, Aneta Cruz, Chris Modafferi, Sarah Billington, Dianna Wilson Sirkovsky, Kira Watson, Brenna Jeanneret, Erin Petti and Breanna Wright – thank you for cheering me on and being a shoulder to whinge on. You're all phenomenally talented and I can't wait to watch you take the world by storm. (But not in a climate disaster type way.)

To Oren and Matt of the Just Shoot it Podcast, thank you for teaching me about the 'bite and smile', which became the 'bite and sming' in this book. To Amos Teo, cheers for all the Broadway road trip playlists – turns out I was listening after all! And to the lovely people of Sweetwater, Tennessee, I hope y'all (is this how I use y'all?) don't mind that I used your town's name (but not its likeness) – it is a charming place indeed.

To all the lovely coffee shop patrons who are kind to baristas, tip well and bus their own tables, thank you for helping add to the tapestry of this book! To the other type: into the roaster with you!

And to you, lovely reader, thank you for sharing your time with me. Wherever you're reading this – plane, train, a comfy armchair, perhaps, dare I say it, even a coffee shop – I hope this book made you laugh, and I'm sorry if that one bit made you cry. (I'm a monster, I know.) I do hope you'll join me for the next one!